Sharon Kendrick started storytelling at the age of eleven and has never stopped. She likes to write fast-paced, feel-good romances with heroes who are so sexy they'll make your toes curl! She lives in the beautiful city of Winchester – where she can see the cathedral from her window (when standing on tip-toes!). She has two children, Celia and Patrick and her passions include music, books, cooking and eating – and drifting into daydreams while working out new plots.

Caroline Anderson's been a nurse, a secretary, a teacher, and has run her own business. Now she's settled on writing. 'I was looking for that elusive something and finally realised it was variety – now I have it in abundance. Every book brings new horizons, new friends, and in between books, I juggle! My husband John and I have two beautiful daughters, Sarah and Hannah, umpteen pets, and several acres of Suffolk that nature tries to reclaim every time we turn our backs!'

Susan Stephens is passionate about writing books set in fabulous locations where an outstanding man comes to grips with a cool, feisty woman. Susan's hobbies include travel, reading, theatre, long walks, playing the piano, and she loves hearing from readers at her website susanstephens.com

Snowbound Christmas Nights

SHARON KENDRICK

CAROLINE ANDERSON

SUSAN STEPHENS

MILLS & BOON

First Published in Great Britain 2025
by Mills & Boon, an imprint of HarperCollins*Publishers* Ltd
1 London Bridge Street, London, SE1 9GF

www.harpercollins.co.uk

HarperCollins*Publishers*
Macken House, 39/40 Mayor Street Upper,
Dublin 1, D01 C9W8, Ireland

Snowbound Christmas Nights © 2025 Harlequin Enterprises ULC.

Cinderella's Christmas Secret © 2020 Sharon Kendrick
Snowed in with the Billionaire © 2013 Caroline Anderson
One Scandalous Christmas Eve © 2020 Susan Stephens

ISBN: 978-0-263-41921-4

This book contains FSC™ certified paper and other controlled sources to ensure responsible forest management.

For more information visit: www.harpercollins.co.uk/green

Printed and Bound in the UK using 100% Renewable Electricity
at CPI Group (UK) Ltd, Croydon, CR0 4YY

CINDERELLA'S CHRISTMAS SECRET

SHARON KENDRICK

In memory of my dearest friend
Mandy 'Gregoire' Morris, who was clever, cultured,
kind, and possessed a wicked sense of humour – qualities
which live on in her four amazing children, Simon,
Katy, Robin and Guy.

CHAPTER ONE

'I CAN'T...' HOLLIE'S words came out as a strangled squeak as she held the dress up.

It was very Christmassy. In fact, it *screamed* Christmas—and not in a good way. Short, bright and very green, it gleamed beneath the garish lights of the hotel where the party was being held. She tried again. 'I can't possibly wear this, Janette.'

Her boss's perfectly plucked brows were elevated. 'Why not?'

'Because it's...' Hollie hesitated. Normally, she was the most accommodating of employees. She was a peacemaker. A facilitator. She worked very hard and did what was asked of her, but surely there was a limit. 'A little on the small side...'

But her boss wasn't interested in her objections. In fact, she was even more self-absorbed than usual and had been in a particularly vile mood since her fingernail had chipped that morning and subsequently snagged one of her super-fine stockings.

'Someone of your age can get away with wearing something as daring as that,' Janette clipped out as she adjusted a low-hanging bunch of mistletoe. 'You might find it suits you, Hollie—it'll certainly make a change from your usual wardrobe choices.'

'But—'

'No buts,' continued her boss smoothly. 'We're sponsoring this party, just in case you'd forgotten. And since one of the waitresses is a no-show and with so many VIPs coming, we can't possibly be short-staffed. All you have to do is to turn up dressed as an elf for a couple of hours and hand out a few canapés. Why, if I were a few years younger I would have worn the outfit myself! Especially as Maximo Diaz has agreed to come.' She flashed a veneer-capped smile. 'Potentially the most valuable client we've ever had. Mr Big. Mr Limitless Bank Account. And if his hotel purchase goes through before Christmas, you're looking at a big fat bonus. Surely you haven't forgotten that, have you?'

Hollie shook her head. No, of course she hadn't. How could she have forgotten Maximo Diaz and all the fuss which surrounded him whenever he made an appearance in the small Devon town where she'd moved after her life's savings had become someone else's pocket money? How could *anyone* ever forget a man who resembled a dark, avenging angel who had tumbled to earth in a custom-made suit? A man who made her heart race with uncomfortable excitement whenever he caught her in the hard, black spotlight of his gaze so that she felt like a butterfly pinned to a piece of card.

She swallowed. She guessed every woman felt that way about him. She'd seen the way he was watched by every female who happened to be in the vicinity, whenever he walked into the estate agency where Hollie worked. She'd noticed the way their eyes were drawn—

reluctantly or otherwise—to the powerful muscularity of his body and the glow of his olive-dark skin. He was a man who seemed to have taken up stubborn residence in her imagination. A man who symbolised a simmering sexuality and virility which scared her and excited her in equal measure—and no matter how hard she tried, she found it impossible to remain neutral to him.

Not that she would have made very much of a mark on *his* radar. Powerful Spanish billionaires tended not to take much notice of nondescript women who beavered away quietly in the background of large offices. Occasionally she'd made him a cup of coffee, accompanied by one of the home-made biscuits she sometimes brought to the office, if her boss wasn't on one of her rigid diets. She remembered him absently taking a bite from a piece of featherlight shortbread and then looking at it in surprise, as if the taste of something sweet was something he wasn't used to. He probably wasn't. Because 'sweet' wasn't really a word you associated with the rugged tycoon. Hard and dark were words which sprang more readily to mind.

But she shouldn't be thinking about Maximo Diaz—not when Janette was still fixing her with that expectant stare, and automatically Hollie smiled back.

'Of course I haven't forgotten Señor Diaz,' she said. 'He's a very important client.'

'Yes, he is. Which is why all the local bigwigs and politicians are so eager to meet him,' Janette said eagerly. 'He's going to have a big impact on this area, Hollie. Especially if he turns the old castle into a hotel like it was before, back in the day. It means we won't have to use this eyesore of a place any more for our official functions—and not before time.'

'Yes, I do realise that.'

'So you'll do it?'

Hollie nodded. It seemed she didn't have a choice and therefore she would accept the situation gracefully. Wasn't that one of life's most important lessons? 'Yes, Janette, I'll do it.'

'Excellent. Run along and get changed. I've popped in a pair of my own shoes—I think we're the same size. You'll never fit into the other ones. Oh, and wear your hair down for once, will you? I don't know why you always insist on hiding away your best feature!'

Tucking the outfit under her arm, Hollie slipped from the room, dodging gaudy streamers along the way, trying to concentrate on the evening ahead rather than her boss's rather overbearing manner. Despite being a whole two months until the holidays, the hotel was decked out with yuletide sparkle, which didn't quite manage to disguise the ugly fittings which had seen better days. Yet she wasn't going to complain about the fact that the festival seemed to come earlier every year, because Christmas was a welcome break in the normal routine. A time for candles and carols and twinkling lights. For pine-scented trees and bells and snow. She might not have any family of her own to celebrate with but somehow that didn't matter. It was a time when strangers talked to one another and it brought with it the indefinable sense of hope that, somehow, things were going to get better—and Hollie loved that feeling.

Fluorescent lights lit the way to a gloomy subterranean cloakroom, which was a bit like descending into hell, but Hollie remained determinedly positive as she shook out the fur-trimmed green dress, the red and white striped tights and Janette's scarlet stilettos, which were scarily high.

Peeling off her shirt dress, flesh-coloured tights and sensible court shoes, she stood shivering in her underwear as she struggled into her elf costume. But by the time she had managed to zip it up, she realised her reservations had been well founded because the person who stared back at her from the mirror was…

Unrecognisable.

She blinked, finding it hard to reconcile this new image of herself—and not just because she was wearing what amounted to fancy dress. The no-show waitress must have been much shorter, because the hem of fake white fur swung to barely mid-thigh—a super-short length, which was exaggerated by Janette's skyscraper heels. The other waitress must have been slimmer too, because the green velvet was clinging to every pore of Hollie's body, like honey on the back of a teaspoon. The rich material moulded itself to her breasts and hugged her waist in a style which was as far from her usual choice of outfit as it was possible to imagine.

She looked…

She cleared her throat, hating the sudden nerves and fear which slammed through her body and made her heart race like a train. She looked like a stranger, that was for sure. The way her mother used to look when she was expecting a visit from her father. As if tight clothes could mask a basic incompatibility—as if adornment were the only thing a woman needed to make a man love her. And it hadn't worked, had it? She remembered the bitterness which used to distort her mother's features after she had slammed the door in his wake.

'You can never make a man love you, Hollie, because men aren't capable of love!'

It was a lesson she'd never forgotten—her mum had made sure of that—but not one she particularly wanted to remember, especially now. She wished she could strip off these stupid clothes and the too-high heels. Skip the party and go home to her rented cottage. She could study that new cake recipe she was planning to try out on the weekend and dream about the time when she could finally open her own business and be independent at last. One more year of frugality and she should have amassed the funds she needed. Only this time she would be sure to go it alone, in a part of the world which she found manageable. A picturesque little Devon town called Trescombe—not some big, anonymous city like London, where it was all too easy for a person like her to slip off the radar and become invisible.

Was it that erosion of her confidence which had led to her not paying attention to what was going on around her—until one day Hollie had discovered that nearly all the money had gone and her supposedly best friend had ripped her off? It had been a harsh and hurtful lesson, but she had learnt from it. Never again would she put herself in the position of being conned by someone she'd thought of as a friend, and have her trust in human nature eroded yet again.

And wasn't that another reason for making sure this party was a success? Because Maximo Diaz's purchase of the old castle on top of the big hill outside town had the potential to herald a new golden age in local tourism and Hollie wanted to be part of it. It hadn't been a hotel for years but was crying out for some love and attention. And if the enigmatic Spaniard was an unlikely candidate to play the part of neighbourhood saviour—well, that was what life was like. Sometimes it threw up surprises and you discovered that people didn't always fit into the little boxes you tried to squeeze them into. Just because a man was an impossibly wealthy global superstar, didn't mean he couldn't also be a good man, did it?

Remembering Janette's parting words, Hollie pulled the scrunchy from her hair and shook her head to let her hair tumble down around her shoulders. It was a colour best described as light brown, though some of the bitchier girls at school used to call it 'mousy'. But it was clean and shiny and it streamed abundantly over her breasts, effectively hiding that rather scary glimpse of cleavage.

The final touch was a red and green hat with a bell on the end and the sound of it jangling like a cash register as she crammed it over her head made Hollie smile. One day soon she would open her very own tea shop and, although she wasn't planning on wearing quite such a revealing uniform, tonight's event would be perfect practice for her future career of serving the public. Wobbling a little in her spindly heels, she headed for the door.

Christmas elf?

How hard could it be?

He didn't want to be here.

Despite the fact that he was poised on the brink of a venture guaranteed to net him even more millions, Maximo Diaz was feeling even more detached than usual.

He looked around at a room which, bizarrely, was decorated with thick streamers of glittering tinsel— even though it was still only October. A giant fir dominated one wall and tiny golden and silver lights twinkled in every available corner of the room. Christmas had, it seemed, come ridiculously early to this one-horse town, with its distant glimpses of the sea and the bleak sweeping moorland which lay to the east.

His mouth hardened.

The truth was, he didn't want to be anywhere right now. Not at either of his homes in Madrid or New York and certainly not here in Devon. Because everywhere he went he took himself with him and 'here' was inside his head, listening to clamouring thoughts which would not be silenced. For the first time in his life, he was finding it difficult to switch off and that disturbed him.

In his past there had been troubles. Of course there had. Everyone had troubles and sometimes he felt as if he'd netted more than his fair share. Bleak, dark events which had come out of nowhere and threatened to blindside him, although in the end they had bounced off him like hailstones on a pavement because he had willed them to. He had schooled himself to cultivate a steely self-control and had always prided himself on his ability to shrug off hardship. To step away from chaos, resilient and untouched, like a phoenix rising from the ashes. But back then youth, hunger and ambition had been on his side, shielding him against hurt and shielding him against pain. He had come to the conclusion that he was one of those lucky few who were immune to hurt. And if that meant people—usually women—were prone to describe him as cold and unfeeling. Well, he could live with that.

Yet who would have thought the death of someone he'd despised could have pierced his heart so ragged? How was that even *possible*? He hadn't seen her in years. Hadn't wanted to—and with good reason. He should have felt anger or injustice or resentment—maybe all three—as he'd said goodbye to the woman who had given birth to him, summoned to her bedside by the nuns who had cared for her during her final days. Yet it hadn't been like that. He shook his head. His reaction had surprised him. And angered him too, because he hadn't wanted to feel that way. As he'd held her papery hand with its dark tracery of veins, he had felt a deep sorrow welling up inside him. He had been overwhelmed by a sense of something lost, which now eluded him for ever.

And he didn't do that kind of emotion. Not now and not ever.

But he had to carry on. To brush off pointless grief and make like it had never happened. What other choice was there for someone who had turned indifference into an art form? He would get over it because he always did. And he would forgive himself for that rare foray into the saccharine world of sentimentality, because that was a place which held no allure for him.

He would continue with his inexorable rise to the top. He would keep on making a fortune from fundamentally changing the infrastructure of different countries. Building roads and building railways and creating a turnover which caused his competitors to shake their heads with frustration and awe. He had added a luxury hotel chain to his portfolio now and was surrounded by the kind of wealth which, strangely and rather disturbingly, had not brought him the satisfaction he'd sought. But it certainly made women's eyes grow wide whenever they stepped over the threshold of one of his homes or slid into the leather-bound luxury of his private jet. And just because he had more money than he would ever need in several lifetimes, didn't mean he wanted to slow down. Because he liked success. He liked it a lot. Not because of the material rewards it reaped, but for the glow of achievement it provided, no matter how fleeting that feeling proved to be. It was as if he was intent on proving himself over and over again, if not to the father and mother who had rejected him, then maybe to himself.

'Can I tempt you with something to eat, Señor Diaz?'

A soft voice broke into Maximo's reverie and, glad to have the dark tangle of his thoughts interrupted, he turned his head to see a woman standing there, a tray of food in her hands. But it wasn't the unappetising fare which caught his attention and held it, as much as her appearance.

Tempt him? She most certainly could.

His narrowed his eyes, because the thought came out of nowhere, especially as she looked faintly ridiculous in her fancy-dress costume. A sudden pulse beat at his temple and he felt the inexplicable drying of his mouth. Ridiculous, yes—but kind of sexy, too. No. Scrub that. *Very* sexy.

For a moment he thought she seemed faintly familiar, but the thought instantly left him because he was finding it difficult not to stare. And difficult to breathe. Who wouldn't when she looked so...*spectacular*? He swallowed as he continued with his silent scrutiny. Rich green velvet emphasised the porcelain paleness of her skin and a band of white fur at her shoulders drew his attention to her creamy flesh—which was unfashion- ably soft and abundant. Maximo allowed his gaze to move down, distracted by long legs which seemed to go all the way up to her armpits, an illusion no doubt helped by her teetering shoes. Sexy, scarlet shoes—and most men didn't bother denying their reaction to *that* kind of footwear.

Yet, in direct contrast to the provocation of those killer heels, she wore not a scrap of make-up on her milk-pale face and the healthy sway of hair which gleamed beneath the fairy lights made Maximo ex- perience something he hadn't felt in quite a while. A stealthy but insistent tug of desire, which pulsed through his veins like sweet, dark honey.

His mouth twisted self-deprecatingly. Surely the healthy libido which seemed to have deserted him of late hadn't been stirred by something as off-the-wall as a woman in fancy dress? Maybe his sexual appetite had become so jaded that he was being tempted by a little seasonal role play.

'Um...we have a selection of delicious canapés on offer,' she was saying, her words tumbling over them- selves, and something about the softness of her voice made his skin prickle with recognition once more. 'We've got pineapple and cheese on sticks and vol-au- vents—or there's mini quiche, if you prefer.'

'Mini quiche?' he echoed sardonically, dropping his gaze to survey something unrecognisable which was stabbed unappetisingly onto the end of a cocktail stick, and maybe she picked up on his tone because when he looked up again, her face had turned very pink.

'I know they're not to everyone's taste—'

His mouth twisted. 'You can say that again.'

'But the tourist board suggested we go with a retro theme,' she defended.

He found himself unexpectedly charmed by her blush, for when was the last time *that* had happened? 'And why would that be, I wonder?'

'Because nostalgia is big, especially at Christmas.' She hesitated, as if establishing whether he really did want to talk to her or whether he was just being polite. 'Isn't that the whole point of it?'

'But it isn't Christmas,' he pointed out. 'Not for weeks.'

'Yes, I know. But the holiday always puts people in a good mood. And everywhere looks better with a few decorations and a Christmas tree.'

'I must beg to differ,' he commented, shooting a disparaging gaze at the glittering fir with its flashing fairy lights, which was nudging the hotel ceiling. He studied the fake presents he could see piled up at the base and couldn't repress a shudder. 'It looks monstrous.'

She hesitated again. 'You sound as if you don't like Christmas?'

'Something of an understatement,' he returned coolly. 'If you want the truth, I loathe it.'

'Oh. Right. Well, that's a shame,' she said and he could see her biting her lip as she struggled to think of a suitably compensatory response. 'In that case, would you like a glass of bubbly? There's plenty over on the bar—I can easily go and fetch you one.'

He could just imagine the quality of wine on offer but something about her worried expression made Maximo bite back the acerbic response which was hovering on his lips. Suddenly he realised it wasn't fair to take his mood out on her. For him, this party was nothing more than a social necessity—an opportunity to meet the local officials who would help facilitate his ambitious plans. It certainly wasn't what he'd call a pleasure, and she was only doing her job, after all.

And then that first faint flicker of recognition crystallised into something more solid, which made him examine her face more closely, because the dark-lashed beauty of her grey eyes had stirred more than a vague memory.

'Don't I know you?' he questioned suddenly.

She wriggled her milky shoulders a little awkwardly. 'You don't exactly *know* me, Signor Diaz,' she said. 'We've met a few times when you've been into the office. I work in the estate agency you're using to purchase the castle. I'm usually—'

'Sitting behind a desk. *Sí, sí*—of course, I remember,' he said, for hadn't she been an oasis of calm during his recent purchase, and as unlike her abrasive and predatory boss as it was possible to be? She'd made him coffee and served him with something delicious to accompany it. But usually her clothes were unremarkable and her thick hair always scraped back in a style so severe, he imagined even a nun might shun it as unflattering. He remembered thinking that if he were planning on moving his business here, she might make the perfect secretary, and perhaps he would have poached her and paid her twice as much as she was currently earning.

He'd had no idea that beneath her drab clothes was a body which was little short of sensational and he was finding it unexpectedly difficult to reconcile these two dramatically different images of the same woman. 'So why the sudden change of role—and the sudden change of outfit?'

'I know. It's awful, isn't it?' she whispered, her stricken gaze glancing down at the clashing colours of red and green.

'I don't know if that's the word I would have chosen,' he answered carefully. 'I think it suits you, if you want the truth.'

'Seriously?' She looked surprised and then shyly delighted.

And wasn't it strange how her obvious self-consciousness was playing sudden havoc with Maximo's senses? The way she was biting her bottom lip was drawing his attention to the cushion of pink flesh which curved so sweetly into a shy smile. Her mouth suddenly looked very inviting. And extremely kissable. Bizarre. He shook his head, reminding himself that there were plenty of women more suitable as recipients of his desire than an office junior in fancy dress. 'Are you moonlighting?'

'You could say that.'

She lowered her voice again so he had to lean closer to hear her, and as he did he caught the faint drift of her scent and wondered how something so light and delicate could smell so unbelievably provocative. 'The waitress who'd been hired to do this let them down at the last minute,' she confided. 'And I was asked to—'

'Ah! There you are, Maximo! Hiding away in the shadows, like some dashing conquistador!'

A shrill voice crashed into their conversation and Maximo looked up to see Janette James bearing down on them, her body language managing to be both sinuous yet determined at the same time. She wore a look on her face which he'd seen the first time he'd walked into her estate agency and every time since. It was an expression he'd encountered many times during his life, but especially from middle-aged divorcees.

'I do hope Hollie has been looking after you?' she was saying. 'I'm sure she has, judging by the amount of time she's been standing here.' She fluttered him another predatory smile before turning to the hapless waitress by his side. 'But there *are* other people in the room, Hollie dear, tempting as it must be to monopolise Señor Diaz. People who are very hungry. So run along, will you? The mayor keeps glancing in your direction and he looks as if he could murder a sausage roll.'

Hollie nodded, aware of Maximo Diaz's burning black gaze on her as she moved away and that the high heels were making her hips sway in a way she hoped wasn't drawing attention to her bottom. Finding the mayor waiting, she kept her smile intact as he popped an entire sausage roll into his mouth, and thought about what her boss had said. *Had* she been guilty of monopolising the Spaniard? Maybe she had. She'd certainly been transfixed by him. Lulled by the timbre of his richly accented voice, she had been unable to tear her eyes away from his darkly beautiful face. But for once it had been a two-way street, because tonight she sensed that she had captured his complete attention. Instead of flicking her his usual dismissive glance, he had been openly staring at her and talking to her and listening to her as if her opinion actually *mattered*.

Had she been gaping at him like a stranded fish in response to that and drinking in all that powerful mastery instead of 'working the room' as Janette had told her to? She turned her head and watched other people moving towards him, as if they too were being magnetised by all that unashamed masculinity.

'Good-looking fellow, isn't he?' observed the mayor wryly, noting the direction of her gaze as he reached for a second sausage roll. 'I've noticed every woman in the room can't seem to stop staring at him.'

Hollie winced. And she had been as guilty as the rest! She had drooled over him like some teenager at a pop concert.

'I guess everyone's interested because he's about to become a local landowner.'

'You think so? Wouldn't have anything to do with the size of his wallet or the fact that he looks like an old-fashioned matinee idol, would it?'

'Of course not,' she said primly, quickly excusing herself to continue her elfish duties with renewed fervour, in an attempt to redeem herself in her boss's eyes. She dispensed the gradually wilting selection left on her tray, topped up glasses and tried to keep busy, but, irritatingly, her thoughts kept flitting back to the man with the black eyes who was currently being monopolised by the local member of parliament. Maximo Diaz had unsettled her and made her feel distinctly disorientated because when he'd looked at her that way, she'd felt…

It was difficult to describe but she'd felt *different*. As if she weren't Hollie Walker at all, but as if another woman had taken over her body. During a brief conversation about the wisdom of serving throwback cocktail snacks, an entirely different narrative had been running through her head. Hadn't she found her gaze straying to the Spaniard's sensual lips, which looked like an invitation to sin, and wondered what it would be like to be kissed by him? Hadn't her curiosity been piqued about how it would feel to be held in the arms of someone who looked so unbelievably strong?

Which was crazy. A man like Maximo Diaz was about as far out of her reach as the cold stars in the heavens. He was an international playboy with girlfriends who featured regularly on the covers of glossy magazines, while she was a twenty-six-year-old virgin. In fact, sometimes Hollie thought she could be defined by all the things she *hadn't* done. Yes, she'd gone to live in London—and just look how *that* had ended—but she'd never been intimate with a man. She'd never lain naked in someone's arms, or shared a giggling breakfast with them next morning, or gone on a mini-break, or been given a sentimental piece of jewellery.

Maybe that was her own fault. She knew people thought she dressed too conservatively for her age, because they'd hinted at it more than once and Janette had come right out and said so on more than one occasion. But they hadn't grown up watching a woman who used sexual allure like a weapon, had they? Who'd painted her face like a courtesan and squeezed her body into clothes bought solely for the intention of showing off her fabulous physique. But it hadn't worked. Her mother had spent years making herself available to a man who didn't want her and, as Hollie had watched her repeat that humiliating spectacle over and over again, she had vowed she was never going to be like that. Women didn't need a man to define them any more and she was going to live her life on *her* terms.

She cleared away empty glasses and plates and the next time she looked, Maximo Diaz was nowhere to be seen and most of the other guests had begun to drift away. Her heart sank. And that was that. She hadn't even seen him go! Feeling curiously deflated, she brushed up the dropped cocktail sticks and pine needles which littered the floor before making her way back to the basement to change, and by the time she'd bagged up her elf costume, the place was almost empty.

Someone had turned off the flashing Christmas tree lights and the hotel seemed deserted as she left by the staff entrance at the back. But as Hollie stepped out into the dark night, she was unprepared for the rain— or rather, the sudden deluge which was tipping from the sky. With no umbrella and a coat which wasn't particularly waterproof, she was quickly soaked through and her windswept progress to the nearby bus stop didn't provide much in the way of shelter. She looked upwards. Why hadn't the council bothered to repair that gaping hole in the roof?

In vain she scanned the horizon for the welcoming light of the bus and was just contemplating digging out her phone to call a taxi—and to hell with the expense— or even braving the elements and walking home, when a large dark car purred soundlessly down the street and came to a gliding halt beside her.

It wasn't a car she recognised. It was sleek and gleaming and obviously very expensive. A car which looked totally out of place in this tiny Devon town, especially as it was being driven by a chauffeur who wore a peaked cap. But Hollie's heart missed a beat as she identified the powerful figure sitting in the back seat.

The electric window slid down and the shiver which rippled down her spine had less to do with the water slowly soaking through her jacket and more to do with the ebony gaze of Maximo Diaz, which was spearing through her like a dark sword. With a crashing heart she registered his thick black hair and the curve of his sensual mouth, which now twisted in what looked like resignation.

'Get in' was all he said.

CHAPTER TWO

'Where to?' Maximo demanded as the woman slid her damp and shivering body onto the seat beside him and his chauffeur shut the door on the howling night.

'I was on my way h-home.'

'I'd kind of worked that out for myself,' he said, steeling himself against the strangely seductive stumble of her words. 'Where do you live?'

'Right on the edge of town, towards the moors.' She turned her face towards his in the dim light of the limousine and he could hear the faint deference in her voice. 'It's very kind of you to give me a lift, Señor Diaz.'

'I'm not known for my kindness,' he told her, with impatient candour. 'But you'd have to be pretty hard-hearted to drive past a woman standing alone at a rainy bus stop on a night like this.' He stared at the raindrops which glittered on her pale cheeks and lowered his voice. 'The question is whether you want me to drive you home, or did your mother warn you never to accept lifts from strangers?'

'You're not exactly a stranger, are you?' she answered primly. 'And since you're offering, then I'll ac-

cept. Thank you. It's a rotten night and it really is very…
nice of you.'

Nice as well as kind? Maximo almost laughed as he
leaned forward to tap the glass and the big car moved
forward. When was the last time he'd been described in
such glowing terms? The nurses who had cared for his
mother in her final days would certainly never have sub-
scribed to such a favourable opinion, but their views on
the world had been as black and white as the habits they
wore. Nice sons did not neglect their dying mother, nor
remain dry-eyed as she shuddered out her last breath.

'Anyway, you can call me Maximo. And put on your
seat belt,' he ordered, dragging his thoughts back from
the painful past to the woman still shivering beside him.

'I'm trying.'

Waving away her fumbling fingers, he leaned over
to slot in her seat belt and as he again caught a drift of
scent which was more soap than perfume, he wondered
if his behaviour really *was* motivated by a stab of chiv-
alry and nothing more. Because wasn't the truth that tonight he had wanted her—and not in some hypothetical
role as his ideal secretarial assistant? Hell, no. Tonight,
all the softness and sweetness he'd previously associated with her had collided with a totally unexpected
raunchy version, which had planted desire stubbornly
in his mind. And he hadn't seemed able to shift it…

Either way, he hadn't intended to take it any further,
for what would be the point? She was a small-town
woman and he was just…passing through. He didn't do
one-night stands. He never had, for all kinds of reasons.
They were too messy and had the potential to be complicated, and complicated was something he avoided

at all cost. So he had left the hotel and the humdrum party and convinced himself he would quickly forget her—at least until next time he ran into her, if indeed he did. Only by then, she would be back to normal. He wouldn't be dazzled by that very obvious visual stimulant of a short, figure-hugging dress, because she would be back in her drab clothes—barely meriting a second glance as he signed off on his castle purchase. And that would be an end to it. *Adios.* He wasn't intending to stay in this claustrophobic town for a second longer than he needed to. He would sign on the dotted line, put his deal into rapid motion—and nobody would see him for dust.

And then fate had conspired to put her directly in his path—quite literally. No longer a red-and-white-stockinged elf, but a wet and bedraggled woman standing by the roadside. Shivering.

'You're cold,' he observed.

'A bit.'

Commanding his driver in Spanish to increase the heat, he turned to her.

'How's that? Any better?'

'Much better.' She wriggled around in the seat a little. 'It's weird but even the seat feels warm.'

'That's because it's heated.'

'Your car seat has a *heater*?'

'It's hardly at the cutting edge of invention,' he said drily. 'Most new cars do.'

There was silence for a moment.

'I've never owned a car.'

'You're kidding?'

'No.' She shook her head and a few raindrops sprayed over in his direction. 'There's never really been any reason to have one. I used to live in London, where it's impossible to park, and I don't need one here. We need to turn left, please. Just there, past the lamp post.'

Maximo met his driver's eyes in the rear-view mirror and the man gave a barely perceptible nod of comprehension as he started to negotiate the turn. 'So how do you manage without one?'

'Oh, it's easy enough. I walk—when the weather's fine. Or I use my bike. These country roads around here are glorious in the springtime.'

Inadvertently, an image strayed into his mind of a woman on a bicycle, her long shiny hair flowing behind her, while pale flowers sprang in drifts along the hedgerows. He had just allowed this uncharacteristically romantic fantasy to incorporate an element of birdsong, when he heard her teeth begin to chatter.

'You're still cold,' he observed.

'Yes. But we're here now. It's the last house—just before the road turns into a mud track,' she was saying, pointing towards a small, darkened house in the distance. 'That's right. Stop just here.'

The car drew to a halt and Maximo saw the chauffeur unclip his seat belt, obviously intending to open the car door, but something compelled him to halt his action with a terse command.

'Permitame...' Maximo murmured, getting out and going to Hollie's side of the car. And even while he was opening the door for her, he was telling himself there was no need to behave like some old-fashioned doorman—not when he'd already played the Good Samaritan and given her a lift home. But somehow he wasn't interested

in listening to reason and indeed, he seemed impervious to the hard lash of rain on his face.

'You're getting wet!' she protested.

'I'll survive.'

That look of hesitation was back on her face again. 'Would you…?' She glanced up at the darkened cottage and then back at him as if summoning up a courage she didn't normally call on. 'Would you like to come in, for a cup of coffee? Just as my way of saying thank you? No, that's an absolutely stupid suggestion. I don't know why I made it. Forget it. Forget I said anything.' She shook her head as if embarrassed. 'I'm sure you have somewhere else you need to be.'

He saw the doubt which crossed her face, echoing the ones which were proliferating inside his own head, because this wasn't his style. Not at all. He didn't frequent houses like this and he didn't know women like her. Not any more. He'd left the world of mediocrity behind him a long time ago and had never looked back.

'Actually, there's nowhere I need to be right now and I'd love a cup of coffee. But quickly,' he amended. 'Before both of us get any wetter.'

As he followed her up the narrow path Maximo told himself it wasn't too late to change his mind. He could get his driver to speed out of town, return to his luxury hotel and lose himself in some work—maybe even call that model who'd been texting him for months. The Christmas elf would let herself into her little home, take off her dripping coat—and that would be that. She would be a little disappointed, yes, and even he might experience the briefest of pangs himself, but it would soon pass. He'd never met a woman he would miss if he never saw her again.

Dipping his head to enter the tiny house, he felt the icy temperature hit him. Did she notice his shoulders bunch against the chilly blast as he closed the door behind him?

'I know. It's freezing. I keep the heating off when I'm not here,' she explained, giving a slightly nervous laugh as she switched on a tall lamp.

He didn't need to ask why. She might claim to be nobly conserving energy as everyone was supposed to be doing these days, but he suspected the real reason was a lack of cash. Why else would she be doing more than one job and living in such humble surroundings? He looked around the room, observing the faded rug on the hearth and noticing that the thin curtains she drew across the window didn't quite meet in the middle. Yet the cushions on the sofa looked home-made and a dark red lily in a pot on the table looked almost startling in its simple beauty. And something about the limitations of the room suddenly seemed achingly familiar to him, even though he had grown up in the north-west of Spain and this was England.

He felt the twist of his heart, for it was a long time since he had been anywhere which wasn't five-star. He had embraced luxury for so long that he'd thought those impoverished memories had vanished into the dark abyss of time. Forgotten. For a long time he'd wanted to forget them—no, had *needed* to forget them—but now they came rushing back in an acrid stream.

He remembered the cold and the hunger. The proud need to survive without letting people know your sweater wasn't thick enough, or that your boots had holes in them. He remembered the slow seep of water making his feet wet and cold. And wasn't that the craziest thing of all—that you sometimes found yourself hungering for the things you no longer had, even if they were bad things? So that when he'd been poor he had craved nothing but wealth and now he had all the money he could ever use, wasn't he guilty of sentimentalising the hardships of the past?

'I'll make you some coffee.'

Her soft words broke into his reverie, her expression criss-crossed with anxiety. Perhaps she'd seen the tension on his face and had interpreted it as disapproval. Maybe that was why she was looking as if she regretted her decision to invite him here. Had he appeared to be *judging* her, when he had no right to judge anyone?

Except maybe himself.

'No,' he said. 'Get yourself dry first. The coffee can wait.'

'But—'

'Just do it,' he reaffirmed harshly.

Unable—or unwilling—to ignore the deep mastery in the Spaniard's voice, Hollie nodded and ran upstairs, her heart pounding with excitement, and started stripping off her sodden clothes, bundling her damp tights into the laundry basket and searching around for something suitable to wear. As her fingertips halted on her best woollen dress, she thought how weird it was to think of Maximo Diaz downstairs, because the only men who ever stepped over the threshold were tradespeople commissioned by her landlord to repair the aging and rather dodgy appliances.

She knew her self-contained behaviour meant she was often regarded as something of an oddity and there were a million reasons she gave to herself and others when asked why she didn't socialise much. She didn't have a lot of spare cash, because she was saving up to start her own business. She hadn't lived here very long, so she didn't know many people. These things were true, but weren't the whole story. The real reason was that her solitary life made her feel safe and protected. It didn't leave her open to pain or deception, or having her life messed up by somebody else.

Yet she had broken the habit of a lifetime and invited Maximo Diaz into her home, hadn't she? A world-famous billionaire financier. She was surprised she'd had the nerve and even more surprised when he'd accepted. And now she had to go down and face him and say... *what*? What on earth did she have in common with the Spanish billionaire?

Yet even though part of her was regretting her impulsiveness, she couldn't deny the slow curl of excitement which was unfurling somewhere low in her stomach. Was it wrong to feel this way about someone she barely knew? She stared in the mirror, her hand automatically reaching for something to tie her hair up, but at the last minute her hand fell back and she left it loose and streaming down her back as she closed her bedroom door behind her.

The creak of the stairs should have warned him she was on her way back down but Maximo didn't appear to have heard her and for a moment Hollie stood immobile on the foot of the stairs. And suddenly it was as though someone had waved a magic wand and filled her ordinary little sitting room with unexpected life and colour, and Maximo Diaz was at the blazing heart of it.

He had lit the fire. Removed his smart suit jacket and put it on the sofa to coax a blaze from the sometimes stubborn little wood-burning stove. Behind the small glass doors, orange flames were licking upwards from the applewood logs and already a blanket of heat was beginning to seep out into the room. Had she thought that a man so rich and so privileged would be unwilling to get his hands dirty? Yes, she had. But it was his stance which surprised her most, for he was sitting back on his heels on the old hearthrug as if he were perfectly comfortable to find himself there. He seemed lost in thought as the flames flickered shadows over his aristocratic profile.

Hollie felt another ripple of excitement whispering over her skin—a sensation as unsettling as that low clench of heat unfurling inside her. She knew she ought to say something but she didn't want to break the spell. At least, not yet. Because surely any minute now he would come to his senses. He would suddenly realise that his driver was waiting in the car outside and it was time to excuse himself.

Silently, she went into the kitchen and made a pot of coffee, which she carried back into the sitting room, and when he glanced up and saw her, something unrecognisable gleamed in the ebony abyss of his eyes. Something which made her feel as shivery as before, as if she were standing outside in the rain again.

Was she imagining it?

Was she imagining the glint of approval as he ran his narrow-eyed gaze over her?

'Come and sit by the fire,' he said.

His rich voice washed over her like dark silk, as Hollie acknowledged what sounded like a direct order. Did he always assume such an air of rightful dominance, she wondered—and was it wrong to find that more than a little exciting? She put the tray down and sank onto the floor beside him and wondered if she was getting herself into something outside her experience, which a sensible person should steer clear of. But she was cold, the fire was hot and the coffee smelt unbearably good. And surely she wasn't misguided enough to think that Maximo Diaz was actually going to make a pass at her!

'Maybe I should have offered you wine,' she ventured.

'Is that what you want?'

She shook her head. She was already distracted by his proximity—wine was the last thing she needed. 'Good heavens, no,' she said briskly. 'This will be fine. Just so long as it doesn't keep you awake.'

His lips curved into a mocking smile. He looked as if he was about to make a comment, then seemed to change his mind, leaning back against the old armchair behind him and spreading his long legs out in front of him.

For a moment everything in the room became very still—like the preternatural calm which sometimes comes before a storm. The crackle of the fire and the pounding of her heart were the only sounds Hollie could hear and, in the soft light, his eyes looked ebony-dark as he turned his head to study her.

'Have you lived here long?' he questioned.

'Just over a year now. I lived in London before that.'

'Where you didn't have a car.'

She beamed, pleased he'd remembered. 'That's right.'

'So what was the lure of a place like Trescombe?'

Hollie wondered how to answer him. No need to tell him she'd been ripped off. Or that a supposed good friendship had hit the skids as a result. Nobody wanted to hear that kind of downbeat detail and she certainly didn't want to start re-evaluating whether she'd been a hopeless judge of character. And wasn't her new-found motto that she was going to look forward, not back?

'My dream has always been to run a traditional English tea shop,' she told him. 'And when London didn't work out, I heard about an opportunity opening up down here. There's a great site in the town but it won't be available until springtime and until that happens I need regular work so I can save up as much as possible. That's why I'm working for Janette. I'm sorry, I should have asked you before—would you like anything to eat to go with that?'

Reluctantly, Maximo smiled in response to her question. He could sense her eagerness to keep him entertained and knew he ought to cut the visit short rather than get her hopes up, yet he stayed exactly where he was. For the first time in a long time, he felt *comfortable*. Uncharacteristically comfortable. The simply furnished room and warm fire were strangely seductive and so too was her undemanding company. In fact, for someone who was notoriously restless, he might have been able to relax completely—were it not for the undeniable tension which had begun to build in the air between them.

His senses seemed heightened. He could see the

thrust of her breasts against the soft jersey of her dress and the pebbled outline of her nipples. He swallowed. It might have been a while since he'd been intimate with a woman but the subliminal message of desire which Little Miss Christmas was sending his way was unmistakable.

And it was driving him crazy.

Was she aware that her eyes grew dark whenever she looked his way, or that she kept trailing the tip of her tongue over her mouth, like an unobserved cat contemplating where its next meal was coming from? And didn't he want to pull her into his arms, to test if those lips tasted as sweet as they looked?

'Why don't you wear your hair down more often?' he said suddenly.

His question seemed to startle her, for she touched her fingers to the silky waves which rippled almost to her waist. 'Because it isn't…' She shrugged. 'I don't know. Practical, I guess.'

'And do you always have to be practical?'

'As much as possible, yes. Life is easier that way,' she asserted, when he continued to look at her. 'You know, more dependable.'

'Really?' he pondered reflectively, the pad of his thumb brushing over the beard-shadowed jut of his jaw—a movement which seemed to fascinate her. 'But surely dependability can get a little boring sometimes. How old are you?'

'Twenty-six,' she said, a little defiantly.

'Don't you ever want to throw caution to the wind and do something unpredictable?'

'I've never really thought about it much, to be honest.'

He noticed that her fingers were trembling, making her coffee cup rattle against the saucer as she quickly put it down on the hearth.

'Well, think about it now,' he said. 'What would you do, for example, if I were to acknowledge the unspoken desire in your eyes and touch you? If I were to brush my fingers against your hair, to discover whether it feels as soft as it looks in the firelight?'

'I can't...' Her words sounded husky and he could see the swallowing movement of her throat. 'I can't imagine you doing something like that.'

'No?' He heard the note of repressed hope in her voice and silently, he answered it, reaching out to imprison a single lock of hair and stroking it between his thumb and forefinger, like a merchant examining a piece of valuable cloth. 'The funny thing is neither can I. But I am. And it does. Like silk, I mean. Rich, dark golden silk.'

'Mr Diaz.'

'I've been thinking about touching you all night long,' he husked unsteadily, skating his palm down over the abundant waves. 'And you like it, don't you? You like me stroking your hair.'

Her shuddered word was barely audible. 'Y-yes.'

For a while he listened to her uneven breathing and felt his own corresponding leap of desire. 'And you know what comes next, don't you?'

She shook her head and gazed at him in silence.

'Yes, you do.'

'Tell me,' she whispered, like a child asking to be told a story.

'I kiss you,' he said, a note of urgency deepening his voice to a growl.

Their eyes met. 'Yes,' she whispered, nodding her head with eager assent. 'Yes, please.'

It was the most innocent yet the most provocative thing he'd ever heard.

And suddenly her hair was a rope and Maximo was using it to guide him towards her waiting lips and he felt his body tense with a sweet and tantalising hunger.

CHAPTER THREE

MAXIMO WAS KISSING HER until she had started to make mewling little sounds of hunger. Until she was moving her body restlessly against him in a gesture of unspoken need.

She should have been nervous about what was about to happen, but fear was the last thing on Hollie's mind as the Spaniard drew away from her, his black eyes blazing with passion in the glow of the firelight.

He laced his fingers through the fall of her hair, and his breath was warm against her lips as he spoke. 'I think it's time we found ourselves somewhere more comfortable, don't you?'

'Yes, please,' she whispered again, and then wondered if she should at least have gone through the motions of pretending to give it more than a moment's consideration.

But that flicker of apprehension fled as soon as he picked her up and carried her upstairs, like the masterful embodiment of all her forbidden dreams. She could hear the powerful beat of her heart and the creak of the wood as he negotiated the narrow staircase.

'Where's your bedroom?' he demanded, once they'd reached the top.

She supposed now wasn't the time to tell him there was only one bedroom—instead she jerked her head in the direction of the nearest door, wishing she had tidied up a bit more. 'In there.'

But as he kicked it open, Maximo didn't seem to notice the cardigan lying on the chair or the pile of cookery books teetering in a haphazard pile on the bedside table. Instead, he set her down and spoke in a voice which suddenly seemed much more accented than before and more than a little unsteady.

'You are wearing far too many clothes,' he growled, skating his fingertips over her trembling body. 'And part of me wishes you'd kept that crazy costume on so I could have had the pleasure of removing it. I've never undressed an elf before.'

Did that mean he didn't like her woollen dress? Probably—it was undoubtedly very staid in comparison, though comparisons were never a good thing, certainly not in her case. But as he peeled it over her head before efficiently disposing of her tights, Hollie suddenly forgot about her insecurities.

'You're shivering,' he observed.

'The upstairs of this cottage is f-freezing.'

'And is that the only reason you're shivering?'

She liked the teasing note in his voice. Was it that which gave her the courage to hook her hand around the back of his head and brush her lips close to his?

'No,' she whispered. 'Not just that, no.'

His soft laugh was tinged with faint triumph as he

pulled back the duvet and pushed her down onto the mattress. 'So why don't you warm up the bed for me?' he suggested as he pulled the duvet over her. 'While I get out of these clothes.'

Hollie studied him hungrily as he peeled off his sweater, her mouth drying to dust as his fingers slipped to the button of his trousers. She was grateful that the room was in semi-darkness, which successfully hid the burn of her cheeks as, slowly, he slid the zip down. And she didn't avert her gaze, not once. Even when he kicked off his boxer shorts to reveal the powerful shaft of his erection, though it was the first time she had ever seen a naked man before.

He climbed into bed beside her and when he took her in his arms, she felt so warm and so…safe—that she buried her head in his shoulder, overcome by a sudden emotion she couldn't put a name to.

'Mi belleza...' he breathed, exploring her trembling flesh with his fingers until she felt as if she were melting, and then unclipping her bra so that her large breasts came tumbling out. And when he put his mouth to her puckered nipple and sucked, Hollie felt as if she were going to dissolve with pleasure.

How could it be that she wasn't feeling the slightest bit shy? Even though she was wearing nothing but a pair of panties, which were growing damper by the second as she clung to him as if her life depended on it. Because that was what it felt like. As if she hadn't known what it was to be properly alive before Maximo Diaz kissed her. As if she'd die if she didn't get more of him. More of *this*…this fierce flame of desire which was arrowing through her body and setting her on fire, making her feel as if she were on the verge of hurtling towards some place of unimaginable bliss.

'Maximo,' she breathed, her voice sounding slurred and nothing like her voice at all. 'That is so…so *incredible.*'

His dark head lifted its attention from her breast and his eyes grew smoky as he moved up the bed to kiss her again, his tongue nudging inside her parted lips. And Hollie let her tongue fence with his, loving this brand-new intimacy as her breasts pressed eagerly against his bare chest, as if her button-hard nipples were trying to communicate some unspoken need to him. And instantly he answered it, his hand reaching down to run his fingertip over the damp gusset of her panties. She quivered as he brushed against her swollen bud through the sodden material and felt the whisper of his words on her lip.

'And so are you.' He shook his head and swallowed. 'I never imagined you'd be so…'

'So, what?' she questioned breathlessly.

He seemed to recover some of his poise, tugging at the elasticated edge of her plain panties. 'Well, you're a little overdressed, for one thing.'

'Am I?'

'Mmm…' For a moment he grazed another teasing fingertip over her damp panties, which made her squirm with delight and frustration, before sliding them off and allowing them to join the tangle of other clothes which were scattered over the floor of her small bedroom. 'But you are also hot. Surprisingly hot. Like my every fantasy brought to life. Who knew?'

'So are you,' she whispered boldly, splaying her fin-

gers over his bare chest and thinking how rich his olive
skin looked in the soft lamplight. Tentatively she rubbed
at one of *his* nipples, silently enjoying his corresponding
shudder of pleasure which gave her the confidence to
return the compliment. 'You are my every fantasy, too.'

For a moment he grew still, then drew his head away
from hers. His black eyes were narrowed but there was
no mistaking the sudden warning which glinted from
their ebony depths. 'But fantasies aren't real,' he said
silkily. 'We both know that, don't we?'

'No, of course they're not. Absolutely they're not.'
Eager to convey her agreement, Hollie nodded, instinctively knowing what he wanted, or, more importantly,
what he *didn't* want. He didn't want her reading too
much into this and falling for him and, to be honest, that
was the last thing she wanted either. She didn't know
much about what made men tick but she'd recognised
from the get-go that Maximo Diaz was the last person
to hitch her star to. Yes, she'd had a crush on him since
the first time they'd met and, yes, that feeling had just
grown and grown—but she certainly wasn't alone in
feeling that way. That she now found herself naked in
bed with him wasn't something she'd imagined would
happen, not in her wildest dreams. That it had happened
in a way which seemed completely natural made her
feel comfortable with her own body for the first time
in her life and she was grateful to him for that. So why
should she deny herself the inevitable outcome of them
being here like this?

Why *should* she?

Always, she'd stuck rigidly to the path of conven-
tion, because life had felt safer that way. But nothing

was ever completely safe and Maximo had been right. For once she wanted to dabble with impulsiveness instead of dependability. She'd never been in love—never wanted to be in love, for that matter—because she'd witnessed the fallout which could result from investing in such an unreliable emotion. She'd never had a boyfriend who had lasted longer than a month and she'd never been turned on enough to get any further than accepting a couple of mechanical fumbles, which had turned her stomach and made her call an instant halt to them.

She'd thought she was one of those women who just didn't feel physical desire. The kind of woman people used to mock and call frigid. But Maximo Diaz was in the process of demonstrating that there was nothing wrong with her body. Nothing at all. Just so long as she didn't start entertaining any unrealistic expectations of some kind of future with the Spanish tycoon. Because that wasn't just impractical—it was stupid.

She closed her eyes as he sank his lips to hers again and moved his hand between her thighs, and Hollie wrapped her arms tightly around his muscular shoulders as if he were her rock and her anchor. How was it possible to feel this good, with a man's tongue in her mouth and his finger strumming at her bare bud with sweetly accurate intensity? But idle reflection was no longer possible, not when a sudden clench of desire was making her heated body as taut as the string of a newly tuned violin.

'Maximo!' she gasped.

He lifted his head, mockery and passion glinting in his eyes. 'What is it?' he husked.

She wanted to tell him to stop. She wanted to tell him

never to stop. But then it was happening. Her body had started clenching around his finger, with swift and perfect spasms, and she was crying out something which sounded as if it had been torn from somewhere deep inside her, as the world splintered into a kaleidoscope of vivid rainbows.

Consciousness receded and then came back again in a slow and sensual comedown. She was dimly aware of him watching her and waiting for her body to grow still. He kissed each tingling nipple in turn and then reached for something he must have put on the locker, which she assumed must be a condom. Because Hollie knew the rules—even if she'd never had to follow them before now—and sex had to be safe.

But his hands seemed to be unsteady as he unpeeled the foil and she watched like a hungry voyeur as he slid the rubber down over his erect shaft. Part of her was wondering why she wasn't experiencing a faint wrench of embarrassment, or some element of misgiving at the reality of what was about to happen. But Hollie felt none of those things. Her current state of being was so dreamy and so...*complete* that she simply opened her arms wide as Maximo came to lie down on top of her, welcoming the warm weight of his body.

He was hard and honed and powerful, yet his skin was silky and warm. She was aware of his rigid hardness pressing against her belly and she could feel her thighs opening for him, as if some inner knowledge was orchestrating her movements, making someone with no experience seem as if she knew exactly what she was doing. He gave a low laugh as he positioned himself over her, his lips brushing over hers as she felt his hard tip seeking entry.

'Do you want me, *mi belleza*?'

'*Sí,*' she answered and this made him smile, but as he thrust inside her the smile faded, his eyes briefly closing before he opened them again.

She could feel the sudden tension in his body as he stared at her with a question furrowing his brow.

'Your first time?' he verified.

She nodded, wondering if she'd imagined the note of disbelief in his voice, the lump in her throat making words impossible, terrified he wouldn't want her now he knew that nobody else ever had.

But in that she was wrong.

Very wrong.

Very deliberately, he changed his position, reaching underneath her to cushion her fleshy buttocks with the palms of his hands and bring her thighs up to his hips, so that their bodies seemed even closer than before. He kissed her long and he kissed her hard and just the feel of his mouth on hers was enough to make her relax into what was happening as her body adjusted around him and his incredible width. He began to move again, each thrust seeming to fill her completely—and the sensation of his flesh inside her flesh, of somehow being at *one* with him, blew her mind as nothing ever had before.

Did she wrap her legs around his waist to make his penetration even deeper, or had he guided her into doing that? Hollie wasn't sure. The only thing she was sure of was that those feelings were building up inside her again, taking her higher and higher towards another incredible peak. And then she reached it. Almost without expecting to, she stumbled over the edge and went into free fall and Hollie screamed out her pleasure—she who had never screamed in her life. As she began to spasm around him, she could feel his body begin to buck with pleasure as he bit out words in fractured Spanish—harsh sounds which seemed to split the night.

His movements seemed to go on and on and never had she been so aware of each and every sensation. She could feel the ragged pull of oxygen into her lungs as she tried to steady her breathing. She could hear the muffled pounding of her heart. There was a fine sheen of sweat on Maximo's shoulders and she could detect a raw and very distinctive masculine scent in the air. And now he was heavy against her—as heavy as her eyelids, which felt as if they had been weighted with lead. A sigh fluttered from her lips as she snuggled into his arms and she must have dozed off. Perhaps he did too, for when she woke it was to the realisation that he was growing hard inside her again and Hollie gave a hungry little yelp of longing. Her arms tightened around him and as she began to writhe against him, she could hear herself making wordless sounds of demand against his skin.

'No.' Cutting short her next wriggle of anticipation with a curt order, he carefully withdrew from her.

She was aware of him rolling away and then, to her horror—he carefully peeled off the condom before getting out of bed. His black hair was ruffled as he stared down at her, his jet eyes unreadable as their gazes clashed.

'Where's the bathroom?'

Startled, Hollie searched her befuddled brain for a

coherent response. 'J-just along the corridor. You can't miss it.'

After he'd gone, she just lay there, her thoughts in a muddle. At first it shamed her to think she'd just been intimate with a man who didn't even know the layout of her house, but Hollie quickly remonstrated with herself. She wasn't going to feel *any* kind of shame—otherwise what would be the point? And she certainly wasn't going to start getting squeamish and wonder what he'd done with the condom. In fact, she refused to feel any negativity at all about what had just happened. She'd just had sex with a man she fancied very much and it had been amazing. Women the world over did this sort of thing all the time. She had joined the party at last—she certainly hadn't done anything *wrong*.

Sitting up in bed, she smoothed down the mussed tumble of her hair and then Maximo walked back into the room—or maybe she should say *sauntered*—looking totally comfortable with his own nakedness, in all its olive-dark gloriousness. She half expected him to reach for his clothes and start getting dressed, and she told herself she would be okay with that—because what choice did she have?—but to her astonishment, he climbed right back into bed beside her. And then Hollie experienced a little shiver of self-recrimination. Did she think so little of herself that she'd thought he would be out of there as fast as his legs could carry him?

She turned to face him, waiting for him to take the lead, because what did a woman *do* in a situation like this? She had no idea and no experience. Was she supposed to praise him, or thank him for the most incredible happening of her entire life? Or act all cool, as if it were no big deal? Why didn't some enterprising person write a sexual etiquette book for virgins? she wondered.

He lay down beside her and for a moment she thought he was about to lean over and kiss her again and, oh, how she wished he would. But instead, he pushed away some of the hair which had fallen into her face and let his gaze scan over her like a dark searchlight.

'Your first time,' he said again.

It was half statement and half question. 'That's right,' Hollie replied, swallowing down her sudden nervousness that this was going to turn into some sort of interrogation session and she would come over as a freak. 'Do you mind?'

'Mind?' He seemed to mull this over in his head. 'Why should I mind? You're an adult. You have free will. You came to a decision that you wanted to have sex with me. I'm flattered, of course, and more than a little interested to know why.'

She wondered if he was fishing for compliments. Did he want her to say he was so gorgeous that she hadn't been able to resist him? *And wouldn't that have been the truth?* But Maximo Diaz needed no boost for his ego, not from her. Certainly not when he was lying there, dissecting what had just happened between them with all the cool detachment of a scientist in the lab. 'Does there have to be a reason?'

He shrugged and the ripple of muscle beneath his broad shoulders was more than a little distracting.

'Most women wait—though I guess you've waited quite a long time already—for a long-term relationship in which they can feel comfortable. Something which has a little more depth.' He paused. 'And history.'

It sounded like an accusation. Or a reproach. Was he somehow *disappointed* that she hadn't made him wait? 'Maybe I'm not most women.'

'No. Maybe you're not. In fact, I would take that as a given. You are certainly very surprising. You confounded my expectations which, believe me, doesn't happen very often.' He gave a short laugh before fixing her with that glittering black gaze again, their bodies still very close, the slick of his sweat-sheened skin sticky against hers. 'So which is the real you, I wonder—the efficient mouse who slaves away behind her desk, or the minxy hostess in fancy dress who wiggles her bottom so provocatively when she walks?'

'It was the shoes which made me walk that way.'

'Ah, so we must blame the shoes, must we?' he questioned gravely.

'I borrowed them,' she explained, when she saw the glint of mockery in his eyes. 'Oh. I see. You're teasing me.'

'Yes, I am teasing you, *mia belleza*,' he said, and his voice suddenly deepened into a velvety note of intent. 'But not for very much longer, because teasing inevitably provokes desire. What I would most like to do to you right now is to kiss you again and then to—'

'Make love?' she put in eagerly, then could have kicked herself for her naivety, which was surely responsible for the sudden tension which had entered his body.

'Well, that is one way of describing what we are about to do, though you need to remember that this has nothing to do with love.' His golden olive features hardened. 'Love is a concept invented by society. As a bribe, or a threat. As a marketing tool used by big businesses. Or as a method of control—a way of regulating women's behaviour.'

Hollie opened her mouth to object to what sounded like pure cynicism, until she realised that she agreed with him. Every single word. Hadn't her own mother carried her supposed 'love' for her father around with her like some dark jewel pressed close to her heart— guarding it and polishing it and making it more important than anything else in her life, including her own daughter?

'What *does* it have to do with, then?' she questioned boldly, because why wouldn't she be bold when she had come this far? When she was naked and glowing with physical satisfaction, even though the turn of the conversation was proving a little too raw for her liking. But then the insistent little clench deep at her core made her realise that she would prefer to stop talking altogether, and start kissing...

Did he read her body language? Was that why he reached out to stroke her face, his thumb whispering to her neck, where it lingered on the frantic little pulse which was beating there? Hollie shivered as he continued with his journey and it seemed to take for ever before he reached her nipple, his eyes not leaving hers as he massaged its diamond hardness, a small smile playing at the edges of his lips as it pebbled beneath his thumb. And she realised he still hadn't answered her question.

'It has to do with sensation. With feeling,' he answered, as if he'd read her mind. 'And this is the best feeling in the world. Wouldn't you agree?'

'Yes.' There was a short silence while she fought and

lost the battle to let the subject go. 'But you've felt it before, I suppose? Probably lots of times.'

He didn't deny it. 'Of course. But not for a while.'

She wanted to ask, but Hollie told herself it was none of her business. That his answers might not be what she wanted to hear. And when she didn't say anything—which seemed to surprise him—he moved closer. So close that at the points where their bodies connected, she could feel goosebumps icing her skin.

'So why don't we enjoy what we have? Just for tonight,' he added softly. 'I could send my chauffeur home and we could enjoy a little more uncomplicated pleasure. I could show you many different ways to achieve orgasm. We could explore and enjoy each other's bodies, because yours is...'

Hollie felt a feeling of power as his finger drifted down over her sternum, to lie possessively on the soft flesh of her belly. 'Mine is what?' she questioned breathlessly, as if she had conversations about the nature of desire every day of the week.

'*Esta magnifica.* So soft, so womanly, so full,' he husked, beginning to knead her flesh with his fingers and making her want to moan with delight. 'I want to be inside you again. Deep inside you. As many times as I can. Do you want that, too?'

Of course she did and she nodded eagerly. Who wouldn't want it? But his husky question came with a coded warning. *Just for tonight*, he had emphasised. Which meant she mustn't expect anything more. His words weren't the stuff of dreams or fairy tales, but that didn't mean she had to shoot them down in flames. At least he was being honest with her. At least he wasn't playing games and messing with her head, which meant something to a person who had been brought up to believe that men were nothing but inveterate liars. And now he was reaching down for his discarded trousers and sliding his phone from the pocket to have a rapid conversation in Spanish, presumably with his chauffeur, laughing briefly before hanging up. What was he laughing about? she wondered. But suddenly her slight paranoia was forgotten because he was pulling another condom from his wallet and in that moment Hollie felt properly grown-up for the first time in her life.

She was having sex! The amazing Spaniard had already given her, not one, but two orgasms—and he was planning on giving her some more! Christmas really had come early!

She settled back against the pillows, anticipation shivering her skin as he began to stroke her, with that look of dark intent on his face which made her melt inside. And then he ruined it all, as he brushed his lips over hers.

'Do you realise,' he mused, his hand reaching comfortably for her breast, 'that I don't even know your name?'

CHAPTER FOUR

HOLLIE'S MOUTH DRIED as she waited. She was trembling. Of course, she was trembling. Who wouldn't be in her situation?

She closed her eyes, uttering some kind of wordless prayer, but when her lids fluttered open, her wish had not been granted. Nothing had changed. She was still staring through the window of her tiny cottage at the dark night outside and the Christmas lights in the window of the house opposite. She was still exactly the same woman she'd been seconds ago.

She swallowed.

Pregnant.

Pregnant with the Spanish tycoon's baby.

Her heart pounding, she knew she couldn't keep putting off the inevitable. She needed to tell Maximo and the longer it went on, the harder it seemed to be.

She was still finding it hard to get her head around what she'd done. After a lifetime of being a virgin, she'd fallen into bed with a man who was practically a stranger. She couldn't have found a more unsuitable man to be her first lover, if she'd tried. An international playboy who had seemed all too eager to put distance between them once their brief encounter was over.

The night had not ended on a particularly good note. She'd hoped he might stay on for a while next morning. She'd thought about making him pancakes for breakfast, with honey or cheese. Or an omelette, maybe—because didn't the Spanish use a lot of eggs in their cooking? Perhaps she'd been secretly hoping to impress him with her undoubted skill at all things cuisine—the way to a man's heart and all that. But no. He had climbed out of bed, all glorious and glowing and naked, when the dawn light had been nothing but a glimmer on the horizon. She must have slipped back into sleep because the next time her eyelids had fluttered open, he had been fully dressed and maybe she should have guessed what was coming from the terse tone of his words.

'I'd better go.'

'Oh. Must you?' Her voice had been little more than a murmur, but afterwards she wondered if she'd sounded a little *needy*.

'I'm afraid I must. I've called my chauffeur to come and pick me up. I have a meeting.'

She remembered thinking it was very early to be having a meeting and then, drugged with satiation and satisfaction, she had fallen into a deep sleep and when she'd woken up, he had gone.

It had taken nearly a week for her to realise Maximo wasn't going to contact her again. He had told her he wouldn't but hadn't there been a stupid glimmer of hope which had taken up stubborn residence in her mind and made her hope he might change his mind? But there had been no phone call. No flowers. No unexpected dropping in at the estate agency to ask whether she might happen to be free for lunch—and of course she would have said yes, because her daily home-made sandwich, which reposed at the bottom of the office fridge, could easily be eaten another day.

But Maximo had done none of these things. The purchase of his castle was now complete and everyone in the town was breathlessly waiting for the refurbishment to begin, when he would turn it into the most talked about hotel in Devon to add to his prestigious group. She assumed that was why he was here today. She'd heard he was having high-powered meetings in the nearby city of Exeter and so, when Janette had left the office to have her nails painted, Hollie had hunted around for the tycoon's telephone number and had sent him a text, asking if she could see him.

His answer hadn't exactly boosted her confidence, or her resolve. It had been blunt and to the point. Some people might even have called it rude.

I'm very busy.

She wished she could have told him to take a running jump, but that was exactly what he would like her to do, she reminded herself bitterly. Her finger had been shaking with rage and she had wasted time correcting several typos as she had furiously tapped out a response.

I'm sure you are, but I need to see you.

She'd been forced to wait for a whole hour before the reluctant reply had come winging back.

I can give you half an hour at six p.m. Where?

That had made her hesitate. Neutral territory would be best. But she couldn't risk any kind of scene, not in a town this small where people would talk. And so even though uncomfortable memories of last time he had visited her cottage wouldn't seem to leave her alone, Hollie forced herself to reply.

Can you come to my cottage? I assume you remember where it is?

And the terse rejoinder.

I'll see you there.

It seemed insane to think about it now, but she'd actually made some biscuits in preparation for his visit, which were currently sitting on her best china plate in the kitchen. She'd told herself it was more to give herself something to do, rather than pacing the floor as she waited for the smooth purr of his limousine. But the insane truth was that she was making shortbread because she knew he liked it.

It was pathetic, really. Did she honestly imagine that the sugary cookie was going to make him smile and tell her everything was going to be okay, and he was fine with the fact that she was carrying his baby after what was only ever supposed to be a one-night stand?

She turned away from the window and glanced around the small sitting room, her gaze coming to rest on the miniature Christmas tree she'd forced herself to decorate, even though she hadn't been feeling remotely festive at the time. Its rainbow lights were pretty and the little baubles she'd crafted herself usually filled her heart with seasonal joy as she dangled them from the pine branches. But she had been so bogged down by a feeling of dread at what she was about to do that not even holiday decorations had been able to lighten her mood.

She heard the sound of a powerful engine and quickly ducked away from the window, not wanting to be seen watching and waiting, like some kind of crazed stalker from a horror film. She drew in a deep breath as she heard the approaching crunch of footsteps and slowly expelled it as the doorbell jangled.

Silently counting to three, Hollie walked calmly towards the door, trying to mentally prepare herself for the sight of Maximo Diaz as it swung open. And even though she had thought about him every single day since their night of passion, Hollie was still unprepared for the visceral impact of seeing him again.

He looked…

Her heart rate, which had already been elevated, now began to pick up into a deafening crescendo as she stared at him.

He looked…incredible.

Dressed entirely in black, he wore jeans and a buttery leather jacket, beneath which was a sweater so soft it could only have been made from cashmere. But that was the only soft thing about him. His body was hard and his face was even harder. Black eyes studied her as coldly as chips of jet and those wickedly sensual lips were set and unsmiling. How weird it was to think of all the pleasures those lips had showered on her while they'd been in bed together, when now they seemed to flatten at the edges with a look of faint disdain. Or was that her imagination?

Hollie knew she had to pull herself together. She couldn't keep catastrophising or trying to get inside his head. She had to act as normally as possible, although that was never going to be easy given what she was about to tell him. How would she have spoken to him if she hadn't had sex with him? How did she used to speak to him when he came into the office, during those easy, uncomplicated days before she'd been stupid enough to allow him to seduce her? With an enormous effort, she fixed a bright smile to her lips, aware of the stupidity of her greeting even as it tumbled from her.

'Good afternoon, Señor Diaz!'

Maximo tried very hard not to react to the instinctive punch to his gut as he studied the woman standing before him. He should be on his guard after her rather embarrassing determination to see him, yet all he could think about was her pale, soft flesh and the thickness of her shiny golden-brown hair as it had tumbled down over her bare breasts. Was that unwanted reaction responsible for his drawled words, which weren't the words he intended? 'Don't you think such formality is a little inappropriate, in view of what happened?'

'Even though you didn't even know my name at the time?' she answered quickly.

Maximo winced. She was right. How had that even *happened*? He still wasn't sure, and looking at her now provided no easy answers. The provocative minx in the towering red heels and thigh-skimming green dress was nothing but a distant memory, for she'd reverted back to her usual sensible look. Her magnificent hair was tied back into a tight bun and her lips were bare. She wore a neat skirt and forgettable sweater, which had obviously not been bought with the intention of emphasising her curves, and her brown leather boots had seen better days. They were obviously old boots which had been carefully polished—and something about that recognition of someone who was 'making do' struck a raw and distant chord deep inside him. She looked unremarkable, yet... He frowned. Wasn't there a glowing inner quality about her, which seemed to transcend her rather drab appearance?

'But I do know your name now,' he said, attempting a placatory smile. 'Hollie.'

'Hollie Walker,' she supplied crisply and then blushed, and that only seemed to emphasise her innocence.

Had he really had sex with her? Taken her virginity in one smooth and delicious thrust? Yes, he had. And it had been amazing. No. That wasn't quite accurate. It had been nothing short of sensational. Turned on and beguiled by those long legs and cascading hair and the startlingly dramatic change in her appearance, Maximo had succumbed to a one-night stand in a way he hadn't done since his teenage years. Her innocence had come as a shock and he still wasn't quite sure why he hadn't extricated himself from the situation as quickly as possible after that first time, doing them both a favour and recognising that someone like him was bad news for a small-town woman like her.

But he hadn't. He had carried on losing himself inside her sweet, tight body for most of the night, over and over again. And when they'd eventually run out of condoms—something which had never happened to him before—he had pleasured her in other ways. He had used his tongue and his fingers and, at one point, an ice cube from the freezer downstairs, he recalled—so that the memory of her shuddered cries of fulfilment had stubbornly lodged themselves in his brain for days afterwards. He'd had difficulty forgetting the way she'd cried out his name and the way her soft thighs had wrapped themselves around his thrusting back. He'd had difficulty concentrating on work too, drifting off into sensual daydreams at the slightest provocation, until he had forced himself to stop thinking about her.

But none of those things addressed his immediate concerns and now a feeling of wariness crept over him as he looked into Hollie Walker's face. Because, why had she asked to see him? Deliberately pushing away the brief cloud of darkness which hovered on the edge of his mind, he met her gaze with a look of polite enquiry.

'So. What can I do for you, Hollie? I meant it when I told you I was busy. There are things I need to get finished before Christmas, which is in a few days' time, as you clearly know.' He forced himself to give a curt nod of acknowledgement in the direction of the smallest tree he had ever seen.

Her mouth was working and her previously glowing complexion had paled. 'There's no easy way to say this. I wish there was.' She clenched her hands into two fists and squeezed them tight until the knuckles grew white. 'I'm pregnant, Maximo,' she husked. 'I'm going to have your baby.'

The world spun and a dull sound inside his head threatened to deafen him. For a minute Maximo thought he must be dreaming, but her trembling body and white face were real enough and told their own story.

For this was no dream. The nightmare had become real.

'You can't be.' His words were icy but the anger growing inside him felt hot and vital and all-consuming. 'We took precautions.'

'Well, obviously those precautions didn't work,' she said. 'Look, I realise this has come as a complete shock to you—'

'But clearly not to you.' He frowned as he did some rapid mental calculations. 'We had sex in—'

'October,' she supplied swiftly, her cheeks flaming. 'Just in case you're muddling me with someone else.'

'There hasn't been anyone else,' he snapped before wondering why on earth he had told her *that*. Because wouldn't it give her more power than she already had if she realised that every other woman had left him cold since he'd exited her bed, that wet dawn morning? Would she mistakenly start thinking she was special, or different?

'Oh. Right,' she said, looking startled.

His gaze skated over her as it had done with so many women in the past, but for once there was only one place it was focussed on. Not on her hair or lips or the curve of her breasts, but on her abdomen. 'Pregnant,' he repeated, as if affirming what his naked eye could not see.

'Eleven weeks.'

He felt as if he were speaking in a language he didn't really understand. As if he had entered a world which was now defined by dates. 'You certainly took your time telling me.'

She nodded. 'I know. I didn't realise for a while. At first I couldn't believe it, because I thought we were so careful. I made myself do three tests, until eventually I had to accept the evidence of what I found. And you weren't around to tell, Maximo. You were supposed to be coming back to Trescombe. Everyone thought work was going to start on the castle before Christmas—'

'What work?' he demanded.

'Well, you're turning it back into a hotel, aren't you? It's been the talk of the town for months. But you just... disappeared.'

'I have a global business,' he informed her coldly. 'Which seems to have gone into overdrive lately.'

'And was that...?' Her face was screwed up and she seemed to be forcing herself to ask the question. 'Was that the only reason?'

Maximo's mouth hardened. Wasn't it better she knew? Better to trample on her foolish dreams rather than to allow them to flourish unchecked? 'Not the only reason, no. If you must know I thought that creating space between us would ensure you didn't get the wrong idea about what had happened. I didn't want you building castles in the air.'

'You're the one with the interest in castles, Maximo,' she said coldly. 'I told you at the time I was okay with it.'

'Women say all kinds of things they don't mean, Hollie. They say them to save face, or sometimes to convince themselves that they actually believe them.'

She glared at him. 'And you were so certain I'd be a thorn in your side with my unwanted devotion that you didn't want to risk a return visit, is that it? Were you worried I'd believe I was hopelessly in love with you?'

'That was always a possibility.'

'Even though you're proving to be so arrogant and unlikeable?'

He shrugged. 'You were an innocent. A virgin. Sometimes a woman's first experience of sex can warp her judgement, particularly if it was as good as yours was. I'd warned you what kind of man I was but I wasn't sure whether you wanted to believe it. But all that is irrelevant now.'

He realised she was looking at him and the reproach on her flushed face suggested she had been hurt by his condemnatory assessment of their night together. But he wasn't going to tell lies in order to spare her feelings. She needed to know the truth, because surely that would limit the painful repercussions of a situation he had been so determined not to create during his own lifetime. The legacy of his upbringing was bitter enough to taint him for ever and he didn't want to feel trapped. Not ever again.

'I've never wanted marriage or children,' he bit out. 'And while the first is within my power to control, the second is clearly not.'

'But I'm not asking you for anything!' she declared furiously, her fists still clenched and looking as if she would like to use them to punch him. 'I can manage perfectly well on my own.'

He glanced around the small room. At the hand-knitted blanket on the battered sofa. At tired-looking walls, which even the rainbow glow from the fairy lights on the Christmas tree couldn't quite disguise.

He remembered the narrow bed in the cold bedroom upstairs, where he had torn the clothes from his body with the eagerness of a boy who had never had sex before. And the speed with which he had made his escape the following morning, issuing a terse directive to his chauffeur to get him the hell out of there when the car had arrived.

And all he could think was—what had he *done*?

'What, here?' he demanded. 'You think you can bring up this baby here, in a place like this?'

'Of course I can! It may not be grand and I may not have a lot of spare cash, but I will manage. I don't know how, but I will. I'm not deluding myself that it's going to be easy, but I'm not afraid of hard work. It won't hurt me to scrimp and save and go without—but there's one thing my baby will never go short of, and that's love!'

An expression of such fierce protectiveness came over her face, that Maximo found himself unexpectedly humbled by her fervour, until he reminded himself that words were cheap. 'Very admirable,' he drawled.

'I'm not seeking your approval.' Angrily, she shook her head. 'In fact, I don't want anything from you, Maximo Diaz. Because I don't need you! Do you understand?'

But he shook his head, as if she hadn't spoken. 'I am not dishonourable enough to desert you in your time of need, just as long as your expectations don't exceed what I am prepared to offer you,' he bit out, withdrawing his wallet from his inside pocket and extracting a business card. He slapped the card down beside the Christmas tree with more force than he had intended, causing the flimsy baubles to jangle before striding towards the front door, barely able to contain the anger which was simmering up inside him.

He pulled open the door. 'You can telephone my office and they will give you contact details of my lawyer, who will fine-tune all the necessary arrangements,' he concluded icily. 'You will have the necessary funds to employ nannies, chauffeurs, cleaners—whatever it is you think you might need to make your life easier once you have a child. But there is one thing you're never going to get, Hollie—at least, not from me—and that's a father for your baby.'

CHAPTER FIVE

'HOLLIE, ARE YOU even listening to what I'm saying?'

Hollie swallowed. No, of course she wasn't listening—not properly, anyway. She hadn't been fully concentrating on Janette's words, just as she hadn't been concentrating on anything lately. Not the news, nor office views, or even the fact that it was Christmas tomorrow. The only thing which was eating up her mind was the terrible showdown she'd had with Maximo a couple of days ago, when she had told him she was expecting his baby and he had reacted with…

Anger?

Disbelief?

Yes, both those things—and more besides. He had been icy with her, and distant. He had seemed to go out of his way to push her away and to view her with coldly dispassionate eyes. Nobody would ever have guessed they'd been lovers. Although, if you didn't even get to share a whole night with a man—did that actually *count* as being a lover?

That had been bad enough but worse was to follow because when she'd arrived at work the next morning, Janette had asked could she make a cake for Maximo, to celebrate his completion on the purchase of the castle. It had been the last thing on earth Hollie had felt like doing, but what excuse could she possibly use for declining?

I'm terribly sorry, Janette, but I'm pregnant with Maximo's baby and he's being so unreasonable that I'd be tempted to tip a dollop of arsenic into the mix.

No, she had nodded her head submissively, even though her heart had wrenched with bitterness and shame. And as she had beaten the eggs and measured out the sugar, she had been unable to flush the image of Maximo's angry face from her mind and to wonder where they went from here. She still had the business card he'd given her, just before he'd made his arrogant assertion that she should contact his lawyers.

He had cold-bloodedly stated that his money would enable her to employ a whole stable of staff, and had ended the conversation by announcing that he had no intention of being a father to his child. Well, that suited her just fine. Did he really imagine she, or her baby, wanted *anything* to do with a man who hadn't bothered to hide his dismay when she'd told him her momentous news?

But surely the most important thing right now was to hang onto her job, at a time when she had never needed work more badly. Which was why she looked up at her boss and forced a weak smile. 'What were you saying, Janette?' she asked.

'I was congratulating you on your cake, Hollie, which is absolutely lovely—though I have to say that it's not quite up to your *usual* standard.'

Hollie nodded. Of course it wasn't. It was unfortunate that a huge salt tear had plopped onto the finished product at the very last minute and Hollie's subsequent attempts at repair work only seemed to have made it worse.

'I know it's not that good,' she said.

'It can't be helped.' Janette's words were brisk. 'I'm sure he won't notice. It's the thought that counts, and this will make him realise that our agency is always prepared to go the extra mile—just in case he's thinking of buying any more local property in the area. Just make sure you deliver it today, can you, dear?'

'D-deliver it?' Hollie could see from Janette's expression that she hadn't quite managed to hide the horror in her voice. 'You mean deliver the cake? To...to Maximo?'

'To *Señor Diaz*,' Janette corrected, frosting her a severe look. 'Since when did you start using first names with clients, Hollie? Of course, I mean you! I thought you'd be delighted to comply after the way you monopolised him at the party. And who else is going to do it?'

'But—'

'Most people are very busy this close to Christmas, but at least you haven't got any family. I'd do it myself except that I have a date through that new site—Flirty at Fifty. I mean, it sounds almost too good to be true, but, still...' Janette's steely-eyed look couldn't quite disguise the unmistakable glint of hope which lurked in her heavily made-up eyes. She shrugged. 'Mustn't look a gift horse in the mouth and all that. Just make sure the cake arrives at the castle this afternoon, will you? There are a few more papers he needs to sign at the same time. But you'd better get a move on.' She shot

a quick glance out of the agency's big glass windows.
'I don't like the look of those clouds and they're fore-
casting snow over the holidays. Dave can drop you at
the bottom of the lane on the way to his four o'clock
appointment and you can easily walk back.'

Behind her frozen smile, Hollie felt as if she were
in pieces, chewed up by a growing feeling of dread at
the thought of seeing Maximo again. Their last meeting
had been bad enough. The awkwardness and embarrassment of facing the reluctant father of her baby was an
episode she wasn't eager to repeat. But without having
to explain *why* she didn't want to go—and just imagine
Janette's reaction if she did *that*—common sense told
her that refusal simply wasn't an option.

Common sense.

How ironic that something she had relied on all her
life had deserted her when she needed it most. If she'd
been sensible she wouldn't have fallen into bed with
him—seduced by a lazy smile and a hard body, and a
smooth line in seduction.

She glanced out of the window, where the main
street was bustling with last-minute shoppers, and as
she looked up at the sky she could see that Janette hadn't
been exaggerating. The heavy pewter clouds looked
bloated and full and there was a strange saffron light
radiating downwards, making the seasonal colours in
the shop windows even more vivid than usual.

Christmas trees were laden with baubles and strings
of fairy lights created magical grottos. Branches
of greenery and berries were swathed in thick, fake
snow—but occasionally a flake of the real stuff fluttered down to lie on the glittery pavement. Strings of

tinsel sparkled as brightly as the midday sun and jolly figures of Santa were tempting little children to tug on their mother's hand to try to get them to linger.

Hollie's heart slammed against her ribcage.

Little children.

That was what she would have before too long. A child of her own. First there would be a baby and then the baby would grow into a toddler and then...

But, no. Before she started trying to imagine an unimaginable future, she needed to deal with the present and there was one thing which couldn't be put off any longer. She would deliver the wretched cake to Maximo and get him to sign the papers. She would do both these things in a calm and outwardly relaxed manner, and if he brought up the subject of his lawyer again, she would tell him that these things would probably be better addressed once the seasonal break was over and the dust had settled.

At just after three, Dave's rather beaten-up old car dropped her off at the bottom of the lane and, carefully clutching the cake box, Hollie began to climb the steep hill towards Kastelloes. From here the ancient grey castle looked faintly forbidding as it dominated the green landscape with its turrets and its towers. It hadn't been a hotel for a long time but Hollie's excitement at the thought of it being brought to life again had been somewhat dampened by the dramatic changes in her own fortune.

She tried to imagine bringing a new life into the world. Would she still be able to open her tea shop with a tiny infant in tow—was that going to be possible, despite all the proud protestations she'd made to Maximo?

As her reluctant steps carried her closer to the castle, she noticed that the snow was starting to fall more heavily and coating her cheeks with big white blobs.

There was no sign of life as she walked over the drawbridge and past the old gatehouse. No Maximo rushing out to relieve her of her burden as she came to a halt in front of the ancient oak door. If he wasn't in, then he wouldn't be able to sign the papers, would he? And Janette would just have to accept that. But an upwards glance showed a golden light gleaming through one of the mullioned windows, indicating that *someone* was home, and, although her heart was plummeting, Hollie knew she couldn't back out now.

She paid the driver and, after putting the cake box down on the doorstep, pulled the bell and heard a faint ringing from somewhere deep inside the castle. She looked around as she waited, trying to enjoy the vision of the falling snow covering the stone pots and statues with a fine layer of white. But more importantly, it allowed her to look away from the door, because she didn't want Maximo opening it and finding her staring up at him with anxiety written all over her face. She needed to show him she was in control, even if she didn't particularly feel that way.

Her hands were cold and she wished she'd remembered to bring gloves with her. Her coat felt inadequately thin and the breath leaving her mouth was coming out in big, white puffs. She was just beginning to wonder if anyone *was* at home when the door of the castle opened with a creak and she turned to see Maximo standing before her, his powerful frame outlined by its arching wooden frame. Hollie felt her stomach somersault and silently cursed—but what could she do about her instinctive reaction? Despite everything which had happened between them, she obviously hadn't acquired any immunity to him. And no wonder. Dressed in his habitual black, he looked as if he had arrived from another age. As if he were thoroughly at home in this windswept citadel, high on a hill. A conquistador, Janette had once called him and, with all that powerful and brooding darkness he exuded, didn't her boss have a point?

'Hollie,' he said. His rich Spanish accent filtered over her skin like velvet but there was a frown creasing his brow. 'This is a...surprise.'

And obviously an unwelcome one, judging by his acid tone. 'I have some papers for you to sign,' she said, instantly on the defensive, determined to ensure he understood she was there because she *had* to be and not because she wanted to be. 'Also...' flushing, she bent to retrieve the large white box from the doorstep, which she held towards him '... Janette wanted you to have this.'

'What is it?' he questioned, eying the box warily.

A few random snowflakes fluttered onto her cheeks and she shuffled from one foot to the other, feeling acutely embarrassed by the cold lack of welcome in his eyes. Suddenly she understood the expression about wishing the ground would open up and swallow you. 'It's a cake.'

'A cake?' he echoed.

'We wanted to...well, it was Janette's idea, actually. She wanted to celebrate the sale of Kastelloes and so she asked me to bake you a cake.'

'And does she ask you to do this for all your purchasers?' he questioned silkily as he took the box from her. 'Or should I be flattered?'

Something about the sarcastic way he said it made Hollie's temper suddenly erupt. She had tried doing this in a polite and professional manner yet he still seemed so full of himself. So full of arrogant provocation and mockery. Did he think she'd concocted some kind of flimsy excuse just in order to see him? She wasn't *that* desperate. 'Christmas is supposed to be a time for giving, isn't it?' she retorted. 'Perhaps that was one of the reasons she asked me to do it. And you don't have to eat it, you know,' she added. 'You can always feed it to the birds. I'm sure they'd appreciate something to line their stomachs in this cold weather.'

'I'm sure they would,' he said. As if on cue, a flurry of snow came cascading down from the straining sky, straight onto her sleek head, and Maximo reluctantly acknowledged the growing tension inside him.

He had come to this ancient castle specifically to escape Christmas, because it was a festival he avoided wherever possible. It provided the ideal bolt-hole and he'd planned to spend a few days there before he had the building razed to the ground. He hadn't imagined that anybody would come near him and he hadn't wanted them to. Yet now Hollie Walker had turned up, reminding him of his harsh new reality. Forcing him to acknowledge the child growing in her belly—a fact which was complicated by the realisation that he would like nothing better than to take her into his arms and kiss her again. To strip her of her drab clothing and reveal the luscious body which lay beneath. To lose himself in her sweetness as he had done on that rain-lashed night.

His mouth twisted, because what would be the point of that? He was not going to be a part of her life, or her child's. He had given her the details of his lawyer, so she could be in no doubt that he would be more than generous. Because providing financially for Hollie and her baby was something he could do. The *only* thing he could do. A child needed love and he did not know how to give love. His heart was damaged—his emotions shredded. He had accepted that a long time ago.

So why not just sign the damned papers, enthuse over the damned cake and then send her on her way, no matter how much he hungered to recreate that night he'd spent in her arms? If he was cold and indifferent towards her, she would soon realise how much better off she was without a man like him. 'You'd better come inside,' he said.

'Don't worry. I'll be sure not to keep you for any longer than I have to.'

'Let's go to the library,' he said, shutting the door on the icy blast outside. 'Unlike most of the castle, at least it's warm in there.'

'Whatever,' she said, with a shrug.

Hollie's heart was heavy as she followed Maximo through the wood-panelled corridors, thinking he couldn't have been more unwelcoming if he'd tried. She thought how abrupt he seemed and she wished she weren't here. In fact, she wished she were anywhere but here—but the instant she entered the library, her concerns were briefly forgotten.

She'd only ever seen the place deserted, when Janette had brought her round to view it just before it went on the market. The fire exit signs from its days as a hotel were faded and the place had always appeared so lacklustre and uninspiring. But not today. Today she found herself noticing the perfect proportions of the room—the intricate carvings of cherubs and sailing ships, and the huge mullioned windows which overlooked the grounds. Was that Maximo's influence? she found herself wondering. Did he have the ability to transmute dull surroundings and turn them into a place which breathed beauty, as he had done the night when she'd taken him home?

Maybe it was just the roaring fire in the grate which had brought the ancient room to vibrant life—illuminating the detailing on the stone fireplace and the bare wall above it, which was just crying out for a painting. A rich landscape in oil, Hollie thought longingly. Or a portrait. You could put a comfortable chair underneath—two chairs, maybe—and sit there in the evenings watching the shadows fall. She felt a wistful wrench of her heart. Couldn't someone turn this castle into a home?

It was unlikely to be Maximo.

She turned to find him studying her, his black gaze fixed on her intently, as if he had never really seen her before. Hollie's heart missed a beat, because wasn't she feeling a bit like that herself? As if this were the first time they'd ever been alone. She felt *awkward* in his presence, which was slightly ridiculous, when you considered all the things they'd done together.

Or maybe it wasn't ridiculous at all. What did she know? She'd thought that what they'd shared had been intimacy, but she had been wrong. In her innocence she had confused sex with real closeness. But you could be naked in a man's arms and it counted for nothing, because right now Maximo Diaz seemed like a stranger. A stranger whose child she carried.

'What exactly do you want me to sign?' he questioned, putting the unopened box down on the table.

'It's right here.' Her hands were trembling as she scrabbled around inside her briefcase and she wondered if he'd noticed as she walked across the room towards him. 'It's the release form concerning the fixtures and fittings. It's just a formality.'

He was reading it. Of course he was. He wasn't the kind of man who would put his signature to something he hadn't studied first. And because he was reading it, it was taking much longer than she had anticipated.

The silence in the room seemed immense and Hollie pulled out her phone and began to look at it, as if there were loads of missed calls she needed to attend to, though in truth the screen was just a blur of mangled words. As a distraction technique it was pretty useless because she couldn't escape the troubled whirl of her thoughts as the minutes ticked slowly by. His dark head was bent and when eventually she heard the scratch of his pen, he looked up, his smile brief and perfunctory.

'I think that's everything you need.'

He can't wait to get rid of you.

He was rising from the chair and Hollie couldn't hold back her shiver as he handed her the document.

'If there's nothing more, I'll see you out.'

'There's really no need. I know my way around.'

'I insist.' He shot her a brief look and something

like pain filtered through his black eyes. 'How are you feeling?'

It might have been funny if it hadn't been so sad and Hollie only just managed to keep a burst of hysterical laughter from her lips. To say there was an elephant in the room didn't come close to it. Was that to be his only reference to the fact that she was pregnant? Because if so she was just going to have to deal with it. From somewhere she managed to produce a smile. 'I'm fine, thanks,' she said. 'The doctor seems very pleased with my progress so far.'

There was a pause. 'Look, I'm aware that my reaction to your news wasn't great and I apologise for that.'

His words were grudging rather than heartfelt, but Hollie told herself she must be generous in her response. 'No, it was hardly the stuff of dreams,' she said drily. 'But that's okay. It must have come as a terrible shock and at least you were being honest. And I'm over it now.'

'My lawyers tell me you haven't made contact yet.'

'No. I thought I'd wait until after Christmas now.'

He inclined his head. 'As you wish.'

As you wish?

Hollie had a whole catalogue of wishes, most of which were never going to come true. She wished he had a heart instead of a lump of cold steel lodged somewhere deep in his chest. She wished…

No. Only a fool would ever wish for love from such an unsuitable candidate.

They had reached the hall and he was opening the door and all Hollie wanted was to get away from him and the way he was making her feel, when his terse exclamation startled her.

'*Es imposible!*'

Hollie followed his gaze and looked outside. Her Spanish was limited to about three words which involved asking for a beer, but even she understood that what he'd just said wasn't true, because it wasn't impossible at all. She felt the jump of her heart. She'd been so busy with her thoughts that she'd barely noticed the time passing, or the increased snowfall. But from here she was aware of how quickly the weather had closed in, and now they seemed to be in a complete white-out.

The landscape had been utterly transformed. Trees, grass and bushes were coated with a mantle of white, which sparkled like diamonds in the fading violet light. The thick fall had turned the place into a winter fairy tale—but one with an underlying threat because, outwardly, everything had changed. No footsteps up the lane. It was as if she'd never been there.

Hollie had only ever thought of snow as a positive thing—as pretty, white and fluffy—but now she saw it as an obstacle, barring her way out of there. And there was no sign of it stopping. She stared up into the darkening sky and uttered a soft curse beneath her breath. All she wanted was to get back to her little cottage because, although it might not amount to very much, at least it was *home*.

'Where's your taxi?' he demanded.

She shrugged. 'I got a lift here and I was planning to walk back.'

He made a soft curse beneath his breath. 'I would take you myself except that I've dismissed the chauffeur for the holidays and he's taken the car.'

'It's fine,' she said, between gritted teeth, thinking

that she'd rather walk home barefoot than be driven home by *him*. 'I've been cooped up in the office all morning, and a bit of snow won't kill me.' With a grimace of stark realisation, Hollie stared down at her feet. 'These boots weren't exactly made for walking, but I guess they'll have to do.'

'Are you out of your mind?' he snapped. 'You can't possibly walk home in this.'

'Watch me.'

'I don't think so. You're pregnant, remember?'

'I'm hardly likely to forget, am I?'

'Do you make a habit of being rescued from bad weather, Hollie?' he demanded. 'Don't you think it's time you invested in one of those clever phone apps?'

'Oh, go to hell!' she snapped back, taking a defiant step forward and immediately sinking into a deep white drift which came almost to the top of her boots. And suddenly Maximo's hands were on her waist and he was lifting her clean out of the snow, and she was staring up into the hard glitter of his black eyes. And wasn't it crazy that, in the midst of all her complicated emotions, her overriding feeling was the hungry throb of her blood in response to his touch? 'Go to hell,' she repeated weakly.

His velvety voice filtered over her skin. 'Even hell would reject a man like me.'

'Please put me down,' she said. 'I want to go home.'

'Well, you can't. You're not going anywhere right now. Not when it's like this. You're going to have to stay here for the time being.' He lowered her to her feet. 'Unless that's what you had in mind all along?'

She moved even further away from him, though that

did little to ease the furious punch of her heart. 'Are you serious? Are you arrogant enough to think I'd deliberately get myself stranded here like this?'

He shrugged. 'Only you know the answer to that, Hollie. But if you're asking whether I think a woman is capable of such manipulation, then I'm afraid the answer has to be yes.'

'Why, you...*cynic*,' she breathed.

'You think so? I prefer to call it realism. But that's irrelevant.' He moved towards the door, his muscular body all honed and rippling strength. 'And rather than standing here debating my perceived defects of character, you'd better come inside, out of the cold.'

CHAPTER SIX

MAXIMO SHUT THE door with more force than he intended, his heart racing with…what? Anger at being stuck with an uninvited guest at the worst time of the year? Yes, there was that. But Hollie was not just any uninvited guest. He stared down at the mutinous tremble of her lips and felt the shimmer of something indefinable spearing at his heart. She was the mother of his child, he reminded himself grimly. A child he had never wanted. Because why would he wish to pass on his cold and emotionless genes to an innocent baby?

Yet his feelings of claustrophobia were complicated by a sensation which threatened to derail his intention to keep his distance from the woman he had seduced, and no matter how firmly he spoke to himself, it was having precisely no effect on him. Because every time he looked at Hollie Walker, he felt that same powerful kick of desire. In spite of everything, he still wanted her. He wanted her badly and yet he still couldn't work out why. He liked his women hard-edged. Tough and sexy. Women who knew the score—not wide-eyed innocents, with lips which trembled when you kissed them.

He preferred considered sex—a careful coupling

rather than wild passion which ran the risk of taking a man hostage. He drew his boundaries from the outset. He preferred to be in the driving seat when it came to relationships and women were so eager for his body and his company that they invariably acceded to his demands. Yet with Hollie Walker, hadn't he already broken one of his self-imposed rules? They said a woman was a mystery until you bedded her and once that happened, she inevitably lost some of that allure. That had always been the case before, so why wasn't it happening now?

Why did he want to discover more about her? And why the hell was he experiencing an overwhelming need to tumble her down and cover her soft body with the hot, hard heat of his own until she cried out his name? She might currently be glaring at him as if he were the devil incarnate, but her anger didn't quite mask her own desire. No. Not at all. The faint flush of her cheeks and the darkening of her spectacular grey eyes was a pretty reliable indicator that she was far from immune to *him*. And since they were stuck with each other until the snow melted, perhaps it might be a good idea to capitalise on that potent sexual chemistry.

They had to do *something* to occupy themselves during the long hours ahead and tomorrow was Christmas Day—a holiday which up until now had always been something he just needed to survive, but now he could see the possibility of transforming it into something else.

Something erotic.

The clench in his gut was sweetly pervasive until the split second when he noticed the flash of vulnerability which had crossed her pale face and silently he remonstrated with himself, forcing himself to listen to reason.

You don't have to have sex with her. You just have to provide shelter until the weather breaks and get through the next few hours.

'I'll show you where you can sleep,' he said tightly.

'I'm sure that won't be necessary,' she said, equally tightly. 'I'm not planning on staying any longer than I need to.'

'You'll stay until it's safe to return and that certainly won't be before nightfall.'

Their eyes met in a silent clash of wills, until eventually she backed down and nodded.

'Then it seems I have no choice.'

'That's right,' he agreed softly. 'You don't. Now come with me.'

Hollie felt chewed up as she trailed behind Maximo up the curving stone staircase which led to the upstairs floor of the chilly castle. She was scared. Scared of the way he made her feel. Scared of wanting to touch him instead of needing to push him away. Because he didn't want her. *He didn't want her.* And that was something she shouldn't forget. His dismay on discovering she was trapped here might have been almost comical to observe, if it hadn't been so hurtful. But she guessed that nobody could ever accuse Maximo Diaz of being duplicitous. He was honest to a fault, which had to be a good thing. And since she was here—maybe she just needed to make the best of it. To look on the bright side. She pressed her lips together.

For both their sakes.

He was pushing open the door of one of the bedrooms and as Hollie stepped inside she was aware of a further drop in temperature. The bed was bare and the room largely empty—there was nothing in the way of decorative furnishing to make it seem inviting or attractive. It certainly wasn't going to be a fairy-tale Christmas Eve, not by any stretch of the imagination.

'You'll find linen in the big wooden cupboard just along the corridor,' he advised, his dark brows knitting together, as if he had just noticed her shiver. 'You're cold?'

'A bit.'

'Let me see what I can do. I've never seen anything quite so archaic as what passes for a heating system here.'

'Don't you have any staff with you?' she questioned curiously.

Black eyebrows were elevated in mocking query. 'You think I travel around with a retinue of servants?'

She shrugged. 'You're a rich man. Apparently, that's what rich men do. And you *do* have a chauffeur.'

'*Si.* I do. But the answer is no, I am completely on my own. Because surely a man is not a true man if he cannot fend for himself. If he cannot live independently of his staff.'

'Christmas is not a time for independence,' she said firmly. 'It's a time for family.'

'And will your family be missing you, Hollie?' he questioned suddenly. 'Is that why you are so eager to get back?'

'I have no family,' she said, deciding it wouldn't be diplomatic or wise to tell him that her desire to get away had been all about his effect on her. Baldly, she gave him the bare facts, the way she always did, just so they could get the inevitable mechanical sympathy out of the way. 'Both my parents are dead.'

'Snap,' he said softly.

It wasn't what she'd been expecting and Hollie almost wished he hadn't told her that, because that was the stupid thing about the mind—it took you down false paths, based on very flimsy evidence. If she wasn't careful it would be easy to start imagining they had something in common, because they were both orphans. When she knew and he knew that they had absolutely nothing in common, other than an inconvenient sexual chemistry and a baby neither of them had planned.

'At least nobody's going to miss us!' she observed brightly, wishing it didn't please her so much to see him smile in response. But the curve of his lips lasted only a second, as though this man was not comfortable with smiling.

'I'll leave you to get settled in,' he said abruptly. 'I'll be downstairs. Come and find me when you've finished. Take as long as you like.'

Settling in seemed a rather over-ambitious term for getting used to such spartan accommodation, but after Maximo had left, Hollie tried to make the bedroom as comfortable as possible. There were no sheets, but she hunted down several mismatched velvet throws and a thick eiderdown, which provided a colourful display against the quiet grey hues of the faded walls. And thankfully she was *used* to sleeping in a chilly bedroom.

The nearby bathroom was ancient, with a noisy cistern and a vast, old-fashioned bath—but the water was piping hot. She washed her hands with a bar of rock-hard soap then stared into the rather mottled mirror above the sink. She was expecting her appearance to come as a shock, but to her surprise her eyes were shining and her cheeks were pink and glowing. She brushed her hair, tempted to leave it loose because wouldn't that provide some essential warmth around her neck and shoulders? But something stopped her and it was the memory of Maximo using a single strand of it as a rope, just before he'd kissed her. Because those kinds of memories weren't helpful. Not helpful at all. Carefully, she wound it into a tight chignon and pinned it into place, before heading downstairs to find Maximo.

He wasn't in the library, but she could smell the aroma of food cooking and Hollie made her way through a series of maze-like corridors towards the kitchen. She could hear movement but when she walked in, the sight which greeted her was the last thing she had expected. What *had* she expected? She wasn't sure—but it certainly wasn't to see the Spanish tycoon with his back to her, his black sweater rolled up to his elbows as he stirred something.

Did she make a sound? Was that why he turned around, his olive skin gleaming from the heat of the hob? And Hollie could do nothing about the instant wrench of her heart, as if she were registering his gorgeousness for the very first time. Because Maximo, holding up a wooden spoon as the conductor of an orchestra might hold a baton, looked insanely sexy. Maybe her hormones were making her respond to him this way. Because right then he looked like the carer and provider. The alpha man. The hunter. The father of her baby. Beneath her sweater she felt her breasts tighten and wondered if he'd noticed. Would that account for the almost imperceptible narrowing of his eyes and the sudden tension which stilled his magnificent body so that he looked almost poised to strike?

'Gosh,' she said.

'*Gosh?*' he echoed, his sardonic tone easing a little of the tension in the air. 'Am I to take that as a very English word of surprise?'

'I suppose I am a bit surprised,' she admitted. 'I didn't have you down as a budding chef.'

'Less of the budding, more of the accomplished.'

'Of course. Silly of me to forget that you probably excel in everything you turn your hand to.'

'You're getting the hang of me, Hollie.'

'Who taught you to cook?'

'I'm self-taught.'

'Wow.' She blew a silent whistle. 'Now I'm even more impressed.'

'Why wouldn't I teach myself how to cook?' he questioned. 'As I told you, my independence is important to me.' His black eyes glittered a challenge at her. 'And isn't your assumption that I'm breaking some sort of mould rather sexist?'

Was it? Hollie wasn't sure. As he turned back to the hob, the only thing she was certain of was a stupid sense of yearning as she feasted her eyes on the black tendrils of hair which brushed against his neck. She didn't want to feel wistful but it was difficult not to. Because if they'd been a real couple they might have done stuff like this—cooked meals and flirted a little. They might have gone out on a few dates, instead of letting passion lead them to a one-night stand with massive consequences. But she wasn't the type of woman Maximo dated, she reminded herself fiercely. She'd seen photos of his girlfriends on the Internet and she was nothing like any of them. She just happened to be a warm and willing body who had made herself available on a night when he'd obviously wanted company.

But those were pointless thoughts. Negative thoughts she wasn't going to entertain. Instead Hollie watched as Maximo chopped onions with rather terrifying dexterity and realised he hadn't been exaggerating about his prowess in the kitchen. 'So what are you cooking?' she asked.

'It's a variation of a dish called *cocido montañéas*. Mountain stew. It comes from northern Spain. From Cantabria.'

'And is that where you come from?'

'It is.' He sliced a wooden spoon through the thick mixture, clearly more comfortable discussing the meal than details about his birthplace. 'It's more of a winter soup really, with pork and chorizo and beans and greens and wine and garlic and pretty much anything else you can find to throw in.'

'It's not...'

'Not?' He turned round again as her words tailed off, only this time his gleaming black gaze pierced through her like a sword. 'Not what, Hollie?'

'Well, it's not the kind of food I can imagine someone like you eating, let alone cooking.'

'Why not?'

Hollie traced her finger along a deep gouge in the ancient table and wondered how long ago it had been put there and by whom. 'It's more I imagine the food a labourer might eat.'

'And I'm no labourer?'

She smiled at the preposterousness of this. 'Obviously not.'

'Maybe,' he said softly. 'But once I was.'

She glanced up from the table, watching as he put a lid on the pot and turned the heat down low. 'You? A labourer?'

Maximo didn't answer immediately, amazed he'd given her an opening to pursue this particular topic because discussions about his past were something he vetoed. Especially with lovers. Women *always* asked questions and he understood why. Knowledge was power and the more you knew about someone, the closer you could presume your relationship to be. Except that any 'closeness' his lovers presumed was all inside their heads. Usually he recommended they consult the Internet if they wanted to discover more about him, confident they'd find out only what he wanted them to know—having successfully kept his online profile deliberately sparse, by employing an IT expert who made sure that happened.

His past was private and his alone—and the only time he connected with it was during this ritual he followed most Christmases, when he cooked up the kind of food which would never feature on the menu of any of the fancy restaurants he frequented these days. At Christmas he went back to basics. He did it because it reminded him of who he had been and where he had come from, and usually it was enough to make him satisfied with his lot and to remind him what he *didn't* want from life.

But something had happened which had changed the

way he thought about everything, and though it pained him to admit it—it all stemmed from his mother's recent passing. Didn't seem to matter that he didn't *want* to be affected by the death of a woman he had despised. Fact was, he was. Ever since it had happened he'd felt... disconnected. Like a tethered balloon whose string had just been cut, leaving him drifting aimlessly and without direction. As if all the money and power he had acquired along the way suddenly meant nothing. Was that why he had taken this provincial office worker to bed and lost himself in a storm of passion so all-pervasive that it had left him feeling dazed and confused the next morning? As if, for the first time in his life, it had felt as if he'd come home.

Wasn't that why he hadn't contacted her again? Because he didn't like the way she made him feel, or because he didn't trust those feelings?

He didn't know and he didn't care and that was why he had walked away. Why he had resisted the surprising desire to contact her again. And time was great for taking the urgency out of desire. It had been easy to lose himself in work and travel and to allow the many projects he juggled to take over his life. To forget about that night and the woman who had temporarily made him lose control.

Yet now, as he stared into the wide grey eyes which were fixed on his, he found himself wanting to tell her stuff. Nothing too deep. No, definitely not that. But it would amuse him to reveal his beginnings to her, to show her some of the real man beneath the fancy patina. Would take his mind off the persistent urge to pull her into his arms and start kissing her, which would complicate his life in a way it didn't need complicating.

'Yes, I was a labourer,' he said. 'And if you know my roots you might be able to understand why. I was the only child of a single mother, and money was scarce. I remember being hungry—always hungry. My need to get food took precedence over schoolwork and the local school wasn't up to much anyway. And when I was fourteen, I started working on the roads.'

'Fourteen?' she breathed, her eyes growing even wider. 'Wow. Is that even *legal*?'

'I doubt it.' He shrugged. 'But there weren't so many checks back then. It was a different kind of world. The guy who owned the construction site didn't know how old I was and if they had, they probably wouldn't have cared.'

'You mean you lied about your age?' she questioned, as if that were important to her.

'I let them believe what they wanted to believe. That's mostly what people do in life, Hollie—haven't you discovered that by now? I was big and strong for my age and looked much older than I was, and it was easy to let my work speak for itself. I started out with a pick and shovel. Breaking up rocks with a big hammer and trying not to inhale the dust. I learnt a lot about construction.' He gave a short laugh. 'But I learnt plenty more about human nature.'

'In what way?'

Her voice was soft. Way too soft to resist—and for some reason, Maximo didn't even try.

'I learnt how to fight,' he admitted. 'I learnt how a man can lose everything through drink, and that gambling is nothing but a short journey to ruin. But mostly I learnt that I didn't want to hang round doing that kind of work for ever.'

'No, I can imagine you didn't. So how did you make the leap, from being a—?'

'Labourer?' Her head was bent as she traced all the scratches on the table with the tip of her finger, as if she were trying not to meet his gaze. And wasn't there a bit of him which was glad about that? Because those beautiful grey eyes were cool and searching and it wasn't easy to ignore their candid gaze.

'It wasn't rocket science,' he continued. 'I made sure I was always the first to arrive and the last to leave and I saved every euro I could to buy my first digger. Eventually that one digger became five, and then twenty— and soon I was the sub-contractor of choice for the big boys.' He gave a short laugh. 'Until I became one of the big boys myself. I started building roads and then railways, and I never really looked back.' Most emphatically he had not looked back.

She absorbed all this in silence for a moment. 'It's not—'

'Not what you expected?' he supplied acidly. 'You imagined I was born with the Spanish equivalent of a silver spoon in my mouth? *Nacer en cuna de oro.* That I grew up with money?'

'Something like that. You seem very comfortable with your wealth. Comfortable in your own skin.'

'Thank you,' he said gravely, and was aware of the warm approbation in his voice as he said it. Her look of surprise indicated she'd heard it too, but then she was unaware that she had just paid him a great compliment—perhaps the greatest compliment of all. For hadn't that been what he had strived for above all else? *To feel comfortable in his own skin.*

But then she ruined it.

'And you have a kind of—I don't know.' She wriggled her shoulders. 'A kind of *aristocratic* look about you.'

Maximo's lips clamped shut, telling himself to be grateful that her perceptive observation had brought him to his senses at last. What was the *matter* with him? Hadn't he been just about to tell her the rest of his pitiful story, lulled by her soft voice and seeking eyes? And why—just because his estranged mother was dead and his equilibrium had temporarily been disturbed?

Hadn't he spent the last two decades eradicating those memories—only to almost blurt them out to a woman who already had too much power over him? Because her pregnancy gave Hollie Walker undue influence in his life, he recognised suddenly—and she could use that influence any way she saw fit.

He gave the pot another stir. He had carefully controlled his image for most of his life. He never gave interviews, never let people too close. He worked hard and played hard and donated generously to charity—and for these qualities he was mostly admired and envied in equal measure. But of himself he gave nothing away. Even during his longest relationships—and none of those had ever been what you'd call lengthy—he had never been anything less than guarded. Hadn't that been part of his appeal—that women saw him as an enigma and a challenge and themselves as the one who would break down those high barriers with which he had surrounded himself?

But Hollie was different. She couldn't help but be different. She was carrying his baby and, inevitably, that was going to cause ripples of curiosity in the circles in which he moved. Sooner or later people were going to find out that this unknown Englishwoman was pregnant with his child. She would be able to present herself to the world however she saw fit. As a victim, if she so desired. And he would have absolutely no control over that.

He felt the sudden knot in his stomach. He had already told her plenty about himself, but of her he knew nothing. Nothing at all. Wasn't it time he did? Not because he particularly cared what made her tick, but because he needed to redress that balance of knowledge.

He pulled out the stool opposite hers and sat down. 'What about you?' he questioned, carelessly.

'Me?'

'I've told you how I started out. Now it's your turn.'

Hollie hesitated. He had divulged much more than she'd expected, though she'd noticed that his story had stopped very abruptly. But he had still surprised her and maybe if he hadn't been so forthcoming she might have brushed over her own background, because it wasn't much to write home about, was it? Even so, it was more than a little distracting to have him sitting so close, making her acutely aware of all the latent power in his muscular body and the devilish gleam of his ebony eyes.

'I was the only child of a single mother, too,' she began and saw a muscle begin working at his temple, as if he thought she was grasping for things they had in common and was irritated by it. Instantly, she sought to emphasise the differences between them. 'We weren't exactly poor, but we weren't exactly rich either. My father…'

'What about your father?' he probed.

She shrugged. 'Well, to be honest, I never knew him very well. He was a bit of a womaniser, I guess. Good-looking. Easy company. One of those men who want to have their cake and eat it. He was a sales manager and so travelled around the area a lot. He had several different lovers, although only one child, as far as I know. He'd tell my mother he loved her and he'd move in with us for a bit and then…' She shrugged. 'I don't know if having a baby cramped his style, or whether he found it stultifying that the whole household always seemed to revolve around him. But the more my mother ran round after him, the more he seemed to despise her. So they'd have a big row and he'd move out and then the whole cycle would start again.'

'That must have been tough on you,' he observed slowly.

'Not really.' Hollie slipped into her best *every-cloud-has-a-silver-lining* attitude. 'It's true that Mum used to go to pieces every time, but it's how I taught myself how to cook, and…'

'Go on,' he said, the faintest of smiles touching the edges of his mouth.

She picked up the story again, thinking that nobody ever really asked her stuff like this. 'One day my father just stopped contacting her and we never found out what happened to him. Like you said, things were different in those days and there was no social media to be able to track someone down. My mum never really got over it and after she died, I sold her little house and went to catering college. Long story short, I made a friend there and used the rest of my savings to go into business with her—we opened a tea shop in London.'

'But? I sense there's a but coming.'

He was insightful, she thought—or maybe such a successful businessman was always going to have an instinct for a duff business venture. 'My partner borrowed a whole load of money on the business and couldn't pay it back.'

'That's theft,' he observed acidly.

'She *meant* to pay it back,' she defended. 'But that was never going to happen and I couldn't bear to waste any more time, or make any more bad memories by chasing her through the small courts. Anyway, we'd chosen a hopeless location. It was more a hip coffee shop sort of area and not really suited to a venue which was serving dinky plates of scones, with cream and jam. It's why I came to Devon, which *is* that kind of place. It's why, no matter what happens, I'm glad you came here too, Maximo.'

He looked startled. 'You are?'

'Yes, I am. Not because of the baby, because I know that's bad news for you.' She ignored the pained expression on his face but resolutely carried on. 'It wasn't meant to happen, but it did—and I will do everything to make sure our child has the best possible life I can give them. And I've lived with a man who didn't want to be a father, which is why I can cope with the fact you don't want to be involved. It's better that way. Better that we're upfront about things from the beginning so everyone knows where they stand—'

'Hollie—'

'No, please let me finish.' She drew a deep breath and stared straight into his fathoms-deep eyes, thinking how thick and black the lashes were. 'What makes me glad is the fact that you've bought Kastelloes, because you'll be injecting life back into this town and local community. So my business—and every other business in Trescombe—will benefit.' He got up quickly to attend to his cooking, an uncomfortable expression crossing his face, and she wondered if she was boring him. 'Gosh, it's seven o'clock already,' she observed, sneaking a glance at her watch. 'Only five more hours to go and it'll be Christmas Day!'

'I can hardly wait,' he said sarcastically.

She watched as he finished cooking the meal, wishing she could tear her eyes away from the graceful agility of his movements and the way his black jeans clung to the hard thrust of his buttocks. But she couldn't. And all the while she was becoming aware of the four walls which surrounded them and the fact that they were completely alone in this beautiful, desolate building. She could feel tension between them mounting—like dark layers of something tantalising, building and building into the promise of something unbearably sweet.

'Let's eat,' he said suddenly.

But his face was still tense as he began to serve up the soup, his shadow seeming to swamp her in an all-consuming darkness. And somehow his abrupt words managed to destroy the fragile harmony which had briefly existed between them.

CHAPTER SEVEN

HOLLIE SHIVERED AS she lay huddled beneath the heap of
the velvet throws, wiggling her toes to stop them from
freezing. It was so *quiet*. Nothing to listen to except the
sound of the distant church bells in nearby Trescombe.
Nothing to distract her from the thought that Maximo
was sleeping just along the corridor and that felt weird.
Was he thinking about her and her predicament, or was
he fast asleep and oblivious to the presence of his unwanted guest? She cocked her ear as the twelfth and
final bell faded into the silent night, announcing to the
world that Christmas day had finally arrived.

Some Christmas! She was stuck in a cold, almost
empty castle with a man who didn't want her there.
She turned her pillow over and bashed it with her fist.
Didn't matter how many sheep she tried to count, she
just couldn't sleep. In fact, she had dozed only fitfully
since she'd retired to bed just after ten last night, leaving Maximo downstairs, working in the library.

Their shared supper had been *awkward*, to say the
least. Oh, the food had been delicious—no doubt about
that. Maximo's Cantabrian mountain stew had hit the
spot and the tycoon had waited on her in a way she

suspected was totally out of character. She had been impressed by his culinary skills and had said so. But Hollie hadn't been impervious to the unspoken words which had seemed to dangle in the air like invisible baubles. Just as she'd been unable to ignore the spiralling tension which curled like smoke in the base of her stomach whenever he came near.

But last night had been about more than sexual chemistry and, although his powerful presence had been impossible to ignore, Hollie had learnt a little more about the father of her child. It had been an illuminating insight to discover that his wealth hadn't been handed to him on a plate, but he was a self-made man, and that revelation had made her feel an undoubted respect towards him. Yet afterwards it was as if he regretted having told her anything at all, because when she had tried to ask him about growing up in those harsh circumstances, he had very firmly changed the subject. And after that, things had become a little stilted.

It hadn't exactly helped that she had nothing to sleep in and when she'd plucked up courage to ask Maximo if he had a pyjama top she could borrow, he had stared at her as if she had taken leave of her senses.

'Are you crazy?' he'd questioned, black eyes narrowed. 'I never wear anything in bed.'

It had proved yet one more awkward moment in a whole series of them and in Hollie's opinion, that was far too much information to take on board, in the circumstances. Berating her naïve stupidity and hiding her sudden blush by leaping to her feet, she had escaped upstairs and run herself a bath—more to get warm than anything else. But when she had returned to her room she had found a T-shirt lying on top of the velvet heap of bedcovers, which Maximo must have left there for her. A black T-shirt with the word *Legend* inscribed across the front. Pulling it on, she had momentarily revelled in the feel of the soft material against her clean skin— even though the garment had swamped her. And wasn't she aware—on some fundamental level—that she got a kick out of wearing it because *he* had worn it, too?

She tossed and turned as the minutes continued to tick slowly by. She looked at her watch to note that midnight had become one o'clock and she was as restless as before and so, wrapping one of the velvet throws around herself, she went to the window and gazed outside. And despite everything, she couldn't hold back the sigh of wonder which escaped from her lips because outside was the most perfect scene she could imagine—like an illustration from a book about winter.

The snow had stopped falling and the moon was huge in the sky, bathing the milky landscape in a bright and silvery light. Against the frosty stillness of the landscape, the tall shapes of the trees rose ghostly and beautiful and for a moment Holly just drank it all in until the dryness in her throat reminded her that she was thirsty. Why hadn't she thought to bring a drink to bed with her?

She stood very still and listened but could hear nothing and surely Maximo must be fast asleep by now. Carefully opening the door to avoid making any noise, she crept along the corridor, clutching her makeshift cloak around her. The whisper of velvet brushing against the stone steps was the only sound she could hear and quietly she made her way to the kitchen, turning the switch on so that it flooded with light. It was neat and clean, all the debris from dinner tidied away. Maximo had obviously cleared up after she went to bed. He really *was* independent she thought, scrolling back through those rare memories of her father to realise that not once had he ever lifted a finger to help her mother.

She poured herself a glass of water and thirstily gulped it down before pouring another and switching off the light. And although the castle was dark and very quiet, Hollie wasn't in the least bit spooked—because the walls felt friendly. She wondered if other women, like her, had wandered these stone corridors in the dead of night and wondered how they were going to cope with an unknown future.

Lost in thought, she had almost reached the end of the passageway when a figure suddenly emerged from the shadows and Hollie jumped. Water arced and splashed against the stone wall and as the glass slipped from her fingers Maximo lunged forward to catch it— cradling the intact vessel in the palm of his hand like a professional cricketer who had just made a sensational catch.

'You scared the life out of me!' she accused, aware that his hair was ruffled as if he'd hurriedly dragged his sweater over his head and that the top button of his jeans was undone.

'I didn't mean to alarm you. I couldn't sleep and I heard something moving downstairs, or rather someone, so I threw on some clothes and came down to investigate.' His shuttered gaze flicked over her. 'You'd better get back upstairs,' he added, and suddenly his voice was tinged with harshness. 'It's cold.'

Hollie nodded but she didn't move. She *couldn't* move. It was as if she had suddenly forgotten how to use her legs.

'It's cold everywhere,' she whispered. 'I've been awake for hours.'

His eyes narrowed and a look of intense calculation darkened his already shadowed features. He looked as if he were fighting some silent inner battle and when he nodded his head, Hollie couldn't decide whether he had won, or lost.

'Maybe we should try and do something about that,' he said. 'What do you think?'

His soft question slid over her skin, snaring her with threads of silk. And he was studying her with that absorbed and shadowed gaze, which was making her grow weak. And all the time, raw desire was pulsing around them, like a living being. Hollie felt breathless. Poised on the edge of something—but she didn't know the rules of this game. She didn't know how to play. 'That depends what you had in mind,' she stumbled.

He smiled. A slow and speculative smile. A smile no sane woman could have resisted. 'There are any number of options. We could go upstairs and I could lend you another T-shirt. We could see if we can find any more of those velvet wraps you seem so fond of. Or you could share my bed and get warm that way. It's up to you. It's your call, Hollie.'

Maybe if he'd asked that same question during daylight hours when he'd made it plain she was an unwelcome guest, then Hollie might have refused. But the darkness had added a strange layer of anonymity, as well as enhancing her already aroused senses. And it was Christmas morning, wasn't it? A time of magic and secret wishes, when anything could happen. She sensed he wouldn't judge her if she said yes, because this was a time out of life and she wanted it. She wanted it very badly.

'Yes, please,' she said simply.

'Which?'

'You know which.'

He made a low growling noise beneath his breath, as if her easy capitulation had pleased him. Then he put the empty glass down on the stone floor, very carefully, and took her in his arms. He brushed her hair from her cheeks, looking down at her for a moment, his gaze crystalline and hard. She'd thought he might kiss her, but he didn't. Instead, he laced his fingers through hers and led her towards the stairs. It felt very grown-up but…it also felt very disappointing and it wasn't until they had reached the upstairs floor that Hollie raised her face to his in question. Because hadn't she secretly been longing for the ultimate castle fantasy of Maximo sweeping her up into his arms and carrying her to his lair?

'You want to know why I didn't carry you this time?' he guessed.

'Yes.' Hollie nodded, marvelling at his perception even as she resented it. Just how many women had he carried to his bed over the years? she wondered.

'Because you're pregnant,' he admitted. 'And I'm terrified of dropping you.'

It was a surprisingly tender admission and Hollie felt her skin grow warm. 'You're way too strong to drop me—and I'm not made of glass, Maximo.'

'I wouldn't bring up the subject of glass right now if I were you.'

His teasing broke a little of the tension until he stared down at her again, his expression dark and unfathomable, and she could see a pulse beating wildly at his temple. 'But since we're on the flat again…'

And this time he *did* pick her up, striding along the corridor to a room just beyond her own, kicking open the door and giving rampant life to her foolish fantasies. It was a room a little larger than her own and just as sparsely furnished, though the bed was much bigger. But Hollie barely noticed the equally haphazard bedclothes, or the thick paperback which was lying open on the locker. All she could see was the man who was lowering her onto the mattress, his aristocratic features dark and shuttered as he made sure she was covered by a feather-soft eiderdown, before stripping his clothes off.

She lay and watched as he peeled off his shirt, his skin gleaming like living metal in the bright moonlight which streamed in through the windows. She observed the line of black hair which arrowed down from his chest to his navel and as he began to slide the zip down, he lifted his head to slant her the sexiest smile she'd ever seen.

'Does it turn you on to watch me undress?' he murmured.

Hollie nodded. She liked that he wasn't treating her as a novice, which essentially she was. Last time they'd had sex it had all been so new and so incredible—as if she hadn't been able to believe that someone like Maximo was in bed with someone like her. But while she might be new to all this, even she could acknowledge the undeniable chemistry which burned between them and she was determined to enjoy every second of what came next. She wasn't going to long for the impossible or wish things had been different. That ship had sailed. She was going to live in the now.

The mattress dipped as he came to lie beside her, taking the baggy hem of the T-shirt she was still wearing and running the tip of his finger over it. 'You have me at something of a disadvantage,' he murmured. 'You're still wearing this, while I am completely naked.'

'Surely it's me that's at a disadvantage,' she returned, lifting her arms above her head without being asked so that he could peel off the offending garment and drop it to one side of the bed.

Maximo pulled her into his arms, brushing aside the thick fall of her silky hair as he pressed his lips into her neck. He hadn't thought this would happen. God knew, he hadn't intended for it to happen—but in the end she had proved too much of a temptation and, besides, which of them was he protecting by resisting something they obviously both wanted? Not her, who was so hungry for him that she was writhing against him like a siren, her breath warm and fast against his skin. Nor himself, either. After all, the damage had already been done and she was pregnant. And if that was a cynical way of looking at it, so what?

He began to explore her body, reacquainting himself with her soft curves and delicious flesh, his fingers sliding over her silky skin. He cupped her breasts in his palms, thinking how full they were—much fuller than last time.

Was that because of the baby?

A rush of something he didn't recognise roared through his blood but deliberately, he blocked it.

He wasn't going to think about the baby. The only thing he was going to think about was pleasure.

So he concentrated on employing every sensual skill he had learnt, tempering blatant provocation with the tantalising whisper of soft promise. So that while his rock-hard erection was pushing against her belly, he was kissing her eyelids, her cheeks, her neck and her ears, making her wait until finally he allowed his lips to plunder hers. Was it the little cry of bliss she gave which made him feel as if he were drowning? As if she were drawing him into some unknown place of dark, sweet honey.

'You are...*deliciosa.*'

'Delicious?' she guessed.

'You are fluent in Spanish now, are you, Hollie?' But as she opened her mouth to doubtless make some equally flippant reply, he kissed away the answer, reaching down to slide his finger between her silken folds, enjoying her gasped frustration as he brought her to the edge of orgasm, over and over again. Only when he could bear his own exquisite torture no longer did he position himself to enter her at last—though more slowly and carefully than he had ever done before. And didn't that make him feel...?

What?

He didn't know and he didn't care because his thoughts were being scatter-gunned by Hollie clenching hard around him, her back arching like a bow as she spasmed, and then he too was jerking helplessly in her arms.

For a while there was no sound other than their ragged sighs, and then she drifted her lips to his cheek.

'Maximo,' she murmured huskily.

'Don't move,' he instructed unsteadily, because already he was growing hard inside her again. 'Stay exactly where you are.'

'I have no intention of going anywhere.'

He gave a soft laugh as he began to move and, while the second time was just as amazing, the third almost defied definition, leaving him gloriously sated and replete.

'I've never done it without protection before,' he observed after a while, lying back against the rumpled bedclothes, his skin warm with satisfaction.

'So that's a first?'

'Well, by my reckoning, it's actually the second.'

His head tipped back against the pillow as she giggled and he must have slept, because when next he opened his eyes, the bright light of a winter's morning had replaced the silvery moonlight of the previous night. He lay there for a moment in silence, aware of Hollie's head on his shoulder—her hair spread out over his chest like satin. He stared down at the twin crescents of her lashes, dark and feathery against her pink cheeks. Her rosy lips were parted, her breathing slow and steady and he felt a twist of something unknown deep inside him.

She was so damned...*unexpected*.

He swallowed.

She had surprised him the first time around with her innocence and she had surprised him this time by being so gloriously accessible. Her body had opened up with a delicious familiarity. It was as if she instinctively knew what pleased him—as if they had been designed to fit together perfectly.

What was the *matter* with him? Almost imperceptibly he shook his head, trying to clear the thoughts which had obviously been skewed by the heady cocktail of hormones which were surging through his bloodstream. But the movement must have woken her, because Hollie's lashes fluttered open and Maximo found himself dazzled by the light shining from her wide grey eyes. He saw a flicker of confusion cross her face, as if she couldn't quite work out where she was, or who with—and then her lips curved into a smile which only made him want to kiss her.

'Happy Christmas!' she said.

'And to you,' he said, his swift smile intended to inform her that he hadn't had a complete personality change during the night. 'Hollie—'

'It's okay,' she said quickly, before moving away from him towards the other side of the bed. 'You don't have to say a word. I know the score.'

'You do?' he questioned.

Hollie couldn't miss the look of surprise which had darkened his features. Was he worried she was about to start planning some sort of future with him, just because they'd had amazing sex? Was he so arrogant as to imagine that a long night of love-making had turned her head?

And wasn't he right to think that way when her heart was full of wonder at the beauty of what had happened? But Maximo would never know that. Not now and not ever—because if he did, it would destroy this fragile relationship of theirs.

'Of course I do,' she answered, her staunch words helping disguise the distracting flutter of her emotions. 'We've already had the discussion. You don't want to be involved with family life and I'm cool with that, for all the reasons I gave before. Nothing has changed. I enjoyed last night and I hope you did too—'

'You know damned well I did,' he growled.

'Well, then.' She raised her eyebrows. 'What's not to like? Has the snow melted? Because if so, I can be on my way and out of your hair.'

Jumping out of bed, she grabbed the nearest velvet throw—which just happened to be scarlet—and wrapped it around herself, before padding over to the window, aware of Maximo's gaze burning into her, watching every move she made.

Part of her wondered if it had all been a dream and the snow nothing but a figment of her imagination. Hadn't she feared that this morning she would look out onto the dull greys and browns of a midwinter garden? But the scene which greeted her was as frozen and as beautiful as it had been the day before. A completely impenetrable world of white. Deep down Hollie knew it would probably be best for everyone if she could make her escape, but she couldn't help the sudden leap of her heart when she realised that wasn't going to be possible. Who could blame her for wanting to eke out this sensual liaison for as long as possible? 'Oh, dear.'

'Oh, dear what?'

'Bad news, I'm afraid. There's no sign of any thaw and it looks like there might even have been a fresh fall during the night. The road out of here is blocked, all right.' She turned back to face him, wondering what had caused his face to darken like that. 'Looks like my departure is going to have to be delayed.'

'You sound almost *disappointed*, Hollie. Are you so eager to get away?'

Hollie gave him the benefit of her brightest smile. Perhaps she was better at acting than she'd thought. Maybe her relationship with Maximo—if you could call it a relationship—was a bit like Christmas. There was all this amazing stuff on the surface, which made you feel fantastic at the time, but after a day or two it was all over, as if it had never happened.

And thinking of Christmas... Hollie sucked in a breath. Just because Maximo had set himself up as some kind of modern-day Scrooge, didn't mean she had to copy him, did it? They might not have a tree, or fancy baubles, but wasn't *adaptable* her middle name? She knew what the score was, which meant that she didn't have to try to impress him. She could just be herself, which she knew from some of her girlfriends wasn't always the case when you were with a man. Wasn't that a liberation of sorts?

So she shot him another smile. 'The only disappointment would be if we weren't going to celebrate Christmas, but that's not going to happen.'

'It isn't?' he questioned, with a frown.

'Certainly not.'

'But there's nothing here. The castle doesn't run to fairy lights,' he said sarcastically. 'And I told you. I don't like Christmas.'

'Maybe you don't, but I do. There's no need for us to

forgo the festivities, just because we're lacking a few resources—and I don't intend to. Just leave it to me.'

The darkness in his eyes had been replaced by a sudden smokiness which Hollie recognised and it was with a feeling of falling—or failing—that she felt her body's instant response.

'I don't care about the damned festivities,' he ground out. 'All I care about is having you back in my bed again. Now come over here, Hollie Walker, before I lose patience.'

Hollie had never been quite so aware of her own power and for a few brief moments she revelled in it. 'Why don't you come and get me?' she said.

CHAPTER EIGHT

'OKAY. YOU CAN open them now.'

The soft hands which had been covering his eyes were removed and Maximo grew still as he stared at the scene in front of him, unable to believe what he was seeing. He shook his head a little, but nothing altered. What the hell had happened? The previously bare room now seemed like a distant memory, replaced by a glittering and shimmering spectacle. Because Hollie had decorated the long table in the castle library for a late Christmas lunch. No. She'd done much more than that. She had actually decorated the whole damned room so that it resembled something you might see on the movie channel throughout the month of December.

Gleaming silver discs and squares hung from the ceiling, suspended by almost invisible pieces of thread. More dangled from a large branch of conifer, which somehow managed to resemble a miniature Christmas tree. And there were sprigs of holly just about everywhere—lying on empty bookshelves and decorously placed on the mantelpiece—plus an enormous bunch which had been stuck into a pottery jug as a centrepiece for the table.

As for the table…

Maximo been entertained many times during his life with no expense spared, because when a woman made you dinner, she seemed to think she was auditioning for a permanent role in your life.

But this was different.

He narrowed his eyes. Echoing the bright holly berries, the table was spread with what looked like the scarlet velvet throw which had adorned her naked body that very morning. Matching red ribbons were tied in festive bows around two snowy linen napkins and everywhere there were candles. Tall candles and squat candles. Some which were near the end of their natural life and others which were clearly brand-new. Their flames flickered upwards and wove intricate shadows against the walls, while more flames came from the fire which was burning brightly in the grate. His gaze moved to the window where outside dusk was falling on the pristine snowy scene, and the contrast with the illuminated interior of the ancient room made the place look almost…magical.

'What have you done?' he husked.

She shrugged. 'I played around with what we had. The candles I found in the scullery. The shiny things hanging from the ceiling are cardboard, covered with silver foil which I discovered in a drawer in the kitchen—and the cotton comes from a sewing kit in my handbag. The napkins were in those hampers you ordered, as were the ribbons—and I found the rest of the stuff in the garden.' She chewed on her lip, anxiety suddenly creasing her brow. 'You do like it?'

'It's…it's a surprise,' he admitted at last. 'It's…well, it's remarkable.'

She looked at him a little uncertainly, as if unsure whether or not that was a compliment. 'Why don't you sit down?' she suggested. 'And I'll bring the food in.'

'I'll help.'

'No,' she said firmly. 'You won't. Humour me, Maximo. You waited on me at dinner last night and now it's my turn. I'm perfectly capable of carrying a dish or two. You can open the wine if you like and pour yourself a glass. I'm just having water—obviously. So let me go and fetch the food.'

Maximo uncorked the bottle and walked across to the fire to hurl an applewood log onto the already crackling blaze, more to distract himself from the spiky carousel of his thoughts than for any other reason. *This* was the reason he always turned down every damn Christmas invitation which ever came his way, because this kind of homely festivity mocked him. Every single time. It reminded him of the lives of others and all the things he'd never had. It made him think of families who cooked and ate together, laughing and talking as they sat around the table. And his discomfort was amplified by Hollie's presence, by her newly discovered sexuality coupled with the fact that she was pregnant with his child.

She returned to the room, carrying a large tray which he took from her, waving away her protests, and he watched while she left for a final journey to the kitchen. Her hips were swaying in unconscious invitation, and she looked almost unbearably sexy in a borrowed sweater of his, which came down to mid-thigh. When he had finally released her from his bed that morning she had bemoaned aloud the fact that she didn't have a change of knickers.

'Then don't wear any.'

'I can't do that!'

'Why not?' His query had been casual, but his heart had been racing like a schoolboy's. And she had looked at him, and he at her, and somehow their getting up had been delayed even further. She had straddled him with abandon and afterwards they had shared a bath and stayed there until their fingertips were wrinkled, and she had squealed with delight when he'd wrapped her in a bathrobe and carried her back into the bedroom.

He couldn't remember ever feeling quite so turned on by a woman and if she hadn't gone to so much trouble with the meal, he might have suggested they postpone it in favour of a far more sensual feast.

But Maximo couldn't shake off a lingering sense of disconnect as he sat down at the table. Because for some reason it felt as if ghosts were joining them and sitting at those empty chairs. The ghost of his mother, so recently dead. His father, too—though he'd only discovered his demise by reading about it in one of the national Spanish newspapers last year. He thought of Christmases past. He stared at Hollie's belly. Of Christmases future.

'There's some of your Cantabrian mountain stew, which I've reheated,' she was saying, shattering his troubled thoughts with her soft English chatter. 'And lots of lovely cheeses and meats from those fancy hampers. Shall I cut you a slice of this Iberico ham, Maximo?'

His tongue felt as if it wouldn't work, as if it were too big for his mouth. He shook his head, taking a sip of wine. Rich, red wine which warmed the blood like soup. He always drank this particular vintage during his preferred solitary Christmases, but tonight, he might as well have been drinking vinegar. Why was he so beset with the past tonight? he wondered with irritation—as if it were a heavy mantle around his shoulders which he couldn't shake off?

'Is something wrong?' she said as he put the barely touched glass down.

He shook his head. 'No, nothing's wrong.'

'Forgive me for contradicting you, Maximo, but something clearly *is*.'

'Let's eat,' he growled. Remembering that they'd missed breakfast, he forced himself to work his way through some of the food, though he noticed that Hollie was tucking into her own meal with a healthy appetite and, on some level, that pleased him. Eventually, she looked up from her plate of cheese and crackers, putting her knife down with a thoughtful expression on her face.

'You know, something has been puzzling me,' she observed slowly.

'Really?' he questioned, injecting a deliberate note of boredom into his voice because her analytical tone suggested she was intending to take the conversation somewhere he didn't want it to go.

'Any ideas?' she ventured.

'I have many attributes, Hollie,' he drawled, 'but mind-reading has never been one of them.'

But his sarcasm didn't deter her. She simply dabbed at the corners of her mouth with her napkin.

'When you told me about how you started in business, about breaking up big rocks in the road, there was something you failed to mention.'

'There were probably plenty of things I didn't mention.'

'Your parents, for one,' she said.

'Maybe that was a deliberate omission.'

'I mean, how did that happen?' she mused, as if he hadn't spoken. 'Because fourteen *is* very young, no matter how old you looked. You haven't explained what your parents had to say about you joining a construction team and working the roads.'

There was a pause. A pause which seemed to last for ever, giving him time to fall back on his familiar strategies for avoiding scrutiny. But something stopped him and he didn't know what. Was it the clearness of her grey eyes—or an expression of something like compassion which had softened her lovely face, rather than judgement? Almost as if she had guessed at the truth. He thought about what she'd told him about her own father—about his failure to be there for her. Maybe he and Hollie Walker had a lot more in common than he'd previously thought, and was it really such a big deal for the mother of his baby to discover a few truths about him?

'They didn't know,' he said.

'But they must have known. How could they not?'

'By that time in my life, my mother and I were estranged—'

'At *fourteen*?'

'Yes, Hollie. At fourteen. It happens.'

'And your father?'

He shrugged. 'He did not really deserve that title, for I only ever had the briefest of relationships with him.'

'Why?' she questioned quietly. 'What happened?'

His mouth tightened because this was the part which

was definitely off-limits. The part he had taken extra care to filter from his life and online presence—confident in the knowledge that nobody else in the picture would disclose it, because it didn't reflect well on them. Very few people knew who his father had been, and that had always suited him just fine.

Yet suddenly he remembered the nurses who had looked at him so contemptuously when he had stood by his mother's deathbed all those weeks ago. Was it that which made him want to break the habit of a lifetime and unburden himself to Hollie? Those nuns who had judged him and found him wanting for his seeming neglect. His mouth hardened. As if anyone who was old and a mother was automatically some kind of saint who deserved unconditional love from her child—a child she had shunned and rejected.

'My mother was never married to my father,' he said baldly. 'I was illegitimate. Not such a big deal now, but pretty big at the time, particularly in the part of the world where I grew up.' He saw her flinch and wondered if she was thinking about her own situation, wondering whether she too would be judged in this small part of Devon which was now her home. 'My father was one of Spain's wealthiest men. Have you heard of the clothes chain Estilo?' he questioned suddenly.

'Yes, of course I have. Practically every woman on the planet has an Estilo piece in her wardrobe.'

'He owned it,' he said and saw her eyes widen in shock. 'He was married, of course. He had any number of lovers—my mother being just one of them.'

'And was she...content with that?'

His narrowed his eyes. 'No woman is ever truly content with being a mistress, Hollie. Maybe that's why she became pregnant.'

'With you?'

He nodded. '*Sí*. With me. He had told her from the very start that he wanted no children, for he already had two daughters—and although he desperately wanted a son, he planned to conceive one with his similarly aristocratic wife. Outwardly, his life was a model of respectability and he had no intention of altering that state. When my mother went to him with news I was on the way, I think she was expecting him to change his mind and divorce his wife, but he didn't. He didn't want the scandal or the damage to his reputation as a family man. So he ordered her from the house and gave her nothing, not even after I was born.' His mouth thinned. 'There was no acknowledgement that I was his child and certainly no maintenance.'

'But...if he was so rich—'

'To have compensated her would have been an admission of liability and that was something he wasn't prepared to do.'

'She didn't go to the papers?'

'Like I said, it was a different world back then and he had most of the media in his pocket anyway.' His mouth hardened. 'So I lived from hand to mouth with a mother who was increasingly resentful that I had ruined her chances of having a "normal" life. Because where we lived, a woman who had a child out of wedlock was shunned.'

Her grey gaze was steady as she flicked her tongue over her lips. 'What happened?' she whispered.

He shrugged. 'My father had no other son and then

his wife died and, behind the scenes, my mother was concocting a plan. I only learned afterwards that she had gone to his home and confronted him. Told him I looked exactly like him—which was true—and that I had his mannerisms. In the extremely macho world in which he operated, she appealed to both his ego and his pride. She asked would he not prefer his only son to inherit his valuable business, rather than his daughters—two women who would be bound to go off and have families of their own. So he agreed to give me a home in his enormous mansion in the centre of Madrid.' He smiled bitterly. 'I guess you might describe it as a trial run. Like taking on an apprentice on a temporary basis, to see whether or not they fit in. To see if I was suitable to be recognised as his son.'

'And what did you do?' she questioned, when the silence which followed his disclosure became elongated. 'Did you go?'

'Life at home wasn't exactly wonderful and I can't pretend that the thought of inheriting one of Spain's most profitable companies didn't appeal to a boy who had known nothing but hardship. So I went to my father's house...' He shrugged as his voice tailed off. 'And quickly realised that the situation I found myself in was untenable.'

'How so?' she whispered.

He was lost now. Lost in the dark memories of the past. He remembered being bemused by the amount of cutlery beside his plate, and cramming food in his mouth as if he were a street urchin. Which was exactly how he had felt. Like a poor boy who had wandered into a parallel universe. He remembered being amazed at marble-decked bathrooms the size of ballrooms and lavish dinners which could have fed a whole village. His stepsisters laughing because he didn't know which knife to use. The servants looking at him with a scorn they hadn't bothered to hide, as if recognising that he was an outsider. *Un bastardo.* And that was never going to change—he'd recognised that instantly. He'd stuck it out for as long as he could but it had felt as if he were trapped inside his own private hell.

'I wasn't made to feel *welcome*,' he summarised acidly and although she looked as if she wanted him to elaborate, he was damned if he was going to do that, for any frailties he possessed, he showed to no one. Nobody would ever see him vulnerable—not even the mother of his child. 'As dawn broke on Christmas Eve, I left to return to my mother and managed to hitch rides from Madrid to A Coruña. I arrived not long before midnight when the night was bitterly cold and the snow was falling. I remember seeing the Belen in the town square... the traditional nativity scene,' he elaborated, when he saw her frown. 'I thought my mother might be out— although I certainly didn't think she'd be on her way to Mass. She was more likely to be drinking in a bar.' He gave a short laugh. 'But she'd gone.'

'Gone?' she echoed. 'Gone where?'

'I never found out. She had cleared out all her stuff the month before and left no word or forwarding address.' It shouldn't have come as a shock, but it did. Because deep down he had always believed that she loved him, because she was his mother. But she did not love him. She never had. He had fallen to his knees in the icy snow and wept and that was the last time he had ever wept. At least he'd had food in his rucksack—the only thing he had taken from his father's house. And then he had begun to walk, though he didn't know where. He had walked on through the night and on Christmas morning he had stumbled across the construction site and waited there for workers to return after the Christmas break. And he had vowed there and then that he would never let anyone close enough to hurt him again.

'She wiped me from her life as if I had never existed,' he continued, the words falling from his mouth like stones. 'It was only much later, when I had started to make money, that she contacted me again.'

'And were you ever...reconciled?'

'We met,' he said tersely, staring down at his fingernails. 'But her main focus was on what I could buy for her, rather than making up for all those lost years. I provided for her throughout the rest of her life but I never saw her again until a couple of months ago.'

'She...died?'

He looked up at her, feeling himself tense up. 'How the hell did you know that?' he demanded.

'Something in your face as you said it. I could see your pain.' Her voice was soft again. How did she make it so damned soft? 'I'm sorry for your loss, Maximo. I know she was cruel to you, but she was still your mother.'

He wanted to deny that he felt anything but she was getting up from the table and walking round to where he sat, sliding onto his lap to face him, one bare leg on either side of his. She looked at him for a long moment before resting her head on his in an age-old gesture which had never come his way before. Maybe he'd

never needed it before. It had nothing to do with sex—
and everything to do with comfort. And it was powerful, he realised. Unbelievably...powerful.

He wanted to shrug her off, to tell her he didn't need
any clumsy attempts at sympathy—but the words remained unspoken, the gesture never made. He could
smell her clean, soapy scent and right then she seemed
to embody all the virtues he'd never really associated
with the women in his life.

Innocence.

Decency.

Kindness.

Suddenly a tension which had been coiled so tightly
inside him started unravelling, like a line spinning
wildly from the fisherman's rod. Something he hadn't
even realised had been stretched to breaking point now
snapped and he held her tightly, losing himself in an
embrace so close that you couldn't have fitted a hair
between them.

He told himself it was desire.

Because it *was* desire. What else could it be? The
powerful beat of his heart and the low clench of heat
were familiar enough, but his urgent need to possess her
was off the scale. With one hand he hooked the back of
her neck and brought her face down to his, revelling in
that first sweet taste of her lips as her satiny hair spilled
over his hands. He deepened the kiss and deepened it
still more, until she was writhing around on his lap—
her lack of panties instantly apparent from the syrupy
wetness which was seeping into his jeans.

'Unzip me,' he urged throatily.

Instantly, she complied, although her fingers were

trembling and it took some careful manoeuvring before he was free, and then at last he lowered her down onto his aching shaft, a ragged groan escaping from his lips as he filled her.

She rode him. She rode him as if she had been born to do just that. Was it instinct which made her so proficient at that age-old rhythm? Because it certainly wasn't experience. Yet she seemed to read him so well. As if she knew exactly when he wanted her to pull the borrowed sweater over her head so that he could drink in every second of her partial striptease and the luscious bounce of her breasts. She shook her hair, so that it moved around her bare shoulders like a shiny ripple of wheat. And then he was coming and so was she. Coming and coming and coming…and it was like no orgasm he'd ever experienced.

His shout of exclamation—or was it exultation?—was harsh. Imprecise. His body bucked helplessly beneath her. And when it was over she didn't say a word, and he was glad. He didn't want her attempting to give meaning to what had just taken place. Because it had no meaning. It was just a manifestation of their extraordinary physical chemistry.

He stirred, wanting to put a little distance between them. Needing space to order his befuddled thoughts. 'Don't you think maybe it's time for dessert?'

'But there isn't…' Her breath was warm against his neck, her words soporific and slightly slurred. 'I'm afraid there isn't any dessert.'

He pulled back from her and frowned. 'Really? I thought you brought cake with you?'

Unwillingly stirred from her sleepy state, Hollie

stared back at him in confusion, suddenly remembering the wretched cake which Janette had insisted on commissioning. 'You really want cake now?'

'Why not?'

Why *not*? She hadn't wanted to present it to him at the time and she was even less inclined to do so now, because it seemed to symbolise some of the things which had been so out of kilter between them. It reminded her of the speed with which he'd left her bed and the way he'd distanced himself afterwards. Worst of all was the memory of his reaction to her pregnancy when he'd been so angry and cold. And she was slightly irritated that he'd asked for it now, because it was hardly the most romantic way to end what had just been the most erotic encounter of her life. But Maximo doesn't do romance, she reminded herself fiercely. He does sex. And that's all he does. Better think about that before you start fabricating any more foolish dreams about him.

'Of course. How could I have forgotten? I'll go and fetch it,' she said, sliding from his lap and plucking his sweater from the floor, before wriggling it over her head. After a detour to the bathroom she hunted down the cake, and when she walked back into the library, she found Maximo still sitting at the table, seemingly lost in thought as he stared across the room at the crackling fire. He looked up as she put the cake on the table, but his expression was shadowed and indecipherable—their mood of lazy sensuality seemingly broken. She wanted to cut him a slice before he had seen it, but he had risen from his seat to look over her shoulder, at the Spanish word for congratulations, which she had laboriously piped onto the white icing.

"Felicidades",' he read slowly, and then pointed to a fuzzy-looking shape beside the word. 'And what's this?'

Did he guess it was a teardrop, which had fallen straight onto the coloured icing at a critical moment? Yesterday she might have concocted some flimsy excuse and told him that she'd been trying to create a star, but not today. Because he had told her stuff. He'd confided in her. Hard, painful stuff. He'd let his guard down, presumably because he'd felt as if, on some level, he could trust her. So maybe she should trust him, too. And besides, it wasn't as if they had any shared illusions about the future which could be tarnished by the truth, was it?

'It was a tear,' she admitted, meeting the seeking expression in his black eyes with a shrug. 'I was feeling a bit sorry for myself.'

'But you're not now?'

'No, I'm not. There's no point. If life gives you lemons, you just have to make lemonade.'

Maximo took the slice she offered him, breaking off a fragment and putting it in his mouth so that it melted in a sugary rush against his tongue. He thought about the days which had led up to this moment, and the days which would follow. His mind began to compose an agenda, just like when he took on a new business deal and had to deal with facts methodically. Whatever happened he would support his child financially—in a way in which his own father had never supported him.

Just financially?

He stared across the table at Hollie, who was studiously picking frosting off her own piece of cake, though not actually eating any. And suddenly he realised that, despite all her outward simplicity, the package she presented was way more complex than he'd first imagined.

He had been the first man to have had sex with her. The only man. That shouldn't have meant anything but the truth was, it did. It made a primitive satisfaction pulse through his body. And although that realisation should have unsettled him, somehow it didn't because it had shone a light onto something else he'd only just realised.

Going forward, he didn't *want* her sleeping with other men. Just as he didn't want his child calling another man Papi. Maybe his attitude could be described as possession but could also be described as pragmatism. Because if the lack of a father had cast dark clouds over his life, hadn't she experienced something similar? And if that were the case, then wasn't it comparatively easy for them to do something about it, to spare their own child a similar kind of heartache?

'Marry me, Hollie.'

She looked up from her crumbled cake, her expression one of shock then confusion, as if she hadn't heard him properly. She knitted her brows together. 'What did you say?'

'I said, marry me, Hollie.'

'Is that an…order?'

'Does my method of asking offend you? Do you want me to pretend?' he demanded huskily. 'To go down on one knee with a ring-pull from a cola can and tell you I'll buy you a thirty-carat diamond ring when we hit the shops?'

'No, Maximo, I don't want you to pretend anything.

I want you to tell me why you've suddenly come out with this extraordinary proposal.'

There was a pause. She'd told him she didn't want him to pretend, so he wouldn't. 'Because I think it's the only sensible solution to our dilemma.'

'*Dilemma?* Is that what you call it?'

'Don't try to gilt-edge a situation which neither of us ever intended to happen,' he said roughly. 'But instead, let's try to make the best of what we have. To make the lemonade, as you said. I don't want this child to grow up thinking his father didn't want him.'

'But you don't, do you?' she questioned baldly. 'Want him. Or her, for that matter.'

He shook his head. 'Now that the shock has worn off, I find that I do.'

'But that isn't enough to justify marriage, Maximo.'

'*No lo es*—I agree. And if it were someone else, I suspect I would not be having this conversation. But I find you easy company, Hollie, and that is rare—for my past relationships with women have not been easy. And believe me, our sexual chemistry is even more rare.'

'But…marriage,' she said. 'Isn't that a rather extreme solution?'

Her continued opposition rather than the instant capitulation he'd been anticipating only spurred Maximo on—because never did he feel quite so alive as when he was having to fight for something. 'I don't think I'll have a problem living with you. Plus my work takes me away a lot, which would give us both space. You will never have to worry about money. Ever. And that will still apply even if you find the situation intolerable and ask me for a divorce.'

He looked at her, his eyes cool and expectant, and Hollie felt the lurch of something she couldn't quite define. Or maybe she just didn't dare to. Because surely she should be feeling offended by his rather brutal words. Surely she shouldn't be excited about the thought of getting wed to a man who was clearly offering marriage out of some archaic form of *duty*? But she was. She couldn't help herself. She might try to talk herself out of her feelings by applying logic, but they were still her feelings.

The truth was that she found him easy company, too. And while she had no experience of sexual chemistry, she didn't imagine it was possible for that side of their relationship to get any better.

But the main thing to consider was her baby.

Their baby.

She touched her fingers to her belly and felt a little spark of hope flickering inside her. Didn't she owe it to this innocent life inside her to offer their child the best possible start in life? To not have to worry about spiralling childcare costs, or the fact that her baby had no contact with a single other blood relative than her. Hadn't she grown up that way and found it lonely and miserable? And Maximo had experienced that too— he'd effectively admitted it to her earlier.

Yet she didn't have a clue about what passed for normal behaviour in the world of this privileged billionaire. For all she knew, he might want what she believed was called an 'open' marriage and some instinct deep in her gut told her she would find that intolerable.

'What about fidelity?' she blurted out. 'Are you intending to be faithful to me?'

'I am and I will,' he said, his voice suddenly growing harsh. 'But I will also be truthful, Hollie. And if ever I meet a woman I desire more than you, then I will tell you so immediately and we will dissolve our marriage.'

It wasn't the answer she'd wanted, but she guessed it would have to do. Because although once again his words were brutal, at least they were true. She thought of the story he had told her and the bitter sadness she had seen in his eyes as he'd recounted it. Maximo had his vulnerabilities too, she realised, just like her. Couldn't they be there for each other—to reach out to each other in times of need—united against a sometimes cruel world?

So Hollie nodded as a sudden sense of calm filled her and the smile she gave him came straight from the heart. 'Then I will,' she said softly. 'I will marry you, Maximo.'

CHAPTER NINE

THE THAW SET in and it was as if the snow had never existed. As if it had all been nothing but a dream. As if Christmas Day and the four days which followed had never actually happened.

Except that they had. At the end of that delicious and sensual sojourn in the ancient castle Kastelloes, Maximo Diaz had asked Hollie Walker to marry him. And her future had changed in an instant. Her image of herself as a plucky but sometimes lonely single mother had crumbled away and instead she was having to get her head around the fact that soon she was going to be the wife of the sexy Spanish tycoon.

Maximo was still sleeping as she slipped silently from the bed, wrapping herself in velvet—green today—before staring out of the window. Water was dripping from branches, from bushes—drip-drip-drip. The dark turrets of the castle were no longer topped by a crown of white and nor did the bushes look like giant white stones. The magic had gone, she realised, a sudden whisper of apprehension prickling over her as she studied Maximo's tousled black head lying against the pillow and all her suppressed fears were suddenly given life.

Would he wake up and regret the resolution they'd come to at the end of Christmas Day, when—possibly affected by the emotional aftermath of the things he'd told her—he had asked her to be his wife? Perhaps it would be better if she gave him the opportunity to retract words he might have delivered too hastily, and she wondered if she could manage to do it in a way which meant that neither of them would lose face.

His lashes fluttered open—so dark against the silken olive of his skin—and mentally Hollie steeled herself against his beauty as he surveyed her through a shuttered gaze.

'The snow has melted,' she said baldly.

'That's good.'

'Good?'

'Sure. Unless you were planning to build a snowman. Don't you need a change of underwear, and don't we need to get to London? If the roads are clear, it means we can go.'

'London?' She looked at him blankly. 'You never said anything about London.'

'My jet is in an airfield on the outskirts of the city, Hollie.' His voice was soft but his words resolute. 'And I'm due back in Madrid for a New Year's party I've promised to attend under pain of death if I don't. As my future wife you'll be coming with me and there's no reason why you shouldn't move in straight away.'

She hadn't considered living in Madrid either. How stupid was that? 'But I thought...'

'What?' he prompted softly, throwing back the pile

of velvet throws to rise from the bed like a magnificent dark and golden statue brought to life, before walking towards her. 'What did you think?'

'That I'd...' It was difficult to think of anything when he was standing so close and so naked. 'Well, I'll have to work out my notice for Janette.'

'Seriously?'

She nodded. 'Of course.'

He shrugged, his eyes shards of glittering jet. 'Even though I could easily arrange for one of my staff to take your place?'

His suggestion made her feel dispensable. As if her job and her old life were of no consequence. And even though it *was* a simple office job which anyone could probably do, and even though Hollie had often found Janette difficult, she had no intention of disappearing in a puff of smoke simply because a rich man was snapping his fingers. If she fell in with his autocratic wishes so readily, it wouldn't bode well for the rest of their lives, would it?

'I'm afraid I can't do that, Maximo,' she said. 'I can't possibly break my contract. I don't want to sneak away from Trescombe under a black cloud.'

His face darkened, as if her determination surprised and slightly irked him. 'I am loath to be apart from you, Hollie—perhaps I've become a little too used to having you in my bed,' he murmured. 'But obviously we can work round it. We'll just have to jet between the two places until you're free to move, if that's what you want.'

Of course it wasn't what she *wanted*. In a way, she was terrified of being apart from him. Terrified that their affair and his subsequent proposal would get diluted by distance and prove as insubstantial as the Christmas snow itself. If she worked out her notice there was the very real possibility that Maximo would change his mind and Hollie didn't want him to change his mind.

She wanted this. Him. The whole package.

She wanted to be his wife. She wanted him to be a father to their baby.

But if Maximo was going to get cold feet, then surely it was better if they discovered it now rather than later.

'The month will soon pass,' she said, with a certainty she didn't feel.

'You think so?' He sighed. 'Then I guess I must be patient—which is not an attribute I've ever been particularly known for. I suppose I must admire your loyalty to your employer, Hollie—but that's all we're going to say on the subject, because I'm taking you back to bed.'

Hollie was still glowing when Maximo's limousine made its way up the hill towards the castle, and she began to get an idea how smoothly the world worked when it was powered by wealth. Decisions which might have taken weeks to evolve were enacted almost before you'd finished making them. Life became seamless and also a little bit scary as she was driven to her cottage and instructed to pack only the things she couldn't bear to be without.

'But we're not leaving Trescombe completely, are we?' she questioned. 'I mean, it's not like we're cutting ties with the place completely. Because when you start renovating the castle—'

'Let's just concentrate on the essentials for now, shall we, Hollie?'

And although his words were a little clipped, Hollie couldn't deny how comforting it was to have someone else make the decisions. She felt the tension leave her body, realising this was the first time she'd ever had someone to lean on. She had cared for her mother and supported her emotionally when she'd gone to pieces, and then she had cared for herself when her mother had died. Why wouldn't she? Yet she couldn't deny how great it was to let someone else take responsibility for a change.

'Okay,' she said. 'I'll go and get my things together. Would you like to come inside?'

'No. I'll wait here in the car. I have a few calls to make.'

It took her less than twenty minutes before Hollie rushed out of the door with her little suitcase, half imagining that the limousine might have disappeared in the interim, like Cinderella's fancy coach turning into a pumpkin. But, no, it was still there—and the six-year-old twin boys who lived in the house opposite were gazing at the shiny black livery as if Santa's reinvented sleigh had made a post-Christmas appearance. As the chauffeur shut the door behind her, Maximo lifted a narrow-eyed gaze from his computer and Hollie got the distinct feeling he had forgotten she was there.

Through towns decked with Christmas finery, they were driven at speed to London, where Maximo announced his intention to buy her a completely new wardrobe, so she could arrive in Madrid suitably clad.

Which left her wondering exactly what was the matter with the way she looked now.

She stared rather moodily at her well-polished brown

leather boots before lifting her gaze to his. 'Because I'll let you down, I suppose?'

'It's not a question of letting me down. You look like a college student,' he informed her, almost gently, his fingertips whispering over her mane of hair. 'Which is undoubtedly a wildly sexy look, just not one which is particularly appropriate for my future wife. If you aren't dressed suitably it will make you self-conscious, for you will be mixing with women who will undoubtedly be wearing very costly clothes.'

'Gosh, you're making our future union sound like it's going to be fun, Maximo.'

He smiled then—a slow, sensual smile which curled over her skin like a wisp of smoke. 'Oh, I can offer you fun, Hollie. Be in no doubt about that. Now wipe that apprehensive look from your face and kiss me instead.'

And wasn't it crazy how his kiss had the power to dissolve every last doubt?

The limousine dropped them at an expensive-looking department store in central London with doormen who looked as if they had stepped straight out of a Victorian novel. And although the post-Christmas sales had just started and there were stampedes of people buying sequinned dresses and puddings which would shortly reach their sell-by dates, Hollie was assigned a personal shopper all to herself, though Maximo's insistence on accompanying her took her a little by surprise.

He watched as she paraded before him in a variety of outfits and the molten smoulder of his eyes when he approved a particular article of clothing was flattering, yes—but his attention quickly turned back to his com-

puter, as though his work was more engrossing than
anything else. Of course it was. He was just dressing
her up like a doll so that she wouldn't disappoint him
in front of all his rich friends.

But she couldn't deny that the exquisite garments felt
wonderful against her skin—more than that, they made
her look like someone she'd never believed she could
be. Why, at certain angles she looked almost…pretty.

'I suppose you've taken lots of women shopping in
the past like this?' she probed.

'Not a single one,' he admitted. 'But then, I've never
asked anyone to marry me before either. Just as I have
never been quite so much in physical thrall to a woman
as I am to you. And so, to avoid unnecessary repetition
of predictable questions, shall I simply assure you that
having my full attention like this is not the way I usually operate? Does that put your mind at rest, as well
as flattering your ego, Hollie?'

It did. It made her feel…*special*. It made her want to
whistle a tune, to sing out loud at the top of her voice.
She felt as if she could conquer the world.

And when the shopping expedition was concluded
and they had eaten lunch in a hushed restaurant with
thick white tablecloths and women who watched him
with predatory eyes, Maximo dropped her back at the
store, where she was whisked off to a basement spa
which smelt faintly of sandalwood and tuberose. There
she had her first ever bikini wax, a pedicure and make-
up lesson, though she begged them to go easy on the
mascara. Next, a sweet girl in a white uniform took her
to the hairdressing section to have a couple of inches

snipped off her mane and some choppy layers added. And when it was all done, she stood in front of the full-length mirror in her new silk dress, with a shiny fall of hair shimmering around her shoulders, and her transformation seemed complete.

She didn't look like Hollie Walker any more.

Neither an uptight office girl nor a giddy Christmas elf stared back at her today.

She looked like an expensive glossy *stranger*.

And when Maximo came to collect her, he must have thought along similar lines because he appeared almost taken aback by her appearance.

'*Bien, bien, bien*—what have we here, *mia belleza*?' he mused, his black gaze travelling over every inch of her, before he slid onto the back seat of the car beside her.

'You don't like it?'

'I didn't say that.' His hand slid over her thigh, his fingers stroking over the navy silk. 'You look out of this world.'

'Like an alien, you mean?'

He laughed. 'No, not remotely like that. Why do you always put yourself down?'

'Perhaps I'm not used to compliments.'

'Then I shall have to make sure you get used to them. Like a beautiful woman at her peak, is that better? My only complaint is that there isn't time for me to prove just how much you have excited my senses, because we need to buy you a ring before the shop closes.'

'We don't really have to do that today, do we, Maximo? Haven't we shopped enough?'

'I'm afraid we do. I was given to understand that

women can never have too much shopping, although maybe you're the exception to the rule,' he added drily. 'But tomorrow, we fly to Madrid and I intend that you should arrive there wearing the biggest diamond in the world.'

Hollie supposed it would be churlish to object to having 'the biggest diamond in the world' on the grounds that she was feeling increasingly detached from reality with all this high-end purchasing power. Yet wasn't this just another example of making sure she was 'good enough' to meet his wealthy friends?

She tried to shake off her insecurity as he took her to a darkened store somewhere near Hatton Garden, which didn't really look like a jeweller's from the outside, and he and the owner began speaking in a language she barely recognised as English. They spoke of *cushion* and *marquise* and *princess*, which she gathered were cuts of diamonds, though when she emerged from the store an hour later, it was with an enormous rock called a *round brilliant* dripping from her finger.

As they were leaving, she saw a woman in the street do a double take when she spotted the size of the jewel. But all Hollie could focus on was the sobering thought that the entire purchase had been conducted with zero emotion. There had been no joy on the face of her husband-to-be as he slipped the priceless ring on her finger—just a glimmer of quiet satisfaction in his eyes as the shop's owner informed him that he had just purchased the finest gem in his collection.

Because there *was* no emotion involved, Hollie reminded herself fiercely as they got into the waiting car. There might be mutual attraction and a determination to do the right thing by their baby, but this marriage was nothing but a solution to their *dilemma*, and she should forget that at her peril.

'So where are we going now?' she asked, slightly dazzled by the rainbow rays which sparkled on her left hand and wondering if she would have to remove it when she was cooking.

He glanced up from his phone, momentarily distracted. 'We'll spend tonight at the Granchester Hotel, for you must be tired after so much travelling?'

'A little,' she admitted.

'And tomorrow we head for the airfield where my jet is ready to fly us to Spain, because it's New Year's Eve and we have a big party to attend.'

'How big a party?' she said, suddenly nervous.

'Very big. The Spanish love to celebrate the start of the new year and since many of my friends will be gathered together in the same place, it means I can introduce you as my bride.' He glanced at his watch. 'We should arrive in Madrid in time for lunch.'

'And that's where you live? In Madrid?' It seemed crazy that soon she would marry him and she didn't actually *know*. There were so many things about him she didn't know.

'Yes, I have an apartment there, very close to the Retiro Park. I think you'll like it.'

Hollie felt dizzy. London for shopping. Madrid for lunch. And a massive New Year's Eve party with, no doubt, all the world's glitterati there. Was this going to be her life from now on? She supposed it was. Would she fit in? Or, even with all her fancy new clothes and hairstyle, would she still look like ordinary Hollie

Walker who worked in an office and baked cakes on the side?

But Maximo had put his phone away and was circling his fingertip over the palm of her hand and making her tremble, and her eyelids were fluttering to a close as he leaned over to kiss her. And really, what more could she possibly want?

CHAPTER TEN

'AND THIS IS my housekeeper, Carmen. Anything you want—Carmen will be able to get for you.' Maximo's eyes glinted as he ushered Hollie inside. 'Within reason, of course.'

'Encantada de conocerte,' said Hollie, using one of the phrases her fiancé had taught her during the flight over from London that morning.

'I'm very pleased to meet you, too. I speak fluent English, by the way,' added Carmen, with a smile.

Hollie beamed. 'Thank goodness for that.'

'And congratulations on your engagement.' Carmen shot a brief smile in the direction of the knuckleduster diamond. 'The staff are all delighted for you and Señor Diaz.'

'I appreciate that, Carmen. And it's wonderful to be here.'

Carmen inclined her head. 'Welcome to your new home.'

'Thank you.' Hollie slid her tongue over her lips. Her new home—a huge and contemporary penthouse apartment overlooking Madrid's beautiful Retiro Park. It was terrifyingly immaculate, with not a single thing out of place, and as she shook the middle-aged housekeeper's hand she wondered if it would ever actually feel like home for her. But at least she was feeling calmer than she had done on the journey here. Their one-night stay at the Granchester Hotel had been unforgettable. Hollie had never stayed anywhere quite so luxurious and they'd been given an incredible suite with reputedly the best view over the London skyline, because Maximo was friends with the owner.

But butterfly nerves had been fluttering in her stomach as her fiancé's jet had touched down in Spain and they had been driven straight from the airfield to his apartment. It had been daunting at first, meeting his staff—Carmen, and a permanent cook as well as a daily cleaner. But they'd seemed very open and friendly, and genuinely pleased to meet her, and that gave Hollie a flare of hope.

I can do this, she thought.

I will do this.

'Would you like to see the rest of the apartment?' asked Maximo softly, once they were out of Carmen's earshot.

'Yes, please,' she said.

'And then, after lunch, I think it is time to introduce you to the very important Spanish tradition of the siesta.'

'Maximo!'

'You do realise that every time you whisper my name like that, it only turns me on some more, so you must never stop doing it? Now follow me and I will show you your new home.'

Hollie nodded, trying to concentrate on her surroundings, wanting to like them more than first impressions had suggested she might. Because although she was aware that she was in one of the most prestigious parts of Madrid, her initial reaction to Maximo's apartment had been one of disappointment. It was so modern and so *functional*. The spaces were vast and curiously impersonal, even thought they housed some pretty stunning furniture and artworks. Huge canvases adorned the giant walls and most of the furniture was dark, soft leather and almost tauntingly masculine. In fact, dark was the theme which predominated—apart from an illuminated wine cellar, which looked more like an art installation, a dining room which overlooked the city lights and a floodlit rectangular lap pool on the sprawling terrace, where Maximo informed her he liked to swim every morning before breakfast.

She tried to find the right words to say. Tried to imagine herself living here with a baby, with all these hard and gleaming surfaces. She thought about smudged little fingerprints clouding the acres of polished glass. 'It's lovely,' she said politely.

'There are plenty of good restaurants nearby and an interesting mix of people.'

'Gorgeous,' she said obediently, using the same tone she used to project in the office when a prospective vendor would canvas her opinion about the house they were just about to market. It wasn't a question of not being honest, it was simply showing consideration for other people's feelings. Because Hollie knew how a person could form a huge emotional attachment to their home. What right did she have to tell Maximo that she thought his apartment was a hideous monument to brutalism, when clearly he loved it? In England they often said an Englishman's home was his castle, well, maybe it was the same for Spanish men.

Yet all she could think about was a *real* castle, back in Trescombe, where they had shared that magical Christmas and candlelight had flickered intriguing shadows across the bare stone walls. Yes, Kastelloes could be chilly and, yes, the grounds were untamed and some of the interiors were crumbling away. But at least it had heart and soul and an artistic symmetry which took her breath away. Perhaps Maximo would capitalise on all those assets when he turned it into a luxury hotel to add to his existing group. She couldn't wait to see what he would do with it.

'Hollie?'

Maximo's voice interrupted her reverie.

'Mmm…?' she said absently.

'Weren't we talking about a siesta?'

She looked up, meeting the narrowed glint in his black eyes, and her heart turned over and melted. Who cared about bricks and mortar when a man looked at you that way? Who cared about anything when he could make her senses sing without even touching her?

'I believe we were,' she agreed and her answering smile seemed to spur him into instant and very masterful action. But she liked it when he made that soft roaring sound at the back of his throat and then carried her into their bedroom like a victor, carrying his spoils.

She liked it a lot.

Maximo watched Hollie's breasts rise and fall in time with her steady, even breathing. Her gleaming golden-brown hair was spread out over the pillow, her cheeks were lightly brushed with roses and she looked...

He swallowed.

Not beautiful, no. Her nose was a little too big and her lips not quite full enough ever to fit that imprecise and elusive definition which women craved and most men sought.

She looked sexy and serene. In fact, very serene and *very* sexy.

Once again he felt the tightening of desire low in his belly.

She had just flicked her tongue over his body and made his large frame convulse with spasms of delight he'd thought were never going to end. And afterwards he had done the same to her. Given swift featherlight licks against the hidden honey at the top of her legs, until she had clutched his bare shoulders with flailing fingertips and cried out his name.

But his remembered satisfaction was tempered by a sudden flicker of apprehension. She was the most perfect lover he could have ever imagined, and there had been a fair number during his thirty-four years of bachelorhood. But Hollie was like no other woman he'd ever known before. She was sweet and uncomplicated and innocent.

And she was having his baby.

His *baby*.

Didn't that give her a particular power—the kind of power he had vowed no woman would ever wield over him again? He could feel a sudden tightness in his throat. He had never wanted a child of his own, reasoning that someone who had never experienced parental love would be incapable of demonstrating any himself. He'd been scared of falling short and hadn't wanted another child to endure what he had endured. Plus, he'd liked his freedom and the ability to do what he wanted, when he wanted.

But now?

Suddenly he felt the winds of change upon him, and a feeling of inevitability blowing in their wake. He could sense a very different world opening up before him and simple, straightforward Hollie at the beating centre of it.

Hollie.

Hollie who seemed so soft and vulnerable. Almost *too* soft. *Too* vulnerable. He wasn't used to a woman looking at him that way, all wide-eyed and wondering. His mouth hardened. He would protect her and their child for as long as he lived, yes. He would give her whatever she wanted—hadn't he told her so just an hour ago, when he had carried her into the bedroom and stripped that provocative lingerie from her delicious body? She would have security for her and their child for the rest of her life, and he would put money in a trust to ensure that his son or daughter's future was secure. But those were practical needs he was able to fulfil, because this was a practical marriage and nothing more. He had made that clear to her when he'd asked her to be his wife and maybe now it was time to remember it himself. He wouldn't let her think this relationship was going to become any deeper than it already was, because that was never going to happen. Far better she get used to reality, rather than having her hopes raised and then dashed by unrealistic expectations. In the short term, wasn't it better to be a little cruel in order to be kind?

He stroked his fingers over the silky flesh of her cheek. 'Hollie?'

At the sound of his voice she began to stir, opening her eyes to find him watching her, and, almost shyly, she smiled. 'That was…amazing,' she said softly.

'Mmm. It certainly was, but now we must move. The party will already be in full swing and they're expecting us. Everyone's going to want to meet my fiancée.'

She bit down on her bottom lip. 'Have you told them we're engaged?'

'Not yet.' He lifted her hand and the dazzle of the large diamond shot bright fire over her hand. 'We'll let this ring announce it for us, shall we?'

'I'm nervous, Maximo.'

'Why are you nervous?'

'What if they don't like me?'

'Why wouldn't they like you? Now go and get ready and I'll ask Carmen to serve us a glass of *casera* before we leave.'

Hollie nodded and made her way towards the bathroom as Maximo's words echoed inside her head. Why wouldn't they like you? he had asked—because he had no comprehension of what it was like to be her. His world was very different and was inhabited by very different people. Would they welcome an unsophisticated stranger like her into their midst, or would they wonder if Maximo had taken leave of his senses?

She turned on the power shower and let the warm water bounce off her skin, telling herself she mustn't catastrophise the evening before it had even begun.

Maximo's staff had already welcomed her with open arms and there was no reason why his friends shouldn't do the same.

She was feeling much better by the time she emerged from the bathroom, to see Maximo already dressed in a dark evening suit—a delectable sight which made her heart twist with predictable longing. He was lounging back in one of the bedroom's dark leather armchairs and looked up from his phone when she entered, clad in nothing but a snowy bathrobe.

'I haven't a clue what to wear,' she said, rifling through the row of new clothes which someone must have hung neatly in the wardrobe while they were having lunch.

'Wear the black,' he said suddenly. 'And put your hair up.'

'I thought you liked it down.'

'In bed, certainly—but tonight, no. Stop frowning at me like that, Hollie. There's a reason.'

'Am I allowed to know what the reason is?'

'In time.' He smiled. 'Be patient, *mia belleza.*'

Hollie began to get ready, fixing her hair and pinning it in place. Half an hour later and she was ready, a loose chignon coiled against the back of her neck, the black silk dress skimming her knees, and a pair of strappy shoes adding extra height. As she leaned towards the mirror to apply a light coat of lip gloss, Maximo walked across the bedroom and placed a small box on the dressing table in front of her.

'Why don't you put these on?' he said.

'These' turned out to be two long and sparkling columns—a pair of exquisite diamond earrings—and she stared down at them in confusion.

'But you've already given me—'

'Put them on,' he emphasised softly. 'I bought them at the same time as we got your ring. It's your Christmas present, Hollie.'

'But...but I haven't given you anything!' she protested, surprised when he leant over and placed the palm of his hand over her still-flat belly and their eyes met in a silent moment, reflected in the mirror.

'Oh, but you have,' he contradicted softly. 'You have given me something money can never buy. My baby.' There was a pause as she was caught in the ebony spotlight of his gaze. 'Would it bother you if we announced it tonight? It would kill speculation and everyone is going to know about it sooner or later.'

Hollie didn't answer straight away. She wasn't sure she agreed because it still felt very...private, as well as very new. Yet it wasn't as though it were a guilty secret, was it? It was nothing to feel *ashamed* about. And if she was surprised by Maximo's desire to tell people, she couldn't think of any reason why he shouldn't— she was past the danger zone, wasn't she? 'No, I don't mind,' she said.

He turned away then, but not before Hollie saw the flash of something unexpected in his black eyes. A look which was hard and dark and very macho.

Was it triumph?

Was that why she felt a faint flicker of foreboding to add to all the others which seemed to be building up inside her? But she forced herself to push away her fears, determined to count her blessings instead. Tomorrow was the first day of the new year and the man she was going to marry was the father of her baby. Wasn't that good enough to be going along with?

He took her to the drawing room, which was situated at the very top of the large house, where they sipped glasses of *casera*—a simple bubbly lemon concoction, which Maximo said was rarely drunk outside Spain and which Hollie found delicious. Afterwards they were driven to the west of the city, to an upmarket area called Pozuelo de Alarcón, where the party was being held. The house was large and modern and surrounded by enormous grounds, with clever lighting focussing on beautiful outdoor statues and surrounding shrubs. Coloured bulbs were looped through the branches of trees, and as the line of luxury cars progressed up the long drive Hollie could see people laughing and drinking through giant plate-glass windows. It looked just like a commercial and Hollie would have defied anyone not to have felt intimidated by it.

Did her shoulders stiffen with tension—was that why Maximo ran a reflective finger over her palm? 'Everything okay?' he verified.

'I'm still nervous,' she admitted.

'Don't be, *mia belleza*. Your innocence will be like a breath of fresh air.'

'Not so very innocent any more,' she reflected ruefully.

'Everyone has to lose their innocence some time.' He reached up and touched his fingertip against one of the diamond strands which dangled like a spill of stars from her ear. 'You know that at midnight we have a big tradition in this country?'

'Like the siesta, you mean?'

'In its way, *las doce uvas de la suerte* is as important as the siesta, *sí*—because, to the Spanish, all traditions are important.'

Hollie nodded, wondering if that was because he'd grown up without any real traditions of his own.

As had she.

'Everyone eats grapes at midnight on New Year's Eve,' he said. 'One for each stroke of the hour—twelve grapes in all.'

'Why do you do that?'

'To bring us luck.' He smiled. 'Rare is the Spaniard who will poison his fate for the following year by failing to complete this simple task.'

'In England, we might be tempted to call that superstition.'

'Then I shall have to persuade you otherwise, won't I?' he said softly as the limousine slid to a silent halt, and she shivered as he whispered his fingertip over her thigh, as if to remind her of what delights lay in store for them later.

Heads turned as they walked into the party—where even the people serving drinks and canapés looked as if they had stepped from the pages of a fashion bible.

Please don't let me make a fool of myself, Hollie prayed.

There was a split-second pause and then conversation resumed as a tall and very handsome man extricated himself from a group of people and came over to greet them.

'Maximo,' he said. 'I'm glad you made it, though I confess to being a little surprised.' His black eyes gleamed with curiosity. 'Since the word is out that there are going to be a lot of very disappointed women here tonight.'

Hollie felt Maximo's fingertips touch the base of her spine.

'Javier, I'd like you to meet my fiancée, Hollie Walker. Hollie, this is Javier de Balboa, a very old friend of mine, who will probably do his best to cause mischief.'

'Pleased to meet you,' said Hollie, her hand straying to her cheek to push away a dangling strand of hair.

'So it *is* true,' breathed Javier, and Hollie knew she hadn't imagined the surprise which flickered in his dark eyes as he spotted the large diamond gleaming on her finger. 'Wow. I am delighted to meet the woman who has tamed this black-hearted rogue after so long. You *do* realise what you're taking on, don't you, Hollie?'

'I think so.'

Her tentative words made both men smile and suddenly Hollie felt a little more comfortable as she asked for a glass of *casera*.

'You won't have champagne?' asked Javier.

'Hollie's pregnant,' Maximo cut in.

'Ah. Of course she is. My congratulations to you both. In that case, I will have someone prepare you a *casera*.'

After he had gone, Hollie just stood very still for a moment, breathing deeply and trying to compose herself. What had Javier meant—*Of course she is*? That it was inconceivable the powerful bachelor would be contemplating marriage unless he was being shotgunned into it? And wasn't that the truth? She could see people watching them and wondered how they saw her. As an upstart who had managed to get her claws into one of Spain's most eligible bachelors? One who was clearly out of her depth, despite her designer dress and the jewels which hung from her finger and her ears?

Maximo turned to talk to someone and, although a nearby couple were eager to chat to her, Hollie felt strangely isolated. She watched as Maximo seemed to command the attention of everyone in the room. People were trying to get near him and she felt as though she were melting into the shadows and gradually becoming invisible. She realised that for him this was truly home, and always would be.

She did her best to join in with the lively party but couldn't quite contain the nerves which were growing inside her. She saw a huge dish of purple grapes gleaming rather menacingly in a corner and prayed she would be able to match everyone else in the room— although eating twelve grapes in such a short space of time did seem a big ask, particularly of someone who was pregnant.

She glanced around the room, thinking that she'd never seen so many stunning women congregated in one place, and found herself remembering what Maximo had once said. He'd told her that if ever he met a woman he desired more than her he would tell her immediately and their relationship would end. Looking around at the model-perfect array of females, she failed to see how that could *not* happen. Surely once the allure of their brand-new sex life wore off, wasn't it inevitable he would be tempted?

She wasn't much of a drinker but right then she would have given anything for a small glass of wine to help quell her spiralling nervousness, but of course she couldn't do that because she was expecting a baby.

And that was the only reason she was here.

All of a sudden Hollie felt as if she were adrift on a life raft, floating on a wide sea. Lost and all alone— despite the proud-featured man at her side who drew the gaze of every woman in the room.

CHAPTER ELEVEN

HER NIGHT WAS RESTLESS—her sleep broken by ill-defined dreams which somehow scared her—and when Hollie awoke it was to find that Maximo had gone. She sat up in bed and blinked, glancing around at the unfamiliar space of his vast Madrid bedroom. Gone where?

As if in answer to her thoughts he walked into the room, dressed in his habitual black and talking on the phone on what was clearly a work call. He palmed her a wave but continued talking in Spanish, obviously distracted—and when Hollie emerged from the bathroom he was still speaking. She walked over to the window and stared out but, despite the beautiful Retiro Park being so close, all she noticed were the buildings and busy roads. She kept telling herself the problem lay with *her* and not the famously beautiful city of Madrid, but that didn't alter her fundamental fear about whether she'd ever get used to living here after the quiet of Trescombe.

Maximo cut the call and walked over to the window to stand beside her. 'You're awake,' he murmured, snaking his arm around her waist, his thumb stroking a slow circle. 'I thought I'd let you sleep. It was a late night. Did you enjoy the party?'

'It was certainly very lively.'

'Who was that woman I saw you talking to?' he enquired, his fingers reaching up to comb through the tangle of her hair.

'Which one? I was talking to lots of people.'

'The one in the green dress. She had blonde hair, I think.'

'Oh. You mean Cristina.' Hollie smiled. It had been one of the highlights of a very challenging evening. An elegant woman had walked across the crowded room and given her a warm and friendly smile. More than that, she had seemed instantly understanding, telling Hollie that she had once been the newcomer at a similar, glittering party. 'It can be a little overwhelming at the beginning,' she had said softly. 'They are a wonderful but rather intimidating crowd. Just give them a chance.'

'Who is Cristina?' prompted Maximo, breaking into her thoughts.

'She owns a shop on the…' she frowned as she tried to remember '…the Calle de Serrano, and wants me to have lunch with her some time, so I gave her my number. I explained I was going back to England tomorrow to work out my notice, but said I could meet her at the end of the month.'

'Good, good,' he said, as he linked his fingers with hers and began to lead her back towards the bed. 'It's important for you to make new friends.'

'What…what are you doing, Maximo?' she questioned, as he laid her down on the mattress and then began to peel off his clothes with impatient fingers.

'What do you think I'm doing? I'm going to make love to you because I am aching to be inside you again.'

'B-but, you've only just got out of the shower.'

'Then I'll just have to get right back in it, won't I?'

She felt the silky collision of his flesh as their bodies collided and heard the deepening of his voice as he brushed his lips over hers.

'Do I taste good, *mia belleza*?'

'You do.' She shivered. 'You t-taste very good.'

His mouth moved to her neck, her belly and then—most daringly of all—between her legs and Hollie's eyes fluttered to a helpless close as she felt that first deliciously precise flick of his tongue. Pretty soon her body was clenching with the explosive pleasure which was now part of her daily life.

How could I have lived without this for so long? she thought dreamily as she lay cradled in his arms afterwards.

How could I have lived without *him*?

But that was a dangerous way to think. Especially when the next few days made her realise that something fundamental between them seemed to have shifted. At first she thought she was imagining it, but gradually she realised that, on some level, their relationship had changed. It was difficult to define but it was definitely there. All the closeness and banter they'd shared over Christmas seemed to have evaporated. It had become functional. She told herself not to keep analysing the situation, but couldn't seem to stop herself. Because despite the undeniable intimacy she felt whenever they were having sex, hadn't Maximo been noticeably more distant with her ever since they'd arrived in Madrid? Hadn't he been obsessed with his work in a way she hadn't witnessed before? He seemed to be out at the office most of the time and when she had questioned him about it, he hadn't been in the least bit contrite.

'Surely you must understand that I have to work, Hollie,' he had replied, with a shrug. 'I am the head of a very big organisation and a lot of people rely on me.'

'And when the baby arrives? What then? Will you still be working around the clock?'

'Who knows? It's possible.' His black eyes were clear and gleaming. 'I'm not going to make any promises I won't be able to keep, *querida*. I'm planning to do the best I can, but I don't know what form being a husband and a father will take. Is that fair?'

It might have been fair, but it wasn't what Hollie wanted to hear—and while his honesty was admirable, it failed to reassure her. It felt to her as if he had achieved what he had set out to achieve—by offering her marriage—and was now free to turn his attention to other things. Would she be expected to build her own separate life here—a life which touched his only in parts? It wasn't what she had envisaged when she had agreed to marry him...

And before she knew it, it was time to fly back to Devon to work out her notice—an intention she had proudly insisted on but was now beginning to regret. Surrounded by luxury, Hollie stared out of the window of his private jet, wondering if Maximo would be relieved to have the apartment to himself again now she'd left. He certainly hadn't given any indication that he was going to *miss* her. And even though he made love to her that morning, and afterwards held her trembling body very tight, she could never remember feeling quite so alone.

It was weird being back in England. Weird yet strangely comforting—like climbing into a warm bath at the end of a long working day. As the limousine purred along the high-hedged country lanes, Hollie realised that people knew her here in Trescombe. She belonged in this little town. When she stopped at the local store to buy some provisions, the owner did a double take before her face broke into a huge smile.

'It *is* you! Why, for a moment I didn't recognise you, Hollie!'

Hollie blushed, realising she hadn't even considered the impact of leaving a fancy car sitting on the kerb waiting, while she purchased her pint of milk wearing a whacking great diamond ring, and a cream cashmere coat which must have been achingly expensive.

She would need to go back to her trusty skirts and blouses tomorrow morning when she started back at work. Her mind flitted over different possibilities as she wondered how she was going to explain what had happened to Janette. Was she going to give her boss the whole story, chapter and verse, and tell her she was engaged and pregnant in a single sentence?

Her boss was so…probing. She would almost certainly pry and ask Hollie what it was like being engaged to someone as charismatic as Maximo Diaz. She might even ask her details about how it had happened.

And Hollie would say—what?

That it had been a one-night stand with far-reaching

ramifications, hence the Spanish tycoon's shock proposal of marriage? She certainly wasn't going to hint at her growing insecurities about her place in Maximo's life or confess that he seemed to be pushing her away from him. Hollie bit her lip. He'd made it clear he didn't want deep, or mushy, or lovey-dovey from their relationship—yet despite knowing those things, it made little difference to the way she felt about him. She still felt dizzy with longing whenever she thought about him.

Perhaps it was the thought of how it had been before which kept her snared—all those evocative memories of a snowed-in Christmas, which had led her to believe in all kinds of possibilities. The way he'd taken her into his confidence and the way he made her feel when she was in his arms... Perhaps it was her lack of experience of sex which made her ultra-susceptible to its influence. Because sometimes, when she was lying close to him, with the powerful beat of his powerful heart slowing in perfect time with her own, Hollie would feel something close to...

Love?

She swallowed. Was it possible to love someone even if you knew that was the last thing they wanted from you?

Was it?

Yes, of course it was possible. People had been falling in love indiscriminately since the beginning of time. And, despite all her mixed-up feelings, Hollie's heart still lifted with joy when she answered Maximo's text asking whether she'd settled in and saying he'd call her later. His brief message made her think. It made her look at the situation from a different viewpoint. Back in Madrid she had convinced herself she was missing her simple life in Trescombe, but the irony was that she was missing Maximo a lot more. Didn't she ache for him with a fierce longing which was almost visceral? And if that was the case, then surely fitting into her new world in Spain wasn't only preferable, but achievable. All she had to do was to give it a decent chance, and that meant giving it time. Couldn't she choose her moment to suggest that he didn't have to work quite so hard—and couldn't they get back the kind of closeness they'd had before?

Feeling suddenly light-hearted, she made herself a sandwich and sat down at the table munching it as she looked around. Her little pine tree was wilting and had deposited most of its needles onto the rug, and two of the baubles had fallen to the floor. Christmas really was over and she was going to have to think about taking all these decorations down before Twelfth Night.

She was just about to leave for work next morning, when she heard her phone vibrate and she slid it out of her handbag to look at it.

It was a number she didn't recognise. An international number—Spanish, she thought. And when she clicked on the call she discovered it was Cristina, the woman she'd met at Javier's party. The woman with the potential to be a new friend. The blonde in the green dress.

'Hi,' said Hollie, a smile entering her voice. 'How lovely to hear from you! How are you?'

'I'm…well. You have returned to England, I think?'

'That's right. I'm just about to go to work. I'm flying back at the beginning of February.'

Cristina's accented voice dipped by a fraction. 'And Maximo. Is he there with you?'

'No, I'm afraid he's not. He's coming over at the weekend.'

'I see.' There was a pause. 'I understand you're pregnant, Hollie? I really should have congratulated you at the party.'

'Yes, I am.' Hollie felt her heart give a little kick. 'I'm twelve weeks along. The scan is on Wednesday.'

There was another pause but this time, Cristina's voice sounded different. It quivered with the air of somebody who knew something. More specifically, who knew something you didn't.

'I like you, Hollie,' she said slowly. 'And I have learned something which is difficult for me to tell you, but which I feel you ought to know.'

'You're scaring me now,' said Hollie, only half joking. 'What is it?'

'It's about Maximo.' There was a pause. 'About the real reason he's marrying you.'

It was an extraordinary thing for someone to say out of the blue like that—especially someone who didn't know you—and for a moment Hollie's only response was silence. Her fingers tightened around the handset and she could feel her throat constrict. She felt faintly disappointed. As if she had misjudged Cristina, who perhaps didn't want to be her friend at all. If she were a different kind of person she might have frostily retorted that it wasn't any of the other woman's business. But she wasn't going to hide from the truth, and if Cristina was expressing what everyone else was thinking, then maybe the subject would be better addressed head-on. 'I'm not naïve enough to believe the wedding would be happening if I weren't pregnant,' she said quietly.

'I'm sure you're not. But he's not just marrying you in order to maintain respectability,' Cristina said, and then the words came out in a rush, as if she was embarrassed to repeat them. 'He's marrying you because he stands to inherit the family business, which will be put in trust for your child. Only the will stipulates that the child must be born within wedlock.'

Hollie froze.

But Maximo had been estranged from his father since the age of fourteen. He'd told her that.

With her free hand, she gripped the back of a nearby chair. 'I don't believe you,' she whispered.

'I'm afraid it's true, my dear,' said Cristina. 'I heard this through Beatriz, one of his stepsisters. It was a hotly contested clause in the will, although the lawyers assured them it was watertight. They are obviously angry that their father's illegitimate son stands to inherit one of the most profitable companies in Spain. I'm sorry, Hollie. I felt it best you should know, but this is not news I would ever wish to be the bearer of.'

'No. Thank you.' Hollie's voice was brisk now. Polite, even. 'I appreciate it, Cristina.'

With a few more robotic words she cut the call, though all the time she was berating herself. How *stupid* she had been. Sorrow clamped its way around her heart like a vice and then she gave a bitter laugh. She might have lost her virginity but that didn't mean she wasn't still laughably naïve, did it? She had stupidly imagined she had no illusions about the opposite sex, but it seemed she was still capable of being blinded by the stars which had temporarily danced in front of her eyes. She had wanted love so badly that she had been prepared to overlook what was blazingly obvious. Because she didn't know Maximo at all, not really. The man she saw was the man she had wanted to see, not the one with hidden depths which he kept concealed from her. He was marrying her to gain control of one of Spain's most successful companies. Of course he was. Although he certainly didn't need the money, maybe he felt it was a justified legacy—to make up for his father's rejection. Payback time. But it didn't alter one key and painful fact...

That he had betrayed her, just as her father had betrayed her mother.

Her knees felt weak and she gripped the back of the chair even harder, afraid they might buckle. But the weirdest thing was that after that moment of dizziness had passed, Hollie felt calm. Icy calm. Almost as if she had been expecting this. As if things had always been too good to be true.

Because they were, weren't they?

Plenty of women got pregnant without getting married. Did she *really* think that someone like Maximo Diaz would ask someone like her to be his wife if he didn't stand to gain something from it, especially when he'd told her right from the start he didn't want a baby? Or had she walked into the self-deceptive trap of thinking they had something special between them, just because she'd fallen in love with him?

She had fallen in love with him.

Well, more fool her.

He stands to inherit the family business. Cristina's words were branded on Hollie's brain like fire.

If he'd told her himself, she might have understood. If he'd said *Look, this baby means that I can get something I've always lusted after*, she probably could have accepted it. If he'd kept it coldly businesslike from the beginning, then perhaps she wouldn't have built up all those fantasies in her head. But he hadn't and that had given her imagination a free rein. No wonder she thought she'd seen a look of triumph on his face when he'd asked if they could announce the pregnancy. He was probably rubbing his hands with glee at the thought of all that new power.

She picked up her phone, turning it over and over in her hand before finally tapping her fingers over the keypad. It took longer than it should have done but that was because her hands were trembling so much. She kept the message short—because, really, it all boiled down to one simple fact whichever way you looked at it.

Maximo…

A tear dripped onto the back of her hand and, impatiently, she shook it away before continuing to type.

Being back in Devon has given me a bit of time to reflect on things and I just don't think it's going to work out between us.

Her finger hovered as she battled between the desire

to put as much distance between them as possible and the knowledge that she needed to act like a grown-up.

If you like we can talk in a couple of days. Hollie.

She didn't put any kisses, and that drove home the realisation that there had never been any of the stuff which defined most *normal* love affairs. No letters or texts of undying devotion. Just sex and a baby and a big diamond ring. She thought about the turrets and towers of Kastelloes and the thick snow which had trapped them there. She remembered how grateful she had been to that inclement weather, because it had brought her into Maximo's arms. She'd been blown away by her Spanish lover, and hopeful when he'd opened up his heart to her. The world had felt tinged with magic, when all the time...

All the time he had been using their marriage as a way of getting his hands on the family business.

What a trusting fool she had been.

Well, not any more.

She had once told Maximo that she could do all this on her own and she would—with or without his financial assistance. Because anything would be preferable to a lifetime of deceit.

She tugged the heavy ring from her finger and it clattered as she put it on the table and then, letting out a shuddered breath, she laid her face against her cradled arms and wept.

CHAPTER TWELVE

A THIN DRIZZLE of rain coated the windscreen in a slimy film as the car turned into the wintry English road. Maximo eased his foot off the accelerator, bringing the powerful vehicle almost to a halt so that it crept along at a snail's pace. He stared fixedly ahead, not caring if he was wasting time. Because he needed time to work out what he was going to do. To assemble his whirling thoughts into some sort of order before he saw Hollie.

To say what?

He still didn't know.

He thought about the bald little message he had received from her.

I just don't think it's going to work out between us...

He had been taken aback by the dark surge of pain which had flooded through him.

He had wanted to lift the phone and demand to know what had made her write it, but something made him change his mind—though he didn't stop to think what that might be. Instead, he sought a solution in action, because that was how he operated. He had ordered his

jet to be made ready and within hours had flown into
Exeter airport, planning his movements with the precision of a cat burglar.

Unobserved, he had watched Hollie leave the office
and a wave of relief had swamped him as he'd seen her
familiar figure walking towards the bus stop. And although every part of him had ached to drive up and tell
her to get in the car, he'd resisted the powerful temptation to do so, because he didn't want any kind of con-
frontation or public spectacle. He didn't want to run the
risk of her refusing to travel with him.

He had seen the chill wind blowing at her hair, but
the tresses were no longer unfettered and free as he
liked them. They had been tamed beneath a hat he'd
never seen her wear before, and the coat she was hud-
dling into was not one of the items he had bought her,
but a well-worn relic from her old wardrobe. It was as
if she had embraced her old life and cut him out completely, he thought, and his heart gave another painful
clench as he increased the speed of the car.

Once he had vowed never to let a woman close
enough to hurt him. What had happened to that fer-
vent vow from which he had never wavered? The vow
he'd made on his knees on that snowy Christmas Eve
in Spain, all those years ago.

You could leave now while there's still time, a cold
and pragmatic voice in his head reminded him.

But he ignored it.

His car slid to a halt outside her tiny cottage and he
crunched his way up the gravel path. Ignoring the twee
little bell which dangled in the porch, he lifted his arm

and began to pound on the door and the mighty sound created by his fist echoed through the still night air.

Someone was knocking at her door and Hollie paused in the middle of washing up her teacup. No, it was more like a pounding. The sound which someone who was in a hurry—or a temper—would make. Someone autocratic and powerful who wouldn't think twice about making enough noise to wake the dead.

Her throat dried. There was only one person she knew who would knock like that. Was that why her heart started racing as she put her teacup down and headed for the door? Or was it just that deep down she'd been expecting this visit and now the moment had arrived, she felt a terrible fatalistic sorrow washing over her?

Drawing in a deep breath, she pulled open the door and there stood Maximo. His hair was windswept and he was dressed in the black clothes which were so familiar, but Hollie had never seen that expression on his face before. It was tense. Brittle. As if he were holding something dark and unwanted inside him. His eyes narrowed, and then he spoke.

'Can I come in, please, Hollie?'

Did he really think she would refuse him entry? That she would *want* to? Because even though she recognised that the final minutes of their relationship were ticking away, Hollie wasn't feeling the things she wanted to feel. Despite the fact that he had used her as a pawn in his ambitious game plan, she wasn't hating him, or not fancying him. Her stupid stomach still turned to mush when he brushed past her, forcing her to shut the door on the drizzly evening outside.

For a minute she was tempted to throw herself into his arms in an effort to blot out all those things she'd discovered. Or even to ask if he'd like some coffee after his long journey, in a futile desire to put off the inevitable. To act as if she were still going to be his wife and make like they were going to be a happy family.

But she couldn't do that any more. She couldn't pretend—not to him—not even to herself.

Especially not to herself.

Uncharacteristically, he seemed almost hesitant as his gaze swept over her. 'Is the baby okay?'

Of *course* that would be his number one concern. 'Everything's fine,' she answered briskly. 'I'm having the scan the day after tomorrow.'

There was a pause, and now the light from his eyes was very hard and very bright. 'Do you want to tell me why you sent that text?'

Hollie tried to think of the right words but there were no right words. Only wrong ones. Harsh, discordant words which had the power to destroy everything and now she was going to have to say them out loud and make it all real.

'Do you want to tell me why you asked me to marry you, Maximo?' she questioned quietly. 'Only give me the *real* reason this time!'

His frown deepened. 'But you know the reason.'

'Yes, of course I do. Because of the baby. Or so I thought. We were supposed to be completely honest with each other, weren't we? We said that truth was going to define our relationship. Yet all the time...'

She swallowed. 'All the time there was this great big secret bubbling away in the background, which you failed to mention.'

'What *secret*?' he echoed. 'You've completely lost me now.'

'Please don't treat me like an idiot!' she snapped.

'Then why don't you stop speaking in riddles? I told you. I don't know what you're talking about.'

'I'm talking about inheriting your father's business!'

He shook his head. 'Nope. Still confused.'

His words sounded genuine but Hollie steeled her heart against them, because men could lie, couldn't they? In fact, men *did* lie. Her father had rarely spoken a true word in his life, according to her mother.

'Cristina rang me up. The blonde in the green dress at the party,' she continued. 'She knows your stepsister, Beatriz.' She heard his sudden sharp intake of breath, which she interpreted as guilt.

'Beatriz,' he said slowly. 'Well, well, well. Now it really *does* get interesting.'

Hollie sucked in a ragged breath. 'Cristina told me about the will. About how your father left you controlling shares of his business, but only if you have a child born within wedlock. So why didn't you tell me that, Maximo? If you'd told me the truth in the first place then maybe I could have lived with it. It's the lies I can't stand.'

But there was no guilt or resignation on his face. No sense of having been found out. In fact, there was nothing on his sculpted features but a look of growing comprehension.

'This is all news to me, Hollie,' he said slowly. 'If there is such a bequest then it has never been on my radar, because I have been estranged from my family for many years and in all that time I haven't spoken to my stepsisters—not since they decided that cruelty towards an impressionable young boy was a sport they relished.' His voice harshened. 'Do you really think I would conceal something like that from you?'

'Yes! If you want the truth, yes, I do!'

Maximo flinched as if she had hit him, but through the slow burn of injustice came a powerful rush of feelings. Uncomfortable feelings he had buried for years and if it had been anyone else, he would have slammed his way out of there and taken his outraged pride with him.

But this wasn't just anyone. This was Hollie. Hollie who knew more about him than anyone else did. He remembered when he'd told her about working on the roads as a teenager and she'd asked him if he had lied about his age, as if it was important. As if it had meant something. Because it *did* mean something. She was used to men lying to her. Her father, for one. Did she think he was cast out of the same mould and that he would deceive her about something as big as this?

And then he wondered how he dared be such a hypocrite. Why *wouldn't* she believe that, when he had done nothing but push her away since she'd arrived in Spain, and maybe even before that? He had been so damned keen to create barriers between them and to ensure she knew never to dare cross them, that he had succeeded in destroying all the ease and the intimacy which had once existed between them. And now she was looking at him warily, with sadness and mistrust written all over her lovely face, and although he knew he deserved all of that—and more—suddenly he couldn't bear the thought that he might have sabotaged, not just his own future, but that of his family. *His family with her.*

'I repeat, I knew nothing about this legacy, and even if I did, do you really think I'd want his damned business? If I had, I might have stayed on in that heartless mansion—enduring the taunts of my stepsisters and the sniggers of the servants who surrounded him. Do you really think that even if I were poor—*even if I were poor*—I would accept the charity of someone who had never wanted me during his lifetime? Do you, Hollie?'

The fierceness of his tone must have convinced her, for she gave a brief and reluctant shrug. 'I guess not.'

But the wariness was still there and Maximo knew he had a long way to go. He could feel his jaw hardening—locking so tight he could scarcely grit the next words out, but then he'd had a whole lifetime of suppressing stuff instead of articulating it.

'I didn't lie to you about the will,' he said slowly. 'But in a way, I was lying to myself.'

Her eyes widened. 'What…what are you talking about?'

'I lied about the way you made me feel. I refused to acknowledge that you touched something deep inside me right from the start. And as that feeling grew, it scared me. It made me feel…powerless—and I had vowed that nobody was ever going to make me feel that way again.' He expelled a long and ragged breath. 'I thought when I took you to Spain—that if I could get back to the way I normally felt, I could deal with it. I was stupid enough and arrogant enough to believe I could just slot you into your own little compartment in my life and you would be content with that. But instead, I drove you away—'

'Yes,' she said. 'You did.'

'I shouldn't have done that,' he ground out.

'No, you shouldn't.' She hesitated. 'But we all say and do things we shouldn't, often because we're scared. You're not the only one, Maximo.'

'Hollie—'

'No, wait.' Her firm tone belied the sudden trembling of her lips and, suddenly, her voice was trembling too. 'Let me confess something to you. Something I'm only just starting to realise—which is that I felt almost *relieved* when Cristina told me about the will.'

'Relieved?' he verified incredulously.

She swallowed and nodded. 'Maybe it suited me to believe that all men were fundamentally liars and you could never trust any of them because that way...' Her eyes had suddenly become very bright and her words tailed off as she looked at him.

'That way you'd never get hurt?'

'Yes,' she whispered. '*Yes.* I didn't want to get hurt and I didn't want my baby—'

'Our baby.'

She bit her lip as if she was about to cry. 'I didn't want our baby to grow up the way I did,' she said huskily. 'In a world of broken promises and no real love. Or one-sided love. I thought it would be easier to go it alone than to do that. Because I want a *real* family, Maximo—not something which just looks like it from the outside—and I'm not going to accept anything less than that.'

This still sounded like bargaining to him and was

not the instant capitulation Maximo had expected to hear. It still felt as if someone were squeezing his heart with their fist—and it hurt. It *really* hurt. He'd spent his whole life avoiding emotional pain and maybe that was why he had built up no resistance against it. Because suddenly he realised that if he wanted Hollie, he needed to really put his feelings on the line. To say things he'd never expected to hear himself say and make sure she knew he meant them.

'I've never told you that I love you, have I, Hollie?' he questioned unevenly. 'I've never told you that first time I lay with you, it felt as if you were touching me with flame? As if you'd unleashed the lick of a potent fire which threatened to melt the coldness deep inside me, which I'd lived with for so long? I'd never felt that way before and it made me feel vulnerable. That's what made me want to push you away.'

'Maximo—'

But he silenced her with a shake of his head because he couldn't allow her forgiving nature to let him off the hook. Not this time. 'You withstood my appalling attitude when I discovered you were pregnant—as if I had nothing to do with it!' He gave a bitter laugh. 'And then you created the kind of Christmas I'd never had and never thought I'd wanted, but it seems I did. For the first time in my life, I discovered what people meant when they talked about coming home. You are my home and I love you, Hollie, and I want to share my life with you and our baby.' He shrugged. 'It's as complicated and as simple as that.'

'Oh, Maximo,' she said, so quietly he could hardly hear her.

He opened his arms to her and she went straight into them, like a bird arriving back on the nest after a long flight away. She buried her head against his shoulder and he held her until she had stopped crying and then he turned her face up towards him, tracing his fingertip over the tracks of her tears. 'But I've been thinking about my bachelor apartment in Madrid and I've recognised it isn't really suitable for a baby,' he mused.

'But it's right next to that beautiful park.'

'*Sí*, it is, but I got the distinct feeling that you're not much of a city girl, which was one of the reasons you left London, wasn't it?'

She shrugged. 'I guess.'

'When I took you there, I felt as if I had plucked a wildflower from a country meadow and transplanted it into a hothouse. Which is why I'm planning to fit into *your* world from now on.'

Her brow creased into a frown. 'Now who's talking in riddles?'

'There's something else you need to know,' he said suddenly. 'Something I should have told you a whole lot sooner. I was never planning to turn the castle into a luxury hotel. That was just an assumption local people made and I didn't bother to correct them. I had planned to demolish it and turn it into a quarry—to use the valuable stone it was built on to build a railway track.'

'You…you were planning to destroy hundreds of years of history just to build a railway?'

'Don't knock railways, Hollie, because we need them—now more than ever.'

'Why didn't you say something before? Why didn't you tell anyone?'

'Because I knew if that fact got out, it would drive up the purchase price.'

She punched a half-hearted fist against his chest. 'That is the most hard-hearted thing I've—'

'I'm a businessman, Hollie,' he interrupted gently. 'And that's what businessmen do. I'd planned to stay there over Christmas because I knew it would provide the solitude I was seeking, and then to sell it in the new year. I wasn't expecting to meet a woman in this one-horse town, and have my life turned upside down by her. You were the reason I couldn't go through with the sale, not when I saw how much the place meant to you. I realised I couldn't take a wrecking ball to the heart of this little community in order to steamroller another money-making scheme.'

'Oh, Maximo,' she said, lifting her left hand to her heart, making him notice she wasn't wearing her engagement ring.

'I have been thinking that we could keep the castle and turn it into our family home, if that's what you wanted. Or maybe turn it into a hotel and buy a big house and garden for our family instead, if that's what you'd prefer. I was waiting for the perfect moment to tell you, only perfect moments have a habit of being elusive. But those things could only happen…' His words tailed off and somehow he was finding it impossible to keep the sudden break from his voice. 'They could only happen if you still wanted me. If you still wanted to be my wife.'

Hollie put her arms around his neck and pressed her face very close to his as a powerful shaft of joy and gratitude shot through her. 'Of course I still want to be your wife. Because I love you,' she whispered. 'I love you in a way I never thought possible, but I never believed you might feel the same way about me.'

'Believe it now.'

'I do.' She looked into his black eyes and saw a look of true understanding, but she knew there was more to tell him. 'When I thought you'd lied to me, I took the coward's way out. I was trying to protect myself against hurt and pain. That's why I sent you that text instead of waiting until you got here and talking it out with you, face to face.'

'*Querida*—'

'No, let me finish.' That was easier said than done when tears were starting to stream down her cheeks—big and wet and salty and dripping on her sweater. 'But the worst hurt and pain I've ever experienced was imaging a life without you…' Once again her words tailed off and it took a couple of moments before she could catch her breath to speak. To articulate the emotion which Maximo had never been shown as a child and convince him that she meant every single word. They had both been damaged in the past, yes, but love was the true healer. Some might say the only healer. 'I love you with all my heart, Maximo Diaz,' she whispered. 'And I'll never stop loving you. Believe me when I tell you that, my darling.'

His slow smile was like the sun coming out and the glint in his eyes warmed Hollie's heart. And when he caught hold of her she felt as if she'd been reborn. As if he were breathing new life in her, to join the life which grew beneath her heart. Blindly, her lips sought his and as they kissed, the salt water of their mingled tears slowly began to dry.

EPILOGUE

'*SLEEP IN HEAVENLY PEACE...*'

The poignant last notes of the carol seemed to hover on the still night air as, fortified by a pitcher of mulled wine and a platter of home-made mince pies, the group of singers began to make their way down the hill towards the town. Hollie glanced up at the sky as several large, feathery icicles drifted against her cheek. The bright moon of last night was obscured by cloud as the first fat flakes of snow started falling. There should be a thick covering tomorrow, she thought with a glow of satisfaction, as she closed the door of her castle home.

In the wood-panelled hallway stood a tall fir tree, decked with plain white lights and tartan ribbons and topped with an organza-robed angel. There was another tree in the library, where tomorrow they would eat a late lunch, illuminated by as many candles as she could lay her hands on, as had now become a yearly festive tradition. Mistletoe dangled in the hallway and there were bunches of holly and fragrant green garlands strewn everywhere. In the kitchen, a large pot of Cantabrian mountain stew was quietly bubbling away—also a tradition. It was Christmas Eve and it was perfect.

'Will Father Christmas come tonight, Papi?' asked a little voice from behind her and Hollie turned around to see her sleepy son nestled snugly in his father's arms.

'*Sí*, he will come to visit every child in the world tonight,' murmured Maximo, meeting her gaze over Mateo's tousled black head. The smile he slanted her was full of promise and Hollie felt a delicious shiver of anticipation. 'But only when you're asleep. So I'm going to take you up to bed right now, which means morning will come faster.'

'*Oh!*'

'Would you like Mamá to come, as well?'

'Yes, please.'

'Come on, then. *Vamos!*'

Mateo giggled as, going past stone walls now covered with artwork, they mounted the beautiful curving stone staircase to his room, which was just along the corridor from their own. Silk rugs lay scattered over the floors, the draughty windows had been fixed and hung with sumptuous drapes and the building was gloriously warm. In fact, Hollie never stopped marvelling how cosy the place felt after its costly refurbishment, which had started just over three years ago.

Work had begun on the neglected castle soon after she and Maximo had vowed their love and commitment to each other, when they'd married in Trescombe's small church, with its sweeping views of the sea. It had been a small and simple ceremony. Hollie had worn a long dress of fine white wool, with a hooded and feather-trimmed cape, to keep out the bitter winter winds. And although they had been well into January, and it hadn't been Christmastime, her bouquet had nonetheless contained sprays of mistletoe, holly and ivy. Maximo's friend Javier had been best man and the ancient church had been filled with the competing sounds of Spanish and English chatter—though the Spanish had undoubtedly been the louder of the two. It had been, everyone said, the most beautiful wedding.

And they had made their life here, in Devon. Maximo continued to run his empire from this rural base—though they kept apartments in New York and Madrid. But he hadn't forgotten his vow to serve the community of his newly adopted home. He had completely refurbished the rather tatty hotel where first they'd met and the resulting five-star establishment now came under the umbrella of the Diaz group and brought many tourists flocking to the small town which nestled between moorland and sea. It had put Trescombe firmly on the map, although the narrow and winding access roads ensured that it was never going to be *too* much on the map, as Maximo drily commented.

Once their son had reached a year, Hollie had opened her tea shop—though someone else ran it for her. She'd fished out her best recipes and helped with batch cooking whenever she got the opportunity. She'd had the jaunty café painted in ice-cream colours of pink and lemon and spearmint, there was mismatched bone china on the tables, the waitresses wore old-fashioned frilly aprons and people came from miles around to taste her featherlight scones.

Her thoughts dissolving, Hollie sighed with pleasure as she watched her husband tuck his lookalike son into bed before going through the various night-time rituals they had evolved, including a very special one tonight, which involved the reading of Clement Clarke Moore's famous Christmas Eve poem. And when the story had finished, and Mateo had fallen sound asleep, Hollie and Maximo crept from the room and into the corridor outside.

There she turned to him, looping her arms around his neck—unable to resist the temptation to plant a kiss on his lips and then to linger there. A feeling of excitement was bubbling up inside her and it was making her heart beat fast. There was something she needed to tell him and she wanted to find the right time, but for now she just kissed him.

'Everything's *almost* ready, I think,' she whispered, drawing her mouth away from his. 'The stockings have been hung—and Javier's room is prepared. I'm sure he's going to cause something of a stir when he arrives in Trescombe tomorrow morning.'

'Like I did, you mean?' he teased.

'I doubt it. Javier's not quite as arrogant as you,' she advised primly.

He laughed as he curved the palm of his hand over her buttock. 'And don't you just *hate* that arrogance, *mia belleza*?'

'Maximo.' Her throat dried as his fingers continued on their inexorable journey. 'What do you think you're doing?'

'What does it look like I'm doing?' His voice was careless, his arms strong. 'I am picking up my beautiful wife to carry her into the bedroom, because I know that kind of macho thing turns her on, and once we get there I am taking her to bed, where I intend to ravish her.'

'But it's Christmas Eve! And we haven't—'

'Haven't what?' he questioned as he kicked open their bedroom door.

'Finished wrapping all the presents, or—'

'Shut up,' he said gently, laying her down on the luxurious red velvet cover she'd bought in homage to their first night there. 'And come here.'

He undressed her, slowly and reverently, and just before he entered her Hollie almost told him. But passion was a strange and beautiful thing. It stopped you having coherent thoughts. It blotted out the world so that all you could see and feel was that person in your arms, and all you could hear were soft moans which gradually became more frantic. And then it was happening, just as it always happened, and she was pulsing around him and his powerful body tensed for one exquisite moment before, finally, he collapsed into her arms.

Her heart was thumping heavily, her head was lying on his shoulder and all Hollie wanted was to go to sleep, but there wasn't time. 'Maximo...' she murmured lazily.

'Mmm...?'

'I've got something to tell you.'

'I know you have.'

'It has nothing to do with wrapping presents.'

'I know that, too.'

She rolled over to look at him and his black eyes were crystalline, hard and very bright. 'What do you know?'

'That you're having my baby again.'

'Yes, I am,' she breathed, slumping back against the pillow. 'But how did you *guess*?'

Maximo smiled, for this was the easiest question he'd ever had to answer. He didn't even have to think about it. 'Because I love you and because I know you. I know the look in your eyes and the smile on your lips when you have a new life growing inside you. And both of them are there now. Or at least, they were until a couple of minutes ago. Hollie, *querida*—what's the matter?' He frowned and smoothed his finger along the line of her quivering lip. 'Why are you crying?'

'You obviously don't know me that well at all! I'm crying because I'm happy, of course!'

And Maximo laughed softly, a feeling of pure joy wrapping around his heart as he brought her soft body closer to his and kissed the top of her silken head.

He had once thought there was no such thing as a perfect moment, but he had been wrong. Because this— *this*—was the perfect moment. These days his life was filled with them.

'And you spread happiness wherever you go, *mia belleza*,' he said softly. 'Happy Christmas, my beautiful wife.'

* * * * *

SNOWED IN WITH THE BILLIONAIRE

CAROLINE ANDERSON

For Angela, who gave me insight into the harrowing
and difficult issues surrounding adoption,
and for all 'the girls' in the Mills & Boon group
for their unstinting help, support, and amazing
knowledge. Ladies, you rock!

CHAPTER ONE

'OH, WHAT—?'

All Georgia could see in the atrocious conditions were snaking brake lights, and she feathered the brake pedal, glad she'd left a huge gap between her and the car in front.

It slithered to a halt, and she put on her hazard flashers and pulled up cautiously behind it, trying to see why they'd stopped, but visibility was minimal. Even though it was technically still daylight, she could scarcely see a thing through the driving snow.

And the radio hadn't been any help—plenty of talk about the snow arriving earlier than predicted, but no traffic information about any local holdups. Just Chris Rea, singing cheerfully about driving home for Christmas while the fine, granular snow clogged her wipers and made it next to impossible to see where she was going.

Not that they'd been going anywhere fast. The traffic had been moving slower and slower for the last few minutes because of the appalling visibility, and now it had come to a complete grinding halt. She'd been singing along with all the old classics as the weather worsened, crushing the steadily rising panic and trying to pretend that it was all going to be OK. Obviously her crazy, reckless optimism hard at work as usual. When would she learn?

Then the snow eased fleetingly and she glimpsed the tail lights of umpteen cars stretching away into the distance. Far beyond them, barely discernible in the pale gloom, a faint strobe of blue sliced through the falling snow.

More blue lights came from behind, travelling down the other side of the road and overtaking the queue of traffic, and it dawned on her that nothing had come towards them for some minutes. Her heart sank as the police car went past and the flashing blue lights disappeared, swallowed up by the blizzard.

OK, so something serious had happened, but she couldn't afford to sit here and wait for the emergency services to sort it out with the weather going downhill so quickly. If she wasn't careful she'd end up stranded, and she was *so* nearly home, just five or six miles to go. So near, and yet so far.

The snow swirled around them again, picking up speed, and she bit her lip. There was another route—a narrow lane she knew only too well. A lane that she'd used often as a short cut, but she'd been avoiding it, and not only because of the snow—

'Why we stop, Mummy?'

She glanced in the rear-view mirror and met her son's eyes. 'Somebody's car's broken down,' she said. Or hit another car, but she wasn't going to frighten a two-year-old. She hesitated. She was deeply reluctant to use the lane, but realistically she was all out of options.

Making the only decision she could, she smiled brightly at Josh and crossed her fingers. 'It's OK, we'll go another way. We'll soon be at Grannie and Grandpa's.'

His face fell, tugging her heartstrings. 'G'annie now. I hungry.'

'Yeah, me, too, Josh. We won't be long.'

She turned the car, feeling it slither as she pulled away across the road and headed back the way she'd come. Yikes. The roads were truly lethal and they weren't going to get any better as more people drove on them and compacted the snow.

As she turned onto the little lane, she could feel her heart rate pick up. The snow was swirling wildly around the car, almost blinding her, and even when it eased for a second the verges were almost obliterated.

This wasn't supposed to be happening yet! Not until tonight, after they were safely tucked up with her parents, warm and dry and well-fed. Not out in the wilds of the countryside, on a narrow lane that went from nowhere to nowhere else. If only she'd left earlier...

She checked her mobile phone and groaned. No signal. Fabulous. She'd better not get stuck, then. She put the useless phone away, sucked in a deep breath and kept on driving, inching cautiously along.

Too cautiously. The howling wind was blowing the snow straight off the field to her right and the narrow lane would soon be blocked. If she didn't hurry, she wasn't going to get along here at all, she realised, and she swallowed hard and put her foot down a little. At least in the fresh snow she had a bit more traction, and she wasn't likely to meet someone coming the other way. She only had half a mile at the most to go before she hit the other road. She could do it. She could...

A high brick wall loomed into view on the left, rippling in and out like a ribbon, the snow plastered to it like frosting on a Christmas cake, and she felt a surge of relief.

Almost there now. The ancient crinkle crankle wall ran alongside the lane nearly to the end. It would give her a vague idea of where the road was, if nothing else, and all she had to do was follow it to the bigger, better road which would hopefully be clear.

And halfway along the wall—there it was, looming out of the blizzard, the gateway to a hidden world. The walls curved in on both sides of the imposing entrance, rising up to a pair of massive brick piers topped with stone gryphons, and between them hung the huge, ornate iron gates that didn't shut.

Except that today they were firmly shut.

They'd been painted, too, and they weren't wonky any more, she realised as she slowed to a halt. They'd always hung at a crazy angle, open just enough to squirm through, and that gap had been so enticing to an adventurous young girl out for a bike ride with her equally reckless older brother.

The gryphons guarding the entrance had scared them, mythical beasts with the heads and wings of eagles and the bodies of lions, their talons slashing the air as they reared up, but the gap had lured them in, and inside the wall they'd found a secret adventure playground beyond their wildest imaginings. Acres of garden run wild, with hidden rooms and open spaces, vast spreading trees and a million places to hide.

And in the middle of it all, the jewel in the crown, sat the most beautiful house she'd ever seen. A huge front door with a semi-circular fanlight over it was tucked under a pillared portico that sat exactly in the centre of the house, surrounded perfectly symmetrically by nine slender, elegant sash windows.

Not that you could see all the windows. Half of them were covered in wisteria, cloaking the front and invading the roof, and the scent from the flowers, hanging delicately like bunches of pale lilac grapes against the creamy bricks, had been intoxicating.

It had been empty for years; with their hearts in their mouths, she and Jack had found a way inside through the cellar window and tiptoed round the echoing rooms with their faded grandeur, scaring each other half to death with ghost stories about the people who might have lived and loved and died there, and she'd fallen head over heels in love with it.

And then years later, when her brother had started to hang out with Sebastian, she'd taken him there, too. He'd come over to their house one day to see Jack but he'd been out, so they'd gone out for a bike ride instead. His idea, and she'd jumped at it, and they'd ended up here.

It had been their first 'date', not really a date at all but near enough for her infatuated sixteen-year-old self, and she'd dragged him inside the still-empty house just as she had her brother.

Like her, he'd been fascinated by it. They'd explored every inch of it, tried to imagine what it would have been like to live there in its hey-day. What it would be like to live there now. They'd even fantasised about the furnishings—a dining table so long you could hardly see the person at the other end, a Steinway grand in what had to have been the music room and, in the master bedroom, a huge four-poster bed.

In her own private fantasy, that bed had been big enough for them and all their children to pile into for a cuddle. And there'd be lots of them, the foundation of a whole dynasty. They'd fill the house with children, all of them conceived in that wonderful, welcoming bed with feather pillows and a huge fluffy quilt and zillion-thread-count Egyptian cotton sheets.

And then he'd kissed her.

They'd been playing hide and seek, teasing and flirting and bubbling over with adolescent silliness, and he'd found her in the cupboard in the bedroom and kissed her.

She'd fallen the rest of the way in love with him in that instant, but it had been almost two years before their relationship had moved on and fantasy and reality had begun to merge.

He'd gone away to uni, but they'd seen each other every holiday, spent every waking moment together, and the kisses had become more urgent, more purposeful, and way more grown up.

And then, the weekend after her eighteenth birthday, he'd taken her to the house. He wouldn't tell her why, just that it was a surprise, and then he'd led her up to the master bedroom and opened the door, and she'd been enchanted.

He'd set the scene—flickering candles in the fireplace, a thick blanket spread out on the moth-eaten carpet and smothered in petals from the wisteria outside the window, the scent filling the room—and he'd fed her a picnic of delicate smoked salmon and caviar sandwiches and strawberries dipped in chocolate, and he'd toasted her in pink champagne in little paper cups with red hearts all over the outside.

And then, slowly and tenderly, giving her time even though it must have killed him, he'd made love to her.

She'd willingly given him her virginity; they'd come close so many times, but he'd always stalled her. Not that day. That day, when he'd finally made love to her, he'd told her he'd love her forever, and she'd believed him because she loved him, too. They'd stay together, get married, have the children they both wanted, grow old together in the heart of their family. It didn't matter where they lived or how rich or poor they were, it was all going to be perfect because they'd have each other.

But two years down the line, driven by ambition and something else she couldn't understand, he'd changed into someone she didn't know and everything had fallen apart. Their dream had turned into a nightmare with the shocking intrusion of a reality she'd hated, and she'd left him, but she'd been devastated.

She hadn't been back here in the last nine years, but just before Josh was born she'd heard on the grapevine that he'd bought it. Bought their house, and was rescuing it from ruin.

She and David had been at a dinner party, and someone from English Heritage was there. 'I gather some rich guy's bought Easton Court, by the way—Sebastian something or other,' he'd said idly.

'Corder?' she'd suggested, her whole body frozen, her mind whirling, and the man had nodded.

'That's the one. Good luck to him. It deserves rescuing, but it's a good job he's got deep pockets.'

The conversation had moved on, ebbing and flowing around her while she'd tried to make sense of Sebastian's acquisition, but David had asked her about him as they were driving home.

'How do you know this Corder guy?'

'He was a friend of my brother's,' she said casually, although she was feeling far from casual. 'His family live in that area.'

It wasn't a lie, but it wasn't the whole truth and she'd felt a little guilty, but she'd been shocked. No, not shocked. Surprised, more than anything. She'd thought he'd walked away from everything connected to that time, as she had, and the fact that he hadn't had puzzled her. Puzzled and fascinated and horrified her, all at once, because of course it was so close to home, so near to her parents.

Too close for comfort.

But a few days later Josh had been born, and then only weeks after that David had died and her whole world had fallen apart and she'd forgotten it. Forgotten everything, really, except holding it all together for Josh.

But every time since then that she'd visited her parents, she'd avoided the lane, just as she had today—until she'd had no choice.

Her heart thudded against her ribs. Was he in there, behind those intimidating and newly renovated gates? Alone? Or sharing their house with someone else, someone who didn't share the dream—

She cut that thought off before she could follow it. It didn't matter. The dream didn't exist any longer, and she'd moved on. She'd had to. She was a mother now, and there was no time for dreaming. She dragged her eyes and her mind away from the imposing gates and the man who might or might not be behind them, flashed her son a smile to remind her of her priorities and made herself drive on.

Except her car had other ideas. It slithered wildly as she tried to pull away, and the snow swirled around them, the wind battering the car ferociously, reminding her as nothing else could just how perilous their situation was. Gripping the wheel tighter, her heart pounding, she pressed the accelerator again more cautiously and drove on, almost blinded by the blizzard.

Before she'd gone more than a few feet she hit a drift with her right front wheel, and her car slewed round and came to rest across the road, wedged up against the bank behind her. After a few moments of spinning the wheels fruitlessly, she slammed her hand on the steering wheel and stifled a scream of frustration tinged with panic.

'Mummy?'

'It's OK, darling. We're just a teeny bit stuck. I need to have a look outside. I won't be long.'

She tried to open her door, but it wouldn't budge, and she wound the window down and peered out into the blizzard, shielding her eyes from the biting sting of the snow crystals that felt as if they were coming straight from the Arctic.

She was up against a snowdrift, rammed tight into it, and there was no way she'd be able to open the door. She shut the window fast and shook the snow out of her hair.

'Wow! That was a bit blowy!' she said with a grin over her shoulder, but Josh wasn't reassured.

'Don't like it, Mummy,' he said, his lip wobbling ominously.

Nor do I. And I don't need them walking in a winter wonderland on the radio!

'It's fine, Josh. It's just snowing a bit fast at the moment, but it won't last. I'll just get out of the other door and see why we're stuck.'

'No! Mummy stay!'

'Darling, I'll be just outside. I'm not going away.'

'P'omise?'

'I promise.'

She blew him a kiss, scrambled across to the passenger side and fought her way out into the teeth of the blizzard to assess the situation. Difficult, with the biting wind lashing her hair across her eyes and finding its way through her clothes into her very bones, but she checked first one end of the car, then the other, and her heart sank.

It was firmly wedged, jammed between the snow-drift she'd run into on the right and the snow that had fallen down behind them, probably dislodged as she'd slid sideways. The car had embedded itself firmly against the right bank, and there was nothing she could do. She could never dig it out alone with her bare hands, not with the snow drifting so rapidly off the field in the howling wind. It was already a few inches deep. Soon the exhaust pipe would be covered, and the engine would stall, and they'd die of cold.

Literally.

Their only hope, she realised as she shielded her eyes from the snow again and assessed the situation, lay in the house behind those beautiful but intimidating gates.

Easton Court. The home of Sebastian Corder, the man she'd loved with all her heart, the man she'd left because he'd been chasing something she couldn't understand or identify with at the expense of their relationship.

He'd expected her to drop everything and follow him into a lifestyle she hated, abandoning her career, her family, even her principles, and when she'd asked him to reconsider, he'd refused and so she'd walked away, leaving her heart behind...

And now her life and the life of her child might depend on him.

This house, the house she'd fallen so in love with, home of the only man she'd ever really loved, was the last place in the world she wanted to be, its owner the last man in the world she wanted to ask for help. She didn't imagine he'd be any more thrilled than she was, but she had Josh with her, and so she had no choice but to swallow her pride and hope to God he was there.

Heart pounding, she struggled to the gate, lifted a hand so cold she could scarcely feel it and scrubbed the snow away from the intercom with her icy fingers.

'Please be there,' she whispered, 'please help me.' And then, her heart in her mouth, she pressed the button and waited.

The sharp, persistent buzz cut through his concentration, and he stopped what he was doing, pressed save and headed for the hall.

This would be the last of his Christmas deliveries. Hurray for online shopping, he thought, and then glanced out of the window and did a mild double-take. When had it started snowing like that?

He looked at the screen on the intercom and frowned. He couldn't see anything for a moment, just a swirl of white, and then the screen cleared momentarily and he made out the figure of a woman, huddled up in her coat, her hands tucked under her arms—and then she pulled a hand out and swiped snow off the front of the intercom and he saw her clearly.

Georgie?

He felt the blood drain from his head and hauled in a breath, then another one. No. It couldn't be. He was seeing things, conjuring her up out of nowhere because he couldn't stop thinking about her while he was in this damn house—

'Can I help you?' he said crisply, not trusting his eyes, but then she swiped the hair back off her face and anchored it out of the way, and it really was her, her smile tentative but relieved as she heard his voice.

'Oh, Sebastian, thank goodness you're there. I wasn't

sure—um—it's Georgie Pullman. Georgia Becket? Look, I'm really sorry to trouble you, but can you help me? I wouldn't ask, but my car's stuck in a snowdrift just by your gateway, and I don't have a spade to dig myself out and my phone won't work.'

He hesitated, holding his breath and staring at her while he groped frantically for a level surface in a world that suddenly seemed tilted on its axis. And then it righted and common sense prevailed. Sort of.

'Wait there. I'll drive down. Maybe I can tow you out.'

'Thanks. You're a star.'

She vanished in a swirl of whiteout, and he let go of the button with a sharp sigh. What the hell was she doing driving along the lane in this weather?

Surely not coming to see him? Why would she? She never had, not once in nine years, and he had no reason to think she'd do it now—unless it was curiosity about the house, and he doubted it. Not in this weather, and probably not at all. Why would she care? She hadn't cared enough to stay with him.

She'd hated him in the end, and he couldn't blame her. He'd hated himself, but he'd hated her, too, for what she'd done to them, for not having faith in him, for not sticking by him just when he'd needed her the most.

No, she wasn't coming to see him. She'd been going home to her parents for Christmas, using the short cut, and now here she was, purely by chance, stuck outside his house and he had no choice—no damn choice at all—but to go and dig her out. And that would mean talking to her, seeing her face, hearing her voice.

Resurrecting a whole shed-load of memories of a time he'd rather forget.

Dragging that up all over again was the last thing he

needed, but just moving here had done that, anyway, and there was no way he could leave her outside in a blizzard. And it'd be dark soon. The light was failing already. He'd dig her out and send her on her way. Fast, before it was too late and he was stuck with her.

Letting out a low growl, he picked up his car keys, shrugged on his coat, grabbed a shovel and a tow rope from the coach-house and threw them into the back of the Range Rover he'd bought for just this sort of eventuality. Not that he'd ever expected to be digging Georgia out of a hole.

He headed down the drive, his wipers going flat out to clear the screen, but when he got to the gates and opened them with the remote control, there was no sign of her. Just footprints in the deep snow, heading to the left and vanishing fast in the blizzard.

It was far worse than he'd realised. There were no huge, fat flakes that drifted softly down and stayed where they fell, but tiny crystals of snow driven horizontally by the biting wind, the drifts piling up and making the lane impassable. He wondered where the hell she was. It would have been handy to know just how far along—

And then he saw it, literally yards from the end of his drive, the red tail lights dim through the coating of snow over the lenses. He left the car in the gateway and got out, his boots sinking deep into the powdery drifts as he crunched towards her. No wonder she was stuck, going out in weather like this in that ridiculous little car, but there was no way she'd be going anywhere else in it tonight, he realised. Which meant he *would* be stuck with her.

Damn.

He felt anger moving in, taking the place of shock.

Good. Healthy. Better than the sentimental wallowing he'd been doing last night in that damn four-poster bed—

Bracing himself against the wind, he turned his collar up against the needles of ice and strode over to it, opening the passenger door and stooping down. A blast of warmth and Christmas music swamped him, and carried on the warmth was a lingering scent that he remembered so painfully, excruciatingly well.

It hit him like a kick in the gut, and he slammed the lid on his memories and peered inside.

She was kneeling on the seat looking at something in the back, and as she turned towards him she gave him a tentative smile.

'Hi. That was quick. I'm really sorry—'

'Don't worry about it,' he said crisply, trying not to scan her face for changes. 'Right, let's get you out of here.'

'See, Josh?' she said cheerfully. 'I told you he was going to help us.'

Josh? She had a *Josh* who could dig her out?

'Josh?' he said coldly, and her smile softened, stabbing him in the gut.

'My son.'

She had a son?

His heart pounding, he ducked his head in so he could look over the back of the seat—and met wide eyes so familiar they seemed to cut right to his soul.

'Josh, this is Sebastian. He's going to get us unstuck.'

He was? Well, of course he was! How could he refuse those liquid green eyes so filled with uncertainty? Poor little kid.

'Hi, Josh,' he said softly, because after all it wasn't

the child's fault they were stuck, and then he finally let himself look at Georgie.

She hadn't changed at all. She had the same wide, ingenuous eyes as her son, the same soft bow lips, high cheekbones and sweeping brows that had first enchanted him all those years ago. Her wild curls were dark and glossy and beaded with melted snow, and there was a tiny pleat of worry between her brows. And her face was just inches from his, her scent swirling around him in the shelter of the car and making mincemeat of his carefully erected defences.

He hauled his head out of the car and straightened up, sucking in a lungful of freezing air. Better. Slightly. Now if he could just nail those defences back in place again—

'I'm really sorry,' she began again, peering up at him, but he shook his head.

'Don't. Let's just get your car out of here and get you inside.'

'No! I need to get to my parents!'

He let his breath out on a disbelieving huff. 'Georgie, look at it!' he said, gesturing at the weather. 'You're going nowhere. I don't even know if I can get your car out, and you're certainly not taking it anywhere else in the dark.'

'It's not dark—'

'Almost. And we haven't got your car out yet. Just get in the driver's seat, keep the engine running and when you feel a tug let the brakes off and reverse gently back as I pull you. And try and steer it so it doesn't go in the ditch. OK?'

She opened her mouth, shut it again and nodded.

Plenty of time once the car was out to argue with him.

* * *

It took just moments.

The car slithered and slid, and for a second she thought they'd end up in the ditch, but then she felt the tug from behind ease off as they came to rest outside the gates and she put the handbrake on and relaxed her grip on the wheel.

Phase 1 over. Now for Phase 2.

She opened the car door and got out into the blizzard again. He was right there, checking the side of her car that had been wedged against the snowdrift, and he straightened and met her eyes.

'It looks OK. I don't think it's damaged.'

'Good. That's a relief. And thanks for helping me—'

'Don't thank me,' he said bluntly. 'You were blocking the lane, I've only cleared it before the snow plough comes along and mashes it to a pulp.'

She gulped down the snippy retort. Of course he wasn't going to be gracious about it! She was the last person he wanted to turn out to help, but he'd done it anyway, so she swallowed her pride and tried again. 'Well, whatever, I'm still grateful. I'll be on my way now—'

He cut her off with a sharp sigh. 'We've just had this conversation, Georgia. You can't go anywhere. Your car won't get down the lane. Nothing will. I could hardly pull you out with the Range Rover. What on earth possessed you to try and drive down here in weather like this anyway?'

She blinked and stared at him. 'I had to. I'm on my way home to my parents for Christmas, and I thought I'd beat the snow, but it came out of nowhere and for the last hour I've just been crawling along—'

'So why come this way? It's hardly the most sensible route in that little tin can.'

She bristled. Tin can? 'I wasn't coming this way but the other road was closed with an accident—d'you know what? Forget it!' she snapped, losing her temper completely because absolutely the last place in the world she wanted to be snowed in was with this bad-tempered and ungracious reminder of the worst time of her life, and she was seriously leaving now! *In her tin can!* 'I'm really sorry I disturbed you, I'll make sure I never do it again. Just—just go back to your ivory tower and leave me alone and I'll get out of your hair!'

She tried to get back in the car, desperate to get away before the weather got any worse, but his hand shot out and clamped round her wrist like a vice.

'Georgia, grow up! No matter how tempted I am to leave you here to work it out for yourself—and believe me, I am *very* tempted at the moment—I can't let you both die of your stubborn, stiff-necked stupidity.'

Her eyes widened and she glared at him, trying to wrestle her arm free. 'Stubborn, stiff-necked—? Well, you can talk! You're a past master at that! And we're not going to die. You're being ridiculously melodramatic. It's simply not that bad.'

It was his turn to snap then, his temper flayed by that intoxicating scent and the deluge of memories that apparently just wouldn't be stopped. He tugged her closer, glowering down into her face as the scent assailed him once more.

'Are you sure?' he growled. 'Because I can leave you here to test the theory, if you insist, but I am *not* leaving your son in the car with you while you do it.'

'You can't touch him—'

'Watch me,' he said flatly. 'He's—what? Two? Three?'

The fight went out of her eyes, replaced by maternal worry. 'Two. He's two.'

He closed his eyes fleetingly and swallowed the wave of nausea. He'd been two…

'Right,' he said, his voice tight but reasoned now, 'I'm going to unhitch my car, drive into the entrance and hitch yours up again and pull you up the drive—'

'No. Just leave me here,' she pleaded. 'We'll be all right. The accident will be cleared by now. I'll turn round and go back the other way—'

His mouth flattened into a straight, implacable line. 'No. Believe me, I don't want this any more than you do, but unlike you I take my responsibilities seriously—'

'How dare you!' she yelled, because that was just the last straw. 'I take my responsibilities seriously! *Nothing* is more important to me than Josh!'

'Then prove it! Get in the car, shut up and do as you're told just for *once* in your life before we all freeze to death—and turn that blasted radio off!'

He dropped her arm like a hot brick, and she got back in the car, slammed the door unnecessarily hard and a shower of snow slid off the roof and blocked the wipers.

'Mummy?'

Oh, Josh.

'It's OK, darling.' Hell, her voice was shaking. She was shaking all over—

'Don't like him. Why he cross?'

'He's just cross with the snow, Josh, like Mummy. It's OK.'

A gloved hand swiped across the screen and the wipers started moving again, clearing it just enough that she could see his car in front of her now, pointing into the gateway. He was bending over, looking for the towing eye, probably, and seconds later he was dropping a loop over the tow hitch on his car and easing away from her.

She felt the tug, then the car slithered round and followed him obediently while she quietly seethed. Behind them she could see the gates begin to close, trapping her inside, and in front of them lights glowed dimly in the gloom.

Easton Court, home of her broken dreams.

Her prison for the next however long?

She should have just sat it out in the traffic jam.

CHAPTER TWO

He towed her all the way up the drive and round into the old stable yard behind the house, and by the time he pulled up he'd got his temper back under control.

Not so the memories, but if he could just keep his mouth shut he might not say anything he'd regret.

Anything *else* he'd regret. Too late for what he'd already said today, and far too late for all the words they'd said nine years ago, the bitterness and acrimony and destruction they'd brought down on their relationship.

All this time later, he still couldn't see who'd been right or wrong, or even if there'd been a right or wrong at all. He just knew he missed her, he'd never stopped missing her, and all he'd done about it in those intervening years was to ignore it, shut it away in a cupboard marked 'No Entry'.

And she'd just ripped the door right off it. She and this damned house. Well, that would teach him to give in to sentiment. He should have let it rot and then he wouldn't have been here.

So who would have rescued them? No-one?

He sucked in a deep breath, got out of the car and detached the tow rope, flinging it back into the car on top of the shovel just in case there were any other lunatics out on the lane today, although he doubted it. He could hardly see his hand in front of his face for the snow now, and that was in the shelter of the stable yard.

Dammit, if this didn't let up soon he was going to be stuck with her for days, her and her two-year-old son, with fathoms-deep eyes that could break your heart. And that, more than anything, was what was getting to him. The child, and what might have happened to him if he'd not been there to help—

'Oh, man up, Corder,' he growled to himself, and slammed the tailgate.

'OK, little guy?'

She turned and looked at Josh over her shoulder, his face all eyes and doubt.

'Want G'annie and G'anpa.'

'I know, but we can't get there today because of the snow, so we're going to stay here tonight with Sebastian in his lovely house and have an adventure!'

She tried to smile, but it felt so false. She was dreading going inside with Sebastian into the house that contained so much of their past. It would trash all her happy memories, and the tense, awkward atmosphere, the unspoken recriminations, the hurt and pain and regret lurking just under the surface of her emotions would make this so difficult to cope with, but it wasn't his fault she was here and the least she could do was be a little gracious and accept his grudging hospitality.

She glanced round as her nemesis walked over to her car and opened the door.

'I'm sorry.'

They said it in unison, and he gave her a crooked smile that tore at her heart and stood back to let her out.

'Let's get you both in out of this. Can I give you a hand with anything?'

'Luggage? Realistically I'm not going anywhere to-night, am I?' She said it with a wry smile, and he let out a soft huff of laughter and started to pick up the luggage she was pulling from the boot.

He wondered how much one woman and a very small boy could possibly need for a single night. Baby stuff, he guessed, and slung a soft bag over his shoulder as he picked up another case and a long rectangular object she said was a travel cot.

'That should do for now. I might need to come back for something later.'

'OK.' He shut the tailgate as she opened the back door and reached in, emerging moments later with Josh.

Her son, he thought, and was shocked at the surge of jealousy at the thought of her carrying another man's child.

The grapevine had failed him, because he hadn't known she'd had a baby, but he'd known that her husband had died. A while ago now—a year, maybe two. While she was pregnant? The jealousy ebbed away, replaced by compassion. God, that must have been tough. Tough for all of them.

The boy looked at him solemnly for a moment with those huge, wary eyes that bored right through to his soul and found him wanting, and Sebastian turned away, swallowing a sudden lump in his throat, and led them in out of the cold.

'Oh!'

She stopped dead in the doorway and stared around her, her jaw sagging. He'd brought her into the old-est part of the house, through a lobby that acted as a boot room and into a warm and welcoming kitchen that could have stepped straight out of the pages of a glossy magazine.

His smile was wry. 'It's a bit different, isn't it?' he offered, and she gave a slight, disbelieving laugh.

The last time she'd seen it, it had been dark, gloomy and had birds nesting in it.

Not any more. Now, it was…

'Just a bit,' she said weakly. 'Wow.'

He watched her as she looked round the kitchen, her lips parted, her eyes wide. She was taking in every detail of the transformation, and he assessed her reaction, despising himself for caring what she thought and yet somehow, in some deep, dark place inside himself that he didn't want to analyse, needing her approval.

Ridiculous. He didn't need her approval for anything in his life. She'd given up the right to ask for that on the day she'd walked out, and he wasn't giving it back to her now, tacitly or otherwise.

He shrugged off his coat and hung it over the back of a chair by the Aga, then picked up the kettle.

'Tea?'

She dragged her eyes away from her cataloguing of the changes to the house and looked at him warily, nibbling her lip with even white teeth until he found himself longing to kiss away the tiny indentations she was leaving in its soft, pink plumpness—

'If you don't mind.'

But they'd already established that he did mind, in that tempestuous and savage exchange outside the gate, and he gave an uneven sigh and rammed a hand through his hair. It was wet with snow, dripping down his neck, and hers must be, too. Hating himself for that loss of temper and control, he got a tea towel out of the drawer and handed it to her, taking another one for himself.

'Here,' he said gruffly. 'Your hair's wet. Go and stand by the Aga and warm up.'

It wasn't an apology, but it could have been an olive branch and she accepted it as that. They were stuck with each other, there was nothing either of them could do about it, and Josh was cold and scared and hungry. And the snow was dripping off her hair and running down her face.

She propped herself up on the front of the Aga, Josh on her hip, and towelled her hair with her free hand while she tried not to study him. 'Tea would be lovely, please, and if you've got one Josh would probably like a biscuit.'

'No problem. I think we could probably withstand a siege—my entire family are here for Christmas from tomorrow so the cupboards are groaning. It's my first Christmas in the house and I offered to host it for my sins.'

'I expect they're looking forward to it. Your parents must be glad to have you close again.'

He gave a slightly bitter smile and turned away, giving her a perfect view of his broad shoulders as he got mugs out of a cupboard. 'Needs must. My mother's not well. She had a heart attack three years ago, and they gave her a by-pass at Easter.'

Ouch. She'd loved his mother, but his relationship with her had been a little rocky, although she'd never really been able to work out why. 'I'm sorry to hear that. I didn't know. I hope she's OK now.'

'She's getting over it—and why would you know? Unless you're keeping tabs on my family as well as me?' he said, his voice deceptively mild as he turned to look at her with those penetrating dark eyes.

She stared at him, taken aback by that. 'I'm not keeping tabs on you!'

'But you knew I was living here. When I answered the intercom, you knew it was me. There was no hesitation.'

As if she wouldn't have known his voice anywhere, she thought with a dull ache in her chest.

'I didn't know you'd moved in,' she told him honestly. 'That was just sheer luck under the circumstances, but the fact that you'd bought it was hardly a state secret. You were rescuing a listed house of historical importance on the verge of ruin, and people were talking about it. Bear in mind my husband was an estate agent.'

He frowned. That made sense. He contemplated saying something, but what? Sorry he'd died? Bit late to offer his condolences, and he hadn't felt able to at the time. Because it felt inappropriate? Probably. Or just keeping his distance from her, desperately trying to keep her in that cupboard she'd just ripped the door off. And now, in front of the child, wasn't the time to initiate that conversation.

So, after a pause in which he filled the kettle, he brought the subject back to the house. Safer, marginally, so long as he kept his memories under control.

'I didn't realise it had caused such a stir,' he said casually.

'Well, of course it did. It was on the at-risk register for years. I think everyone expected it to fall down before it was sold.'

'It wasn't that close. There wasn't much wrong with it that money couldn't solve, but the owner couldn't afford to do anything other than repair the roof and he hadn't wanted to sell it for development, so before he died he put a restrictive covenant on it to say it couldn't be divided or turned into a hotel. And apparently nobody wants a house like this any more. Too costly to repair, too costly to run, too much red tape because of the listing—it goes on and on, and so it just sat here waiting while the executors tried to get the covenant lifted.'

'And then you rescued it.'

Because he hadn't been able to forget it. Or her.

'Yeah, well, we all make mistakes sometimes,' he muttered, and lifting the hob cover, he put the kettle on, getting another drift of her scent as he did so. He moved away, making a production of finding biscuits for Josh as he opened one cupboard after another, and she watched him thoughtfully.

We all make mistakes sometimes.

Really? He thought it was a mistake? Why? Because it had been a money-sink? Or because of all the memories—memories that were haunting her even now, standing here with him in the house where they'd fallen in love?

'Well, mistake or not,' she said softly, 'I'm really glad you're here, because otherwise we'd still be out there in the snow and it's not letting up. And you're right,' she acknowledged. 'It could have ended quite differently.'

He met her eyes then, his brows tugging briefly together in a frown. He'd only been back here a couple of days. And if he'd still been away—

'Yes. It could. Look, we'll see how it is tomorrow. If the wind drops and the snow eases off, I might be able to get you to your parents in the Range Rover, even if you can't get your car there for now.'

She nodded. 'Thank you. That would be great. And I really am sorry. I know I was a stroppy cow out there, but I was just scared and I wanted to get home.'

His mouth flickered in a brief smile. 'Don't worry

about it. So—I take it you approve of what I've done in here?' he asked to change the subject, and then wanted to kick himself. Finally engaging his brain on the task of finding some biscuits, he opened the door of the pantry cupboard and stared at the shelves while he had another go at himself for fishing for her approval.

'Well, I do so far,' she said to his back. 'If this is representative of the rest of the house, you've done a lovely job of rescuing it.'

'Thanks.' He just stopped himself from offering her a guided tour, and grabbed a packet of amaretti biscuits and turned towards her. 'Are these OK?' he asked, and she nodded.

'Lovely. Thank you. He really likes those.'

Josh pointed at them and squirmed to get down. 'Biscuit,' he said, eyeing Sebastian as if he didn't quite trust him.

'Say please,' she prompted.

'P'ees.'

She put him on the floor and took off his coat, tugging the cuffs as he pulled his arms out, but then instead of coming over to get a biscuit from him, he stood there next to her, one arm round her leg, watching Sebastian with those wary eyes.

He opened the packet, then held it out.

'Here. Take them to Mummy, see if she wants one.'

He hesitated for a second then let go of her leg and took the packet, eyes wide, and ran back to her, tripping as he got there and scattering a few on the floor.

'Oops—three second rule,' she said with a grin that kicked him in the chest, and knelt down and gathered them up.

'Here,' he said, offering her a plate, and she put them on it and stood up with a rueful smile, just inches from him.

'Sorry about that.'

He backed away to a safe distance. 'Don't worry about it. It was my fault, I didn't think. He's only little.'

'Oh, he can do it. He's just a bit overawed by it all.'

And on the verge of tears now, hiding his face in his mother's legs and looking uncertain.

'Hey, I reckon we'd better eat these up, don't you, Josh?' Sebastian said encouragingly, and he took one of the slightly chipped biscuits from the plate, then glanced at Georgia. 'In case you're wondering, the floor's pristine. It was washed this morning.'

'No pets?'

He shook his head. 'No pets.'

'I thought a dog by the fire was part of the dream?' she said lightly, and then could have kicked herself, because his face shut down and he turned away.

'I gave up dreaming nine years ago,' he said flatly, and she let out a quiet sigh and gave Josh a biscuit.

'Sorry. Forget I said that. I'm on autopilot. In fact, do you think I could borrow your landline? I should call my mother—but I can't get a signal. She'll be wondering where we are.'

'Sure. There's one there.'

She nodded, picked it up and turned away, and he glanced down at the child.

Their eyes met, and Josh studied him briefly before pointing at the biscuits. 'More biscuit. And d'ink, Mummy.'

Georgia found a feeder cup and gave it to him to give Sebastian. 'What do you say?' she prompted from the other side of the kitchen.

'P'ees.'

'Good boy.' Sebastian smiled at him as he took the

cup, and the child smiled back shyly, making his heart squeeze.

Poor little tyke. He'd been expecting to go to his loving and welcoming grandparents, and he'd ended up with a grumpy recluse with a serious case of the sulks. Good job, Corder.

'Here, let's sit down,' he said, and sat on the floor, handed Josh his plastic feeder cup, and they tucked into the biscuits while he tried not to eavesdrop on Georgie's conversation.

She glanced over her shoulder, and saw Josh was on the floor with Sebastian. They seemed to be demolishing the entire plateful of biscuits, and she hid a smile.

He'd never eat all his supper, but frankly she didn't care. The fact that Josh wasn't still clinging to her leg was a minor miracle, and she let them get on with it while she soothed her mother.

'Mum, we're fine. The person who lives here is taking very good care of us, and he's been very kind and got my car off the road, so we're warm and safe and it's all good.'

'Are you sure? Because you can't be too careful.'

'Absolutely. It's just for tonight, and it'll be clear by tomorrow. They've got a Range Rover so he's going to give us a lift,' she said optimistically, crossing her fingers.

'Oh, well, that's all right, then,' her mother said with relief in her voice. 'I'm glad you're both safe, we were worried sick when you didn't ring, so do keep in touch. We'll see you tomorrow, and you stay safe. And give my love to Josh.'

'Will do. Bye, Mum.'

She cut the connection and put the phone back on

the charger, then turned and met his eyes. A brow flickered eloquently.

'They?' he murmured.

'Figure of speech.' And less of a red flag to her
mother than 'he'...

He humphed slightly. 'You didn't tell her where you
are.'

She blinked. 'Why would I?'

The brow flickered again. 'Lying by omission?'

She shrugged off her coat and draped it over a chair
next to his at the huge table. 'It's not a lie, it's just an
unnecessary fact that changes nothing material. And
what she doesn't know...'

He didn't answer, just held her eyes for an endless
moment before turning away. The kettle had boiled and
he was making tea now while Josh cleaned up the last
few crumbs on the plate, and she picked it up before
he could break it.

'Here—your tea.' Sebastian put her cup down in the
middle of the table out of Josh's reach and picked up
his coat.

'Give me your keys. I'll put your car away in the
coach-house. Is there anything else you need out of it?'

'Oh. There's a bag of Christmas presents. There are
some things in there that don't really need to freeze.
It's in the boot.'

'OK.' She passed him the keys and he went out, and
she let the breath ease out of her lungs.

Just one night, she told herself. *You can do this. And
at least you know he's not an axe murderer, so it could
have been worse.*

'Mummy, finished.'

Josh handed her his cup and she found him a book in
the changing bag and sat him on her lap. She was read-

ing to him when Sebastian came back in a few minutes later, stamping snow off his boots and brushing it off his head and shoulders.

She put her tea down and stared at him in dismay. 'No sign of it stopping, then?'

He shook his head and held out her keys, and she reached out to take them, her fingers closing round his for a moment. They were freezing cold, wet with the snow, and she shivered slightly with the thought of what might have been. If he hadn't been here…

'Sebastian—thank you. For everything.'

His eyes searched hers, then flicked away. 'You're welcome.' He shrugged off his coat and hung it up again. 'I'll go and make sure your room's ready.'

'You don't need to do that just for one night! I can sleep on a sofa—'

He stared at her as if she'd sprouted another head. 'It's a ten-bedroomed house! Why on earth would you want to do that?'

'I just don't want you to go to any more trouble.'

'It's no trouble, the rooms are already made up. Where do you want these?'

'Ah.' She eyed the presents. 'Can you find somewhere for them that's not my room? Just to be on the safe side.'

'Sure. If you need the cloakroom it's at the end of the hall.'

He picked up all her bags and went out, and she let out her breath on another sigh. She hadn't realised she'd been holding it again, and the slackening of tension when he left the room was a huge relief.

She felt a tug on her sweater. 'Mummy, more biscuit.'

'No, Josh. You can't have any more. You won't eat your supper.'

'Supper at G'annie's house?' he said hopefully, and she shook her head, watching his face fall.

'No, darling, we're staying here. Grannie sends you her love and a great big kiss and she'll see you tomorrow, if it's stopped snowing.' Which it had better have done soon. She scooped him up and kissed him.

'I tell you what, why don't we play hide and seek?' she suggested, trying to inject some excitement into her voice, and he giggled and squirmed down. As she counted to ten he disappeared under the table, his little rump sticking out between the chair legs.

'I hiding! Mummy find me!'

'Oh! Where's he gone? Josh? Jo-osh, where are you?' she called softly, in a sing-song voice, and pretended to look. She opened the door Sebastian had got the biscuits from, and found a pantry cupboard laden with goodies. Heavens, he was right, they were ready for a siege! The shelves were groaning with expensive food from exclusive London shops like Fortnum's and Harrods, and the contents of the pantry were probably equal to her annual food budget.

She shut the door quickly and went back to her 'search' for the giggling child. 'Jo-osh! Where are you?'

She opened another cupboard, and found an enormous built-in fridge, then behind the next door a huge crockery cupboard. It was an exquisitely made hand-built painted kitchen, every piece custom made of solid wood and beautifully constructed, finished in a muted grey eggshell that went perfectly with the cream walls and the black slate floor. And rather than granite, the worktops were made of oiled wood—more traditional, softer than granite, warmer somehow.

The whole effect was classy and elegant at the same time as being homely and welcoming, and it was also well designed, an efficient working triangle. He'd done it properly—or someone had—

'Mummy! I here!'

'Josh? Goodness, I'm sure I can hear you, but I can't see you anywhere!'

'I under the table!'

'Under the table?'

She knelt down and peered through the legs of the chairs, bottom in the air, and of course that was how Sebastian found her when he came in a second later.

'Georgie?'

She closed her eyes briefly. *Marvellous*. She lifted her head and swiped her hair back out of her eyes as she sat back on her heels, her dignity in tatters. She could feel her cheeks flaming, and she swallowed hard. 'Hi,' she said, trying to smile. 'We're playing hide and seek.'

He gave a soft, rueful laugh. 'Nothing much changes, does it?' he murmured, and she felt heat sweep over her body.

They'd played hide and seek in the house often after that first time, and every time he'd found her, he'd kissed her.

She remembered it vividly, so vividly, and she could feel her cheeks burning up.

'Apparently not,' she said, and got hastily to her feet, brushing the non-existent dust from her jeans, ridiculously flustered. 'Um—I could probably do with changing his nappy. Where did you put our bags?'

'In your room. It's the one at the end of the landing on the right—do you want me to show you?'

'That might be an idea.'

Not because she needed showing, but because she didn't want to be tempted to stray into his room. He would have the master suite in the middle at the front, overlooking the carriage sweep, and the stairs came up right beside it.

Too tempting.

She called Josh, took his hand in hers and followed Sebastian up the elegant Georgian staircase and resolutely past the slightly open door of the bedroom where she'd given him her body—and her heart…

Why on earth had he brought up the past when she'd mentioned hide and seek?

Idiot, he chided himself. He'd already had to leave the kitchen on the pretext of putting the cars away when she'd taken her coat off and he'd seen the lush, feminine curves that motherhood had given her.

She'd always had curves, but they were rounder now, softer somehow, utterly unlike the scrawny beanpoles he normally came into contact with, and he ached to touch her, to mould the soft fullness, to cradle the smooth swell of her bottom in his hand and ease her closer.

Much closer.

So much closer that he'd had to get out of the kitchen and give himself a moment.

Now he realised it was going to take a miracle, not a moment, because when he'd run out of things to do he'd walked back in to the sight of that rounded bottom sticking up into the air as she played under the table with the baby, and then she'd straightened, her cheeks still pink from bending over, and he'd seen straight down the V neck of her sweater to the enticing valley between those soft, rounded breasts and lust had hit him like a sledgehammer.

'Here,' he said, pushing open the door of her room. 'It's got its own bathroom, but I haven't put up the travel cot, I'm afraid. I wouldn't know where to start—is that OK? Can you manage?'

'Oh. Yes. That's fine. Um—I don't suppose you've got a small blanket—a fleecy one or something? And a sheet? I don't have any bedding with me because my mother keeps some at hers.'

'I'm sure I can find something. I'll see you in the kitchen when you're done,' he said, and left them to it.

She looked around at the lovely room, beautifully furnished with antiques, and wondered who'd sourced everything. Him? It seemed unlikely. He'd probably paid an interior designer an obscene amount of money to do it, but that was fine, he had it.

He'd been outrageously successful, by all accounts, made a killing on the stock market in the early days and re-invested the money in other businesses. He had a reputation for being fair but firm, and companies that he'd taken over had been turned around and sold for vast amounts, or retained in his portfolio to earn him a nice little income.

Not that she'd been keeping tabs on him...

She sighed. 'Come here, Josh. Let's do your nappy.'

But Josh was exploring, investigating the utterly decadent bathroom with its free-standing white-enamelled bateau bath, the vintage loo with ornate high level cistern and gleaming brass downpipe, the vintage china basin set on an old marble-topped washstand painted the same soft grey as the kitchen and the outside of the bath. There was a rack piled high with sumptuous, fluffy white towels, and expensive toiletries stood on the side of the washstand.

Gorgeous. Utterly, utterly gorgeous. She eyed the bath longingly. Maybe later.

'Come on, tinker. Let's change you.'

But he ran off, giggling, and she had to chase him and catch him and pin him down, squirming like an eel and brimming with mischief. No wonder she didn't need the gym! Even if she had time, which she didn't. She hitched his trousers back up victoriously, mission accomplished, and grinned at him.

'Right, let's go back downstairs and have that tea, shall we?'

And see Sebastian again.

She bit her lip. He was being polite but distant, and she told herself it was what she wanted. Well, of course it was.

Except apparently her heart didn't think so, and a tiny corner of it was disappointed that he hadn't seemed pleased to see her. Well, what had she expected? She'd dumped him because he was too ambitious, too driven, too different from the boy she'd fallen in love with four years earlier, and he hadn't even tried to understand how she'd felt.

She obviously hadn't been that important to him then, and she certainly wouldn't be now, toting another man's child.

She rounded Josh up, took his hand and led him towards the stairs, but then he slipped out of her grasp and ran through a doorway.

The doorway to the master bedroom, she realised, and her heart sank.

'Josh? Come out. That's not our room.'

Silence.

Which left her no choice but to go in...

She pushed the door open and looked around, and the first thing she saw was the bed, huge, beautiful, piled high with snowy white linen and taking her breath away. To be fair, it would have been hard to miss even in such a large room, but it dominated the space, leaping out of her fantasies and taunting her with its perfection, and she felt her cheeks burn.

She dragged her eyes away from it and looked around.

There was no sign of Josh—but the cupboard was there in the corner, the cupboard where she'd hidden, where Sebastian had found her and kissed her the first time.

And there, in front of the fireplace, was where he'd spread the blanket covered in petals and—

'Mummy, find me!'

She pressed a hand to her chest and sucked in a slow, steadying breath. What on earth was she *doing*? Why was she there? She shouldn't be here, in this room, in this house, with this man!

With her memories running riot—

'Mummy!'

She let out her breath, drew it in again and pinned a smile on her face, because he could always tell if she was smiling.

'Ready or not, here I come,' she sang, and heard the words echo down the years, ringing in the empty corridors as she'd hidden in the cupboard and held back her innocent, girlish laughter.

And then he'd kissed her and everything had changed…

CHAPTER THREE

THEY WERE TAKING ages.

Maybe she'd decided to unpack, or bath Josh, or perhaps she was lost.

He gave a soft snort. As if. She knew the house like the back of her hand. More likely she was exploring, giving herself a guided tour. She'd always considered the house to be her own private property. The concept of trespass never seemed to occur to her.

He went to look for her, taking the soft woollen throw he'd found for Josh's bed, and saw his bedroom door standing wide open and voices coming from inside.

'Josh, now! Come out from under there this minute or I'm going downstairs without you.'

Irritated, he walked in and was greeted yet again by that delectable bottom sticking up in the air. Was she doing it on purpose? He dragged his eyes off it. 'Problems?' he asked crisply.

She jerked upright, her hand on her heart, and gave a little gasp. 'Oh—you startled me. I'm *so* sorry. The door was open and he ran in here and he's hiding under the middle of the bed and I can't reach him.'

She sounded exasperated and embarrassed, and he gave her the benefit of the doubt.

'Two-pronged attack?' he suggested with a slightly

strained smile, and went round to the other side of the bed and lay down. 'Hello, Josh. Time to come out, little man.'

Josh shook his head and wriggled towards the other side, and then shrieked and giggled as his mother's hand closed over his arm and tugged gently.

'Come on, or you won't have supper.'

'Want biscuits.'

Sebastian opened his mouth to offer them and caught the warning look she shot him under the bed, and winked. 'No biscuits,' he said firmly. 'Not unless you come straight out and eat all your supper first.'

He was out in seconds, and Georgie scooped him up and plonked him firmly on her hip. She was smiling apologetically, her hair wildly tangled and out of control, those teeth catching her lip again, and he wanted her so much he could hardly breathe.

The air was full of tension, and he wondered if she was remembering that he'd kissed her here for the first time. They'd been playing hide and seek, and she'd hidden in the cupboard beside the chimney breast. He'd found her easily, just followed the sound of her muted laughter and hauled the door open to find her there, hand over her mouth to hold in the giggles, eyes so like Josh's brimming with mischief and something else, something much, much older than either of them, as old as time, and he'd followed her into the cupboard, cradled her face in his hands and kissed her.

He thought he'd died and gone to heaven.

'You kept the cupboard,' she said, her eyes flicking to it briefly, and he knew she was remembering it. Remembering, too, when he'd spread a picnic blanket on the middle of the bedroom floor and scattered it with

the petals of the wisteria that still grew outside the bedroom window and laid her gently down—

'Yes. Well, it's useful,' he said gruffly, and dragged
in some much-needed air. 'I put the kettle on because
your tea was cold. It'll be boiling its head off.'

She seemed to draw herself back from the brink of
something momentous, and her eyes flicked to his and
away again, just as they had with the cupboard.

'Yes. Yes, it will. Come on, Josh, let's go and find
you some supper.' She spun on her heel and walked
swiftly out, the sound of her footsteps barely audible
on the soft, thick carpet, and he didn't breathe until he
heard her boot heels click hurriedly across the hall floor.

Then he let the air out in a rush and sat down heavily on the edge of the huge four-poster bed his interior designer had sourced for him without consultation
and which haunted him every time he came in here.
He sucked in another breath, but her scent was in the
air and he closed his eyes, his hands fisting in the soft
woollen throw, and struggled with a tidal wave of need
and want and lust.

How was he going to survive this? The snow hadn't
let up at all, and the forecast was atrocious. With that
vicious wind blowing the snow straight off the field
and dumping it in the lane, there was no way they'd be
out of here in days, Range Rover or not. Nothing but a
snow plough could get past three foot drifts, and that's
what they'd been heading towards an hour ago.

Maybe the wind would drop overnight, he thought,
but it was a vain hope. He could hear it now, rattling the
windows in the front of the house, sweeping straight
across from Siberia like a solid wall.

He swore under his breath, hauled in another lungful of air, straightened his shoulders and headed down-stairs.

He'd keep out of her way. He could be polite but distant, give her the run of the kitchen and her bed-room and hide out in his study. Except he didn't want to, he discovered as he reached the hall and followed the sound of voices to the kitchen as if he'd been drawn by a magnet.

She turned with a wary smile as he walked in, and set a mug down on the table.

'I made you tea.'

'Thanks. What about Josh? What will he eat?'

'I don't know what you've got.'

He laughed softly and rolled his eyes. 'Everything. I gave my PA a guest list, a menu plan and a fairly loose brief. She used her initiative liberally.'

'I don't suppose she got any fish fingers?'

He felt himself recoil slightly. 'I doubt it. There's smoked salmon.'

She was suppressing a smile, and he could feel him-self responding. 'So—shall I just look?' she suggested, and he nodded and gestured at the kitchen.

'Help yourself. Clearly I would have no idea where to start.'

He dropped into a chair and watched her and the child as she foraged in the cupboards and came up tri-umphant.

'Pasta and pesto with cherry tomatoes, Josh?'

Josh nodded and ran to a chair, trying to pull it out.

'I have to cook it, darling. Five minutes. Why don't you sit and read your book?'

But reading the book was boring, apparently, and he came over to Sebastian and leaned against his legs and looked up at him hopefully. 'Hide and seek?' he asked, and Sebastian stared at Georgie a trifle desperately because the very *last* thing he wanted to play was hide and seek, with his memories running riot—

'Won't he get lost?'

'In here? Hardly.'

'Just in here? There's nowhere to hide.'

'Oh, you'd be surprised,' she said, her laugh like music to his ears. 'Go and hide, Josh. Sebastian will count to ten and look for you.' She met his eyes over the table, mischief dancing in them. 'It's simple. He "hides",' she explained with little air quotes, 'and you look for him. I'm sure you can remember how it works.'

Oh, yes. He could remember how it all worked, particularly the finding part. She'd never made that difficult after the first time…

He closed his eyes briefly, and when he opened them she'd looked away and was halving cherry tomatoes.

'Well, go on, then. Count!'

So he counted to ten, deluged with memories that refused to stay in their box, and then he got to his feet, ignoring the giggling child under the table, and said softly, 'Ready or not, here I come!'

Their eyes met, and he felt his heart bump against his ribs. The air seemed to be sucked out of the room, the tension palpable. And then she dropped the knife with a clatter, bent to pick it up and turned away, and he found he could breathe again.

'Has he settled?'

'Finally. I'm sorry it took so long.'

'Don't worry about it. It's a strange place. Will he be all right up there on his own?'

'Yes, he's gone out like a light now and I've got the baby monitor.'

He nodded. He was sprawled on a chair by the Aga, legs outstretched and crossed at the ankle, one arm resting on the dining table with a glass of wine held loosely in his fingers, watching the news.

He tilted his head towards the screen. 'The country seems to be gridlocked,' he said drily.

'Well, that's not a surprise. It always is if it snows.'

'Yeah. Well, there's over a foot already in the courtyard and the wind hasn't let up at all which doesn't bode well for the lane.'

'Which means you're stuck with us, then, doesn't it?' she said, her heart sinking, and swallowed. 'I'm so, so sorry. I should have left earlier, paid more attention to the weather forecast.' Gone the other way and stayed in the traffic jam, and she'd have been home by now instead of putting them both in this impossibly difficult situation.

He shook his head. 'They got it wrong. The wind picked up, a high pressure area shifted, and that was it. Not even you could cause this much havoc.'

But a wry smile softened his words, and he slid the bottle towards her. 'Try this. It's quite interesting. I've found some duck breasts. I thought it might go rather nicely.'

She poured a little into the clean glass that was waiting, and sipped. 'Mmm. Lovely. So—do you want me to cook for us?'

'No, I'll do it.'

She blinked. 'You can cook?'

'No,' he said drily. 'I have a resident housekeeper and if she's got a day off I get something delivered from the restaurant over the road—of course I can cook! I've been looking after myself for years. And anyway, my mother taught me.' He uncrossed his legs and stood up.

'So—how does pan-fried duck breast with a red wine and redcurrant *jus* on root-vegetable mash with tender-stem broccoli and julienne carrots sound?'

'Like a restaurant menu,' she said, trying not to laugh at him, but she had to bite her lips and he balled up a tea towel and threw it at her, his lips twitching.

'So is that yes or no?'

'Oh, yes—please. But only if you can manage it,' she added mischievously.

He rolled his eyes. 'Don't push your luck or you'll end up with beans on toast,' he warned, and rolled up his sleeves and started emptying the fridge onto the worktop.

'Can I help?'

'Yes. You can lay the table. I'll let you.'

'Big of you.'

'It is. Do it properly. The cutlery's in this drawer.'

She threw the tea towel back, catching him squarely in the middle of his chest, and he grabbed it and chuckled, and for a second the years seemed to melt away.

And then he turned, picking up a knife, and the moment was gone.

It was no hardship to watch him while he cooked.

She studied every nuance of his body, tracking the changes brought about in nine years. He'd only been twenty-one then, nearly twenty-two. Now, he was thirty-one, and a man in his prime.

Not that he'd been anything other than a man then, there'd been no doubt about that, but now his shoulders under the soft cotton shirt seemed broader, more solidly muscled, and he seemed a little taller. The skilfully cut trousers hugged the same neat hips, though, and hinted at the taut muscles of his legs. She'd always loved his legs, and every time he shifted, her body tightened in response.

And while she watched, greedily drinking in every movement of the frame she'd once known so well, he peeled and chopped and sliced, mashed and seasoned, deglazed the frying pan with a sizzle of the lovely red, stirred in a hefty dollop of port and redcurrant sauce and then arranged it all with mathematical precision on perfectly warmed plates.

'Voilà!'

He set the plates down on the places she'd laid, and she smiled. 'Very pretty.'

'We aim to please. Dig in.'

She dug, her mouth watering, and it was every bit as good as it looked and smelled.

'Oh, wow,' she mumbled, and he gave a wry huff of laughter.

'See? No faith in me. You never have had.'

Georgie shook her head. 'I've always had faith in you. I always knew you'd be a success, and you are.'

Even if she hadn't been able to live with him any more.

He shrugged. There was success, and then there was happiness. That still eluded him, chased out by a restless, fretful search for his identity, his fundamental self, and it had cost him Georgia and everything that went with her. Everything she'd then had with another man—and he really didn't want to think about that. He changed the subject. Sort of.

'Josh seems a nice little kid. I didn't know you'd had a child.'

She met his eyes, her fork suspended in mid-air. 'Why would you unless you were keeping tabs on me?'

A smile touched his eyes. 'Touché,' he murmured

softly, and the smile faded. 'I was sorry to hear about your husband. That must have been tough for you.'

Tough? He didn't know the half of it. 'It was,' she said quietly.

'What happened?'

She put her fork down. 'He had a heart attack. He was at work and I had a call to say he'd collapsed and died at his desk.'

He winced. 'Ouch. Wasn't he a bit young for that?'

'Thirty-nine. And we'd just moved and extended the mortgage, so things are a bit tight.'

'What about the life insurance? Surely that covered the mortgage?'

Her mouth twisted slightly. 'He'd cancelled it three months before.'

That shocked him. 'Cancelled it? Why would he cancel it?'

'Cash flow, I presume. Property wasn't selling, and because he'd cancelled the insurance of course they won't pay out, so I'm having to work full-time to pay the mortgage. And it's still not selling, so I can't shift the house, and I'm stuck.'

He rammed a hand through his hair. 'Oh, George. That's tough. I'm sorry.'

'Yeah, me, too, but there's nothing I can do. I just have to get on with it.'

He frowned, slowly turning his wine glass round and round by the stem with his thumb and forefinger. 'So what do you do with Josh while you're at work?'

'I have him with me. I work at home—mostly at night. He goes to nursery three mornings a week to give me a straight stretch of time, and it just about works.'

He topped up her glass and leaned back against the chair, his eyes searching her face. 'So what do you do?'

She smiled. 'I'm a virtual PA. My boss is very under-standing, and we get by, but I won't pretend it's easy.'

'No, I'm sure it's not.' For either of them. He thought of how he'd manage if he and Tash weren't in the same office, and then realised that they weren't for a lot of the time, but that was because he was the one out of the office, not her, and she was there in the thick of it and able to get him answers at the touch of a button.

The other way round—well, the mind boggled.

'How old was Josh when it happened?'

'Two months.'

Sebastian felt sick. 'He won't remember him at all,' he said, his voice sounding hollow to his ears. 'That's such a shame.'

'It is, it's a real shame. David was so proud of him. He would have adored him.'

'You will tell Josh all about him, won't you?'

'Of course I will. And he's got grandparents, too. David's parents live in Cambridge. Don't worry. He'll know all about his father, Sebastian. I won't let him grow up in a vacuum.'

He felt the tension leave him, but a wave of grief fol-lowed it. He hadn't grown up in a vacuum, but he'd been living a lie and he hadn't known it until he was eigh-teen. And then this void had opened up, a yawning hole where once had been certainty, and nothing had been the same since. Especially not since he'd been privy to the finer details. Not that there was anything fine about them, by any stretch of the imagination.

Had his father been proud of him? Had his mother? Had her voice softened when she talked about her little son, the way Georgie's did?

Who was he?

Endless questions, but no proper answers, even after

all this time, and realistically he knew now that there never would be. He sucked in a breath and turned his attention back to the food, but it tasted like sawdust.

'Hey—it's OK,' she said, frowning at him, her face concerned. 'We're doing all right. Life goes on.'

'Were you happy together, you and David?' he asked, wondering why he was beating himself up like this, but she didn't answer, and after a moment he looked up and met her eyes.

'He was a good man,' she said eventually. 'We lived in a nice house with good neighbours, we had some lovely friends—it was good.'

Good? What did that mean? Such an ineffectual word—or maybe not. Good was more than he had. 'And did you love him?'

Her eyes went blank. 'I don't think that's any of your business,' she said softly, and put her cutlery down, the food unfinished.

'I'll take that as a no, then,' he said, pushing it because he was angry about Josh, angry that she'd been playing happy families with someone else while he'd been alone—

'Take it as whatever you like, Sebastian. As I said, it's none of your business. If you don't mind, I think I'll go to bed now.'

'And if I mind?'

She stood up and looked at him expressionlessly. 'Then I'm still going to bed. Thank you for my meal and your hospitality,' she said politely. 'I'll see you tomorrow.'

He watched her go, and he swore softly and dropped his head into his hands. Why? Why hadn't he kept his mouth shut? Getting angry with her wouldn't change anything, any more than it had nine years ago.

He was reaching for the wine bottle when the lights on the baby monitor flashed, and he heard a sound that could have been a sigh or a sob or both.

'Why does he care, Josh? It's none of his business if I was happy with another man. *He* didn't make me happy in the long term, did he? He could have done, but he just didn't damn well care.'

Sebastian closed his eyes briefly, then picked up the baby monitor and took it upstairs, tapping lightly on her door and handing it to her silently when she opened it.

'Oh. Thanks.'

'You're welcome. And, for the record, I did care. I never stopped caring.'

She swallowed, and he could see the realisation that he'd heard everything she'd said register on her face. She coloured, but she didn't look away, just challenged him again, her voice soft so she didn't disturb the sleeping child.

'You didn't care enough to change for me, though, did you? You wouldn't even talk about it. You didn't even try to understand or explain why you never had time for me any more.'

No. He hadn't explained. He still couldn't. He wasn't sure he really knew himself, in some ways.

'I couldn't change,' he said, feeling exasperated and cornered. 'It wasn't possible. I had to do what I had to do to succeed, and I couldn't have changed that, not even for you.'

'No, Sebastian, you could have done. You just wouldn't.'

And she stepped back and closed the door quietly in his face.

He stared at the closed door, his thoughts reeling.

Was she right? Could he have changed the way he'd

done things, made it easier for her to live the life he'd had to live?

Not really. Not without giving up all he'd worked for, all he'd done to try and find out who he really was, deep down under all the layers that had been superimposed by his upbringing.

He was still no closer to knowing the answer, and maybe he never would be, but until then he couldn't stop striving to find out, to explore every avenue, every facet of himself, to push himself to the limit until he found out where those limits were.

And on the way, he'd discovered he could make money. Serious money. Enough to make a difference to the people who mattered? Maybe. He hoped so. The charities he supported seemed to think he was making a difference to the kids.

But Georgie mattered, too, and she was right, there hadn't been time for her in all of this.

OK, it had been tough—tough for both of them. He'd had a hectic life—working all day, networking every evening in one way or another. Dinner out with someone influential. Private views. Trade fairs, cocktails, fundraising dinners—a never-ending succession of opportunities to meet people and forge potentially beneficial links.

To do that had meant working eighteen-hour days, seven days a week. There'd been hardly any down time, and of course it had meant living in London, And that hadn't been compatible with her view of their relationship, or her need to follow her career—although there was no sign of that now.

She'd wanted to stay at university in Norwich, get her Biological Sciences degree and work in research, maybe do a PhD, but now it seemed she was a virtual PA with a 'very understanding' boss.

So much for her career plans, he thought bitterly.

Hell, she could have been his PA. She would have been amazing, and with him, by his side every minute of the day and night, and Josh would have been his child. That would have been a relationship worth having. Instead she'd chosen her career over him, and then gone on to live her dream with some other man who hadn't had the sense to keep his life insurance going to protect his family.

Great stuff. Good choice, Georgia.

Shaking his head in disgust, he turned away from the door and went downstairs to the kitchen. It was in uproar, the worktops covered with the wreckage of their meal and its preparation, but that was fine. He needed something to do, and it certainly needed doing, so he rolled up his sleeves and got stuck in.

The bath was wasted on her.

It should have been relaxing and wonderful, but instead she lay in the warm, scented water, utterly unable to relax, unable to shift the weight of guilt that was crushing her.

She got out, dried herself on what had to be the softest towel in the world and pulled on clean clothes. Not her night clothes—she wasn't that crazy—but jeans and a jumper and nice thick slipper socks, and picking up the baby monitor she padded softly downstairs to find him.

The kitchen door was ajar and she could hear him moving around in there—clearing up, probably, she thought with another stab of guilt. She shouldn't have stalked off like that, not without offering to help first, but he'd been so pushy, so—angry?

About David?

She opened the door and walked in, and he turned and met her eyes expressionlessly. 'I thought you'd gone to bed?'

She shook her head.

'I wasn't fair to you just now. I know you cared,' she said quietly, her voice suddenly choked.

He went very still, then turned away and picked up a cloth, wiping down the worktops even though they looked immaculate. 'So why say I didn't?'

'Because that was what it *felt* like. All you seemed to worry about was *your* career, *your* life, *your* plans for the future. There was never any time for *us*, just you, you, you. You and your brand new shiny friends and your meteoric rise to the top. You knew I wanted to finish my degree, but you just didn't seem to think that was important.'

He turned back, cloth in hand. 'Well, it doesn't seem important to you any longer, does it? You're doing a job you could easily have done in London, that's nothing to do with your degree or your PhD or anything else.'

'That's not by choice, though, and actually it's not true, I am still using my degree. I'm working for my old boss in Cambridge. I'd started my PhD and I was working there in research when I met David.'

'And then you had it all,' he said, his voice curiously bitter. 'Everything you'd always wanted. The career, the marriage, the baby—'

'No.' She stopped him with one word. 'No, I didn't have it all, Sebastian. I didn't have you. But you'd made it clear that you were going to take over the world, and I just hated everything about that lifestyle and what it had turned you into. You were never there, and when you were, we were hardly ever alone. I was just so unhappy. So lonely and isolated. I hated it.'

'Well, you made that pretty clear,' he said gruffly, and turned back to the pristine worktops, scrubbing them ferociously.

'It wasn't you, though. You weren't like that. You'd changed, turned into someone I'd never met, someone I didn't like. The people you mixed with, the parties you went to—'

'Networking, Georgia. Building bridges, making contacts. That's how it works.'

'But the people were *horrible*. They were so unfriendly to me. They made me feel really unwelcome, and I was like a fish out of water. And *so* much of the time you weren't even there. You were travelling all over the world, wheeling and dealing and counting your money—'

'It wasn't about money! It's never been about money.'

'Well what, then? Because it strikes me you aren't doing badly for someone who says it's not about money.'

She swept an arm around the room, pointing out the no-expense-spared, hand-built kitchen in the house that had cost him ridiculous amounts of money to restore on a foolish whim, and he sighed. 'That's just coincidence. I'm good at it. I can see how to turn companies around, how to make things work.'

'You couldn't make our relationship work.'

Her words fell like stones into the black pool of his emotions, and he felt the ripples reaching out into the depths of his lonely, aching soul, lapping against the wounds that just wouldn't heal.

'No. Apparently not.' He threw the cloth into the sink and braced his hands on the edge of the worktop, his head lowered. 'But then nor could you. It wasn't just me. It needs give and take.'

'And all you did was take.'

He turned then and met her eyes, and she saw raw pain and something that could have been regret in his face. 'I would have given you the world—'

'I didn't want the world! I wanted you, and you were never there. You were too busy looking over the horizon to even see what was right under your nose.'

'So you left me. Did it make you happy?'

She closed her eyes. 'No! Of course it didn't, not then, but gradually it stopped hurting quite so much, and then I moved to Cambridge and met David. I was looking for somewhere to live and I went into his office, and we got talking and he asked me out for a drink. He was kind and funny, and he thought that what I was doing was worthwhile, and we got on well, and it just grew from there. And he really *cared* about me, Sebastian. He made me feel that I mattered, that my opinion was valid.'

'That was all it took? Kind and funny?'

She gave him a steely glare. 'It was more than I got from you by the end.'

A muscle in his jaw flickered, but otherwise his face didn't move and he ignored her comment and moved on. 'So what happened to your PhD?'

'I found out I was pregnant, but he'd been moved to the Huntingdon office by then and I was commuting, which wasn't really satisfactory, and then the housing market collapsed. So I contacted my professor and he offered me this job, which kept us going, and then just after I had Josh, David died.'

'And do you miss him?' he asked. His voice was casual, but there was something strange going on in his eyes. Something curiously intense and disturbing. Jealousy? Of a dead man? 'Yes, of course I miss him,' she said softly. 'It's lonely in the house by myself, but life goes on, and I've got Josh, and I'm OK. He was a nice man, and I did love him, and he deserved more from me than I was ever able to give him, but I never felt the way I did with you, as if I couldn't breathe if he wasn't there. As if there was no colour, no music, no poetry. No sense to my life.'

His eyes burned into hers. 'And yet you walked away from me. From us.'

'Because it was *killing* me, Sebastian. *You* were killing me, the person you'd become. You never had any time for me, we never went anywhere or did anything that didn't serve another purpose. It was all about business, about making contacts that would make more money. I felt like an ornament, or a mistress, someone who should just be grateful for the crumbs that fell from your table. But I didn't want crumbs, I wanted you, I wanted what we'd had, but you shut me out, and you broke my heart, and I never want to let anyone that close to me ever again.

'So, no, I didn't feel for David the way I did for you. I didn't *want* to. He didn't give me what I'd thought I wanted when I was little more than a kid and everything was starry-eyed and rose-tinted, but he loved me, and he took care of me, and he made me happy.'

'And he cancelled the life insurance.'

Damn him! 'He had no choice! We were really struggling—'

'Did he tell you he was doing it? Did you discuss it? Or did he just do it and hope for the best? Because I would *never* have done that to you, Georgia,' he said passionately. 'I would never have left you so unprovided for. Would never have compromised your safety or security like that.'

'You have no idea what you would have done in those circumstances—'

'I know I'd starve before I did that—'

'You have no right to criticise him!'

'You were mine!' he said harshly. 'And you gave him all the things you'd promised me. Marriage. A child. Hearth and home and all of that—hell, George, we had so many dreams! How could you walk away? I loved you. You knew I loved you—'

His voice cracked on the last word, and her eyes flooded with tears; she closed them, unable to look at him any longer, unable to watch his face as he bared his soul to her. Because she *had* left him, and he *had* loved her, but she hadn't been mature enough or brave enough to cope with what he'd asked of her.

'I'm sorry,' she said, her heart aching with so many hurts and wrongs and losses she'd lost count. 'If it helps, I loved you, too, and it broke my heart to leave you.'

She heard him swear softly, then heard the sound of his footsteps as he walked up to her, his voice a soft sigh.

'Ahh, George, don't cry. No more tears. I'm sorry.'

She felt his hands on her shoulders, felt him ease her close against his chest, and with a ragged sigh she rested her cheek against his shirt and listened to the steady thudding of his heart. His arms closed around her, cradling her against his warmth and solidity, the mingled scent of his skin and the cologne he'd always used wrapping her in delicious, heart-wrenching familiarity.

She slid her arms around his waist, flattening her palms against the broad columns of muscle that bracketed his spine, and he held her without speaking, while their breathing steadied and their hearts slowed, until the tension left them.

But then another tension crept in, coiling tighter, pushing out everything else until it was the only thought, the only reason for breathing.

The only reason for being.

She felt his head shift, felt the warmth of his lips press tentatively against her forehead, and she tilted her head and met his blazing eyes.

CHAPTER FOUR

THE KISS WAS inevitable.

Slow, tender, fleeting, their lips brushing lightly, then gradually settling. Clinging. Melding into one, until she didn't know where she ended and he began.

She curled her fingers into his shirt, felt his fingers tunnel into her hair and steady her head as he plundered her mouth, taking, giving, duelling with her until abruptly, long before she was ready, he wrenched his head back and stepped away.

She pressed trembling fingers to her aching, tingling lips. They felt as if his had been ripped away from them, tearing them somehow, leaving them incomplete. Leaving her incomplete.

She looked up, and his eyes were black as night, his chest rising and falling unsteadily. She could hear the air sawing in and out of his lungs, see the muscle jumping in his jaw as he took another step away.

'I think you'd better go to bed,' he said gruffly, and handed her the baby monitor from the table.

She nodded, her heart thrashing, emotions tumbling one over the other as she turned and all but ran back to her room.

What had she been thinking of, to let him kiss her? After all that had happened, all the water under the bridge of their relationship, everything that had happened since—she must have been mad!

She'd finally found peace, after years of striving, of what had felt like settling for second best—which was so unfair on David, *so* unfair, but how could he compete with Sebastian? He couldn't. And, to be fair to him, she'd never asked him to. But still, it had felt like that, and it was only with Josh's birth and the bond that had formed between them after David's death that peace had finally come to her.

And now Sebastian had snatched it away, torn off the thin veneer of serenity and exposed the raw anguish in her heart. Because she still loved him. She'd always loved him, and now she was hurting all over again, her heart flayed raw by the knowledge of what she'd lost and what she'd done to him, but there was no way she could go back to that lifestyle, to the way he lived and the man he'd had to become.

She changed into her pyjamas and crawled into bed, lying there in a soft cloud of goose down and Egyptian cotton while her thoughts tumbled endlessly and went nowhere.

She heard him come upstairs to bed at something after midnight, but the sound didn't wake her because she was still lying awake, listening to the wind howling round the house, battering the windows with its unrelenting assault. There was no way she was getting out of there any time soon. The lane would be full to the top by now, the snow trapped against the crinkle-crankle wall with no escape, piling up endlessly as the wind drove it off the field.

Trapping her and Josh inside with Sebastian.

Oh, why had she let him kiss her?

Or had she kissed him? She wasn't sure, she only

knew it had been the most monumental mistake. It had broken down the barriers between them, ripped away her flimsy defences, opened the Pandora's box of their relationship, and try as they might, they'd never get the lid back on it in one piece.

She closed her eyes. She was *so* not looking forward to tomorrow…

He just couldn't sleep.

Well, there might have been a few minutes here and there, but mostly he just lay awake trying not to think about that kiss while he listened to the wind battering the house and blocking them in forever.

There was no way he was getting her out of here today. No way at all. Which was all made a whole sight more difficult by the fact that he'd let his guard down and weakened like that.

He should have kept his mouth shut, not dragged it all out again. And his voice cracking like that! What the hell was that about? He was *over* her…

Liar.

He sighed harshly. OK, so he wasn't over her, not totally, but he hadn't had to tell her that quite so graphically. He *certainly* hadn't needed to kiss her!

And now they were stuck here, forced together, with no prospect of escape for days. He rolled onto his front and folded his arms under his head, banging his forehead gently on them to knock some sense into himself.

Not working. So he lay there, fuming at his stupidity and resigning himself to a fraught and emotionally draining couple of days ahead.

It could have been worse. At least they had Josh there between them. They could hardly fight over his head, and he'd just have to make sure they were only together when he was around.

Although that was a problem in itself, because Josh, with his mother's eyes and engaging personality, was a vivid and living reminder of all he'd lost when she'd walked away. Josh could have been his son. *Should* have been his son. His first known living relative.

His family.

He swallowed hard, the ache in his chest making it hard to breathe.

It was no good. He'd never get to sleep again. He threw off the covers, tugged on his clothes and went downstairs. If nothing else, he could get some work done.

But he couldn't concentrate, and he ended up in the kitchen making yet more coffee at shortly before six in the morning. He put in some toast to blot it up a bit and give his stomach lining a rest, then sat at the table to eat it.

Not a good idea.

Little boys, he discovered, woke early, and he ended up with company.

Georgia, sleep-tousled, puffy-eyed and with a crease on one cheek, stumbled into the kitchen with Josh on her hip and came to an abrupt halt.

'Ah. Sorry.'

Not as sorry as he was. She was wearing pyjamas, but they were soft and stretchy and the child's weight on her hip had pulled the top askew and exposed an inviting expanse of soft, creamy flesh below her collar bone that drew his eyes like a magnet.

She followed the direction of his gaze and tugged it straight, colour flooding her cheeks, and he dragged his eyes away and jerked his head at the kettle.

'It's just boiled if you want tea?'

'Um—please. And do you have any spare milk? Josh usually has some when he wakes up.'

'Sure. I tell you what, why don't I get out of your way while you do whatever you want to do in here? Just help yourself to whatever you need.'

He left the room with almost indecent haste, and Georgie put Josh down on the floor and let her breath ease out of her lungs on a sigh of relief. She'd forgotten just how good he looked, how sexy, with his hair rumpled and his jaw roughened with stubble.

And tired. He'd looked tired, she thought, as if he'd been up all night. Because of the kiss? Or the wind, hammering against the house until she thought the windows were coming in? Between the kiss and the wind, they'd made sure she hadn't slept all night, and she'd only just crashed into oblivion when Josh had woken.

She hadn't realised it was so early until she saw the kitchen clock, because the snow made it lighter, the moon reflecting off it with an eerie, cold light that seemed to seep through the curtains for the sole purpose of reminding her of the mess she was in.

Why had she let him kiss her?

'Biscuit,' Josh said, and she sighed. They had this conversation every day, but he never gave up trying.

'No. You can have a drink of milk and a banana. There must be some bananas.'

She opened the pantry cupboard and found the fruit in a bowl. She pulled off a banana and peeled it and broke it into chunks for him, and left him kneeling up on a chair and eating it while she made some tea and warmed his milk in a little pan. She would have given it a couple of moments in the microwave, but she couldn't find one. She'd have to ask about that.

She sat down with her tea next to Josh, in the place where Sebastian had been. He'd left half a slice of toast on the plate, with a neat bite out of it, and she couldn't resist it. She should have finished her supper the night before instead of running out on him, and she was starving.

'Me toast,' Josh said, eyeing it hopefully, and she tore him off a chunk and ate the rest.

'More.'

'I'll make you some in a minute. Let's go and get dressed first.'

She took him upstairs, protesting all the way, and heard water running. Sebastian must be showering, she realised, and tried really, really hard not to think about that, about the times she'd joined him in the shower, getting in behind him and sliding her arms around his waist—

'Right. Let's get you dressed.'

'Then toast?'

'Then I have to get ready, and then you can have toast,' she promised, but she dragged out the dressing and teeth cleaning and face washing as long as possible, then sat Josh on the bed with a book while she washed and dressed herself and tidied the room.

The sound of running water from Sebastian's room had stopped, she realised as she tugged the bed straight. There was no sound at all, no drawers shutting or boards creaking. He must have finished in the shower and gone downstairs again. With any luck he was in the study, and if not, he could show her where the toaster was to save her scouring the kitchen for it.

She retrieved Josh from the bathroom where he was driving the nailbrush around on top of the washstand like a car.

'Toast?' she said, and he beamed and ran over to her, taking her outstretched hand. He chattered all the way down the stairs and into the kitchen, and she was suddenly really, really glad that he'd been with her in the car, that she hadn't been stuck here with Sebastian on her own.

Not with all the fizzing emotions in her chest—

She found the bread, but there wasn't a toaster and he wasn't around. She was still standing there with the bread in her hand and contemplating going to find him when Sebastian came back into the room.

She waved the bread at him. 'I can't find the toaster.'

'Ah. There's a mesh gadget for that in the slot on the left of the Aga. Just stick the bread in it and put it under the cover, and then flip it. It only takes a few seconds each side so keep an eye on it.'

He pulled the thing out and handed it to her, then headed into the boot room.

'I'm just going to check the lane,' he said. 'See how bad it is.'

'Really? It's almost dark still.'

Except it wasn't, of course, because of the eerie light from the snow and the fact that she'd dallied around for so long getting ready.

Even though she'd resisted putting make-up on…

The door shut behind him, and she put the bread between the two hinged flaps of mesh, laid it on the hotplate and put the cover down. Delicious smells wafted out in moments, and she flipped it and gave it another moment and then buttered the toast while the kettle boiled again.

It smelt so good she made a pile of it, unable to resist sinking her teeth into a bit while she worked, and all the time she wondered how he was getting on and what he'd found at the end of the drive.

Sheesh.

He stood inside the gates—well inside, as he couldn't actually get near them without a shovel and a few hours of solid graft—and stared in shock at the lane beyond.

He was already up to his knees in snow and it was getting deeper with every step. Beyond the gates, the snow reached to head height at either side of the entrance. It only dipped opposite the gates because the snow had had somewhere to go.

Straight across the entrance, through the bars of the gates and right up the drive.

There was at least a foot everywhere, but it wasn't smooth and level. It was sculpted, like sand in the Sahara, swirls and peaks and troughs in shades of brilliant white and cold bluey-purple in the light of dawn.

Beautiful, fascinating—and deadly. If he hadn't been here they could have been trapped inside the car, buried alive in the snow, slowly and gradually suffocating in the freezing temperatures—

He shut off that line of thought and concentrated on the here and now. It wasn't good.

In a freewheeling part of his brain that he hadn't even consulted he realised Georgie wouldn't even be able to get away if they landed a helicopter in the field opposite, despite the fact that it was virtually bare of snow now, because the snow in the lane was so deep they'd never cross it. Not that he'd really contemplated hiring a helicopter on Christmas Eve to take her and Josh away and bring his family back, but even if he had...

And the snow wasn't going anywhere soon. Although the wind had finally died away, it was cold. Bitterly, desperately cold, the change from the previous few days sudden and shocking, and he shrugged down inside his coat with a humourless laugh.

He hadn't needed a cold shower. He should have just come out here. Naked. That might have done the trick. The shower certainly hadn't.

He gave the lane one last disparaging look and waded back to the house, walking in to the smell of toast and the sound of laughter, and for a moment he felt his heart lift.

Crazy. Stupid. She left you.

But even so, he'd still have her there for another twenty-four hours at least. More, probably, and nobody was going to worry about this tiny little lane given that it was as bad elsewhere in the county as it was here. He'd already known it, he'd seen it on the news, and only wild optimism had sent him down the drive to check…

He swept the snow which had fallen in through the doorway back out into the courtyard, shut the door, stamped the snow off his boots and put them on the rack, hung up his coat and went back into the kitchen.

She'd made a pot of tea and was sitting at the table with Josh and a pile of hot buttered toast, playing peeka-bo behind a slice of toast. Josh, his face smeared with butter and crumbs, was giggling deliciously and Sebastian felt his heart squeeze.

'Smells good,' he said, rubbing his hands together to warm them, and Georgie looked up and searched his face.

'And the answer is?' she asked, the laughter fading in her eyes, and he shook his head.

'We're going nowhere. The lane's full to head height.'

'Head height?' she gasped, and her eyes looked

shocked. As if she was imagining being out there with Josh, trapped in the car, seeing what he'd seen in his mind's eye?

'Hey, it's all right, I was here,' he said softly, reading her mind, and she looked up at him again and their eyes locked.

'But what if…?'

'No what ifs. Don't go there, George.' He certainly wasn't going there again. Once was enough. He took a mug out of the cupboard. 'Any more tea in the pot?'

'Mmm. And I made you more toast. I wasn't sure if you'd want it but I made it anyway because we interrupted your breakfast.'

He dropped into the chair opposite her and reached for a slice. 'That's fine, I could do with more,' he said, and sank his teeth into it, suddenly hungry.

Hungry for all sorts of things.

Her warmth. Her laughter.

Her little boy, so like her, so mischievous and delightful, a part of her. What did that feel like? To have someone to love, someone who was part of you?

He looked quickly away and turned on the television to give himself something to do.

So much for his defences. They were in tatters, strewn around him like an old timber barn after a hurricane, and she and her child had walked straight through them as if they'd never even existed.

Maybe they hadn't. Maybe they'd just never been tested before, but they were being tested now, with bells on.

Jingle bells.

She was watching the screen, looking at the pictures of snow sent in by viewers of the local breakfast news programme. Not just them, then—not by a long way. And tomorrow was Christmas Day.

'There's no chance we'll be out of here by tomorrow, is there?' she said flatly.

Had she read his mind? Probably, as easily as he'd read hers. They'd always been good at it. Except at the end—

'I think it's very unlikely. I'm sorry. Your parents will be disappointed.' She nodded. Josh was playing on the floor now, driving a piece of toast around like a car, and she met Sebastian's eyes, worrying her lip again in that way of hers.

'They will be disappointed,' she said softly, lowering her voice. 'So will yours. Was it just them coming?'

'No. My brothers were coming up from London— well, Surrey. I expect they'll spend it together now. They live pretty close to each other. What about your family? Was it just your parents, or was Jack going to be there?'

'No, just them. Jack's got his own family now.' She sighed. 'I really wanted this Christmas to be special. Josh was too small to understand his first Christmas, and last year—well, it just didn't happen really, without David. It seemed wrong, and he was still too young to understand it, so we just spent it very quietly with my parents. But this year...'

'This year he's old enough, and you've moved on,' he murmured.

She nodded. 'Yes. Yes, I have, and he is, and it was going to be so lovely—'

She broke off and swallowed her disappointment, and he couldn't leave her like that. Her, or a little boy who'd lost his father. He had no idea how his own first Christ-mases had been spent. He didn't even know the religion of his real parents, their nationality, their age. Nothing. Just a void. And he couldn't bear the thought that Josh would have a void where Christmas should have been. He'd make sure that didn't happen if it killed him.

He took a deep breath, buried his misgivings and smiled at her.

'Well, we'll just have to make sure it *is* lovely,' he said. 'Heaven knows we've got enough food, and I've got all the decorations and there's a tree outside waiting to come in, if I can find it under the snow. And we can't do anything else. My family aren't going to be able to get here, and you can't get away, so why don't we just go for it? Give Josh a Christmas to remember.'

She stared at him, taking in his words, registering just what it must be costing him to make the offer—although she might have known he would. The old Sebastian, the one she loved, wouldn't have hesitated. The new one—well, she was beginning to realise she didn't know him at all, but he might not be as bad as she'd feared.

'That would be lovely,' she said softly, her eyes welling. 'Thank you. I know you don't—'

He lifted his hand, silencing her. 'Let it go, George. Let's just take it at face value, have a bit of fun and give Josh his Christmas—no strings, no harking on the past, no recriminations. And no repeats of last night. Can we do that?'

Could they? She wasn't sure, but she wanted to try.

She felt the tears welling faster now, and pressed her lips together as she smiled at him. 'Yes. Yes, we can do that. Thank you.'

He returned her smile a little wryly, and got to his feet.

'So—want to help me decorate the house?'

* * *

He gave them a guided tour of the ground floor.

Josh loved it. There were so many places to hide, so much to explore. And Georgie—well, she loved it in a different way, a bitter-sweet, this-could-have-been-ours way that made her heart ache.

No what ifs.

His words echoed in her head, and she put the thoughts out of her mind and concentrated on what he'd done to the house.

A lot.

'Oh, wow!' she said, laughing in surprise when they went into the dining room. 'That's a pretty big table.'

'It extends, too,' he said, his mouth twitching, and she felt her eyes widen.

'Really?' She went to the far end and sat down. 'Can you hear me?'

His smile was wry with old memories. 'Just about. Probably not with the extra leaves in.'

Their eyes held for just a beat too long, and she felt a whole whirlpool of emotions swirling in her chest. She got up and came towards him, running her fingers slowly over the gleaming wood, avoiding his eyes while she got herself back under control. 'Did you get the grand piano for the music room?' she asked lightly, and looked up in time to catch a flicker of something strange in his eyes.

He shook his head. 'No. It seemed pointless. I don't play the piano, but I do listen to music in there sometimes. It's my study now. I prefer it to the library, the view's better. Come and see the sitting room—the old one, in the Tudor part. I think it's probably where I'll put the tree.'

'Not in the hall?'

He shrugged. 'What's the point? I'm never in the hall, I just walk through it. And I thought, over Christmas, we might want to sit somewhere warm and cosy and less like a barn than the drawing room. It's huge, if you remember, and a bit unfriendly. It'll be better in the summer.'

She nodded. It *was* huge, but it was stunningly elegant and ornate in a restrained way, and it had a long sash window that slid up inside the wall so you could walk out through it onto the terrace. She'd loved it, but she could see his point.

In winter, the little sitting room—which was still twice the size of her main reception room—would be much more appropriate. Next to the kitchen in the same area of the house, it was beamed and somehow much less formal than its Georgian counterpart, and it had a ginormous inglenook fireplace big enough to stand inside.

He pushed open the door, and she went in and sighed longingly.

'Oh, this looks really cosy.' Huge, squashy sofas bracketed the inglenook, and there were logs in the old iron dog grate waiting to be lit. She could just imagine curling up there in the corner of a sofa with a book, with a dog leaning on her knees and Josh driving his toy cars around on the floor.

Dreaming again.

'Where are you going to put the tree?'

'In this corner. There's a power socket for the lights, and it's out of the way.'

'How big is it?'

He shrugged. 'I don't know. Eight foot?'

Her eyes widened. 'Will it fit under the beams?'

He grinned and shrugged again. 'Probably. I can always trim it. Only one way to find out.'

'Finding out' turned out to be a bit of a mission. It was in the courtyard, close to the coach house, but the snow was deep except by the back door where it had all fallen in earlier.

'A shovel would make this a lot easier,' he said, standing at the door in his boots and eyeing the snow with disgust.

'I thought you had a shovel in the car?'

'I do. Look at the coach-house.'

'Ah.' Snow was banked up in front of the doors, and digging it out without a shovel wasn't really practical.

'I should have thought of that last night,' he said, but of course he hadn't, and nor had she, because they'd had quite enough to think about already.

She didn't want to think about last night.

She picked Josh up and stood in the kitchen watching through the window as Sebastian ploughed his way through the snow to a huge, shapeless lump in the corner by the coach-house door. He plunged his arm into the snow, grabbed something and shook, and a conical shape gradually appeared.

'Mummy, what 'Bastian doing?'

'He's finding the Christmas tree. It's buried under the snow—look, there it is!'

'Oh..!' He watched, spellbound, as the tree emerged from its snowy shroud and Sebastian hauled it out of the corner and hoisted it into the air.

She went to the boot room door.

'Can I help you get it in?'

'I doubt it. I should stand back, this is going to be wet and messy.'

She moved out of the way, and he dragged it through

the doorway, shedding snow and needles and other debris all over the place. Then he emerged from underneath it, propped it in the corner and grinned at them both.

'Well, that's the easy bit done,' he said. There was a leaf in his hair, in amongst the sprinkles of snow, and she had to stuff her hand in her pocket to stop from reaching out and picking it off.

'What's the hard bit?' she said, trying to concentrate.

'Getting it to stay upright in the stand, and finding the right side.'

She chuckled, still eyeing the leaf. 'I can remember one year my mother cut so much off the tree trying to even it up she threw it out onto the compost heap and bought an artificial one.'

He laughed and turned his back on the tree and met her eyes with a smile. 'Well, that won't happen here. There's no way I can find the secateurs, and the compost heap's far too far away.'

'Well, let's hope it's a good tree, then,' she said drily. 'How about coffee while it drip-dries? And then, talking of my mother, I really should phone her and tell her what's happening.'

'Do that now, although I expect she's worked it out. The news is full of it. The entire country's ground to a halt, so at least we're not alone. And at least you're both safe. There are plenty of people who've been stuck on the motorways overnight.'

'Really?'

'Oh, yeah. It's bad. Go on, ring her, and I'll make the coffee,' he offered, so she picked up the phone and dialled the number, and the moment she said, 'Hi, Mum,' Josh was clamouring for the phone.

'Want G'annie! Me phone!'

'Oh, Mum, just have a quick word with him, can you, and then I'll fill you in.'

'Are you stuck there? We thought you must be. It's dreadful here.'

'Oh, yes. Well and truly—OK, Josh, you can talk to Grannie now.'

She handed over the phone to the pleading child, and he beamed and started chatting. And because he was two, he just said the things that mattered to him.

'G'annie, 'Bastian got a big tree!'

Oh, no! Why hadn't she thought of that? She held out her hand for the phone. 'OK, darling, let Mummy have the phone now. You've said hello to Grannie.'

But he was having none of it, and ran off. 'We got snow, and we stuck,' he went on, oblivious. 'And we having a 'venture, and 'Bastian got biscuits—'

Biscuits. That was the way forward.

She grabbed the packet off the table and waved them at him. 'Come and sit down and give me the phone and you can have biscuits,' she said, and wrestled the receiver off him.

'Hi. Sorry about that. He's a bit excited. Anyway, Mum, I'm really just ringing to say we're stuck here for the foreseeable. The lane is head high, apparently, and there's just no way out, so we aren't going to be able to get to you until it's cleared, and I very much doubt it'll be today—'

'Did he say Sebastian?'

Oh, rats. Trust her to cut to the chase. 'Uh—yeah. He did.'

'As in Sebastian Corder? At Easton Court? Is that where you are?'

'Uh—yeah.' Her brain dried up, and she ground to a

halt, but it didn't matter because her mother had plenty to say and no hesitation in saying it.

'I can't believe you didn't tell me last night! Are you all right? Of all the places to be stuck—is he OK with you? And you said "they"—is there someone else there? His family? A woman? Not a woman—oh, darling, do be careful—'

'Mum, it's fine—'

'How can it be fine? Georgia, he broke your heart!'

'I think it was pretty mutual,' she said softly. 'Look, Mum, I know it's not what you want to hear, but we're OK, and we're alive, which is the main thing, and he's being really generous and it's fine. And there's nobody else here, just us. His family were coming today. Don't stress. Nothing's going to happen.'

Nothing more than the kiss they'd already exchanged, but they'd promised each other no repeats...

'You can't just tell me not to stress, I'm your mother. That's what we do! And he's—' Her mother broke off and floundered for a moment, lost for a definition.

'What?' Georgie prompted softly. 'An old friend? And at least we know he's not a serial killer.'

'He doesn't need to be. There's more than one way to hurt someone.'

And didn't she know that. 'Mum, it's fine. I'm a big girl now. I can manage. Look, I have to go, he's made coffee for us and then we're going to decorate the tree. I'll give you a ring as soon as I know what's happening with the snow, OK? And give Dad a hug from us and tell him we'll see him soon. I'll ring you tomorrow.'

She hung up before her mother could say any more, and turned to find Sebastian watching her thoughtfully across the table.

'I take it she's not impressed.'

She rolled her eyes. 'You'd think you were holding us hostage, the fuss she's making.'

'She's your mother. She's bound to stress.'

'That's exactly what she said.' She sat down at the table with a plonk and gave a frustrated little laugh. 'I'm so sorry.'

'About your mother, who you have no control over, or the weather, for which ditto?' He smiled wryly and pushed the biscuits towards her.

'Here, have one of these before your son finishes them all, and let's go and tackle this tree.'

CHAPTER FIVE

Easier said than done.

It took the best part of an hour to wrestle the tree into the room and get it in the right position, and by the end of it he was hot, cross and had a nice bruise on his finger from pinching it in the clamp.

'Look on the bright side,' Georgie said, standing back to study it critically. 'At least it's a nice soft fir and not a prickly old spruce. And it fitted under the beam.'

He stuck his head out from underneath it and gave her a look. 'Just don't tell me to turn it round again,' he growled, and she smiled sweetly and widened her eyes.

'As if. It looks good. It's even vertical. That's a miracle in itself. So, where are the decorations?'

He worked his way out from under the tree and stood up, brushing bits of vegetation off his cashmere sweater. Probably not the best choice of garment for the task in hand, but with Georgia in the house he didn't seem to be able to think clearly. 'In my study. Come and have a look.'

She followed him to the room that they'd christened the music room, under her bedroom. There was a desk in there positioned to take advantage of the views over the garden, and apart from the laptop on the desk, there was nothing to give away that it was an office. She wondered how much work he did here, or was planning to, or if it was just a weekend cottage.

Some cottage, she thought drily.

There was a stack of boxes beside the desk, and he pulled one of the boxes off the pile and opened it on the desk. 'I'm not convinced they're child-friendly.'

Probably not, she thought, eyeing the expensive packaging. The decorations were all immaculately boxed, individually wrapped in tissue paper and made of glass. Beautiful though they were, she wasn't in a hurry to put them in reach of Josh.

'Not good?' he asked, and she shrugged.

'They're lovely. Beautiful, but they aren't really safe within his reach. He's a bit small to understand about cutting his fingers off.'

Sebastian winced. 'We could put them higher up, out of his reach.'

'We could. And we could decorate the lower part with other things. And they aren't all glass. Look, these ones are traditional pâpier maché, it says. They'll be all right, and I can make gingerbread stars and trees, and decorate them with icing—have you got icing sugar and colourings?'

He raised his hands palm-up and pulled a face. 'How would I know?'

'You put the stuff away in your kitchen?'

He shook his head. 'My mother put a lot of the food away. She was here when it arrived. I was still in London.'

'Ah. Well, in that case we'll have to go and look or be imaginative. There are fir trees in the grounds. We can find fir cones and berries and things—'

'May I remind you that everything in the garden is submerged under a foot of snow?' he said drily, and she smiled.

'I'm sure you'll manage. Coloured paper? Glue? Sticky tape?'

He had a horrible feeling the tree was going to end up looking like a refugee from a craft programme on the television, but then Josh crawled through the knee-hole of the desk pushing his stapler along the floor and making 'vroom vroom' noises, and he suddenly didn't care what the tree looked like. He just wanted Josh to be safe, and happy, and together they could have fun making stuff for the tree.

Well, Josh could. He wasn't sure he'd be so thrilled by it, but hey. Josh was just a kid, and Sebastian wasn't going to put his own feelings before the child's. No way.

'Let's put this lot on the top half,' he suggested, 'and I'll go and see what I can find in the garden while you make the biscuits. I'm sure I've got ribbon and sticky tape and coloured wrapping paper left from the presents.'

She smiled, her whole face softening. 'Thanks. That would be great. OK, Josh, let's go and make the tree pretty, shall we?'

'Lights first,' Sebastian said, picking up the box.

'Do they flash?'

'No they don't,' he said, appalled. 'Nor are they blue. Christmas tree lights should be white, like stars.'

'Stars twinkle,' she pointed out, and started singing 'Twinkle, twinkle, little star', but he'd had enough. Laughing in exasperation, he turned her shoulders, gave her a little push towards the door and followed her back to the sitting room, trying really, really hard not to breathe in the scent of her perfume.

'Your mother rang.'

He paused in the act of tugging off his boots and met her eyes. 'Ah. I sent her a text earlier saying the lane was impassable and Christmas wasn't going to happen tomorrow. What did you say to her?'

She rolled her eyes at him. 'Nothing. I'm not that stupid. She rang the house first, and I heard the answerphone cut in, and then she rang your mobile. It came up on the screen.'

'Right. OK. I'll go and call her.'

'So did you find fir cones and berries?'

'Fir cones. Not berries. The birds were all over them, and I thought their need was greater, but I've got some greenery. I've left it all out here to drip for a bit. Something smells good.'

'That's the biscuits.'

'Mmm. They probably need testing. Did you make spares?' he asked hopefully.

She shook her head, then relented and smiled at him when he pulled a disappointed face. 'I'm sure there'll be breakages.'

He felt his mouth twitch. 'I'm sure it can be arranged even if there aren't. Stick the kettle on, I'm starving and I could do with a drink. I'll go and call my mother and then we can have lunch.'

He went into the study and picked up the phone, listened to the message and rang her. 'So how is it? Are you cut off, too?'

'Yes, and your brothers aren't here, either. They were coming up last night but of course they watched the news and thought better of it. They're spending Christmas together, though, so they'll be fine.'

'So you'll be alone?'

'Well, we hope not. We were still hoping you might be able to get out with your Range Rover to collect us.'

'No chance. It's head high in the lane and I don't see it thawing with the weather so cold and clear. We're going to have to postpone Christmas for days, I'm afraid. It could be ages before they get through here with a snow plough.'

'Oh, darling, I'm so sorry, how disappointing. And I can't bear to think of you spending your first Christmas there on your own.'

Except, of course, he wouldn't be, but there was no way he was telling her that. 'I'm more worried for you,' he said, hastily moving the subject on. 'I don't know what you're going to eat, I've got all the food here at this end.'

'Well, don't try and keep it. Just have it and enjoy it and we'll worry about restocking later. At least it's only us, and I'm sure I've got things in the freezer. We'll be fine, but be careful with all that food at yours and freeze anything you can't use in time. You don't want to get food poisoning eating it past its use-by date—'

'Mum,' he said warningly, and she sighed.

'Sorry, but you can't stop me worrying about you. Big as you are, you're still my son.'

If only that was true, he thought with a pang, but he didn't go there because he knew that in every way that mattered, he was. Well, his heart knew that, and now, after all these years, he was finally able to accept it. His head, though—that still wanted answers—

He heard a noise and realised that Josh had followed him into the study and was crawling around on the floor with the stapler vrooming again, and he swivelled the chair round and watched him out of the corner of his eye while he listened to his mother making alternative plans and telling him how they were going to get together with the neighbours and it would all be fine, and they'd see him soon.

And then Josh stood up under the desk and banged his head, and started to cry.

'Hang on.' He dropped the phone and scooped Josh up into his arms, cross with himself for not anticipating it so that now Josh was hurt, and cross with Georgia for letting him out of her sight so that it could happen in the first place.

And he was hurt. Real tears were welling in his eyes, and without thinking Sebastian sat back in his chair, cuddled him close and kissed his head better, murmuring reassurance. Josh snuggled into him, sniffing a little, and from the phone on the desk he could hear his mother's tinny voice saying, 'Sebastian? Sebastian, whose child is that?'

Why hadn't he just hung up? But he hadn't, and there was no way round this. He picked up the receiver with a sigh and prepared himself for an earbashing.

'It's Georgia Becket's little boy—'

'Georgie's? I didn't know you were seeing her! How long's this been going on?'

'It's not. It isn't,' he told her hastily. 'She was on her way home for Christmas yesterday afternoon and the other road was blocked so she tried the short cut and got stuck outside the gates. And it was almost dark, so the obvious thing to do was let them stay. I was going to take her home today, but the weather rather messed that up so we're just making the best of it, really.'

Shut up! Too much information. Stop talking!

But then of course his mother started again.

'Oh, Sebastian! Well, thank goodness you were there! Who knows what would have happened if you hadn't been—it doesn't bear thinking about, her and her little boy—'

'Well, I was here, so it's fine, and it's only till the snow clears so don't get excited.'

'I'm not excited. I'm just concerned for her. How is she? That poor girl's been through so much—'

'She's fine,' he said shortly, and then added, 'She's making gingerbread decorations for the tree at the moment.'

Why? Why had he told her that? It sounded so cosy and domesticated and just plain happy families, and his mother latched onto it like a terrier.

'Oh, how lovely! She always was a clever girl. She was so good for you—I never did understand why you let her go, but you were behaving so oddly then, I expect you just drove her away. I don't suppose you ever talked to her, explained anything?'

He said nothing. He didn't need to. His mother was on a roll.

'No, of course you didn't. You weren't talking to anyone at that time, least of all us.' She sighed. 'I wish we'd told you sooner. We should have done.'

'You should.'

His voice was harsh, and he heard her suck in her breath. 'Well, whatever, you be nice to her. Don't you dare hurt her again, Sebastian, she doesn't deserve it. And—try talking to her. Tell her what was going on then, how you were feeling about the adoption and everything. How you still feel. I'm sure she'll understand. She's a lovely girl and it would be wonderful if you got back together. I'd love to see you happy, and that poor little boy of hers...'

He swallowed hard, pressing his lips briefly to Josh's dark, glossy hair. 'Well, you can put all that out of your head. It's over. It was over years ago, and it's just not going to happen. Look, I'll give you a call when I know more, but in the meantime you take care and don't let Dad overdo it shovelling snow. I know what he's like about clearing the drive.'

'I'll pass it on, but I can't guarantee he'll listen. And I'm sorry we aren't going to be with you, but I'm really glad Georgie is. And her little boy. You'll have so much fun together. How old is he?'

'Two. He's two—well, two and a bit.' *The same age I was...*

His mother sucked in a breath. 'Oh, Sebastian! He's going to love it! I remember your first Christmas with us—'

'Mum, I've got to go. I'm expecting a call. I'll ring you tomorrow.'

He ended the call abruptly and put the phone down, and then swivelled the chair to find Georgie standing there watching him thoughtfully.

'What's not going to happen?'

'Us,' he said shortly, and put Josh back on his feet. 'What can I do for you?'

She could think of a million things, none of which he'd want to hear and all of them disastrous for her emotional security. 'Nothing. I was looking for Josh and I heard him crying. What happened?'

'He stood up under the desk. He's fine now, aren't you, little guy?'

Josh nodded, and she held out her hand to him. 'Lunch is ready when you are,' she told Sebastian. 'Come on, Josh. Let's go and have something to eat.' And she left him to follow them in his own time.

Great. His mother must have heard Josh cry and asked who he was, which would have opened a whole can of worms.

She'd have to apologise for that because it was her fault, of course, for letting Josh run off like that, but she'd been busy rescuing the biscuits from the Aga and one minute he was there and the next he was gone.

Interestingly, though, it sounded as if his mother, unlike hers, wanted them back together. Well, as he'd said, it just wasn't going to happen. It was *so* not going to happen! Been there, done that, and had the scars to prove it.

And so did he, and from the sound of his voice he wasn't any more keen than she was. He'd certainly cut his mother off short when she started asking questions about Josh.

She towed him back to the kitchen and shut the door to keep him there so he didn't cause any more havoc, and sat him down at the table. She'd made cheese and caramelised onion chutney sandwiches, a big pile of them, and there were little golden brown trees and stars cooling on a wire rack on the worktop.

There were even a few failures. Sebastian would be pleased. Or he would have been. Now, with his mother sticking her oar in and putting him on the defensive, things might not be so jolly. She sucked in a deep breath when she heard the door open and forced herself to smile.

'You got lucky,' she told him. 'Some of the ginger-bread trees were cracked so we can't use them for decorations. And I found some packets of stock cubes which would make perfect tree ornaments if I wrapped them up. Can you spare them for a few days?'

'Probably. You could take some out just in case we need them, but no, that's fine, go for it.' And dropping into a chair, he picked up a sandwich and bit into it. 'Nice bread.'

She raised an eyebrow at him. 'Well, don't look at me, I just raided the kitchen. It was entirely your PA's choice. I suggest you give her a substantial bonus.'

'I already did.'

She laughed and shook her head, then put the kettle on again to make tea and sat down opposite him. 'I'm sorry I let Josh give me the slip. It must have been—awkward with your mother.'

He rolled his eyes. 'You know what she's like.'

'I do. She loves you, though, even though you fight with her all the time. You do know that?'

'Of course I know that.' He frowned and pushed back his chair. 'Look, I've got work to do, so I might just take a pile of sandwiches and disappear into my study. I'll see you later.'

Oh, great, she'd driven him out. It wasn't hard. All she had to do was mention his mother and it was enough to send him running. She felt her shoulders drop as he left the room, and let out a long, slow breath.

They'd agreed to spend Christmas together and ignore the past for Josh's sake, but the past just kept getting in the way, one way or the other, and tainting the atmosphere, as if it was determined to have its say.

She looked out of the window, but the snow was still there, and it was even snowing again lightly, just tiny bits of dust in the air. Was it ever going to thaw so they could escape?

Not nearly soon enough. She cleared the table, gave it a wipe and smiled at her son.

'Are you going to help me ice the decorations for the tree?' she asked, but he was more interested in eating them, so she gave him a pile of little bits to keep him occupied and piped white 'snow' onto the trees and the stars through the snipped-off corner of a sandwich bag, which seemed to work all right until it split and splodged icing on the last one.

She saved it for Sebastian and took it in to him with a cup of tea, knocking on the open door before she went in.

He didn't seem to be working. He was sitting with his feet on the corner of the desk, his fingers linked and lying loosely on his board-flat abdomen, and he glanced at her and frowned.

'Sorry. My mother just got to me.'

'Don't apologise. It was my fault for not keeping a closer eye on Josh. Here. I messed up one of the biscuits. I thought you might like it, and I've brought you a cup of tea.'

'Thanks.'

He dropped his feet to the floor and sighed. 'I wish this damn snow would clear,' he muttered, and she gave a short laugh.

'I don't think there's any chance. I think it's got it in for us. It was snowing again a moment ago.'

'I noticed.' He looked around. 'Where's Josh?'

'Eating broken biscuits.'

'I thought they were mine?'

'You walked out, Sebastian.'

'Well, it makes a change for it to be me.'

She sucked in a breath, took a step back and turned on her heel and walked away. She got all the way to the door before she stopped and turned back.

'I didn't walk out,' she reminded him. 'You drove me out. There's a difference. And if you had the slightest chance, you'd do it again, right now. But don't worry. The moment the snow clears, I'll be out of here, and you'll never have to see me again.'

'Wait.'

His voice stopped her in the doorway, and she heard the creak of his chair as he got up and crossed the room to her.

She could feel him behind her, just inches away, unmoving. After a moment his hands cupped her shoulders, but he still didn't move, didn't say anything, just stood there and held her, as if he didn't quite know what to say or do but wanted to do something.

She turned and looked up into his eyes, and they were troubled. Hers probably were, too. Goodness knows there was enough to trouble them. She let her breath out on a long, quiet sigh, and lifted her hand and touched his cheek, making contact.

Even though he'd shaved that morning she could feel the tantalising rasp of stubble against her palm, and under her fingers his jaw clenched, the muscle twitching.

'I'm sorry,' he murmured. 'I know it wasn't just you. I know I wasn't easy to live with. I'm not. But—we have to do Christmas for Josh, and I really want to do it right, and I know I said we wouldn't talk about it and I just broke the rule. Can we start again?'

She dropped her hand. 'Start what again?'

He was silent for long moments, then his mouth flickered into a smile filled with remorse and tenderness and pain. 'Christmas. Nothing else. I know you don't want more than that.'

Didn't she? Suddenly she wasn't so sure, but then it wasn't what he was offering, so she nodded and stepped back a little and tried to smile.

'OK. No more snide remarks, no more cheap shots, no more bickering. And maybe a bit more respect for who we are and where we are now?'

He nodded slowly. 'Sounds good to me,' he said

gruffly, and he smiled again, that same sad smile that brought a lump to her throat and made her hurt inside.

How long they would have stood there she had no idea, but there was a crash from the kitchen and she fled, her heart in her mouth.

She found Josh on the floor looking stunned, a biscuit in his hand, the wire rack teetering on the edge of the worktop and a chair lying on its side, and guilt flooded her yet again.

'Is he all right?'

'I think so.' She gathered him up, and he clung to her like a little monkey, arms and legs wrapping round her as he burrowed into her shoulder and sobbed. 'I think he's probably just frightened himself.'

And her. And Sebastian, judging by the look on his face.

He reached out a hand and laid it gently on Josh's back. 'Are you OK, little guy? You're really in the wars today, aren't you?'

'I've told him so many times not to climb on chairs.'

'He's a boy. They climb. I was covered in bruises from falling off or out of things until I was about seventeen. Then I started driving.'

She gave him a dry look. 'Thanks. It's really good to know what's in store.'

He smiled at her over her son's head, and this time it was a real smile. His soft chuckle filled the kitchen, warming her, and she sat down on the righted chair and hugged Josh and examined him for bumps and bruises and odd-shaped limbs.

Just a fright, she concluded, and a little egg on the side of his head, but that could have been from standing up under the desk.

'Tea?' Sebastian offered, and she nodded.

'Tea sounds like a good idea. Thank you.'

'Universal panacea, isn't it? When all else fails, make tea.'

He put the kettle on and went back to his study to bring his mug and the uneaten biscuit, pausing for a moment to take a few deep breaths and slow his heart rate. He'd had no idea what they'd find, and the relief that Josh seemed to be OK was enormous.

Crazily enormous. Hell, the little kid was getting right under his skin—

He strode briskly back to the kitchen, stood his mug on the side of the Aga so it didn't cool any more and made her a fresh mug.

'How is he?'

'He's fine, aren't you, Josh? It's probably time he had a nap. I usually put him down after lunch for a little while. I might go up with him and read for a bit while he sleeps.'

He frowned as he analysed an unfamiliar emotion. *Disappointment? Really? What was the matter with him?*

'Good idea. I'll get on with my work, and then we'll decorate the tree later.'

'Mistletoe?'

He'd cut mistletoe, of all the things! Like that was *really* going to help—

'I know, I know,' he sighed shortly, 'but it is Christmassy, and everything else was out of reach or too tough, and I could cut it with scissors, and I have no idea where the secateurs might be. I made sure it didn't have berries on, either, in case Josh should try and eat them, because they're poisonous. But there is one bit of holly—for the Christmas pudding.'

She tipped her head on one side and eyed him in disbelief, trying not to laugh. 'The Christmas pudding?'

'Absolutely. You have to have a bit of holly on fire in the middle of the Christmas pudding when it's brought to the table. It's the law.'

She suppressed a splutter of laughter. 'Is that the same law that says that lights must be white? My, aren't we traditional?' she teased, but he just folded his arms and quirked a brow.

'Absolutely. Christmas is Christmas. It has to be done properly. Have you got a problem with that?'

She smiled slowly. 'Do you know what? You've got a good heart, Sebastian Corder, for all you're as prickly as a hedgehog. And no, I don't have a problem with that. Not at all.'

He cleared his throat. 'Good. Right. So, what's next?' he asked, avoiding her eyes and fluffing up his prickles.

Still smiling, she handed him the boxes of stock cubes and a few other little things she'd found that could be wrapped, and they sat down at the table, gave Josh a piece of paper and a pencil to do a drawing, and made little parcels for the tree.

She'd snapped off some twigs from a shrub outside the sitting room window, and once the other parcels were done they made them into little bundles to dangle on the tree.

'Finger,' he demanded, and she put her finger on the knot and he tugged the gold ribbon tight, and made a loop to hang it by.

'You're good at this. You might have found your vocation.'

'I have a vocation.'

'What, making money?'

He sighed and put the little bundle of sticks down on the growing pile.

'George—'

She raised her hands. 'It's OK, I'm sorry, cheap shot.'

'Yes, it was. And I don't just spend it all on myself. I employ a lot of people, and I support various charities and organisations—and I really don't need to explain myself to you.'

She searched his eyes. 'Maybe you do,' she said softly. 'Maybe you always did, instead of just rushing off and doing.'

'Yeah, well, there's been a lot of water under the bridge since then, and as you were kind enough to point out to me when I was asking about David, it's actually none of your business. Now, are we going to finish this tree or not?'

He got to his feet, scooping the little parcels up in his big hands and heading out of the door. She grabbed the fir cones, ribbon and scissors and stood up. He was never going to change, never going to compromise. The word wasn't even in his vocabulary.

'Josh, come on, we're going to decorate the tree,' she told her son, and he wriggled down off the chair and followed her into the sitting room.

CHAPTER SIX

'It looks good.'

She put the baby monitor on the coffee table, sat down at the other end of the sofa and studied the tree with satisfaction.

Not exactly elegant, with its slightly squiffy little parcels and random bunches of twigs and soggy fir cones—well, the top half wasn't so bad, although there were a few odd bits up there just to link it in so it didn't look like a game of Consequences—but it looked like a proper, family Christmas tree.

And that brought a huge lump to her throat.

Josh had had so much fun putting all their home-made bits and pieces on there, and Sebastian hadn't turned a hair when he'd pulled too hard and the whole tree had wobbled. He'd just got a bit of string and tied it to a hook on the beam above so it couldn't fall.

'It does look good,' she said softly. 'It looks lovely. Thank you.'

Sebastian turned his head and frowned slightly at her. 'Why are you thanking me? You've helped me decorate my tree.'

'And we've done it for my son, which has meant not being able to use all your lovely decorations and smothering the bottom of it in all sorts of weird home-made bits and pieces, which I'm perfectly sure wasn't your intention, so—yes, thank *you*.'

The frown deepened for a moment, then cleared as he shook his head and looked back at the tree.

'Actually, I rather like all the home-made things,' he said after a moment, and she had to swallow the lump in her throat.

'Especially the gingerbread trees and stars,' she said, trying to lighten the moment. 'And don't think I haven't noticed that every time you "accidentally" bump into the tree another one breaks so you get to eat it. Between you and Josh there are hardly any left.'

He grinned. 'I don't know what you mean. And if we're running out, it's your fault. I told you to make plenty.'

She rolled her eyes and rested her head back against the sofa cushions with a lazy groan. 'This is really comfortable,' she mumbled.

'It is. I love this room. I think it's probably my favourite room in the whole house.'

Because they'd never made any plans for it? Maybe, she thought, considering it. Or had they? Hadn't there been some mention of it being a playroom for all the hordes of children? But they hadn't spent any *significant* time in it. Not like the bedroom. Maybe that made the difference.

Or maybe he just liked it.

She rolled her head towards him and changed the subject.

'So, what's the programme for tomorrow? Since you have such strong opinions on how it should be done…'

Another grin flashed across his face. 'Cheeky.' He hitched his leg up, resting his arm on the back of the sofa and propping his head on his hand so he was facing her, thoughtful now.

'I think that probably depends on you and Josh. What are you going to do about presents for him? Are you going to wait until you're with your parents?'

'I don't know. I don't think so. He was really excited about the tree and he knows there will be presents under it because they had them at nursery, so I think there probably should be something for him to find tomorrow, otherwise it might be a bit of an anti-climax.'

'You don't think it will anyway, with just us and a few presents instead of a big family affair? Wouldn't you rather wait?'

'Do you think I should?'

He shrugged. 'I don't know. It's up to you, but it makes me feel a bit awkward because there isn't one from me, and it'll look as if I don't care and I'd hate him to think that, but obviously I haven't got anything to give him. Either of you.'

She stared at him, unbearably touched that he should feel so strongly about it—and so wrongly. She reached out a hand to him, grasping his and squeezing it.

'Oh, Sebastian. You're giving us Christmas! How much more could we possibly ask? You've opened your home to us, let us create absolute havoc in it, we've taken it over completely so you haven't even been able to work, and—well, frankly, without you we might not even be alive for it, so I really don't think you need to worry about some gaudy plastic toy wrapped up and stuck under the tree! In the grand scheme of things, what you've given him—given us—is immeasurable, and whatever else is going on between us, I'll never forget that.'

Sebastian frowned again—he was doing that a lot—and turned away, his jaw working.

'He's just a kid, George,' he said gruffly.

'I know,' she said softly. 'And for some reason that really seems to get to you.'

He shrugged and eased his hand away, as if the contact made him uncomfortable. 'I don't like to think of kids being unhappy at Christmas. Or ever. Any time. And as I've said, I've got nothing else to do and nowhere else to be. So—presents, or not presents?'

She thought about it for a moment. Her parents had spoiled him on his birthday just four weeks ago, and he'd had so many presents he hadn't really known what to play with first. And there was nothing here in the house, really, that he could play with safely.

And then she had an idea that would solve it all. 'I think—presents? Or some of them, at least. I've got him a wooden train set, and it comes in two boxes. There's the main set, and there are some little people and a bench and trees and things in another box. You could give him that, if you're really worried about him having something from you under the tree.'

'Don't you mind?'

She laughed. 'Why should I mind? He's still getting the toy, and it would give him something constructive to play with while we're stuck here. And I've got a little stocking for him from Father Christmas. That ought to go up tonight because he's bound to get up early.'

'Does he even know who Father Christmas is?'

She smiled ruefully. 'I don't know. We went to see him, but I'm not sure he was that impressed. He looked a bit worried, to be honest, but it might make him like the old guy a bit better if he brings him chocolate.'

They shared a smiled, and he nodded.

'You could hang it from the beam over the fire.'

'I could. We might need to let the fire go out first, though, so the chocolate buttons don't melt.'

'Ah. Yes, of course. Good plan. Well, if we let it die down now, it should be all right by the end of the evening. It can go at the side, out of the direct heat. And, yes, please, if I can put my name on the other box of train stuff, that would be good. But you must let me pay you for it.'

She just laughed at that, it was so outrageous. 'You have to be kidding! The amount you're spending on us already? I'll have you know I eat a lot on Christmas Day.'

'Good. Have you seen the size of the goose?'

'We have goose?' she said, her jaw dropping open in delight. 'Oh, wow, I love goose! What stuffing?'

'Prune and apple and Armagnac,' he told her, and she sighed with contentment and slumped back onto the sofa cushions, grinning.

'Oh, joy. Deep, deep joy. Bring it on…'

He laughed and stood up, slapping her leg lightly in passing. 'That's your job. I have no idea how to cook a goose, especially not in an Aga, so I was hoping you'd do it. Shall I get the presents?'

'I'll come. I only want a few. Where did you put them?'

'In my room.'

Ah.

Was her face so transparent? Because he took one look at her and smiled and shook his head.

'You're perfectly safe, George. I'm not going to do anything crazy.'

No. And wishing she wouldn't be quite so perfectly

safe was crazy. Utterly crazy. Good job one of them was thinking clearly.

She nodded slowly and stood up. 'OK. We'll just get the train set boxes and the stocking and leave the rest for when I'm with my parents. Then I can just put the whole bag in the car when I leave.'

He didn't want her to leave.

It dawned on him suddenly, with a dip in his stomach, as they went upstairs to the bedroom, walking up side by side as if they were going to bed.

And he needed to stop thinking about that right there before he embarrassed them both.

He pushed the door open and flicked on the light. 'They're in here,' he said, and let her through the communicating door into his dressing room. It had been cut in half, the half with the window becoming the bathroom, this half now lined out with wardrobes fitted with racks and shelves and hanging space.

He'd dumped the bag of presents inside one of the practically empty cupboards, and he pulled it out and turned to find her looking around, studying the wardrobes minutely.

'Useful. Really useful. What sensible storage. They're great.'

'They are. How anybody managed with that little cupboard in the bedroom I have no idea.'

'Maybe they didn't have as many clothes. Or maybe they just used it to play hide and seek?' she said lightly.

She was bending over the presents as he held them, and he stared down at the top of her head and tried to work out what was going on in there. Why had she said that? Why chuck something so contentious into the mix?

Although it was him that had raised the subject of the cupboard in the first place...

He had to get out of there. Now.

'Right, why don't I leave you to sort out what you want to bring down, and I'll go and get on. I've got a few loose ends to tie up before tomorrow. Just stick them back in the cupboard when you're done.'

And he handed her the bag and left. Swiftly, before he gave in to the temptation to grab her by the shoulders, haul her up straight and kiss her senseless.

'Here. This is the train set stuff. Did you want to wrap yours in different paper?'

She put the boxes down on the kitchen table and he studied them thoughtfully. 'Does it matter if they're the same?'

'Not necessarily.'

He gave a slight smile. 'I'll do whatever, but I have to say my wrapping paper doesn't really compete with little trains being driven by Santas.'

She smiled back. 'Probably not. And he won't think about the fact that they're the same. He'll just want to unwrap them. He knows what presents are now, having just had a birthday.'

'When was his birthday?'

'Three days after yours.'

His eyebrows crunched briefly together again in another little frown, and she wondered what she'd said this time. Was it because she remembered his birthday? Unlikely. She'd always remembered everyone's birthdays. That was what she did. Remembered stuff. It was her forte, just as his was making money.

She gave up trying to work him out.

'So, lunch tomorrow or whenever we're having it.

Are we going for lunchtime, or mid-afternoon, or evening, or what?'

He turned his hands palm up and shrugged. 'Look, this is all for Josh. I don't care what time we eat, so long as we eat. I'm sure we'll manage whenever it is. Just do whatever you think will suit him best.'

'Lunch, probably, if that's OK? What veg do you have? And actually, where is the goose? It's not in the fridge so I hope it's not still frozen.'

'It's in the larder.'

'Larder?' The kitchen had been so derelict she hadn't even realised it'd had a larder. Or maybe he'd created one?

He walked across to what she'd assumed was a broom cupboard or something, and opened the door. A light came on automatically, illuminating the small room, and she saw stone shelves laden with food. So much food.

'Wow. And this was just for you and your family?'

He gave a wry smile. 'I told you my PA had gone mad.'

Not that mad, she thought, studying the shelves. Yes, there was a lot of food, but much of it would keep and it was only the goose and the fresh vegetables that might struggle.

She shivered. 'It's chilly in here. Ideal storage. I didn't even know it existed. Was it here?'

'Yes. It had one slate shelf and I had the others put in, and it's got a vent to the outside and faces north, which keeps it cool.'

'Which is why it feels like a fridge.'

He smiled. 'Indeed. Perfect for the days when fridges didn't exist. So—there you are. Feel free to indulge us with anything you can find.'

'Oh, I will.'

She ran her eye over it all again, mentally planning the menu, then shut the door behind them and sat back down at the table to write a list.

'Do you really want Brussels sprouts?'

'Definitely. Christmas isn't Christmas without sprouts.'

'And burnt holly.'

'And burnt holly,' he said with a grin.

She bit down on the smile and added sprouts to the list, then looked up as he set a glass of wine down on the table in front of her.

'Here, Cookie. To get you into the festive spirit.'

'Thank you. And talking of Cookie, are you about to cook, by any chance, or was that a hint for me?'

'I've done it. There's a pizza in the oven and some salad, and we could have fruit or icecream to follow. I thought I'd let you off the hook, seeing as you'll be doing quite enough tomorrow.'

'How noble of you.' She sipped her wine and glanced at her list. 'Is the goose stuffed already?'

'So I was told. Ready to go straight in the oven. It says four hours.'

'I thought you didn't know how to cook it?' she asked drily, and he smiled, his eyes dancing with mischief.

'I didn't want to do you out of the pleasure—and this way you get all the glory.'

'What glory?'

'The glory of basking in my adoration,' he murmured, and she wasn't sure but there seemed to be a mildly flirtatious tone in his voice.

She held his eyes for a startled moment, then gave a slightly strained little laugh and looked away. 'Always assuming I don't burn it.'

'You won't. I'll make sure of that. Right, let's label that present with a new tag, and you go and stick them under the tree and I'll dish up.'

But what to write? His pen hovered for a moment over the tag he'd found. Did it matter? The child couldn't read.

'To Josh from Sebastian' would do.

But he put *love* in there, just because it seemed right. Weirdly right.

'OK, that's done, we need to eat or the pizza will be ruined.'

He slid the box across the table to her, pushed back his chair and made himself busy. So busy he didn't have time to think about what he'd written.

Or why.

She put the presents under the tree while he dished up, and then after they'd eaten and cleared away they peeled sprouts and potatoes and parsnips and carrots, until finally he called a halt.

'Enough,' he said firmly, took the knife out of her hand, replaced it with her wine glass and ushered her through to the sitting room.

The fire was low, the embers glowing, and they sat there with just the faint glow of the fairy lights and the occasional spark from the fire, his arm stretched out along the back of the sofa, his head turned towards her as they talked about the timetable for tomorrow.

If he moved his fingers just a millimetre—

'Tell me about the renovations,' she said then, and shifted, settling further into the corner, and he reached for his glass and pulled his arm back a little, out of temptation, and as he told her about the house and what he'd had done to it, he watched her and wondered just how much he was going to miss her when she left…

* * *

Josh woke early.

He always did, but she'd sat up with Sebastian talking about the house and the building work and what his plans were for the gardens until the fire had died away to ash and her eyes were drooping.

He'd hung the little stocking up on the beam, off to one side so the chocolate didn't melt, and then he'd taken himself off to his study while she'd come up to bed.

She'd heard him come up later, but not much later, and she'd turned on her side then and fallen sound asleep until Josh's cheerful chatter had woken her.

Bless his darling heart, she loved him so much but she could have done with another half hour. She prised open her eyes and he beamed at her and stood up in the travel cot, holding up his arms.

'Happy Christmas, Josh,' she said softly, gathering him up and hugging him tight. He gave her a big, sloppy kiss, and she laughed and kissed him back and tickled him, then she changed his nappy and took him down to the kitchen.

To her amazement the lights were blazing, the kettle was on and there was a wonderful smell of baking.

And it was after seven! How did that happen?

'Biscuit, Mummy,' Josh said, just as Sebastian came back into the kitchen.

He was wearing checked pyjama trousers and a jumper, his hair was rumpled and he definitely hadn't shaved, but he'd never looked so good, and her heart squeezed.

No! Don't fall in love with him again!

But then Josh ran over to him and he scooped him up and hugged him, tolerated the sloppy kiss with amazing grace and even kissed him back. 'Happy Christmas, Tiger,' he said, ruffling his hair, and Josh growled at him and made him laugh.

He growled back, and Josh giggled and squirmed down and ran back to her. 'Biscuit, Mummy! Bastian want biscuit too.'

'Ah. Sebastian's actually cooking croissants and pain au chocolat,' he confessed, his eyes flicking to hers in apology.

She smiled. 'It's Christmas. And they smell amazing.'

'They are. And they'll be burnt if I don't take them out. Coffee or tea?'

'Both. Tea first. I'll make it. What do you want?'

'Same. Tea, then coffee. I'll put a jug on for later.'

How domesticated, she thought, getting out the mugs and making the tea while he rescued the pastries and found plates and butter and jam, and she poured the tea and he sat Josh down and pulled up his pyjama sleeves so he didn't get plastered in butter.

We're like an old married couple, she thought, *just getting breakfast together on Christmas morning, and in a minute we'll go through to the sitting room and open Josh's presents and play with him, and the goose will cook and...*

She cut herself off.

This was a one-off. They weren't married. They were never getting married. And she needed to stop dreaming.

The train set was a hit.

They moved a table out of the way, and Sebastian got down on the floor with Josh and helped him set up the track, and she sat with her feet tucked up under her bottom, still in her pyjamas, cradling a cup of coffee and watching them.

Josh had opened his stocking, with the little cars and a packet of chocolate buttons and a satsuma she'd taken from the fruit bowl, and Sebastian had lit the fire and thrown the peel on it and it smelled Christmassy and wonderful.

So wonderful.

Her eyes filled. What had happened to him to make him change so much, to become so driven, so remote, so focused on something she couldn't understand that their love had withered and died?

He wasn't like that now. Or not today, at least. He'd been pretty crabby out in the lane in the snow, but since then he'd made a real effort.

Or maybe it was just because of Josh, to make him happy. That seemed really important to him, but was there more to it than that?

He'd written 'love from Sebastian' on the gift tag.

Just a figure of speech, the thing everyone always writes? Or because he meant it?

She had no idea, she just knew, watching him, listening to the two of them talking, that he'd really taken her little boy to his heart, and she found it unbearably touching.

'Right. Time to put the goose in,' he said, and she yanked herself out of her thoughts and put the cup down.

'I'll do it.'

'No. It's heavy. I'll put it in. You can do the tricky stuff later.'

He went out, taking their mugs, and came back a few minutes later with a refill and a handful of satsumas.

'Is that an attempt to compensate for the croissants?' she said drily, and he chuckled and lobbed one over to her, dropping down onto the other sofa and turning so he could watch Josh over the back.

'He chatters away, doesn't he?'

'Oh, yes. He didn't talk very early, but boys don't, I don't think. And they stop talking again in their teens, of course, and just start grunting.'

He frowned again, looking thoughtful for a moment. 'I'm sure I didn't grunt. Nor did my brothers, as far as I'm aware.'

'My brother did. He was monosyllabic for years. It made a refreshing change from all the arguments.'

'How is he? We lost touch when—well, then.'

She ignored his hesitation. 'Fine. He's working in Norwich. He's a surveyor. He's stopped grunting now and he's quite civilised. He's married with two children and a dog.'

He looked away. 'Lucky Jack.'

'He is. He's very happy.'

'I'm glad. Give him my regards.'

'I will. How are your brothers?'

'Better now they've grown up. They both work for me. Andy's an accountant, and Matt's a sales director.'

'Don't they mind answering to you?'

He laughed softly. 'It makes for interesting board meetings sometimes,' he confessed, and she laughed too.

'I'm sure. Talking of families, I ought to ring my parents. They'll want to say Happy Christmas to Josh.'

'How about doing it from my computer with the web-cam, so they can see you?'

'Can we? That would be brilliant!'

'Well, since they know you're here, you might as well. Do it in my study.'

She looked down at herself, suddenly aware of what

she was wearing. 'I might get dressed first. Just so they don't think we're hanging out all day in PJs.'

And then she looked up, and his eyes were on her, filled with a dark emotion she didn't want to try to understand, and she took Josh upstairs, protesting all the way, and washed and dressed him.

She needed a shower, really, and her hair washed, but she didn't like to let Josh run riot and she could hear water running in Sebastian's room, so she told him to stay there and look at a book, shot into the bathroom and showered and came out to find the door open and no sign of him.

'Josh? Josh, where are you?'

She ran out onto the landing, clutching the towel together, and slammed straight into Sebastian's chest. His bare, wet chest. His hands came up and steadied her, and she stared, mesmerised, as a dribble of water ran down through the light scatter of hair across his pecs and disappeared into the towel at his hips.

'If you're looking for Josh, he's in my room.'

His voice, low and gravelly, cut through her thoughts and she sucked in a breath. *What was she doing?*

He let go of her shoulders and stepped back, and she hitched her towel up and blushed. 'He is?'

'Yes. Don't worry. He came to find me. You take your time, we're fine.'

'Are you sure? Because I really need to—' She waved a hand vaguely at her towel, and his eyes tracked over it and he smiled slightly.

'Yes. You do.'

She glanced down, and saw it was gaping. Dear God, could it get any worse?

Blushing furiously and clutching it together, she went back into her room and closed the door, leant back against it and shut her eyes, humiliation washing over her. How could she have gone out there with her towel flapping open and revealing—well, everything, pretty much!

Not that he'd been exactly covered. Had he always looked that good naked?

Yes. Always. He was more solid now, but he'd always looked good. Tall, broad, muscular, without an ounce of spare flesh on him.

And she really, really didn't need to be thinking about that now! She pushed away from the door, dried herself quickly and wrestled her still-damp body into jeans and a jumper.

Her hair needed careful combing and drying, but it wasn't going to get it.

Or was it? There was a knock on the door and it opened a crack.

'There's a hairdryer in the top drawer of the bedside table. I'm taking Josh downstairs. There's no rush. We're going to play with the train set.'

She sat down on the edge of the bed and sighed. Well, it would give her time to dry her hair properly and put on some make-up. And gather herself together a little. Her composure was scattered in all directions, and she was ready to die of humiliation.

Too right she'd take her time. She was in no hurry to face him again!

Her towel had slipped.

Not far enough. Just enough to taunt him, not enough to see anything. He'd gone back into his room, found Josh under the bed giggling and got dressed before Georgie had time to come looking for him again and caused another incident.

And Josh was more than happy to come downstairs and play with his trains. So was Sebastian. Only too happy, because it reminded him of all the reasons why getting involved with Georgie again would be such a mistake.

She'd walked out on him once, but they'd been the only ones who could get hurt in that situation, and he knew he'd been at least partly responsible. OK, maybe largely responsible, but not solely. He wasn't taking all the blame for her lack of sticking power.

But this time, Josh would be involved. And he was so open, so trusting, so vulnerable. Two was a bad time for your world to fall apart. He knew that, in some deep, inaccessible but intrinsic part of him that still ached with loss.

Wounds that deep never really healed. And that was another reason to keep his distance.

So he played with Josh until she came down, and then he went into the kitchen and started putting the lunch together.

She followed him, Josh in tow. 'You said I could hook up with my parents,' she reminded him, and he nodded, put the timer on for the potatoes and took her to the study, connected her up and left them to it. Five minutes later they were back.

'I thought I was supposed to be cooking?' she said, but he shook his head.

'Don't worry about it. It actually looks pretty straightforward and the instructions are idiot-proof.'

'Are you sure? I thought that was the deal?'

'There's no deal,' he said shortly. 'Go and play with your son. It's Christmas. He needs you, not me. I'll do this.'

In fact there wasn't that much to do, to his regret.

He parboiled the potatoes and parsnips, put them in a roasting pan with some of the goose fat and put them in the oven, moving the goose to the bottom oven to continue cooking slowly.

And then there was nothing to do for an hour.

Well, he had two choices. He could spend his Christmas Day sitting alone in the kitchen, or he could go back into the sitting room with Georgie and Josh and try not to remember what he'd seen under her towel...

The sitting room won, hands down.

CHAPTER SEVEN

GEORGIE SAT BACK and sighed happily.

'Sebastian, for someone who claims not to know how to cook a goose, that was an amazing lunch. Thank you so much.'

His shoulders twitched in that little shrug of his that she was getting so used to. 'Good ingredients. I can't take any credit.'

That was rubbish and they both knew it, but he'd always been modest about his achievements. For such a high achiever, it was a strange trait, and rather endearing. She smiled at him.

'Nevertheless, it was delicious and I'm washing up.'

'No. The dishwasher's washing up. And the sun's out and it's warmer, so let's not waste the day in here. Has Josh got anything he can wear outside?'

'Yes. Wellies and overalls, in the car, and I brought my wellies, too—hey, we could make snow angels!'

He chuckled. 'I think you'll find if we put him down in the snow, he'll vanish without trace, unless we can find a bit where it's not so deep. Right, let's go!'

So they abandoned the devastated kitchen, wrapped themselves up and headed out into the garden. Sebastian hoisted Josh up onto his shoulders and the little boy anchored his chubby fingers into Sebastian's hair, his happy grin almost splitting his face in half.

'Wait, let me take a photo,' she said, and pulled out her phone. They posed dutifully, and she carried on, snapping off several shots of them as he turned and walked through the archway into the sunlit garden.

And it was glorious. He was right, it would have been criminal to miss it. The wind had died away completely and the sun shone with real warmth, sparkling on the snow and blinding them with its brilliance.

She scooped up a handful of snow and let Josh touch it, probing it with his finger. He was wary, but fascinated, and Sebastian lifted him down on the grass in the little orchard where the snow wasn't so deep and lowered him carefully into it, and Josh watched his feet disappear and giggled.

Then Sebastian turned and looked at her, and she knew what was coming.

She saw it in his eyes, saw the way he carefully gathered up a great big handful of snow and showed Josh how to squash it into a snowball.

'No. Sebastian, no! I mean it—!'

It got her right in the middle of the chest.

'Oh, you rat!' she squealed indignantly, and he just picked up her giggling son and laughed, his head tilted back, his mouth open, his face tipped up to the sun as Josh laughed with him, and if she could have bottled it, she would.

Instead she whipped out her phone and took a photo, the instant before he set Josh back in the snow.

Then she filed her phone safely in her pocket, because this was war and she wasn't taking any prisoners.

Sebastian's eyes were alight with mischief, and she scraped up a handful and hurled it back, missing him by miles. The next one got him, though, but not before his got her, and they ended up chasing each other through the snow, Sebastian carrying Josh in his arms, until he cornered her in one of the recesses of the crinkle-crankle wall and trapped her.

'Got that snowball, Josh?' he asked, advancing on her with a wicked smile that made her heart race for a whole lot of reasons, and he held her still, pinning her against the wall with his body while Josh put snow down her neck and made her shriek.

'Oh, that was so mean! Just you wait, Corder!'

'Oh, I'm so scared.' He grinned cockily, turning away, and she took her chance and pelted him right on the back of his neck.

'Like that, is it?' he said softly, and she felt her heart flip against her ribs.

But he did nothing, because they found a clear bit of snow where it wasn't too deep, and one by one they fell over backwards and made snow angels.

Josh's angel was a bit crooked, but Sebastian's was brilliant, huge and crisp and clean. How he stood up without damaging it she had no idea, but he did, and she looked down at it next to Josh's little angel and then hers, and felt something huge swelling in her chest.

And then she got a handful of snow shoved down the back of her neck, which would teach her to turn her back on Sebastian, and it jerked her out of her sentimental daze.

'Thought you'd got away with it, didn't you?' he teased, his mischievous grin taunting her, and she chased him through the orchard, dodging round the trees with Josh running after them and giggling hysterically.

Then he stopped, and she cannoned into him just as

he turned so that she ended up plastered against him, his arms locking reflexively round her to steady her.

And then he glanced up. She followed his gaze and saw the mistletoe, but it was too late. Too late to move or object or do anything except stand there transfixed, her heart pounding, while he smiled slowly and cupped her chilly, glowing face in his frozen hands and kissed her.

His lips were warm, their touch gentle, and the years seemed to melt away until she was eighteen again, and he was just twenty, and they were in love.

She'd forgotten.

She, who remembered everything about everything, had forgotten that all those Christmases ago he'd brought her here, to the orchard where that summer they'd made love in the dappled shade under the gnarled old apple trees, and kissed her.

Under this very mistletoe?

Possibly. It seemed very familiar, although the kiss was completely different.

That kiss had been wonderfully romantic and passionate. This one was utterly spontaneous and playful; tender, filled with nostalgia, it rocked her composure as passion never would have done. Passion she could have dismissed. This...

She backed away, her hand over her mouth, and spun round in the snow to look for Josh.

He was busy squashing more snow up, pressing his hands into it and laughing, and she waded over to him and picked him up, holding him against her like a shield.

'Oh, Josh, your hands are freezing! Come on, darling, time to go back inside.' And without waiting to see what Sebastian was doing, she carried Josh back to the relative safety of the house.

As she pulled off their snowy clothes in the boot

room, she noticed the little heap of mistletoe on the floor. It was still lying in the corner where he'd left it yesterday, and she'd forgotten all about it. Had he? Or had he taken her to the orchard deliberately, so he could kiss her right there underneath the tree where it had been growing for all these years? Where he'd kissed her all those Christmases ago?

If so, it had been a mistake. No kisses, she'd said, and he'd promised. They both had. And it had lasted a whole twenty-four hours.

Great. Fantastic. What a result...

Sebastian watched her go, kicking himself for that crazy, unnecessary lapse in common sense.

He hadn't even put up the mistletoe in the house because in the end it had seemed like such a bad idea, and then he'd brought her out here and they'd played in the snow just as they had eleven years ago, right under that great hanging bunch of mistletoe.

And he'd kissed her under it.

In front of Josh.

Of all the stupid, stupid things...

'Oh, you *idiot*.'

Shaking his head in disbelief, he made his way back inside and found she'd hung up their wet coats in front of the Aga to dry. Josh was playing on the floor with one of the cars out of his stocking, and she was pulling up her sleeves and getting stuck into the clearing up.

'I've put the kettle on,' she said. 'I thought we could do with a hot drink.'

'Good idea,' he said, but he noticed that she didn't look at him, and he only noticed that out of the corner of his eye because he was so busy not looking at her.

No repeats.

That had been the deal. He'd give Josh Christmas, and there'd be no recriminations, no harking back to their breakup, and no repeats of that kiss.

So far, it seemed, they were failing on all fronts.

Idiot! he repeated in his head, and pushing up his own sleeves, he tackled what was left.

'I'm sorry.'

The words were weary, and Georgie searched his eyes.

She'd put Josh to bed, waited until he was asleep and then forced herself to come downstairs. She'd hoped he'd be in the study, but he wasn't, he was in the kitchen making sandwiches with the left-over goose and cranberry sauce, and now she was here, too. Having walked in, there was no way of walking out without appearing appallingly rude, and then he'd turned to her and apologised.

And it had really only been a lighthearted, playful little kiss, she told herself, but she knew that she was lying.

'It's OK,' she said, although it wasn't, because it had affected her much more than she was letting on. She gave a little shrug. 'It was nothing really.'

'Well, I'll have to do better next time, then,' he said softly, and her eyes flew back to his.

'There won't be a next time. You promised.'

'I know. It was a joke.'

'Well, it wasn't funny.'

He sighed and rammed his hand through his hair, the smile leaving his eyes. 'We're not doing well, are we?'

'You're not. It was you that raised the walking out issue, you that kissed me. So far I think I've pretty much stuck to my side of the bargain.'

'Apart from running around in a scanty little towel that didn't quite meet.'

She felt hot colour run up her cheeks, and turned away. 'That was an accident. I was worried about Josh. And you didn't have a lot on, either.'

'No.' He sighed again. 'I have to say, as apologies go, this isn't going very well, is it?'

She gave a soft, exasperated laugh and turned back to him, meeting the wry smile in his eyes and relenting.

'Not really. Why don't we just draw a line under it and start again? As you said, it was warmer today. It'll thaw soon. We just have to get through the next day or two. I'm sure we can manage that.'

'I'm sure we can. I thought you might be hungry, so I threw something together.' He cut the sandwiches in quarters as he spoke, stacked them on a plate and put them on a tray. Glasses, side plates, cheese, a slab of fruit cake and the remains of lunchtime's bottle of Rioja followed, and he picked the tray up and walked towards her. 'Open the door?'

She opened it, followed him to the sitting room and sat down. This was so awkward. All of it, everything, was so awkward, pretending that it was all OK and being civilised when all they really wanted to do was yell at each other.

Or make love.

'George, don't.'

'Don't what?'

He sat down on the other sofa, opposite her, and held her eyes with his. 'Don't look like that. I know it's difficult. I'm sorry, I'm an idiot, I've just made it more uncomfortable, but—we were good friends once, Georgie—'

'We were lovers,' she said bluntly, and he smiled sadly.

'We were friends, too. We should be able to talk to each other in a civilised manner. We managed last night.'

'That was before you kissed me again.'

He sighed and rammed his hand through his hair, and she began to feel sorry for it.

'The kiss was nothing,' he said shortly, 'you know that, you said so yourself. And I'm sorry it upset you. It just seemed—right. Natural. The obvious thing to do. We were playing, and then there you were, right under the mistletoe, and—well, I just acted on impulse. It really, really won't happen again. I promise.'

She didn't challenge him on that. He'd promised to love her forever, and he'd driven her away. She knew about his promises. And hers weren't a lot better, because she'd promised to love him, too, and she'd left him.

What a mess. *Please, please thaw so we can get away from him…*

She reached for a sandwich and bit into it, and he sat forward, pouring the wine and sliding a glass towards her.

'You didn't tell me what you thought of this wine at lunch.'

'Is it important?'

He shrugged. 'In a way. I've got shares in the bodega. It's a good vintage. I just wondered if you liked it.'

'Yes, it's lovely.' She sipped, giving it thought. 'It goes well with the goose and the cranberries. It is nice—really nice, although if it's fiendishly expensive it's wasted on me. I could talk a lot of rubbish about it being packed with plump, luscious fruit and dark chocolate with a long, slow finish because I watch the television, but I wouldn't really know what I was talking about. But it is nice. I like it.'

He laughed. 'You don't need to know anything else. You just need to know what you like and what you don't like, and I like my wines soft. Rounded. Full of plump, luscious fruit,' he said, and there was something in his eyes that made her catch her breath and remember the gaping towel.

She looked hastily away, grabbing another sandwich and making a production of eating it, and he sat back and worked his way down a little pile of them, and for a while there was silence.

'So,' he said, breaking it at last, 'what's the plan for your house? You say you can't sell it at the moment, but what will you do when you have? Buy another? Rent?'

'Move back home.'

'Home? As in, come back and live with your parents?'

'Yes. I'll have childcare on tap, they'll get to see lots of Josh and I can work for my boss as easily here as I can in Huntingdon.'

He nodded, but there was a little crease between his eyebrows, the beginnings of a frown. 'Wouldn't you rather have your independence?'

She put down the shredded crusts of her sandwich and sighed. 'Well, of course, and I've tried that, but it doesn't feel like independence, really, not with Josh. It's just difficult. Every day's an uphill struggle to get everything done, hence watching the television when I'm too tired to work any more. There's no adult to talk to, I'm alone all day and all night except for the company of a two-year-old, and after he's in bed it's just lonely.'

The frown was back. 'He's very good company though when he is around. He's a great little kid.'

'He is, but his conversation is a wee bit lacking.'

Sebastian chuckled and reached for his wine. 'We don't seem to be doing so well, either.'

'So what do you want to talk about? Politics? The economy? Biogenetics? I can tell you all about that.'

'Is that what you do?'

'A bit. I don't really do anything any more. I just collate stuff for them and check for research trials and see if I can validate them. Some are a bit sketchy. It's an interesting field, genetic engineering, and it's going to be increasingly useful in medicine and agriculture in the future.'

'Tell me.'

So she talked about her work, about what her professor was doing at the moment, what they'd done, and what she'd been studying for her PhD before she'd had to abandon it.

'Would you like to finish it?' he asked, and she rolled her eyes.

'Of course! But I can't. I've got Josh now. I have other priorities.'

'But later?'

She shrugged. 'Later might be too late. Things move on, and what I was researching won't be relevant any longer. Things move so fast in genetics, so that what wasn't possible yesterday will be commonplace tomorrow. Take the use of DNA tests, for example. It's got all sorts of forensic and familial implications that simply couldn't have been imagined not that long ago, and now it's just accepted.'

His heart thumped.

'Familial implications? Things like tracing members of your family?' he suggested, keeping his voice carefully neutral.

'Yes. Yes, absolutely. It can be used to prove that people are or aren't related, it can tell you where in the world you've come from, where your distant ancestors came from—using mitochondrial DNA, which our bodies are absolutely rammed with, most Europeans can be traced back down the female line to one of a handful of women if you go back enough thousands of years. It's incredible.'

But not infallible. Not if you didn't know enough to start with. And not clever enough to give a match to someone who'd never been tested or had their DNA stored on a relevant database. He knew all about that and its frustrations.

Tell her.

'So, tell me about this bodega,' she said, settling back with a slab of fruitcake and a chunk of cheese, and he let the tension ease out of him at the change of subject.

'The bodega?'

'Mmm. I've decided it's a rather nice wine. I might have some more when I've finished eating. I'm not sure it'd go with cake and cheese.'

'I'm not sure cake and cheese go together in the first place.'

'You are joking?' She stared at him, her mouth slightly open. 'You're not joking. Try it.'

She held out the piece of cake with the cheese perched on top, the marks made by her even teeth clear at the edge of the bite, and he leant in and bit off the part her mouth had touched.

He felt something kick in his gut, but then the flavour burst through and he sat back and tried to concentrate on the cake and cheese combo and not the fact that he felt as if he'd indirectly kissed her.

'Wow. That is actually rather nice.'

She rolled her eyes again. 'You are so sceptical. It's like ham and pineapple, and lamb and redcurrant jelly.'

'Chalk and cheese.'

'Now you're just being silly. I thought you liked it?'

'I do.' He cut himself a chunk of both and put them together, mostly so he didn't have to watch her bite off the bit his own teeth had touched.

Hell. How could it be so ridiculously erotic?

'So—the bodega?'

'Um. Yeah.' He groped for his brain and got it into gear again, more or less, and told her all about it—about how he'd been driving along a quiet country road and he'd broken down and a man had stopped to help him.

'He turned out to be the owner of the bodega. He took me back there and contacted the local garage, and while we waited we got talking, and to cut a long story short I ended up bailing them out.'

'That was a good day's business for them.'

He chuckled. 'It wasn't a bad one for me. I stumbled on it by accident, I now own thirty per cent, and they're doing well. They've had three good vintages on the trot, I get a regular supply of wine I can trust, and we're all happy.'

'And if it's a bad year?'

'Then we've got the financial resilience to weather it.'

Or he had, she thought. They'd been lucky to find him.

'Where is it?' she asked. 'Does Rioja have to come from a very specific region?'

'Yes. It's in northern Spain. They grow a variety of

grapes—it's a region rather than a grape variety, and they use mostly Tempranillo which gives it that lovely softness.'

He opened another bottle, a different vintage, and as he told her about it, about how they made it, the barrels they used, the effect of the climate, he stopped thinking about her mouth and what it would be like to kiss her again, and began to relax and just enjoy her company.

He didn't normally spend much time like this, and certainly not with anyone as interesting and restful to be with as Georgie. Not nearly enough, he realised. He was too busy, too harassed, too driven by the workload to take time out. And that was a mistake.

Hence why he'd turned off his mobile phone and ignored it for the last twenty-four hours. It was Christmas. He was allowed a day off, and he intended to take advantage of every minute of it. Tomorrow would come soon enough.

He peeled a satsuma from the bowl and threw it to her, and peeled himself another one, then they cracked some nuts and threw the shells in the fire and watched it die down slowly.

It seemed as if neither of them wanted to move, to call it a night, to do anything to disturb the fragile truce, and so they sat there, staring into the fire and talking about safe subjects.

Uncontroversial ones, with no bones of contention, no trigger points, no sore spots, as if by mutual agreement. They talked about his mother's heart attack, her father's retirement plans, his plans for the restoration of the walled garden, and gradually the fire died away to ash and it grew chilly in the room.

'I ought to go up and make sure Josh is all right,' she said, although the baby monitor was there on the table and hadn't done more than blink a couple of times, just enough so they knew it was working.

But he didn't argue, because they were running out of safe topics and it was better to quit while they were winning and before he did something stupid like kiss her.

He got to his feet, gathered up their glasses and put them on the tray with the plates, made sure the fire guard was secure and carried the tray through to the kitchen.

She was getting herself a glass of water, and he put the tray down beside the sink and turned towards her.

'Got everything you need?'

No, she thought. She needed him, but he wasn't good for her, and she certainly hadn't been good for him. Not in the long term. 'Yes, I'm fine,' she said, and then hesitated.

His eyes were unreadable, but the air was thick with tension. It would have been so natural, so easy to lean in and kiss him goodnight.

So dangerous.

So tempting...

She paused in the doorway and looked back, and he was watching her, his face shuttered.

'Thank you for today,' she said quietly. 'It's been really lovely. Really lovely. Josh has had a brilliant time, and so've I.'

'Even the kiss?'

She laughed softly. 'There was never any doubt about your kisses, Sebastian. None at all.'

'Wrong place, wrong time?' he suggested, and she shook her head.

'Wrong time.'

'And the place?'

'You can never go back,' she said simply, and with a sad smile, she closed the door and left him standing there in what should have been their kitchen, gazing after the woman he still loved but knew he'd lost forever.

'Damn,' he said softly.

It was a fine time to discover that he still wanted her, that he still loved her, that he should have done more to stop her leaving. But his head had been in the wrong place then, and hers was now.

You should have told her.

He should. But he hadn't, and now wasn't the time.

It was too late. She'd moved on, and so had he.

Hadn't he?

He poured himself another glass of wine and left the kitchen, retreating into his study and the thing that kept him sane. Work. Always work. The one constant in his life.

He turned his phone on, and it beeped at him furiously as the emails and messages came pouring in. Even on Christmas Day. He was obviously not the only workaholic, he thought drily, and then he opened them.

Greetings. Christmas greetings from family, friends, work colleagues.

And he'd meant to contact all of them, and so far had only rung his immediate family.

He'd do it now. He had nothing better to do, either, and it beat lying in bed next to Georgie's room and listening to the sounds of her getting ready for bed. Although even in his study he could hear her, because she was immediately overhead.

He listened to the sound of water running, the creak of the boards as she crossed the room to the bed. A different creak as she climbed into it and lay down.

He tried to tune it out, but it was impossible, so he put

the radio on quietly. Carols from King's College, Cambridge, flooded the room and drowned out the sound of her movements.

Pity they couldn't drown out his thoughts…

CHAPTER EIGHT

'MUMMY! MUMMY, WAKE up!'

She prised her eyes open. Light was leaking round the edges of the curtains, and it looked—astonishingly—like sunlight. She propped herself up on one elbow and scraped her hair back out of her eyes.

'Hello, Mummy!'

He was beaming at her, and she felt her heart melt. 'Hello, darling. Are you all right? Did you sleep well?'

He nodded vigorously. He was standing in the cot, bobbing up and down with unchannelled energy, and he looked bright-eyed and bushy-tailed.

'Want Bastian,' he said. 'Play in snow.'

The cot rocked wildly, and she sat up and grabbed the edge to steady it. 'Let's get up first, shall we? Nappy, drink, clothes on? Then we'll see.'

He nodded and held up his arms, and she lifted him out. He was warm and he smelled of sleepy baby, and she breathed him in and snuggled him close for a moment, but he wasn't having any of it. There was snow outside with his name on it, and he wanted out.

Now.

She changed his nappy, hesitated for a moment and pulled on his clothes, then dressed herself quickly, just in case Sebastian was around. That almost-kiss last night was still tormenting her as it had been all night so she wasn't going to tempt fate, but Josh was starving and in a hurry.

Teeth and a quick wash could wait till after breakfast, she decided, and opened the bedroom door to the wonderful smell of bacon cooking. And toast, the aromas wafting up the stairs and making her mouth water.

He turned as she went in, frying pan in hand, and smiled at them. 'You're up bright and early.'

'Well, someone is,' she said drily, as Josh ran over to Sebastian and put his arms round his legs, tilting his head back and looking up pleadingly.

'Want snow,' he said, and Sebastian gave a slightly stunned laugh.

'Whoa, little fella, it's a bit early for that. How about some nice breakfast first?' He looked across at Georgie. 'Does he like bacon sandwiches?'

She laughed. 'Probably. He's never had one, but he likes bacon and he eats sandwiches. And I certainly do.'

His smile was a little twisted, his voice soft. 'I know.'

Of course he did. They'd had bacon sandwiches for breakfast every Sunday morning when they'd been together, either at home or in a café. And he hadn't forgotten, apparently, any more than she had.

Those dangerous emotions swirled in the air for a moment, carried, like the memories, on the smell of frying bacon, and she pulled herself together with an effort.

'Can I do anything?' she asked briskly. 'Make tea? Coffee?'

'Tea. I've had coffee. I've been up a couple of hours.'

'Really?'

She glanced at the old school-style clock on the wall and did a mild double-take.

'It's after eight! When did that happen?'

'While you were sleeping?' he said, his eyes gently mocking. 'I was about to come up and open the bedroom door when I heard Josh chatting. I knew you wouldn't be long if I let the smell of bacon in.'

'Like one of Pavlov's dogs?'

'If the cap fits...'

'You are so rude.' She stared at the worktop blankly. 'What was I doing?'

'Making tea?' he offered, his mouth twitching, and she threw the tea towel at him and put the kettle on while he moved the bacon to the slower burner and sliced some bread.

In the time it took her to make the tea and give Josh a drink of milk, he'd flipped the bacon out onto kitchen paper to drain, cracked some eggs into a pan and scrambled them while the toast cooked, sliced some tomatoes, split the toast and made a stack of club sandwiches.

'He might be happier with bread,' she said, but Josh reached out, his little hand opening and closing frantically. 'Me have Bastian sandwich,' he said.

He was getting a serious and rather worrying case of hero worship, she realised with a sigh, but she shrugged and cut him off a chunk. She didn't think he'd eat it, but he did, and demanded more.

'I'm not sure I'm going to give him any more, this is soooo good,' she mumbled through a mouthful, and Sebastian just laughed and handed Josh the rest of his own.

Just like a father would.

She blinked, sucked in a quiet breath and gave herself a mental shake. He was *not* Josh's father, and he wasn't going to be his stepfather, or surrogate father, or even a best uncle! He was nobody to Josh except an old friend of hers who'd rescued them one Christmas, and that was the way it had to stay if she didn't want to risk him getting hurt. Hero worship notwithstanding.

Frankly, he'd lost enough already. And so had she.

'Right, I'm going out to clear the drive. The snow's beginning to soften slightly. It didn't freeze last night, and with the sun on it the drive might thaw if I can get most of the snow off it. I wouldn't be surprised if they don't clear the lane tomorrow.'

'Not today?' she asked, sort of hopefully, although a part of her definitely didn't want it cleared yet.

'Not on Boxing Day,' he said. 'It's unlikely. They'll be clearing the main roads still, making sure the urban areas are safe for the majority of the population. This lane is incredibly small potatoes in comparison. It's probably not even on their to-do list so it might be a local farmer.'

She nodded slowly. That made sense, and if the farmer had stock, he might be too busy with them to worry about the lane for days.

And she wasn't at all sure how that made her feel.

Yes, she was!

She had to get out of here before—well, before it got any worse. Before Josh's idolisation of Sebastian got out of proportion. And before one or other of them cracked big-time and gave into the magnetic tug of attraction that time didn't seem to have done anything to weaken. And that meant being able to get the car out.

'If you've got another shovel, can I give you a hand?'

'I haven't, but you can come out and cheerlead if you like. I'm sure Josh'll have fun out there playing in the snow, won't you, Josh? There aren't any roses or anything lurking under the snow to hurt him, not near the drive, so he can't come to any harm.'

'Me snow!' he begged, bouncing up and down beside her, his eyes pleading, and she gave up the unequal struggle. They didn't have to stay out there for long.

'Teeth first, and then we'll go outside. OK?'

'OK!'

He ran off, heading towards the stairs, with Georgie in hot pursuit, and as they left the kitchen Sebastian found himself smiling.

Why?

Because he was happy?

Because they were coming outside to help him clear the drive, and he'd get to play with Josh again?

Not to mention Georgie...

Stop it!

They could make a snowman, he thought, dragging his mind back to the child, and he tracked down a carrot for his nose and two Brussels sprouts for eyes, then wrapped up warm and went outside to get started.

The snow wasn't quite as deep as it had been, but there was still quite enough of it and the first thing he did was cut a path through to the gates and clear around the bottom of them so they had room to swing open.

Assuming the mechanism wasn't frozen solid. It had better not be, he'd paid enough for them to be restored and the electric openers to be fitted.

He wouldn't test them. Not yet, not until the sun had time to get on them and warm them up a little, but he could clear the rest of the snow from in front of them.

He'd hardly started when Georgie and Josh arrived. He'd heard them coming, Josh's excited chatter reaching him long before Georgie's mellow tones.

'How are you doing?'

'OK. It's slow.'

'Is it OK if we build a snowman?' she asked.

He straightened up and turned to look at them. Josh

was busy making a snowball, crouched down with his little bottom stuck out and perched on the snow, and Georgie, bundled up in her coat and gloves, looked so like she had all those years ago when they'd played in the orchard right here that his heart tugged.

He pulled out the carrot and sprouts. 'Great minds think alike,' he said with a smile, and handed them to her.

'What's that?' Josh asked, peering at them, the snow-ball forgotten.

'His nose and eyes,' he said, and got a sceptical look, but Georgie just laughed, the sound rippling through him like a shock wave.

'You'll see, Josh. Now, where shall we build him?'

'Over there?' Sebastian suggested, pointing at a piece of ground he knew was firm and flat, so they went over to it, and she started rolling up a ball to make the body while he carried on shovelling the drive.

'Gosh, it's heavy!'

He turned to watch her. She was shoving it with both hands, and after a moment her feet slipped and she face-planted into the snow.

He had to laugh.

He couldn't help it, and nor could Josh, the laughter bubbling up inside them irresistibly, but then he re-lented and went over and held out a hand, hauling her to her feet.

Her eyes were laughing, even though she was pre-tending to be cross with them, and she brushed herself off and straightened, just inches from him. There was a trickle of melting snow on her cheek, and he wiped it gently away with his thumb.

Their eyes met and locked, and for a moment time

seemed suspended. Then Josh floundered over to them, and the spell was broken, and he breathed again.

'Need a hand with your snowman?' he asked.

'I never turn down muscle when it's offered,' she said, and he chuckled.

'I take it that's a yes,' he said and, abandoning the shovel, he joined in the fun.

'There!'

He'd rolled up a smaller ball for the head, heaved it on top of the body and set it in a little hollow so it didn't rock off, and she'd pushed in the carrot and sprouts to make his face and found a stick for a pipe.

They were standing back to admire their handiwork, and Georgie frowned.

'He needs a scarf,' she said, and he shrugged and unravelled the scarf from round his neck.

She blinked. 'I can't use that,' she said, sounding scandalised. 'It's a really nice one. It feels like cashmere.'

He shrugged again. 'It's fine.'

It meant he wouldn't have one until the snow went, but that didn't matter. He could rescue it then, and it could be washed. Even if it got ruined, which it probably would, he realised he didn't care.

Didn't care at all, because Josh was giggling and having a brilliant time, and that was all that mattered.

But then the brilliant time came to an end. His fingers were cold, his nose was bright red and he was hungry, and Georgie took him back inside, leaving Sebastian to his shovelling.

He studied the drive, assessing the task.

Monumental, really. He would be there all day, but

it needed doing, and the hard physical exertion was a distraction from his thoughts.

It worked well, until he had to stop for a while, straightening up with a groan and shoving his hands in the small of his back and arching it out straight.

'Ouch.' Clearly not as fit as he imagined he was.

He turned to look at the snowman, and found himself smiling.

His eyes weren't on the same level, his nose was bent, his head wasn't quite in the middle, but the scarf looked good.

He gave a wry huff of laughter. So it should, but it had been worth it just to see the little boy's face. And Georgie's.

He felt a wash of emotion that he didn't really want to analyse. It felt curiously like happy families, and it felt good, and that wasn't a great idea. Not at all.

Damn. It's not going to happen. Don't go there.

He went back to the shovelling, working until the burning in his back muscles forced him to stop. He creaked up straight, studied the drive again and shrugged.

The gates had opened when he'd tested them, and the area beyond the gates was cleared, as was the drive for the first thirty or so feet. His car would get through the uncleared bit if he took it steady. All he needed now was for the farmer to come and clear the lane, and he was home free.

Or, rather, she would be.

He ignored the stab of something that he didn't want to think about, and headed inside into the warm. Not that his body was cold, but his nose and ears were a bit chilly and his hands were cold where the gloves had got soaked making the snowman.

With any luck, he thought as he kicked off his boots, Georgie and Josh would be in the little sitting room and he could go straight into his study and distract himself in there.

They weren't. They were in the kitchen, Josh playing on the floor with a little car, and the air was full of the aroma of freshly brewed coffee.

She walked over to the boot room door and leant on the frame with a smile. 'You've saved me a journey,' she said. 'I was just about to bring you a drink.'

'I'm done. My back aches and I've cleared enough.'

She tsked under her breath. 'I knew you'd do too much. Where does it hurt? Do you want me to rub it for you?'

He gave her an incredulous look. 'I don't think that's a good idea.'

'But you're hurting.'

He sighed softly and met her eyes, his dark with all manner of nameless emotions that made her heart lurch in her chest. 'Let me put it in words of one syllable,' he said slowly. 'I am trying-'

'That's two,' she said, trying to lighten the stifling atmosphere.

He rolled his eyes. 'OK,' he said, his voice ultrasoft so Josh wouldn't hear. 'I. Need. To. Keep. My. Hands. Off. You. And. If. You. Touch. Me. That. Will. Not. Help!'

And without waiting for her to make some sassy reply, he cupped her shoulders in his hands, moved her out of his way and forced himself to walk away from temptation.

Georgie closed her eyes and blew out her breath slowly.

What an idiot she was! Of course he didn't want her

touching him! It was hard enough as it was. Throw any more fuel on the fire between them and it would rage out of control like a bushfire. And neither of them needed that.

Yes...!

No! No, no, no, no, NO!

She poured a coffee for him, told Josh she would only be a moment and followed him to his study, her heart pounding.

She knew he was there because the music was on and she could hear it from the kitchen doorway. She tapped, pushed the door open and went in, leaving the door open for safety.

'Coffee,' she said, setting it down on the mat on his desk, and he turned his head and looked up at her.

'George—I'm sorry. It's just...'

'I know. It's my fault. I wasn't thinking. I'll see you later for lunch. Half an hour OK?'

He nodded. 'That would be great. Thanks.'

She took herself back to the kitchen, poured a coffee for herself and took Josh back into the little sitting room to play with the train set for a few minutes. It was nearer to Sebastian, but they weren't making a lot of noise and she didn't think they'd disturb him, especially not over the music.

But then the door opened and he came in, cup in hand, and joined them.

Why?

Because he couldn't stay away?

'I've just spoken to the local farmer. He's going to clear the lane. He'll make a start today, but it might be tomorrow before he gets to the gate.'

'Oh. Right.' She forced a smile. 'Well, that's good to know. I'll tell my mother to expect us.'

'So—shall I get lunch?'

'Goose sandwiches?' she teased, but he shook his head.

'We had sandwiches for breakfast and for supper. It might be time for something more imaginative. We have a whole groaning larder to choose from.'

They did.

She made a winter salad tossed in a honey and mustard dressing to go with the goose which he shredded and crisped in the oven, and Josh had a little of it with some pasta and pesto and a handful of cherry tomatoes.

'That was nice and healthy,' she said, and he laughed and got out the Christmas cake.

'It was. And I'm starving. You can be too healthy. Want cheese with it?'

'Mmm. And tea.'

She cubed some cheese for Josh, gave him a sliver of the cake without icing and then cut them both a chunk.

Sebastian was munching his way through a slab the size of his hand when he glanced up and frowned.

'It's raining!'

'What?'

She turned and looked out of the window.

Rain. Only light rain, but rain, not snow. And that meant a sudden thaw.

'It could flood tomorrow,' she said.

'It could, if it keeps on. In the meantime, I guess my activities on the drive are over.'

'Well, it won't be necessary anyway if it's going to rain hard. It's a pity, though. I was hoping I could take Josh outside again for a bit more running around.'

Sebastian shrugged. 'There's plenty of room in the house. He can run around in here, can't you, Josh?'

'Well, that's true,' she said. 'If he just tears up and down the hall he'll wear himself out in half an hour.'

'Play hide and seek?' Josh said hopefully, and Sebastian smiled indulgently at him.

'Sure. Heaven knows there are plenty of places to hide,' he said drily, his eyes flicking up to Georgie's.

There were. More than enough. And she'd hidden in all of them, and he'd found her.

And kissed her.

She looked hastily away.

'I think we could stick to the ground floor.'

'Or the attic?'

'The attic? Have you done anything with it?'

'Not much. It's been cleaned out and repaired when the roof was sorted, but it's pretty much as it was. I thought the house was big enough for me with just two floors.'

'What's a tick?' Josh asked, looking puzzled, and Georgie suppressed a smile.

'Not a tick, an attic. It's—well, we'll show you, shall we? It's just the very, very, very upstairs.'

'Oh.'

Sebastian chuckled softly. 'I can hear the cogs turning.'

'Oh, yeah. Watching him learn is amazing. Let's go and show him.'

He opened the door at the top of the stairs, and Georgie followed him and looked around, her eyes wide.

'Gosh. It looks enormous now you can see it all. It used to be full of cobwebs and birds' nests and clutter.'

'It was—especially the clutter. We lost count of the number of skips it took to take it all away.'

'Was there anything interesting?'

'There was, but most of the stuff was damaged because the birds had got in. I've got some of the things that were rescued downstairs, but most of it was beyond saving. And there was a lot of rubbish. You know what people are like. They put stuff away and leave it "just in case", and then forget it.'

She walked slowly through the rooms, Josh's hand firmly in hers, and checked that it was safe. It was. There was nothing that could harm him, and so she let go of his hand.

'Right. Are we going to play hide and seek?'

'Yay! Hide and seek! Yay!'

Josh was bouncing on the spot, and she put her hands over her eyes and peeped through her fingers.

'You peeping!' he said, and she laughed.

'I'm going to count. Josh, Sebastian, go and hide!'

He grabbed Josh by the hand and grinned. 'Come on. I know a good place.'

He did. It was under the eaves, behind the chimney, and he pulled Josh in there and held him close.

'Ready or not, here I come!'

He could hear her footsteps coming, and Josh started to giggle.

'Shh,' he whispered. 'Don't make a sound.'

He could hear her footsteps coming, going into another room, then coming closer, closer...

Like the walls, closing in on him, the small boy leaning on his leg, a voice saying 'Shh,' the sound almost inaudible in the silence.

Silence broken only by the sound of footsteps...

A sudden wave of panic came out of nowhere, and he tried to swallow it, but it wouldn't subside, and with a sudden rush he straightened and burst out of the tight space and into the light.

'Sebastian?'

She was right there, staring at him curiously, her mouth moving, but he could hardly hear her through the pounding of his heart. It was running like an express train, deafening him, and he made some vague excuse about having something to do and walked swiftly away on legs like overcooked spaghetti.

Georgia stared after him.

Busy? It was Boxing Day, all businesses except retail outlets were closed.

No. It was just an excuse not to be with her and Josh. Maybe he felt she was just sucking him in again?

But it had seemed like more than that. Much more. There had been something in his eyes...

No matter. He'd left, claiming pressure of work, and so she left him to it and played with Josh for a while, hiding in easy to find places, making enough noise to give him a clue, and they giggled and hugged and had fun.

And all the time, in the back of her mind, was Sebastian. And she was troubled, for some reason.

'Right, that's enough of hide and seek. It's very dirty up here. Shall we go and play with your train again?'

'Bastian play with me?'

'No, darling, he's busy, but I will. Of course I will.'

But first, she had to find Sebastian. She sorted Josh out, settled him down with the train set and went to find him.

He was in the study, of course, doing something on his computer, and he glanced up at her and carried on.

'OK, what's going on?'

'Nothing. I'm fine. I'm just busy.'

'No, you aren't. Sebastian, talk to me. What's the matter? What happened back there?'

'Nothing. I just don't like being shut in. You know that. It's why I never go in a lift.'

'I know, but—'

'But nothing. It's fine.'

'It's not fine. You ought to see someone about that,' she told him softly. 'They can do things about claustrophobia.'

'I take the stairs. It's good for me.'

'But—'

'Georgia, leave it.'

Georgia. Not George, not Georgie.

She hesitated a moment, then gave a defeated little shrug and walked away. He was shutting her out again, shutting her out as he always did.

Well, she was tired of fighting him. With any luck the rain which she'd heard gurgling in the gutters was washing away the snow on the roads, and first thing in the morning, as soon as the lane was clear, she was off, because she just couldn't do this any more.

He didn't appear again that day. She cooked supper for Josh, then took him up and bathed him and put him to bed, and when she came down she could see that Sebastian had helped himself to something.

A goose sandwich, ironically, she thought from the evidence left scattered about on the worktop. And carefully timed for when she was out of the way.

She shrugged. Oh, well, if he didn't want her company, she wasn't going to force it on him. And even though she didn't really need another sandwich, she made herself one and ate it at the table. Just in case he was in the little sitting room.

He wasn't.

She realised that after she'd finished her sandwich and cleared up the kitchen. She'd made a cup of tea, and picking up the baby monitor she went out into the hall. It was dimly lit, and she could see light coming under the study door, but the door to the little sitting room was open and it was dark inside.

Fair enough. She'd sit in there, watch the television and start packing up Josh's toys.

Once the lane was cleared, she didn't want to be here a minute longer than necessary. They'd clearly outstayed their welcome, and she felt emotionally exhausted.

So exhausted, in fact, that she went up to bed as soon as she'd dismantled the little train set. Josh didn't stir when she went in, and she turned off the monitor, put it down on the bedside table and got ready for bed in the bathroom.

She would have liked to read, but her book was in the car and anyway she doubted she'd be able to concentrate. She lay down, closed her eyes and tried not to think about him, but it was impossible.

Her mind was full of images—him playing in the snow with Josh, shovelling snow, laughing at her as she fell on her face, kissing her under the mistletoe—and coming out from behind the chimney in the attic as if the hounds of hell were after him. He'd always been claustrophobic, but it had looked like more than that.

No. He'd never liked being shut in. He never went in lifts, as he'd reminded her, and he'd never hidden anywhere cramped when they'd been playing hide and seek.

He'd been rubbish at hiding. Good at finding, but rubbish at hiding. And he'd been hiding with Josh, in behind the chimney. It was tight in there, tight and dark, and although she'd never been afraid of it, she could see why he might have been.

Well, it had been his idea to go in the attic, and a bit of claustrophobia wasn't going to have kept him holed up in his study for the rest of the day.

No, he was sick of them being there, interrupting his routine, cluttering up his house and his life and just generally taking over. Well, just a few more hours and she'd be gone. She'd looked out of the bathroom window and the snow was patchy already. By the morning, it would be clear and she could get away.

And she wouldn't need to see him again.

The noise woke her.

Not a scream, more of a muffled shout, a cry of pain.

Sebastian.

She grabbed the baby monitor and tiptoed out of the room, closing the door behind her. His door was never completely closed, but as she opened it further she could hear him breathing fast, muttering in his sleep, wordless sounds of distress.

The dream again. 'Sebastian?'

She switched on the bedside light and reached for him, shaking his shoulder gently.

'Sebastian? Wake up. It's a dream. It's just a dream.'

His eyes flew open and locked on hers, and then he turned away, throwing his arm up over his eyes, his chest heaving.

He looked awful. His face was ashen, his eyes wary, and he was breathing hard, as if he'd been running, and it shocked her.

'Sebastian?'

She reached out a hand and touched him tentatively,

and he dropped his arm and dragged a hand down over his face.

'I'm all right. I didn't mean to disturb you. Go back to bed.'

'You had the dream again, didn't you?'

He swallowed hard.

'I'm fine.'

'No, you're not. Do you want a cup of tea?'

He shook his head. 'No. You need to be with Josh.'

But he was shaking all over, his skin grey, and she turned on the baby monitor and put it on the bedside cabinet, then got into bed beside him and pulled him into her arms.

'It's OK,' she said, murmuring to him as she would to Josh. 'It's OK. I've got you.'

He shuddered, and then slumped his head against her shoulder, letting the tension out of his body in a rush. 'I'm sorry.'

'Don't be. I wish you'd talk to me.'

'No. I don't want to talk about it.'

But he needed her, and she was there, just there, in his bed, in his arms, and he gave up fighting. His hand came up and cradled her face, his fingers still shaking, and then his mouth was on hers, her body under his, her hands running over him as she made desperate little pleading noises.

He lifted his head and she followed him, her mouth searching for his, her lips clinging, and he followed her back down to the pillow and let go of the last shred of his self-control.

CHAPTER NINE

WHEN HE WOKE in the morning, he was alone.

Had he dreamed it?

Dreamed it all, not just *the dream*—hell, he hadn't had it for ages, but last night—and then afterwards…

Had she come to him?

No.

Or had she? It had seemed so real…

He rolled his face into the pillow and breathed in, and the faint, lingering scent of her perfume dragged him right back to the dream.

No. Not the dream. The thing that wasn't a dream. The thing that had been a really, really bad idea.

Damn.

He rolled onto his back and stared at the ceiling. It was dark outside, and he could hear the rain falling, but his watch had beeped ages ago which meant it was long after six.

He peered at the hands. Six forty-eight. Nearly seven.

He threw back the bedclothes and hit the shower, standing under the pounding blast and letting it wash away the fog of fear and confusion that lingered in the corners of his mind.

And with the washing away of the fog came clarity, and with it, the realisation of just what he'd done.

He must have been crazy! How could he have let himself do that? Of all the stupid, stupid things—

He turned off the water and stepped out, burying his face in the towel for a long moment before towelling himself roughly dry.

He heard something—machinery?—and strode to the window, yanking the curtain out of the way.

There were lights on the lane; a tractor, clearing the snow in the almost-dark. The drive looked almost completely free of snow.

Which meant Georgie could leave.

Good. That was good, he told himself, but it didn't feel good, and just underlined how big a mistake he'd made last night. Well, never again. He was done with breaking his heart over Georgia Beckett.

He was up.

She could hear him moving around in his room, hear the water running. Josh was playing on the floor, and she'd showered and dressed and she was packing their things.

His cot, with the bedding Sebastian had lent her. All their wash things. Random toys and bits and pieces scattered about all over the room by Josh.

She checked under the bed and found the nappy cream she'd lost last night, and put it in the changing bag. Time he was potty trained, anyway. She'd do that as soon as she was home, but she hadn't wanted to do anything when he was out of routine. Not a good time to set yourself up for a fall.

And talking of doing that, what had she been thinking about last night? Why get into bed with him? *On* the bed, maybe, but *in* it?

Asking for trouble, and she'd got it, with bells on.

He needed you.

And you needed him, every bit as much.

'Josh, come on, let's take these things downstairs and we can go and have breakfast with Grannie and Grandpa!'

'Now?'

She nodded, dredging up a bright smile from somewhere. 'Yes. Look. The farmer's cleared all the snow from the lane. We can get out now, and go to Grannie's house.'

'Bastian come?'

Oh, here we go. 'No, darling. Sebastian lives here.'

'Us live here.'

'No. We can't, Josh. It's not our house, and anyway, we've got a house already.'

He stuck his chin out. 'Want Bastian.'

So did she, but it wasn't going to happen in this lifetime.

She picked up the travel cot, slung the changing bag over her shoulder and pulled up the handle on her case. 'Come on, downstairs, please.'

She trundled the case to the top of the stairs, then picked it up and struggled down the first few steps.

Then a firm hand on her shoulder stopped her, the case was removed from her grasp, the travel cot removed from the other hand and Sebastian carried them down to the kitchen without a word.

'Anything else up there?'

He met her eyes, but warily, and she felt hers skitter away. 'No. That's everything. There's just the train set. I packed it up last night. Oh, and the bag of presents in your room.'

He nodded, went and got everything and returned, putting the train set boxes on the big kitchen table where they seemed to have shared so many important moments in the last few days.

Josh was trailing him, talking to him non-stop, asking if they could live there, if he was coming for breakfast with Grannie, if they were coming back.

He either didn't understand Josh, which was possible, or didn't want to understand, which was much more likely.

'Josh, leave Sebastian alone, we can't stay here and he's not coming with us,' she said softly, and he started to cry.

'Hey. Don't cry, little guy,' Sebastian said, finally relenting and crouching down to Josh's level. 'Mummy's right. You can't stay here, you have to go home to your house, and I can't come with you because I have to stay here in mine.'

'Me stay here,' he said, and he wrapped his arms tightly round Sebastian's neck and hung on.

A pained expression crossed his face for a fleeting second, and he hugged him briefly, but then he gently but firmly disentangled the little boy's arms and prised him away, setting him down on the floor and standing up. 'Come on, Josh, don't cry. You're going to see your Grannie.'

But Josh's arms were wrapped round his legs now, and Georgie unwrapped them and picked him up, sobbing piteously, and Sebastian pushed past her and pulled on his coat and sloshed across to the coach-house to get her car out.

He was gone longer than she expected, but then she heard the car pull up. 'The traction seems fine, the slush is really wet,' he said as he came back in, leaving the car running just by the door. 'The drive's fine and the lane's clear. I just drove down to have a look. You should be OK.'

OK? She doubted it, but she nodded and pulled her coat on, one arm at a time with Josh still in her arms, and then while Sebastian put their luggage in the car, she sat down on a chair to put Josh's coat on.

He wasn't having any of it.

'Come on, Josh,' she pleaded, but he just made it even harder, burrowing into her and hiding his hands, so she carried him out to the car as he was and strapped him in.

'Will he be all right without it?'

'He'll be fine,' she said crisply. 'Look, I think I've got everything but it's really hard with Josh, he carts stuff about all over the place. If you find anything, maybe you could pile it all up and my father could come and collect it.'

He nodded. 'Or I can post it to you.'

'They can do that,' she said, reluctant to give him her address. She really, really didn't need any more scenes like this one.

And then there was nothing more to say but good-bye, and thank you.

For what?

For opening his home to her, but not his heart?

For making love to her one last time, so she could treasure it in the cold, lonely hours of the nights to come?

For saving her son's life?

'I'll miss you,' he said gruffly. 'Both of you.'

Her eyes flooded with tears, and she nodded. She couldn't speak. Couldn't move. Couldn't do anything except stand there mutely and blink away the stupid, stupid tears—

His thumbs were gentle as he wiped them away.

'Don't cry, George. We're no good for each other.'

But they had been. All this time, the last few days, they'd got on really, really well. Except for the times they hadn't.

She tried to smile, but it was a shaky effort.

'Goodbye, Sebastian. And thank you. For everything.'

Going up on tiptoe, she pressed a gentle, rather wistful kiss to his lips, and then turned and walked out of the door, her head bowed against the rain, her eyes flooding with tears as she left the man she'd never stopped loving standing on the step behind her.

She didn't look back.

He was glad. If she had, he might have weakened, said something.

Like what? Begging her to stay?

He opened the gates remotely from the hall, watched on the security camera as her car turned out of the drive and headed left, the direction the farmer had cleared already.

The car slithered a little, and he frowned. He had his coat on. His keys were in his pocket. He had to make sure she was safe.

He followed her, staying well behind out of sight, and ten minutes later he cruised by the end of her parents' drive.

Her car was there, and her father was carrying her things in, her mother was holding Josh and Georgie was lifting the bag of presents out of the front of the car.

She was safe. Home, and safe.

Duty discharged.

He went home, turned into the drive and saw the

soggy remains of the snowman wilting gently on the lawn beside the drive. His nose had fallen out, and one of his eyes, and the scarf had definitely seen better days.

He left it there. It seemed wrong to take it off until the snowman had gone completely, and anyway, it was already ruined.

Everything, he discovered, seemed wrong.

The house, which until Monday had seemed calm and peaceful and a haven, was silent and empty.

The kitchen echoed to his footsteps. The boot room had a little coat, a snuggly jacket and two pairs of wellies missing from it. And under the table was a toy car.

He picked it up, tossing it pensively in his hand. It was a toy Josh might never have played with, if things had been different. If he hadn't been here. If the snow had come a little earlier, or she'd stopped a little later.

If nothing else, Josh and his mother were still alive, they still had each other and they could move on with their lives. And so could he.

Even if the house echoed with every sound he made.

He made some toast and coffee, took it through to the study and paused en route to check the little sitting room.

And saw the Christmas tree, festooned with all the little toys and sticks and fir cones Georgie had made at the kitchen table and Josh had put on the tree.

There were no gingerbread trees or stars left.

Or at least, only one. High up, out of Josh's reach.

He left it there, left it all there and went into the study and phoned his mother.

'Hi. The lane's clear. When do you want to come?'

'Oh. That was quick. Are you all right?'

'Of course I'm all right. Why wouldn't I be?'

'You tell me, darling,' his mother said softly. 'How's Georgie?'

'She's fine. Look, I don't want to talk about this. Are you coming over, or not?'

'Oh, we're coming, whenever you're ready for us. Andrew and Matthew are here, too. Shall we come now?'

'That would be fine. Come as soon as you like.'

'Do you have anything left to eat, or do you want us to get something on the way?'

He gave a slightly strangled laugh. 'There's plenty here. I've got a joint of beef. We can have it for dinner tonight.'

And maybe having a full house would drown out the echoes…

'I knew it.'

'Knew what?'

'That you'd be upset.'

Georgie put the tea towel down on the worktop and rolled eyes. 'Mum, don't start—'

'Sorry. I'm sorry, but you look so—'

'Mum…'

'OK. Point taken. I'll back off. So—how was your Christmas?'

Wonderful. Heartbreakingly wonderful.

'I don't really want to talk about it,' she said. 'He did us a huge favour, he made a real effort to be nice to Josh who's completely idolised him as you might have guessed, and it's over now and I'd rather just forget it. How was yours?'

'Oh, quiet. We missed you. We were on our own, of course, so I put the turkey in the freezer, but I've got a chicken in the fridge so we could have it for supper or even a late lunch. We've still got most of the trimmings. We could still make it a proper Christmas dinner.'

She forced a smile. She wasn't really hungry, but she owed her mother the courtesy of good manners. 'That would be lovely. Thank you. Want me to peel some potatoes?'

'If you like. It would be nice to have your company, and Josh seems happy enough for now with his Grandpa and the train set.'

Except for the word 'Bastian' that seemed to crop up in every conversation...

He went back to London as soon as his parents and brothers went.

He hadn't intended to, but the empty house was driving him insane, so he loaded up the car with a ton of fresh food out of the pantry and took it to the refuge. He was never going to get through it, so there was no point in wasting it.

He also took back a lot for the office staff, things his PA had over-supplied in her enthusiasm but that would keep until the office reopened and yet more for the refuge. Tash had really overdone it.

And then he went back to work.

He hadn't intended to do that, either, but he was there before the office reopened, sitting at his desk filling his time and his mind with anything rather than Georgie and her apparently rather lovable little boy. Not that there was a lot to do until everyone was back, so in the end he gave up and just walked the streets and went to the theatre and the odd art exhibition, watched the fireworks on New Year's Eve from the window in his apartment and wondered what the New Year would bring.

Nothing he was about to get excited about.

Then he went back into the office at the crack of dawn on the second of January, champing at the bit and ready to get on. Anything rather than this agonising limbo he seemed to be in.

Tash sashayed into his office, humming softly to herself, and stopped dead. 'Hey, boss, what are you doing back? I thought you'd be there till next week. I wasn't expecting you in till Monday.'

He looked up and met his PA's astonished eyes. Her hair was pink this week. Last week it had been orange—or was it the week before? 'It's a bit quiet in the country.'

She frowned, and perched on the edge of his desk, twisting her hair up and anchoring it with a pencil out of the pot.

'Really? I thought you liked that.'

'I do.' He did. He had. Until Georgie came.

'So how was the food? Did you get through it all?'

He laughed. 'Not really. I've brought a lot in for everyone—I thought we could have a sort of random buffet to welcome everyone back.'

He'd got more, too, in the back of the car, but he'd drop that off later at the refuge, to kick the New Year off.

Pity he couldn't seem to kick his year off. Off a cliff, maybe.

'So how was your Christmas?' he asked belatedly.

She gurgled with laughter. Positively gurgled, and flashed a ring under his nose.

He grabbed her hand and held it still, studying the ring in astonishment. 'He did it?'

'He did. In style. Took me to a posh restaurant and went down on one knee and everything.'

He chuckled, and stood up and hugged her. 'I'm really pleased for you, Tash. That's great news.'

Her smile faltered and she pulled a face. 'Yeah. That's the good news.'

'And the bad?' he said, with a sense of impending doom.

'He's got a job offer. He's moving to America for a year—to Chicago—and he wants me to go with him.'

He sat down again, propping his ankle on his knee, his foot jiggling. This was not good news—well, not for him. 'When?'

'As soon as you can replace me.'

He shook his head slowly. 'I'll never be able to replace you, Tash, but you can go as soon as it's right for you. I'll manage.'

'How?'

He grazed his knuckles lightly over her cheek. 'You're not indispensable,' he said gently. 'But I will miss you and there'll always be a place for you here if you want to come back.'

'Oh, Sebastian, I'll miss you, too,' she said, and flung her arms around his neck. 'I wish you could be happy. I hate it that you're so sad.'

'I'm not sad,' he protested, but she gave him a sceptical look.

'Yes, you are. You've been sad ever since I've known you. You don't even realise it. I don't know who she was, but I'm guessing you've seen her over Christmas, because your eyes look even sadder today.'

He looked away, uncomfortable with her all too accurate analysis.

'Since when were you a psychotherapist?' he asked brusquely, but it didn't put her off. Nothing put Tash off, not when she felt she was on the scent. Maybe it was just as well she was leaving—

'Is she married?'

He gave up. 'No. Not any more.'

'Well, there you are, then. Do you love her? No, don't answer that, it's obvious. Does she love you?'

Did she?

'Yes. But we're not right for each other. Sometimes love's just not enough.'

'Rubbish. It's always enough. Talk to her, Sebastian. I know you. You never talk about anything that matters to you, not really. The only thing you get really worked up about is the refuge, and you never talk about why.'

'It's a good cause.'

She rolled her eyes and pulled the pencil out, shaking her hair down around her shoulders in a shower of shocking pink.

'Go and see her,' she said, stabbing him repeatedly in the chest with the end of the pencil to punctuate every word. 'And talk. *Properly.*'

She dropped the pencil on the desk and swished out of the door. 'Want a coffee before you go?' she asked over her shoulder.

Go? 'Who said anything about going?' he yelled after her, but she ignored him, so he sat down again and stared out of the window at the river.

It was brown with silt from all the run-off after the thaw, and it looked bleak and uninviting.

Like his house.

Was Tash right? Was he sad all the time?

He swallowed hard. Maybe. He hadn't always been. Not while he was with Georgie. She'd taken away the ache, made him feel whole again. And this Christmas, with Josh—he'd been happy.

'Forget the coffee,' he said, snagging his coat off the hook in Tash's office on the way past. 'Don't forget the food. It's in the board room. Share it out. And tell Craig he's a lucky man.'

'Break a leg,' she yelled after him, and he gave a little huff of laughter.

He wasn't really sure what he was doing, and he was far less sure that it would work, but he had to do something, and dithering around for another nine years wasn't going to achieve anything.

It was time to talk to Georgie. Time to tell her the truth in all its ugly glory.

He went home first.

Not to his flat, but to the house.

He'd dropped off the extravagant goodies at the refuge on the way, and wished them all a happy New Year, and then he drove back up to Suffolk and let himself in.

He needed the files, so he could show her. And the test results. Everything.

And then he just had to convince her parents to give him her address in Huntingdon.

It wasn't easy. Her mother was like a Rottweiler, and she wasn't going to give in without a fight.

'Why do you want to see her?'

'I need to talk to her. There are things I need to tell her.'

'You've hurt her.'

He opened his mouth to point out that she'd left him, and shut it. 'I know,' he said after a pause. 'But I want to put it right.'

'How?'

'That's between me and Georgie, Mrs Becket. But

I don't want to hurt her, and I especially don't want to hurt Josh.'

'But you will. If you go there, you will.'

'Not if I don't go when he's awake.'

She seemed to consider that for a moment, but then her husband appeared behind her shoulder and frowned at him.

'I don't know whether to shake your hand for saving their lives or punch your lights out,' he growled, and Sebastian sighed.

'Look, this is nothing to do with Christmas. This is about me, and things about me that she doesn't know. Things I should have told her years ago.'

'So why didn't you?' his mother asked.

He shrugged, swallowing hard. 'Because it's not easy.'

She said nothing for a long moment, then gave a shaky sigh.

'It never is easy, making yourself vulnerable. 42 Wincanton Close.'

'Thank you.' He let his breath out slowly, then sucked it in again. 'Don't tell her I'm coming. I don't want her to do anything silly like go out. I'll ring her when I'm there, tell her I want to talk to her, ask if she'll see me. I won't just rock up on the doorstep. Not if she doesn't want me to.'

Her mother nodded. 'Good. Don't hurt her again, Sebastian. Whatever you do, don't hurt her again.'

'Don't worry, Mrs Becket. I won't hurt her. Not intentionally. I love her. I've always loved her.'

'I know that. If I didn't, I wouldn't have given you her address.'

And taking him completely by surprise, she leant forwards and kissed his cheek. 'Good luck.'

He swallowed. 'Thank you. I have a feeling I'll need it.'

'I don't think so. It's been too long coming, but she'll hear you out. She's always been fair.'

He nodded, shook her father's proffered hand and got back in the car. On the seat beside him were a handful of Josh's toys. The car he'd found under the kitchen table. A train carriage, a piece of track, a little wooden tree. And George's shampoo out of the corner of the shower cubicle in her room.

He'd nearly kept it, just in case she kicked him out, because the smell of it reminded him so much of her.

42 Wincanton Close, Huntingdon. He punched it into the satellite navigation system in the car, reversed carefully off their drive and hit the road.

No rush.

He had well over an hour before Josh was in bed, maybe more. Plenty of time to work out what he was going to say.

He laughed at himself.

He'd had years. Nine, for the worst bits. Thirteen for the rest, all the time he'd known her. If he didn't know what to say now, he never would.

'Oh, man up, Corder. She can only kick you out.'

His gut clenched, and he shut his eyes briefly. He didn't need to think about failure. Not now.

He just needed to see her. Everything else would follow.

CHAPTER TEN

HE FOUND THE house easily. It was the one with the 'For Sale' board outside, and the lights were on.

He slowed down to a crawl with a sigh of relief, and looked around.

She was right, it was in a nice neighbourhood. Tree lined roads, pleasant modern detached houses in different styles each with their own garage, arranged at different angles to soften the lines.

Respectable, decent. Safe.

He was glad she was safe. Safe was important.

He drove past, turned round and pulled up not quite opposite the house, where he could see it and she could see him, and spent a moment gathering his thoughts.

Hell, it was hard. His heart was pounding, his mouth felt dry and his gut was so tight it almost hurt.

It was time.

He pulled the phone out of his pocket and dialled her number.

She didn't answer the first time he rang, so he rang again. He knew it was her phone number, because he'd found her phone lying around and she'd got the number stored under 'me'.

He smiled. Predictable George, to keep the same number. All she had to do was pick up.

She didn't, so he sent her a text, and sat and waited.

The text just said, 'Call me' and gave his number, just in case her phone didn't come up with it. Unlikely, but he wasn't giving her any excuses. Not at this point. There was too much riding on it.

And then she rang him, just when he thought she wouldn't.

'Sebastian? What is it? I've had two missed calls from you and a text. What's going on?'

'I need to see you. We need to talk.' He paused, then went on, his voice gruff. 'There are things you should know. Things I should have told you years ago. Well, one thing, really, the only one that really matters.'

There was a second of shocked silence. 'Can you wait an hour? Just until I've fed Josh and got him to bed? We've been out and I'm on the drag.'

He nodded, although she couldn't see him. 'It's kept for thirteen years. It'll keep another hour.'

'I'll call you.'

'Don't bother. I'm outside, in the car. Just flash the porch lights and I'll come over.'

He saw the curtain twitch, and heard her swift intake of breath. 'OK. I'll see you later.'

He was here.

She couldn't believe it. Her heart was thrashing, and yet there was something dawning that could have been hope.

'Josh, do you really want any more of that?' she asked, and he pushed the plate away and shook his head.

'Can I play trains?'

'No. You can have a bath, and I'll read you a story and you can go to sleep. You've got nursery in the morning and it's late.'

'Want trains,' he said, but he trailed upstairs anyway and sat on the loo on his toddler seat while she ran the bath.

She washed his hair because he'd managed to get ketchup in it, and then she dried him and dressed him in his night nappy and pyjamas, curled up with him on the chair in his room and read him a story, and then snuggled him into his cot.

His eyes were wilting, and before she was out of the door he was asleep.

She gave it five minutes, though, because she didn't want him waking up and interrupting what she instinctively knew was probably the most pivotal conversation of her life.

Cripes.

She went into her bedroom, turned on the bathroom light and studied her face.

She'd been out, and she'd put on a light touch of make-up. Nothing fancy, nothing elaborate, just a touch of eyeshadow and a flick of mascara.

She combed her hair, though, wrestling out the tangles, and eyed her clothes critically. Jeans, a nice jumper, socks.

Hardly dressed to kill, but if he'd wanted that he would have given her notice. And it really, really didn't matter. Not now. There were far bigger fish to fry.

Her heart in her mouth, she went downstairs and flashed the porch light.

Game on.

He got out of the car, ran a finger round his collar and crossed the road, locking the car as he walked.

The door swung open, and he stopped on the step.

'Are you OK with this?'

She searched his eyes, and nodded. 'Come in. Just don't talk too loudly. He's only just gone down.'

Talk too loudly? Now he was here, he didn't want to talk at all, but that had always been his problem.

She led him into the sitting room, closing the door behind them, and he looked around.

'Nice house.'

'Thank you. Can I get you a drink?'

He was dying of thirst. His mouth felt like the desert. 'Mineral water?'

She nodded and went out, returning a moment later with a bottle and two glasses. She set them down on the coffee table, filled the glasses and then perched on the edge of the sofa, waving her hand at the other end of it.

'Sit down, Sebastian. You're cluttering the place up.'

He sat, clearing his throat, sipping the water.

Wondering where to start…

He's nervous, she realised. It surprised her, and it was somehow comforting. Working on the principle that nature abhorred a vacuum, she didn't speak, supressing the urge to fill the silence in the hope that he would.

He did. He gave a short and utterly humourless laugh, and lifted his head.

'I don't know where to start.'

She shifted closer and took his hand, squeezing it gently, her heart pounding. 'So why don't you start with saying it straight out, whatever it is, like, I'm gay, or I've got cancer, or whatever? And then explain.'

He gave a hollow laugh and his fingers tightened in hers. 'OK. Well, for a start I'm definitely not gay, and as far as I know I don't have cancer. I just—I don't know who I am.'

'What?' She searched his eyes, trying to read them,

but they were bleak and empty. Lost. And that scared her. She gripped his hand tighter. 'Sebastian, talk to me.'

He hesitated, then sucked in a breath and said the words that had been dammed up inside him for so long.

'I'm adopted.'

She stared at him. 'You're *what?* When did you find out?'

'When I was seventeen, nearly eighteen. I had no idea until I wanted to get a driving license. We'd never been abroad, I'd never needed a passport, but I wanted to learn to drive, and my parents procrastinated, and then they had to tell me, because I needed my birth certificate and—well, basically it's a fabrication.'

She frowned. 'A fabrication? How?'

He let out a shaky sigh, and his fingers tightened on hers, as if this was the hard bit. 'Because nobody knew anything about me. I was found,' he said carefully. 'In a cubicle, of all places, in the Ladies' room in a department store.'

'Oh, Sebastian! That's so sad. Did they never find your mother? Had she given birth to you in the loos?'

'No, she hadn't just given birth to me. I wasn't a baby. And I was with my mother. She was dead,' he said, his voice hollow. 'Dead, and pregnant, and she'd been beaten up. The cleaner found us in the morning, when the department store opened.'

She pressed a hand to her mouth, the shock rippling through her like an explosion. 'You'd been there *all night*?'

He swallowed, looked away, then looked back at her, and she could see an echo of the horror lurking in the back of his eyes.

He nodded. 'I must have been. I was two, or there-abouts.'

'Josh's age,' she whispered, feeling sick.

He nodded again. 'They didn't know exactly, of course, but they gave me a birth date based on my calculated developmental age, and the place of birth is the town where I was found. They never managed to identify my mother. No woman answering her description was ever reported missing, and nobody's looked for her since. She had no ID of any sort on her, no handbag, no wallet. Nothing.'

She didn't know what to say. Shock held her rigid, and it was long seconds before she started to breathe again, short, shaky breaths of horror. She rested her head on his shoulder, and his other hand came up and cradled it tight. She could feel the tremors running through him, the shaking of his hand, the jerky breaths.

What on earth had he gone through in those long, dark hours? She thought of her baby, her precious, darling baby, trapped alone with her dead body in a public toilet cubicle, and silent tears cascaded down her cheeks. She lifted her free hand and found his jaw, cradled it in her palm, turned her head and kissed him.

His tears mingled with hers, and for a long time they sat there holding each other, cheek to cheek, just letting the shockwaves die away. Then he eased away from her and scrubbed his face with his hands, swiping away the tears and sucking in much-needed air.

'My parents didn't tell me that all at once. They just told me I was adopted, that I'd been found and nobody knew who my mother was. I assumed she'd abandoned me, so I spent three years hating her, and three years hating my parents for not telling me, for letting me think I was theirs. And then I found out the truth. The whole, ugly, sordid truth, and other things started to make sense. The dreams I'd had all my life. The claustrophobia, the fear of being in a tight space in the dark.'

'Which is why you freaked out when you were in the attic with Josh.'

He nodded. 'I heard your footsteps coming, and I said to Josh, "Shh, don't make a sound," and we held our breath, and suddenly I had this rush of—I don't know. Memory? Or just an overworked imagination? But it suddenly seemed so real, as if I recognised the words. And I hear it in my dreams, someone telling me to hush, and the footsteps, and hidden in there with his tiny body next to mine—I just had to get the hell out. Was he all right?'

'Yes, he was fine, but I wondered what on earth had happened. I knew about your claustrophobia, but it looked—I don't know. Worse. You looked awful, but you wouldn't talk to me.'

'I couldn't. I'm sorry. I find it really hard to talk about. And I couldn't talk then, apparently. I didn't talk until I was nearly three—or what they'd decided was nearly three, although apparently I might have been younger. They kept a growth chart and you're supposed to be half your adult height at two, and I wasn't half my current height until I was supposedly two and five months, so I was probably younger than they thought when I was found.'

'So maybe not even talking at that point.'

'No. But I was silent, George. It wasn't just that I didn't talk, I didn't cry, or laugh, or babble. I didn't make a sound—and telling Josh to shush—did she tell me not to make a sound? My mother? Probably, because shut in there with Josh it all felt terrifyingly familiar, so maybe I was just too afraid to speak in case something else bad happened.'

Poor, poor little boy. She shook her head slowly, rubbing the back of his hand with her thumb, slowly, rhythmically, her heart aching for him. Oh, Sebastian...

'So what happened to you, after you were found? Where did you go?'

'My parents fostered me. I was put with them straight away, and they moved heaven and earth to adopt me, and gradually I grew more confident and turned into a normal, healthy child, but they never told me. All those years I thought I was theirs, all those birthday parties that weren't my birthday at all, and then this huge hole opened up underneath me, this void where I'd had security and certainty and a sense of history, of belonging. And it was all a lie. It was only later I learned there had been even more lies, covering up the bits of the truth that even then they didn't feel they could tell me.'

Her fingers tightened on his. 'They weren't lying to you, Sebastian. They were protecting you. Doing what they felt was best.'

'I know. I know that, and I know they love me, and don't get me wrong, I love them, too, and I'm deeply grateful for everything they've done for me, but—I'm not theirs, and I thought I was, and that really hurts. If they'd told me the truth, right from the beginning, that my mother was dead and that they didn't know who she was, then it wouldn't have been such a shock when I heard it.'

'So when did you find out about your mother? Was that when you changed, when you went so funny on me? You said three years after you first realised you were adopted, so you would have been—what? Twenty? Nearly twenty-one?'

He nodded. 'Yes. And I just retreated into myself.'

'Why didn't you tell me?' she asked, desolate now that he'd carried this all alone for so long. 'Oh, Sebastian, why didn't you tell me? You should have trusted me. I would have understood.'

'Because I didn't want anything to change. I felt that you were the only person who loved me for myself. You weren't hiding a guilty secret from me, you had no obligation to me, and I was afraid to tell you in case it changed things. That's why I bought the house, because the time I spent there with you was the happiest time of my life.'

He looked down at her, his eyes tender. 'I fell in love with you there, on our first date, when you took me there and showed it to me.'

'That wasn't a date!'

'Yes, it was. I knew Jack wasn't going to be around, and you'd always been friendly towards me. I'd just found out I was adopted, and I needed to get out, give myself time for it all to sink in. And there you were, in a skimpy little top and shorts, your skin kissed by the sun, and when you suggested we went out for the bike ride I thought all my Christmases had come at once.'

'It *was* just a bike ride.'

'No. It was you showing me your secret hideaway, letting me into your dreams, sharing your fantasies, and we made fantasies of our own. I was still reeling from the news that I was adopted, and it was an escape from it, a different reality. In the next few weeks it became our own world, somewhere safe that I could go. And suddenly it all seemed plausible. If I could get rich enough, so I could afford it, we could buy the house and live there and found our dynasty, yours and mine, and I would have a real family, my own flesh and blood.'

She touched his cheek, wiping away the last trace of their tears. 'You should have told me, Sebastian.'

He looked away, his face bleak, and she let her hand fall.

'I know, but I didn't want to change things. You knew who you were. You look like your parents. You're part of them, they're part of you. And I don't have that. My brothers do—they aren't adopted. Nature seemed to have sorted itself out for my parents by that point, and there's no question that Matt and Andy are theirs, but not me. For me, my identity, my origins, even my nationality will always be a mystery. I'm a cuckoo in the nest, Georgie, and I never forget how much I owe them, but they should have told me.'

'They had their reasons. Maybe they thought it would hurt you more? It must have been really traumatic—you were hardly more than a baby, but much more aware than a baby would have been. The impact must have been horrific, and they would have wanted to protect you.'

'I know. Logically, I know, but I didn't feel logical. Suddenly I didn't belong, and that was so shocking to me. It rocked me to my foundations. And when I found out the rest, when I saw my adoption file and the police file, and it was so sordid and harsh, it was even worse. How could I tell you that? I didn't want to distress or disgust you-'

'Disgust me? It wouldn't have disgusted me!'

'I didn't know that. I still don't know that. She could have been anyone, George. She could have been a prostitute or a drug addict, a murderer, even-'

'She was somebody's *daughter*,' she said, appalled that he could think that she was so shallow that his mother's plight would put her off him. 'However she ended up there, she was just a girl—how old was she?'

He shrugged. 'Early twenties, they thought, maybe younger?'

Her eyes flooded again. 'Poor, poor girl. She must have been so terrified. And she must have loved you— she tried to protect you, shut you away in a public place where a man couldn't get to you without drawing attention to himself, and it cost her her life.'

He nodded slowly. 'Yes, it did. And I'd spent three years hating her for something she hadn't done. I didn't realise how much it had changed me, thinking I'd been abandoned, that she hadn't loved me enough to keep me. Why not? What kind of vile child had I been that I wasn't I lovable? But then I heard the truth, and I just needed to find out all I could about her, but there's nothing. I still don't know who she was, and nobody's launched any kind of official search for anyone answering her description in all this time.'

'What about DNA?' she asked, finally on solid ground. 'I know it can't tell you much, but it can tell you something about where you're from.'

'Northern Europe, probably England. No more than that. And if nobody's looked, then the trail's lost and I'll never know who she was, or who I am. And that's the worst thing. I have no idea who I really am. My name, my place and date of birth—not even what nationality I am. Just speculation, all of it.'

'No! You *know* who you are,' she said fiercely. 'And *I* know who you are. I've always known. It wouldn't have made any difference to me where you'd come from, what you were called, what date you were born. You were you, and you've always been you, and it's you I loved. You should have *told* me, Sebastian. You should have trusted me.'

He turned his head slowly and looked at her, his eyes bleak. 'But I did trust you. And you left me.'

She opened her mouth to argue, but then shut it again, because it was true. She had left him. She'd walked away and left him, when she'd promised to love him forever.

Well, that hadn't been a lie. She loved him still, but she'd left him when he'd needed her the most, and it tore her apart.

'I'm so sorry,' she said brokenly. 'I had no idea what you were going through. I wish you'd told me, shared it with me. I would never have left you if I'd known. I loved you so much, I've always loved you. You're a good man, and you always have been, and you must never doubt that—look what you did for Josh and me over Christmas—but still you didn't let us into your heart. You gave us so much, and you didn't need to do that, but you held yourself back like you always do, because everyone you've ever loved has let you down, haven't they, one way or another? No wonder you don't trust your feelings or give your heart to anyone, least of all me.'

'I gave my heart to you,' he said quietly. 'I gave it to you thirteen years ago, and you still have it. That offer stands.'

She shook her head. 'But I left you. I don't deserve it.'

'Yes, you do. I was a nightmare. I know that. But I needed you, and I loved you, and I still do, Georgia. And I know you love me. What I don't know is if you can forgive me, or if you can live with a man from nowhere.'

'Oh, Sebastian. Of course I can forgive you. And whether or not I can live with you is nothing to do with where you've come from so much as where you're going and how. That was what changed. That was the problem, the thing I couldn't live with.'

'I know. I'm sorry. But there was a reason I was so driven.'

'A reason you didn't share with me!'

'I know. I should have.'

'You should. I could have helped you with the DNA research. It's my field, Sebastian. I might have been able to find out more.'

'I doubt it. I've paid a fortune for the best advice-'

'The best isn't necessarily commercially available. And I'm on the inside. Don't overlook that.'

He nodded. 'I won't. But it can't alter the way I was then, how driven I was—still am. After I found out what had actually happened to my mother, the emphasis changed. I needed to make more money—much more, not for me, but to make sure it couldn't happen again, that there'd be somewhere safe for women to go. I support various charities, for women and children who are victims of domestic violence, and I set up a refuge which I fund and maintain. I had to, to stay sane. I couldn't just let it go, and it was eating me up, but now I'm doing something, and making a difference, and I feel I've got my priorities right.'

'You have. You've settled down.'

'Grown up?' he said drily, and she laughed.

'Probably. I prefer to think you've developed a more mature and balanced perspective. And I have, too, so before you start worrying, I'm sure I can live with you now even if I couldn't then.'

'You can?'

'Of course I can—and I could have done then if you'd shared this with me. I think it's a fabulous cause, and I would have supported you and worked with you on it, but you never gave me a chance.'

His eyes were filled with shadows. 'I know. I'm sorry. I just didn't know how to say it, and the longer it went on, the harder it got. And after you went I was so hurt and angry that you'd left me, there was no way I was going to tell you. Then I heard you were married, and I thought you'd moved on.'

'No. I'll never move on from loving you. I've loved you for thirteen years—I fell in love with you on that first date, too, and I promised to love you forever. That hasn't changed, even though I couldn't stay with you then. I still love you. I've never stopped loving you.'

'Even though you were married to David?'

She shrugged. 'He was a nice man, and we were both lonely. You wouldn't let me in, you'd done nothing but shut me out for months. Years later, you still hadn't contacted me again and I had no reason to suppose you ever would. And if we hadn't been snowed in together this Christmas, I don't know that that would have ever changed.'

'No. Maybe not. As I said, I just assumed you'd moved on.'

'Only in a way. Not in my heart. It was a compromise, a rationalisation, and I can't regret it because it's given me Josh, but it was only ever a way of finding a measure of happiness. You were my first love, my only true love, but I was never going to have you, and I didn't want to be alone, and if David hadn't died, we would have been together forever. But he did die, and we're talking, at last, and maybe finally sorting out what we should have sorted out years ago.'

She reached up and cradled his cheek in her hand. 'I

love you, Sebastian. And if you're asking me to marry you, the answer's yes.'

'I asked you years ago.'

'No, you didn't. You promised me we'd be together forever, and we talked about being married, but I don't believe you ever asked me.'

He gave a soft laugh, and eased off the sofa, landing on one knee at her feet. He took her hand in his and stared up into her eyes with a wry smile.

'Georgia Becket Pullman, I love you now as much as I've ever loved you, more than life itself. Without you I'm nothing. With you, I can conquer the world. Marry me. Have my children, to keep your little Josh company and give him a whole host of brothers and sisters. Our dynasty. My very own, real family.'

His smile faded, and his eyes grew bright.

'Marry me, George? Please?'

Her eyes filled. 'Oh, Sebastian—of course I'll marry you! I've already said yes.'

'You made me ask you,' he accused.

'Only because I wanted to hear you say it,' she laughed, but the laugh hiccupped into a sob, and she slid off the sofa onto her knees and went into his arms, hugging him tight to her heart, aching for the little boy he'd been and the strong, courageous man he'd become.

He shifted onto the sofa, lifting her easily onto his lap and cradling her close. 'It's a pity you've got a job,' he said.

She tilted her head and peered at him. 'Why? It might be useful to you in the future, trying to track your family. I've got all the right contacts.'

A week ago, that would have made his heart race faster. Now, he found he didn't care, because he had the only thing that could ever matter this much to him.

"I could still use your skill and expertise now,' he said. 'Why?'

He smiled. 'Because my PA's leaving. She's getting married and moving to Chicago, and I'll need someone to fill in until I can replace her. But that's only short term. Long term, of course, we've got a dynasty to work on. Maybe you'd better warn your boss.'

She laughed and rested her head on his shoulder. 'Yes, I better had. The first little Corder is due on the nineteenth of September.'

He went utterly still, and then he gave a shaky, incredulous laugh and hugged her tight. 'Really? You're having my baby?'

'It would seem so. I did the test this morning. It was very faint, but it was positive.'

'Wow.' He laughed again. 'I didn't even think—that night, when I had the dream?'

'When else? There was only the once.'

'And you're sure? The test can't be wrong?'

'No. You can have a false negative, but never a false positive. I deliberately got a very sensitive test kit.'

'Have you told your mother?'

She shook her head. 'No. Not before you. I was trying to work out how to tell you, but I knew you'd go all Neanderthal and insist on marrying me, so I really wanted to talk to you first and get you to open up to me so I'd know you wanted it for the right reasons.'

'And I came to you. You'd better thank Tash for that. She said she wished I wasn't always sad. I said I wasn't. She pointed out that I was. I am. I have been for years, and the only time I'm not sad is when I'm with you.

'It's like you said to me once, when you were talking about David. He was a nice man, and you loved him, but you didn't feel as if you couldn't breathe if he wasn't there. As if there was no colour, no music, no poetry. No sense to your life. That's how I feel when I'm with you. As if my life has colour and music and poetry, and it all makes sense, and after you'd gone everything was grey and empty and silent. It took Tash to point it out to me.'

'You *really* owe her a bonus now.'

He laughed and hugged her closer. 'I tell you what, they're going to have a cracker of a wedding present.'

'Good. I hope we get invited to the wedding. I want to thank her.'

'That's easy.' He pulled his phone out of his pocket, hit a speed dial number and smiled. 'Tash? My fiancée would like a word with you.'

EPILOGUE

'HAPPY CHRISTMAS, Mrs Corder?'

His arms slid round her from behind, his chin resting on her shoulder. She felt his lips nuzzle her ear, and she laughed and leaned back into him.

'*Very* Happy Christmas, Mr Corder.' She turned in his arms with a smile, and found it reflected in his eyes. 'Where's Evie?'

'Sleeping. On my mother.'

'Not mine, then.'

'For a change, not,' he said with a lazy smile. 'Come and sit down. You've done enough in the kitchen today.'

'I've hardly done anything,' she protested as he towed her down the hall. 'You wouldn't let me.'

'You're a nursing mother.'

'Yes. Not an invalid.'

He smiled indulgently. 'Humour me. I like looking after you. I've got a lot of years to catch up on. So, how do you think it's going?'

'Christmas? Brilliantly. Nobody's had a fight yet, everyone's enjoyed the food-'

'I should hope so. I let Tash loose on the ordering again, remember.'

She chuckled. 'Yes. She's good at it. Impeccable taste.'

'She just knows what I like.'

'So modest.'

He gave a soft huff of laughter and hugged her closer to his side. From down the hall they could hear the hubbub of conversation, interspersed with laughter and the occasional raised voice as someone tried to put their point.

The family were all gathered in the drawing room in front of a roaring fire, playing silly games and getting over the monumental feast that had been Christmas lunch. There wasn't room in the smaller sitting room for all of them, and even the enormous dining table had been filled to capacity.

The house was straining at the seams, all ten bedrooms occupied. Both sets of parents had come to share the celebrations, together with her brother Jack and his wife and two children, Sebastian's brothers Andy and Matt and their girlfriends, and Tash and Craig, who were honorary family members. Including them and Josh and Evie, that made eighteen—nineteen if you counted Tash's burgeoning bump. Twenty-one if you counted the dog and cat.

Not bad for a start at family life, she thought contentedly.

He pulled her to a halt in the hall, next to the Christmas tree. It was decorated with last year's stock cube parcels and bundles of twigs, fresh gingerbread trees and stars and little home-made angels that dangled around the lower branches.

The sophisticated glass baubles were safely near the top of the tree, glinting in the light from the enormous crystal chandelier that hung above it, and it looked wonderful.

She sighed happily. 'What a lovely tree.'

'Isn't it?'

He glanced up, and there overhead, dangling from the landing bannisters above, was a sprig of mistletoe.

'Well, now, would you look at that?' he murmured, his eyes twinkling with mischief, and threading his hands into her hair, he lowered his head and kissed her...

* * * * *

ONE SCANDALOUS CHRISTMAS EVE

SUSAN STEPHENS

For Pippa Roscoe, Mother of Wolves, amazing author of Mills & Boon, and whipper-upper of enthusiasm for more Acostas. If we hadn't been chatting over tapas in a Spanish restaurant called Lobos (Wolves), Team Lobos might never have taken to the saddle.

Thank you to all involved for bringing back the dangerous glamour of the Acostas clan!

CHAPTER ONE

THE SHADOW OF a helicopter briefly dimmed the sunshine of a crisp November day. Jess Slatehome's breath hitched. The logo on the side, a shield of gold on a ground of black, stated boldly, Acosta España.

The Acostas were *back*!

It had been a long ten years since Jess had last met up with the Spanish Acosta family—four handsome brothers with an elegant sister at home—when they had come to trial some ponies on her family farm in Yorkshire.

When she had kissed one of them.

Closing her eyes briefly on that embarrassing thought, Jess knew she had to focus on today, and an idea born of desperation. Sell the stock, save the farm had become her mantra. A seal of approval from the Acostas would assure the success of the big family event Jess had arranged to showcase her father's prize-winning polo ponies, in the hope of selling at least some of them, in an attempt to stave off the bank and bail her father out of financial trouble.

Jess's father, Jim Slatehome, was a much-loved local character and everyone from the village had pitched in to help. Using every penny of her savings, as well as a small bequest from her mother, with the invaluable assistance of an army of volunteers, Jess had been able to plan big. Sending out dozens of invitations in the hope of attracting the glitterati of the polo circuit, she had made it her goal to return her father to the spotlight he deserved. Before her mother's death Jim Slatehome had been the go-to trainer and breeder of world-class ponies. Felled by grief, he had retreated from the world and it had taken all Jess's persuasion to persuade him that five years was long enough to shut himself away, and that today marked his return.

Success hovered tantalisingly within their grasp now. Gazing up as the helicopter prepared to land, she knew that if a member of the Acosta family bought some ponies her father would be back on top. But who would step out of that aircraft?

Jess's mouth dried as she thought back ten years to when the gleam of wealth and success blazing from the Acosta brothers had almost blinded her when they arrived on the farm to buy horses. Finding herself alone with Dante Acosta in the stable, some fan girl craziness had prompted her to launch herself at him and plant a kiss on his mouth. He'd stepped away with a huff of disbelief. The scorch of humiliation felt as keen today as it had done then. But she'd never forgotten the kiss. Or that for a moment—and she was never quite sure if she imagined this or not— Dante Acosta had responded.

Jess tensed as the aircraft door swung open. This was madness, she told herself firmly. And yet she waited, breath held, to see if the fiery superstar of the polo world would descend the steps. She'd followed his career keenly since that first memorable encounter between a naïve seventeen-year-old country girl with a head full of daydreams and a mouth full of cheek and a youth who already boasted the dazzling glamour for which he had since become famous. Dante Acosta's intuition where horses were concerned was said to be second to none, like his success with women. With an army of glamorous female admirers, would he even remember the first time they'd met? Jess's idea of glamour was a night down the pub with her dad, jingling the change in her pocket as she tried to work out if she had enough money to buy him a lemonade.

'Jess—'

She almost jumped out of her skin as she spun around. 'Yes?' It was one of the helpers from the village.

'Your father needs you in the house. I think he's nervous about his welcoming speech.'

'Don't worry. I'll come now and go through it with him.'

It was a relief to drag her attention from the helicopter. Ten years was a long time. These days, she was a fully qualified physiotherapist with a blossoming career, specialising in treating athletes, a fact that would soon bring her face to face with Dante Acosta, whether he appeared today or not. Because of her recent successes in restoring injured athletes to full strength, the Acosta family had chosen Jess to treat their brother's damaged leg, which meant travelling to Spain to Dante's fabulous *estancia*. How he'd feel about the identity of the therapist they'd chosen for him remained to be seen.

She couldn't think about that now. There was today to get though first. Whoever climbed out of the helicopter, it was more likely to be a foreman from one of the Acosta ranches rather than a member of such a wealthy and successful family. Jess's focus was saving the farm, so her father could recover in his own time without upheaval. There were plenty of helpers around to direct the latest arrival to the hospitality marquee where her father was soon to give what Jess passionately hoped would be the sales pitch of his life.

Dante's expression darkened as the cane he was forced to use sank into the claggy mire of a churned-up field. With a vicious curse, he accepted the regrettable conditions. This was no state-of-the-art facility but a beat-up farm in the middle of nowhere.

A farm that boasted some of the best horses in the world, he reminded himself as he ploughed on, which was why he was here. He'd be a fool to miss an opportunity like this. He was always on the lookout for exciting new bloodlines to improve his stock. Aside from playing polo, breeding ponies was his passion, and was the only lure that could drag him out of hibernation after his accident on the polo field. That and the fact that his people had told him the farm was in trouble, and that now would be a good time to buy. He was receiving a constant stream of information from his team to keep him up to speed with any likely competition, as well as likely downsides to a potential purchase. As of now, he was only interested in buying stock.

Another colourful curse heralded a pause as he eased the cramp in his damaged leg. Glancing around, he surveyed the motley throng of farmers, local families and the elite of the horse world, jostling happily alongside each other. They all had one thing in common, which was a deep love of the animals they had come to see, and the sport they provided. A local band added to the upbeat atmosphere. Only Dante's scowl was out of place.

Someone had done a good job of arranging entertainment for the assembled guests, he conceded, taking in the food stalls and all the gaudy trappings of a fairground. This posed a disadvantage for him. He hadn't expected quite so many people. Briefly, he considered the humiliation of the great *El Lobo*, or The Wolf as Dante was known in polo circles, showing himself to the world, staggering along with a cane.

He brushed this off with a snarling curse. Everyone was paparazzo these days. He stood as much chance of being photographed on his *estancia* as he did here.

Dante's stubble-blackened chin lifted at the sound of a young colt neighing. He studied the ponies running free in

a field. Young, hard-muscled and spirited, they were perfect. *That* was why he was here.

Really?

Shrugging off the attention of a marshal who had raced
to his aid with the offer of a lift in a service vehicle, he
asked for Jim Slatehome, the owner of the farm.

'Jim's still in the farmhouse,' the man told him with a
shrug. 'Probably running through his speech—'

Dante was already on his way. He hadn't travelled from
Spain to indulge in fairground sport or well meaning but
ultimately dull parochial chitchat. Nor had he the slightest
intention of being last in line when it came to nailing the
best stock. A deal would be arranged within the next hour
or so, and then he was out of here.

*Was he? Was buying new stock the only reason he was
here?*

The monotony of life since the accident was wearing him
down. He needed a distraction. Any distraction. An unsophisticated young country girl stood a chance of taking his
mind off the fact that his brothers and sister had gone over
his head to arrange a physiotherapist to treat him back in
Spain. Dante had discharged himself from hospital prematurely, so his siblings had decided to bring the hospital to
him. They knew he wouldn't refuse family. The Acostas
were tight and stood by each other always.

Dante's hard mouth tugged with faint amusement as
he approached the ramshackle farmhouse with its peeling paint and crooked roof. It was ten years since he'd
been here. Was it likely he'd find the little vixen he'd first
encountered in the stable? Would she be married now?
Engaged? Would he find a significant other by her side?
Maybe he should have put his team to work on these details
too. The worst he could imagine was that Jim Slatehome's
daughter had mellowed to the point of boring, though with
her abundance of fiery auburn hair and those flashing em-

erald eyes he thought it unlikely. One thing was certain. He and Jess Slatehome had unfinished business between them. With this in mind, he planted his cane and lurched on.

'I can't stay long. I have to get back to the marquee to keep people happy until you're ready to give your speech,' Jess explained when her father looked at her with anxiety glistening in his eyes.

He shouldn't be here in the kitchen, nursing a mug of tea, when there were potential buyers for the ponies outside, waiting to meet him. 'Everyone's looking forward to your speech,' she enthused, kneeling by his side at the kitchen table. 'You can do this,' she stated firmly as she got up, wishing she felt as confident as she sounded.

Her father had aged since her mother's death, which was years ago now. It was as if he'd lost hope. He hadn't even shaved today, and his outfit for such a big occasion comprised a random mix of ancient tweed, a greasy flat cap and worn corduroy trousers.

But that was his charm, Jess reminded herself. Jim Slatehome had used to be the go-to trainer and breeder of the best polo ponies in the world, and she was determined to see him back on top again. Her father was every bit as special and unique as the glossiest billionaire newly arrived in his state-of-the-art helicopter, and she loved him to bits.

Yes. Dante was a billionaire. The Acostas were a massively wealthy family, thanks to land holdings, an international tech company, and their skill on a world stage with horses. But this small farm was equally precious to Jess. It had been in her family for generations and she would defend it to the end.

Leaning down to give her father a hug, she was shocked to see tears in his eyes.

'Those ponies mean everything to me, Jess. I can't bear to let them go.'

'But you have to, if you want to keep the farm,' she explained gently. 'Come on; you can do this,' she coaxed.

He gave her a heartbreaking look. 'If you say so. I suppose I'd better go and clean up. I won't let you down, Jess.'

'I know that,' she whispered.

Her father was up and down the stairs in double-quick time and nothing about his appearance had changed, as far as Jess could tell. Apart from his determination, she was relieved to see. 'You're right. I can do this,' he stated firmly. 'I'll go ahead. You stay here. I don't want our guests thinking I need you to prop me up because I've lost confidence in my ponies.'

'Good idea,' Jess agreed.

She was just clearing up their tea things when the kitchen door swung open. She froze on the spot. Breath hitched in her throat. She must have turned ashen, though heat was surging through her veins. Dante Acosta, looking grimmer and tougher than she remembered, was standing in the doorway.

'Dante!'

'Jess…'

Those eyes…that voice…that powerful, compelling presence.

His deep, sonorous voice with its seductive Spanish sibilance rolled across her senses like black velvet brushed lightly, yet so effectively across every sensitive zone she had. His eyes were black pools of experience, while his mouth was a straight, hard line. There was nothing soft or yielding about Dante Acosta—there never had been, she remembered.

Everything in the room disappeared except him. Dante Acosta was the essence of masculinity, the living embodiment of sex. New scars—she guessed they must have been gained on the polo field at the same time as the damage to his leg—cut livid stripes from the upswept tip of one ebony brow to the corner of his firm, cruel mouth. Wind had whipped his thick black hair into such disarray that it had caught on his stubble. A gold hoop glittered in his right ear, adding to a barbaric appearance that seemed at odds with his aura of wealth. But this was no effete billionaire. This was a man of fierce passion and resolve. Beneath his rugged jacket, she knew from the popular press that Dante, like the other members of his polo team, bore a tattoo of a snarling wolf over his heart. This was the insignia of his polo team, Lobos. The team name alone was enough to strike terror in the hearts of their opponents. Lobos was the Spanish word for wolves—a pack of merciless wolves. On the back of Dante's neck, beneath copious glossy whorls of pitch-black hair, he had another tattoo of a skull and crossed mallets, a warning that Team Lobos took no prisoners, and confidently expected to win every match.

A clatter distracted her. The cane he'd discarded by the door had fallen. Jess frowned. He should be cured by now, with no need for a cane. No wonder his siblings were concerned. Fortunately, they'd sent on his medical records, so she knew the extent of his injury. If Dante hadn't discharged himself from the hospital prematurely, he'd be done with that cane by now.

'Dante,' she said politely, reaching out to shake his hand when he shifted position impatiently. 'How nice to see you again.'

Taking both her hands in a firm grip, he drew her towards him and proceeded to inspect her as if she were a potential purchase like the ponies.

Would you like to examine my teeth? ran through her mind, though she knew that for the sake of any potential purchase she had to mind her manners and remain calm. That wasn't easy when she was practically drowning in charisma, so she closed her eyes.

'Let me look at you…'

That voice again. She jerked her hands free. Dante Acosta was a exciting force of nature but he knew it and had no shame when it came to wielding his power. It was up to Jess to resist him. *If she could.* She hadn't made too good a job of resisting him ten years ago and, seeing him again, she was inclined to forgive her teenage self.

Her hands had felt so small and safe in his—which was all part of the illusion. This was no time to be seduced by a man with more money than Croesus and the morals of an alley cat. How would that help her father? If there was one thing she'd learned since returning home to take care of her father, it was that vultures were always circling. Everyone was out for a deal. Why should Dante Acosta be any different?

'Jess?'

'Apologies. Sorry. I'm forgetting my manners. Welcome—welcome to Bell Farm. Would you like a drink? I expect you've had a long journey.'

'From Spain?' A casual shrug of his massive shoulders hinted at executive travel in the most luxurious of circumstances. 'Not so bad.'

Why did everything about Dante Acosta make her feel like this? She was always blasé about men. Because none could compare with Dante Acosta, as she had discovered ten years ago when she kissed him.

'Tea, surely?' she said to distract herself from the insistent throb between her legs.

'Can't stand the stuff.'

'Oh.' That took her by surprise. 'Something else, perhaps?'

'What have you got?'

From any other lips those words could be taken as an innocent request for a verbal menu. When they came from Dante Acosta the prompt was laden with deadly charm.

'Whatever you like,' she said brightly. 'The stalls outside sell pretty much everything.'

As one corner of his mouth tugged slightly as if to say *Touché*, she knew he'd feel like velvet steel beneath her hands.

Had nothing changed in ten years? Was she still as reckless?

Far from it, Jess told herself firmly. She was no longer a reckless teen but a medical professional who had left a successful career at a leading London teaching hospital to come home to help her father.

'I'm sure you want to see my father, not me,' she said pleasantly. 'Would you like me to take you to him?'

'There's no need,' Dante said with a narrow-eyed look. 'I'll find my own way.'

As he turned, Jess felt as if she'd been appraised and discarded. That was fine. This wasn't about her. She'd arranged the event with the specific intention of attracting an Acosta or the like, someone with a deep love of horses and plenty of money to bail her father out of trouble by buying up his stock. If Dante didn't bite she'd have to find someone who would.

So, Dante mused as he wove his way through the crowd to reach the show ring—if a hastily tidied up paddock with a rickety fence could be described as such a thing—the little vixen he remembered had matured into a beautiful, understated, though rather too serious woman. He missed the mischief in Jess's eyes, as well as the excessively impulsive nature that had prompted her, at the tender age of seventeen, to stand on tiptoe to plant a kiss on his lips.

His senses surged, remembering. He had reined in those senses then and would do so again. He wasn't here to waste time on a serious-minded woman. He wasn't ready to take any woman seriously. Why restrict his diet when the menu was so varied?

Leaning on the hated cane, he paused to greet some fellow polo players. Jess had attracted a motley crowd, from locals to minor royals and celebrities as well as sightseers from far and wide. Towering men in black suits with earpieces and suspicious bulges beneath their jackets followed hot on the heels of a well-known sheikh. Dante had never relied on security personnel for his safety, preferring to rely on his own skills to protect him.

One career had foundered while the other had soared, he mused, moving on when he spotted Jess walking arm in arm with her father. His team had informed him that the farm was in serious financial trouble. They were already working on the ins and outs and would advise him on the questions he'd pose before the day was out.

One thing was certain. Jess had left her job and risked her career to come here to save her father and the farm. She was unusually determined, and he admired that.

He also detested loose ends. If Jess hadn't been seventeen ten years ago, who knew what might have happened between them?

The marquee was already crowded by the time he entered. He recognised more horse breeders, trainers and players like himself jostling to get to the front under Jim Slatehome's nose. He wouldn't have it all his own way today. There would be stiff competition for the better horses.

So he'd go one better.

He could offer double—triple—what anyone else could without feeling a pinch. He could easily afford it. Jim had sold him some good stock in the past, and what he'd seen of the ponies in the field so far suggested Jim had never really gone away, but had made himself invisible so he could nurse his grief.

The urge to help Jim Slatehome overwhelmed him suddenly. To fend off the competition meant putting something else in the pot. After the most recent text from his team an idea was already brewing. How would Jess take his idea, if he went ahead and bought the farm? Not well, he suspected as watched her standing like a protection officer at her father's side. It had cost her everything to be here, financially, career-wise, every which way. His team had filled him in on the details. She'd qualified top of her class as a physiotherapist specialising in sports injuries. Her first job was at a prestigious teaching hospital in London, but she'd given that up to go freelance, which could be tricky. Rumour said she was successful. If she was as good as her reputation suggested, she could guarantee an endless stream of patients from the battleground of polo alone. The thought of those soft hands tracking right up his legs was—

Out of bounds, Dante told himself sternly. He was here for business and nothing else. He'd seen the vixen and satisfied his curiosity, and that had to be enough.

Thankfully, the Sheikh sidled up to him at that moment and as they got talking about horses Dante grew more determined than ever to win the day. He'd handle Jess's objections. As her father mounted the podium and began his speech, Dante stared at Jess.

CHAPTER TWO

HER FATHER'S SPEECH went well. He seemed buoyed up. Maybe the brief chats he'd managed to snatch with Dante had served as a reminder that Jim Slatehome had once been great and would be so again. That was Jess's dearest hope as she congratulated her father, and prompted him to start discussing specific ponies with potential buyers.

'Be patient,' he implored. 'I'm going to speak to Dante while you circulate amongst our guests. Keep them happy while I'm away. This talk is important, Jess,' he added with a significant look.

'I'd rather stay with you.' She glanced at Dante, standing waiting for her father to join him, and felt the same punch to her senses, added to which was the fear that they were cooking something up between them. Dante's expression betrayed nothing beyond a cool stare in her direction.

'This is still my farm, Jess.'

The reminder struck home. Anything she could do to see her father back on top had to be all right with Jess. 'Promise me you won't do anything silly before you and I have talked it through.'

'Like fortune-telling in a tent under the name of Skylar?' her father suggested, lifting one bushy brow.

'You've got me there,' Jess admitted wryly as she checked her watch to make sure she had time to chat to the guests before she was due to inhabit the small gaudy tent that would house the mysterious Skylar.

'Go,' her father prompted urgently.

With a last suspicious glance at the tall, dark man in the shadows who made her heart pound like crazy, she planted a kiss on her father's cheek and did as he said.

The day had turned cold Jess discovered when she stepped out of the marquee. Or maybe apprehension was chilling her. The sky was blue. There wasn't a cloud to be seen and if the air wasn't exactly tropical it was still warm for the time of year in this part of England. In honour of the heatwave Jess had dressed in a thick sweater, a down gilet and a padded coat. Even in summer it could be frigid on the moors.

It would have been a great time to appreciate how well the event was going, had it not been for the turmoil in her head. Seeing Dante again had affected her more than she could ever have imagined, bringing back those few moments in the stable ten years ago, when just for a moment Dante had responded, spoiling her for all other men. There had been men—of course there had, she was almost twenty-seven—serious men, driven by the need to educate; nerdy men obsessed with their phones; *bon viveurs* whose sole aim in life appeared to be preserving their bodies by pickling them in alcohol; gym bunnies and those she would have been wiser to swerve. But none compared to the brigand with attitude, known to one and all as The Wolf.

And now he was even more attractive. And more elusive. With homes across the world, Dante Acosta could pitch up anywhere.

Face it, the gulf between them was a mile wide.

Jess threw herself back into chatting with as many of their visitors as she could. Her reaction to seeing Dante again was an overreaction.

Tell that to her heart. Tell that to her body. Tell her stubborn mind, that doggedly refused to accept it. Making her excuses to the smiling guests, she moved on. What better way to take her mind off Dante Acosta than to get stuck into some fortune-telling, Jess concluded wryly as she headed back to the house to change into Skylar's costume.

Perhaps she could tell her own fortune. Although surely that could easily be predicted. Dante Acosta could, and probably would, disappear from her life again as swiftly as he had recently appeared.

The ground was hard with frost and the views between the field and the farmhouse far-reaching and mesmerising. Jess stopped briefly to admire them, and to chat silently to her mother, as she so often did. Her mother had been dead for more than five years but her presence remained constant in Jess's heart.

She reviewed the promises she'd made—to complete her studies, to look after her father and make sure he kept the farm. Generations of farming ran through her father's blood. He'd have no purpose in life and nowhere to live, her mother had impressed upon her, so these were sacred vows as far as Jess was concerned.

She had never cried at the loss of her mother, Jess realised as the wind whipped her face, prompting her to move on. Her father had cried enough for both of them, but Jess had bottled up her grief deep inside because her father's tears had solved nothing. They hadn't brought her mother back or sent the bank packing. She had to save him, as she'd promised, and so she mourned silently and dealt firmly with the bank. So far she'd managed to stave off repossession of the farm, but for how long? A good sale today might postpone the inevitable, but it wouldn't solve the problem, which meant there was a possibility they might have to sell off some of the land.

Jess's mood lifted when she turned to see how many people were grouped around her father. He looked as happy as she'd ever seen him, dispensing advice and answering questions. Jim Slatehome was back! People in the horse world who mattered were hanging on his every word.

But there was no sign of Dante. Had he lost interest? There was no time to dwell. She had to prepare to tell fortunes.

When Jess came downstairs after changing into Skylar's colourful costume of voluminous, ankle-length skirt strewn with bells and a heavy fringed shawl to wrap around her shoulders, Dante and her father were sitting in the kitchen. The way the two men fell silent the moment she walked in made her instantly suspicious. What were they up to?

Dante's incredulous stare made her self-conscious. She doubted he'd seen many women with scarves and bells tied around their hair, dressed in shapeless clothes that looked as if they belonged in a jumble sale—which was actually where she'd found them. Even in jeans and workmanlike boots, he managed to look like a king amongst men. But her father seemed happy enough and what else mattered?

'I'm doubly glad I came,' Dante murmured, tongue firmly planted in his cheek.

'And we're extremely glad you could find time to come to our event, aren't we, Dad?' she responded politely through gritted teeth.

Her father was definitely hiding something. She knew that guilty look. And she had only succeeded in sounding ridiculous, like Eliza Doolittle trying to please Professor Higgins, when Dante deserved no such consideration with that smirk on his face. 'It's nice to see you again,' she added, aiming for casual.

'*Nice?*' Dante queried in a deep, husky tone that ran tremors through every part of her. Why wasn't her father helping out? Why must she deal with this man on her own?

'Is the apron to protect you from the kittens?' Dante asked straight-faced.

His comment launched her back to the past and the first time they'd met, when Jess had been caring for a litter of kittens. One of them had chosen the precise moment Dante walked into the stables to pee down her front.

'It's part of my costume,' she said primly.

When she'd almost lost hope that her father might find some way to ease the tension between Jess and Dante he sprang back to life. 'Come on,' he urged, standing up. 'I'll escort you to the fortune-telling tent. I might even be one of your first clients.'

'Do you read tea leaves?' Dante enquired, still holding back on that laugh.

'Jess is a dab hand with a crystal ball,' her father explained, oblivious to the war of hard stares currently being exchanged between Jess and Dante. 'She's great at telling fortunes. You should try her.'

'I might do that,' Dante murmured with a long look at Jess.

He infuriated her but melted her from the inside out too, which was inconvenient. Dante Acosta was a storming force of nature that commanded her attention whether she wanted him to or not.

Jess stalked ahead of her father to the fortune-telling tent. She was annoyed with her wilful body for responding so enthusiastically to Dante. Her nipples had tightened into taut, cheeky buds, while her lips felt swollen and her breasts felt heavy. And that was the least of it.

The sky was clouding over but in spite of the rapidly worsening weather there was a long line waiting for Jess outside Skylar's tent. There was nothing like a bit of supernatural hocus pocus to put the seal of success on a day out like this. Jess's father really believed she'd got a gift, while her mother had dubbed her Skylar years ago, saying Jess should have a magic name to go with her gift. Jess had always suspected that this was just her mother's way of putting steel in the spine of a painfully shy child.

It must have worked, she concluded, thinking back ten years to when she'd launched herself at the most eligible bachelor on the planet.

Ten years on, was she running away from him?

She glanced over her shoulder before ducking inside the tent. No one was following. Dante was as disinterested in her now as he had been then. It was time to forget him and get on with the job.

For the first time ever he was having trouble concentrating as he struck a deal with Jess's father. Jess remained on his mind as he wove his way through the crowd to discover what his future held.

Okay, he was a cynic when it came to telling fortunes, but that didn't stop him wanting to see Jess. Ten years back, he'd been twenty-two and dismissive of potential mates unless they satisfied his demanding criteria. Jess with her paint-free face, scraped-back hair and clothes smelling of cat pee, not to mention the mouth on her like a paint-stripper, had been as far from his ideal as it was possible to get.

Until she kissed him.

That had been one big surprise, and a kick to his senses, reminding him not to overlook something when it was right under his nose.

The long line in front of Skylar's tent stopped him in his tracks. He wasn't a man to queue.

With that kiss he'd had the good sense to curtail ten years ago nagging at his mind, he wasn't a man to wait either. No longer a naïve teen, Jess was a beautiful and intriguing woman. Shapely and soft on the outside, the intrigue came from the will of steel that blazed from her eyes.

That same determination had enabled her to save the farm. According to his team, Jess had no funds other than her meagre savings. She'd stripped these bare to put on this show and save her father. Using persuasion, and bartering her physiotherapy services where necessary, she had managed to recruit practically every member of the village to ensure today's success. The result was this confidence-boosting exercise for Jim Slatehome that should put him firmly back on the map.

He stopped in front of the small, gaudily decorated tent. A large banner hung from the turret, declaring boldly: *Skylar Slates—fortune-teller to the stars!* His cynical smile was back. He guessed he qualified. Now his only problem was how to crash the line.

Retracing his steps, he bought a pack of water from a stall. 'I can handle it,' he snapped at the woman behind the counter when she gazed at his stick. Clamping the unwieldy bundle beneath one arm, he stabbed his stick into the ground and set his sights on his goal.

'Water for the fortune-teller,' he announced as he approached the ever-lengthening line in front of Skylar's tent. 'To keep her voice running smoothly,' he explained, mustering every bit of his rusty charm. The throng parted like the Red Sea to allow the unfortunate man with his lurching gait to move through them with his awkward burden. He vowed on the spot that this would be the one and only time that he viewed his injury as a benefit.

Having arrived at his destination, he rested his cane against the canvas wall and, drawing the flap aside, he ducked his head and walked in.

'Excuse me,' Jess rapped with the paint-stripping look he remembered so well. 'I'll call you in when I'm free.'

'Oh, no, no, please,' the woman seated at the table opposite Jess insisted, getting up to make way for him.

'What do you think you're doing?' Jess demanded, shooting emerald fire his way.

He would have known those flashing eyes anywhere, and those lips that formed a perfect Cupid's bow of possibility. The urge to taste the creamy perfection of Jess's rain-washed skin and rasp his stubble against its soft perfection was overwhelming right now. But he had business to transact. 'I'm here to cross your palm with silver and your lips with a bottle of water,' he explained.

'You're asking me to tell your fortune?' she asked with surprise.

Having put the bottles down, he delved in his pocket for some coins to toss on the table, but his casual air was halted by a bolt of pain.

'You'd better sit down,' she said. 'Where's your cane?'

'Thank you for reminding me.'

The look she gave him told him she understood what it must have cost him to come here today with his cane, in front of all these people. And yet what was pride when there was a deal to be done? They measured each other for a few moments and then she reached out to take his hand. Full marks to Jess, he conceded, for retaining her composure, and remembering that he might save the farm. She had guts, and to spare, he reflected.

'Are you sure you want this?' she asked.

'I wouldn't be here if I didn't,' he assured her, while his senses prompted him to take her somewhere where they could be alone. 'Why does that surprise you?'

'I can't believe Señor Acosta is incapable of predicting his own future.'

'Oh, but I can.' He held Jess's gaze locked in his and was rewarded when she blushed deeply.

'You crashed the line,' she scolded.

'I did,' he agreed with a shrug. How beautiful she was, even with what looked like a piece of Christmas tinsel wrapped around her head. Her hair glowed like fire in the soft light of a lamp, over which she'd draped a piece of red chiffon, while her eyes were deep pools of unfathomable green.

'Stop staring at me. I'm supposed to be reading you, not the other way around.'

'Then get on with it,' he suggested.

She reached across and rattled an old biscuit tin that had an opening cut in the top. 'Put your money in here—those pieces of silver,' she reminded him.

'Of course...'

He added a few more coins to those he'd already tossed down on the table. She still held out the tin. 'A twenty should do it,' she prompted bluntly.

'Twenty?' He pulled his head back with surprise.

'Can't you afford it?'

Her lips curved in the first real smile he'd seen and her eyes danced with laughter. That was the Jess he remembered from the stable ten years ago—feisty and free to speak her mind, rather than constrained by the fact that he might be her father's last hope when it came to saving the farm. He preferred this Jess.

'Every penny goes directly to charity,' she explained. 'Nothing I take in this tent will be kept for the farm.'

'Then you can have all my cash.' Levering himself to his feet, he reached into his back pocket to bring out a wad of notes. He fed them into her tin. 'This had better be worth it,' he warned.

But fortune-telling wasn't on Jess's mind now. 'Your leg,' she said with concern. 'You really must agree to treatment. Please don't be stubborn if the appropriate therapy is offered to you, or you could be left with a permanent limp.'

'Did you see that in your crystal ball?' he demanded edgily as he sat down again.

'I don't need a crystal ball to see that. I'm a fully qualified physiotherapist, more than used to dealing with injuries like yours. Which is why I can tell you with authority that you can't afford to leave this any longer,' she added before he could get a word in.

'Well, thank you for your advice, *Skylar*,' he gritted out, 'but that's not what I'm paying you for. What *can* you see in that crystal ball...if anything?'

'A very difficult man,' she fired back.

They glared at each other, and for a good few moments fire flashed between them. Just like ten years ago, it seemed they were destined to strike sparks off each other whenever they met.

'You'll have to be quiet or I can't concentrate,' she said.

'That's the best line I've heard yet,' he muttered as he settled back in his seat.

But Jess did appear to compose herself, before dipping her head and cupping her hands around the ball. His groin tightened at the sight of slender fingers caressing the inanimate object. This was ridiculous. He'd never reacted like this.

Then Jess looked up and made things ten times worse. Her green eyes flayed him before she even spoke, and then she exploded, 'No way!' Pushing the crystal ball away, she snapped, 'This session is at an end.'

'I'm sorry?' he queried dryly. 'Did I miss something, only you don't seem to have told me anything yet.'

Standing up, she stared pointedly at the exit. 'There are people waiting outside. Thank you for your contribution, but—'

'But get lost?' he suggested. 'Is that any way to treat a prospective buyer?'

'If you'd seen what I've seen, you'd be begging to go.'

'All that money and I don't get a second chance?'

'Believe me. You don't want a second chance,' Jess assured him.

He felt a frisson of something as he stared at her, but dismissed it out of hand. No one could foretell the future. This was all an act.

'I can tell you one thing,' she said. 'Like your namesake The Wolf, you should shed your old winter coat, to be ready for spring and changes.'

'Claptrap.'

'Is it?' she challenged, eyes flashing fire as they re-focused on his face. 'Or are you afraid to face what lies ahead?'

'Frightened?' he queried with a short, humourless laugh. 'Are we talking about therapy for my leg?'

'Might be. You must accept treatment before it's too late.'

'Is that what you do?' He gestured around the tent. 'Offer advice under the guise of fortune-telling?'

Jess sighed softly. 'Is that so terrible? Sometimes it's the only way people will hear and take in what they need to. I don't mean any harm.'

'I'm sure you don't,' he agreed grimly. 'But, thank you very much, my siblings have arranged something for me, so you don't need to worry about my leg.'

'That's good news,' she said.

He grunted. 'Don't keep your other mugs waiting.'

'Let's hope they're politer than you.'

But Jess said this with a smile and a genuinely concerned look, which made it hard to remain angry for long. The most annoying teen had grown into a most annoying, hot as hell woman.

CHAPTER THREE

So Jess was unmarried and unattached. Why that should please him, he couldn't say. After all, it wasn't as though he was interested in a relationship with her. Still, his conversation with her father when he returned to the farmhouse hadn't been solely confined to business, and Jim Slatehome had confided that Jess was single. Jim was proud of his daughter, and eager to talk about what she'd achieved. 'Without anyone's help,' he told Dante. 'I just feel sometimes that I'm holding her back. Jess has a big heart. She should share it with a family of her own.'

He fell silent, and the pause was only broken by the crackle of the fire and an old clock ticking on the mantelpiece. And then Jess walked in.

Her father visibly brightened. 'Come and join us,' he said, pulling out a chair.

'When I've showered and changed,' she promised.

Without sparing him a glance, she gathered up the mudsoaked hem of her skirt and dashed upstairs.

She didn't take long to return. Still glowing from the shower, she radiated energy and purpose, and even in a pair of old jeans, scrappy slippers and a nondescript top she was beautiful. She'd made no attempt to impress, which was probably what impressed him most of all.

'Talks between you two go well?' she prompted with

seeming unconcern, but there was an edge of tension in her voice.

'Extremely well,' her father enthused, which only succeeded in making Jess pale.

'Well?' she pressed. 'Aren't you going to tell me what you've decided? Are you buying the horses, Dante?'

'All in good time,' her father promised, thwarting Jess's attempt to turn the spotlight on him. 'Deal or no deal, Dante's still our guest, and he doesn't want to go over the details time and time again. We'll have plenty of chance to discuss it when he's gone.'

Jess's jaw worked as if she disagreed, but she sensibly remained silent. The chance of a deal could not be risked, and she was wise enough to know this.

'Did Skylar do well in the end?' he asked to break the ice when she sat with them in silence.

'You tell me,' she said, fixing him with a look. 'Did you find me convincing?'

'I mean financially,' he explained, matching her no-nonsense look and raising it with serious concern of his own. 'You said it was for charity, so I hope you raked in lots of money.'

'Your generous donation helped,' she admitted. 'I don't think we've ever raised so much.'

'You'll have to come back every year,' her father put in.

Jess drew in a settling breath. 'Yes, why don't you?'

'I intend to.'

'That's good,' her father exclaimed, thumping the table in his enthusiasm. 'Now we'll never lose contact again. The day's been a huge success, and that's all down to you, Jess.'

'And your wonderful ponies, and our helpers from the village,' she insisted, shaking off her father's praise as if she didn't deserve it.

'Sometimes, just say thank you,' he advised good-humouredly.

She shot him a narrow-eyed look, and now her father looked guilty as hell.

'What's going on?' Jess challenged.

'Going on?' her father echoed in a splutter. 'Absolutely nothing,' he protested. 'We've struck a wonderful deal.'

As if to confirm this, the sound of helicopters roaring overhead prevented conversation for a while.

'So all the other potential purchasers are leaving,' Jess commented, staring skywards. She stabbed a look into his eyes. 'So, it's all down to you.'

'Stop fretting, Jess,' her father insisted. 'Dante bought all the horses.'

'All of them?' she murmured, frowning. 'Why do I get the feeling there's something more?'

'Shake his hand, Jess. The farm is saved. The deal is done.'

If looks could kill, the Acostas would be short one member of the family. Jess could afford to show her true feelings now. Standing up, she extended her hand for him to shake. As he captured the tiny fist in his giant paw he was surprised to discover how strong she was. This was no soft, vulnerable individual, but a worthy opponent. That pleased him. He was tired of sycophants and creeps. Extreme wealth came with disadvantages, not least of which was its effect on other people. He couldn't count the times he'd been fawned over, when all he required was to be tested and judged on his merits as a man.

'You can let me go now,' she said.

Realising they were still hand-clasping, he released her. 'Skylar was right about one thing,' he admitted.

'Oh?' Jess's green stare pierced his.

'The deal I struck with your father marks the start of a new chapter in my life.'

'Does that happen every time you buy a few horses?' she demanded suspiciously.

'These aren't just any horses,' her father interrupted, clearly keen to bring Jess's line of questioning to an end. 'These are Slatehome ponies.'

Jess hummed, her suspicion by no means satisfied.

'How did you come by the name Skylar?' he enquired, to break the tension between them when, at her father's insistence, Jess sat down again.

'It was a nickname my mother dreamed up for me when I was heading into my shell and she wanted me to shine. She said Skylar was a witchy name for people with The Sight and it would give me special powers. We laughed about it, and I never felt shy again, because I had this other person inside me: Skylar Slates, fortune-teller extraordinaire. Even now the name reminds me of my mother and the many ways she had to make people feel good about themselves. That was her gift. Skylar's predictions try to encourage hopes and dreams and soothe worries. It seems to help,' she added with a self-deprecating shrug, 'but that's all thanks to my mother.'

'You must miss her terribly.'

'I do.'

For a second he saw that, in one area at least, Jess was vulnerable. The raw wound of loss had never healed. It had been some time since her mother's death. He didn't know exactly. He was guilty of losing touch with anything outside his privileged cocoon and had become even more isolated since the accident.

'My ancestors on my mother's side were *gitanos*,' he revealed. 'Mountain people. Some would call them gypsies. Many of them have The Sight.'

'Jess is shrewd and intuitive, but her magic is confined to making the best cup of tea in Yorkshire,' her father interrupted with his broadest hint yet.

'Make mine coffee,' he reminded Jess.

Having arranged three mugs on the range, she absentmindedly filled them all with tea from the pot. 'Oh, look at me!' she exclaimed with impatience.

He was having difficulty doing anything else.

After making a coffee for Dante she left the two men in the kitchen. She didn't mean to listen in on her return. Who ever did? Her father was telling Dante it was time for him to say goodbye to the last of his guests, and the moment the kitchen door closed behind him Dante was on the phone. 'It's all done,' he said. 'Everything wrapped up to my satisfaction. Notify the lawyers and have the contract drawn up ASAP.'

The covering certificate for each individual pony was already to hand, Jess reasoned with a frown, together with all the requirements for any valuable pedigree horse changing hands. This included a DNA hair sample from both the Sire and Dam to confirm the pony's parentage. The deed of sale was a straightforward matter that would be handled by her father's lawyer. So why was more paperwork necessary?

She barely had chance to reason this through when there was a crash in the kitchen, followed by an earth-shattering curse. Bursting in, she rushed to Dante's side. 'Let me help you up.' Crossing the kitchen without his cane, he'd tripped over a chair leg.

When he snapped tersely, 'My cane, please,' she let it go. The loss of face on a daily basis for a man like Dante Acosta had to be monumental. If he refused treatment, nothing would change.

Handing him the cane, she stood back.

'And no bloody lectures about accepting treatment,' he warned.

'Just do it,' she suggested mildly.

This was rewarded by a grunt. 'Let me look at that leg,' she insisted. 'You might have caused more damage when you fell. Please,' she added when Dante looked at her in silence.

'Very well,' he agreed reluctantly.

She knelt on the floor in front of him, while Dante sat down on the chair. Rolling up the leg of his jeans, she quickly reassured herself that no further damage had been done.

'*Gracias*,' he grated out when she told him this, and got up.

'It's my job,' she said with a shrug. 'Here,' she said when he began to rise. 'Don't forget your cane.'

He took hold of it, and for some reason she didn't let go. For a few potent seconds they were connected by a length of polished wood. Then, to her horror, he began to reel her in. She could let go but she didn't, and Dante only stopped when their faces were almost touching. Closing her eyes, she wondered if she'd have the strength to resist him, or if she would follow the urges of a body that had been denied release and satisfaction for far too long.

'You like playing with fire, don't you, Skylar?' Dante murmured,

She dropped the cane like a red-hot poker. 'I'm trying to help.'

'Yourself?' Dante suggested.

'I don't know what you mean.'

'I think you do,' he argued. 'And if you play with my fire you will definitely get burned. Is that what you want?'

She gave a short huff of incredulity. 'My interest in you is purely professional.'

Furious with herself for succumbing to the notorious Acosta charm, she crossed the room and reached for her coat. Ramming her feet into boots, she went to join her father in saying goodbye to their guests, leaving the mighty Dante Acosta to sort himself out.

He refused to go unless Jess came with him. She plagued his mind and tormented his body, and until she agreed to accompany him to Spain he wasn't going anywhere.

*How was that supposed to happen when they weren't
on speaking terms?*

He'd find a way.

Confined to the house long enough, he gritted out a
curse and heaved himself to his feet.

He found Jess riding in the outside arena. From the look
of concentration on her face he guessed she found solace
as he did, by twinning her soul with a horse. Animal and
human moving as one, with scarcely a visible adjustment
on Jess's part to suggest she was directing the intricate
moves, was the most healing activity he could think of. She
was a master equestrian. He should have expected that. He
was impressed.

Worthy sentiments were soon surpassed by a flash of
triumph as he reflected that all this belonged to him now.
Jess didn't know the extent of his deal with her father. Jim
Slatehome had asked that they keep it between themselves
for the time being that Dante had bought the farm and everything on it. 'She can be difficult, our Jess,' her father
had explained. 'She's had a tough time. I'll know when it's
the right time to tell her. Until then, say nothing. I don't
want her upset after all she's done.'

Triumph yielded to lust as Jess brought her pony alongside him at the fence. 'This is our best horse. Her name is
Moon,' she informed him.

'You handle her well.'

She smiled. 'High praise indeed.'

'I mean it.'

This was possibly the first relaxed conversation they'd
had, and it allowed him to press forward with his plan;
rather than alienating Jess, he had to form a connection
with a woman who could be useful to him. There were
always vacancies for top-class riders in one of his teams.
'Show me what she can do,' he encouraged.

'I just did.'

'Please,' he coaxed, dialling up the charm.

'As it's you…' But she was smiling.

He leaned on a fencepost as Jess put the promising mare through her paces. The pony could be difficult and liked to show off. Sensing he was watching her, Moon kicked out her back legs and bucked. Jess remained perfectly balanced throughout.

'Good job,' he said when she returned to his side.

'I love the challenge of a spirited pony,' she enthused as she reined in.

'I love a challenge full stop.'

She blushed.

'You've got a good seat.' She had a great seat. It would fit his hands perfectly. 'Do you play?'

'I take it you're referring to polo?'

'What else?' he asked, throwing her a surprised look.

'I used to play,' she admitted, 'but I'm usually too tired by the end of each day, so I read instead, play the piano, or crash out in front of a soap.'

'Everyone needs fresh air. You should get out more.'

'Says you?' she jibed.

Humour drained from his eyes. It was common knowledge that Dante Acosta had been housebound since discharging himself from hospital, and that this was his first appearance in public. 'Don't make me regret accepting the invitation to come here today.'

Jess had the good sense to say nothing. She didn't need to. Her eyes spoke eloquently, telling him, *I'm not sure yet what's in it for you, but you would have left by now if the answer was nothing.*

'What are you doing?' she asked as he opened the gate to join her in the paddock.

'I want to see Moon close up for myself.'

'Take care; she bites.'

'You or the horse?'

'She won't like your cane.'

'Then may I suggest you dismount and hand her over to a groom?'

'A groom?' Jess intoned. 'Where do you think you are? This is a working farm, not some billionaire's playground.'

His hackles lifted. 'I live on a working ranch. My business life and home life are very different. Do you want me to trial her or not?'

'You already own her.'

'I do.'

'Then she's all yours,' Jess said with a shrug, but as she turned he saw that accepting the inevitable wasn't easy for Jess. She loved these animals and couldn't bear the thought of never seeing them again.

'Be careful,' she said as he vaulted into the saddle using only the strength of his arms. 'Moon can be tricky.'

'You care?' he asked as he soothed the horse.

'I care about Moon,' she told him.

'Hey, *querida*, let's see what you can do,' he whispered, adding soothing words in Spanish. The pony's flattened ears pricked up at the sound of his warm, encouraging tone and she didn't disappoint, though each swerve and bounce jangled his damaged nerve-endings.

'A good enough reason to accept treatment?' Jess suggested as he made sure not to stumble as he dismounted, by taking the weight on his one good leg.

'She'll make the first team,' he said, ignoring her question.

'Your reputation is well deserved,' she commented as he handed over the reins.

'Do you mean I can ride?' he suggested with a grin.

'Like a master,' she said frankly.

'Your father has lost nothing when it comes to his gift for breeding and training some of the best horses in the world, and some of it's rubbed off on you.'

'Only some of it?' she said, smiling.

'All right…' With a conciliatory gesture, he smiled too. That connection he'd wanted was on the rise.

'Do you want to trial any more ponies?' Jess asked.

'I'll leave that to my grooms. I trust a practised eye and intuition.' And his leg couldn't take any more today.

'How will you transport the ponies to Spain?' Jess asked with concern, glancing at his helicopter in the next field.

'The same way my grooms arrived today. In a specially adapted jet,' he revealed.

'You haven't wasted much time,' she observed suspiciously.

'I never do.' He let the silence hang for a few seconds before adding, 'You should come with me when I go back to Spain—to settle the horses,' he went on before she could argue.

'Can't your grooms do that?'

'I thought you'd like to do it. The ponies know you. They don't know my grooms yet.'

She couldn't argue with that, but she did raise one objection. 'I have work commitments.'

So it wasn't a flat no, he registered with satisfaction.

'And luckily they dovetail nicely.'

Well, that was a surprise. 'So you're saying yes?'

'I believe I am,' Jess confirmed, as if all the advantage in coming to Spain with him was on her side.

CHAPTER FOUR

JESS HAD NEVER seen her father looking so relaxed. He looked ten years younger, as if all his worries were behind him. She'd just sat down when Dante entered the kitchen.

'It was good of you to judge the children's pony race,' her father exclaimed as Dante sat next to her.

Tingling apart, she was surprised to learn that the great Dante Acosta had joined in to such an extent. 'I didn't know you'd been so busy,' she admitted.

'I enjoyed it,' Dante confessed with a sideways look that heated her up from the inside out. 'We'll have to make it an annual event. You were busy being Skylar,' he reminded her.

'It must have been a bit different to your usual afternoon,' her father ventured with a laugh.

'I enjoyed every moment,' Dante assured him with a look at Jess.

'Dante picked prize winners in each different age group,' her father revealed, 'and spent extra time with a little girl who forfeited her race to go back and help her younger brother.'

Saint Dante? Jess reflected, amused in a good way. What Dante had done today had put him in the spotlight, which couldn't have been easy for him, but the children would have loved having one of polo's biggest stars taking an interest in them.

'That was very good of you,' she said frankly.

'So. Transport tomorrow,' he said.

'*Tomorrow?*' Jess hadn't expected to be leaving the farm quite so soon.

'I don't waste time. Remember?' Dante prompted.

Only an Acosta could make things work as fast as this. Jess's spine prickled. What was she getting into?

'You'll find my jet comfortable, and the ponies will have the best care possible.' Dante was continuing as if there was nothing unusual in making a decision one minute, a plan the next, and executing that plan the following day. 'A vet and her assistant will be on duty throughout, while my grooms will be in constant attendance. You'll have very little to do, other than to keep a watchful eye on the animals and inform my grooms if they have any quirks or preferences.'

'But I must be home for Christmas.' Dry-mouthed and backtracking fast as the extent of her commitment to a man she hardly knew, who lived in a country she wasn't used to, hit home, Jess added, 'I won't leave my father on his own.'

'How old do you think I am, Jess?' her father protested. 'You have to stay in Spain until you're sure those animals are happily settled. You know how much they mean to me.'

And there was that contract she'd signed for the Acostas, which could keep her in Spain a lot longer than that. 'I'll be back for Christmas,' she stated firmly.

Jess managed to convince herself that this trip made good sense. She was going to reassure herself and her father that the horses were properly settled. That was important. She also had to find the right opportunity to break the news to Dante that she was his new therapist. He wouldn't thank her. The regime she'd mapped out would be punishing. He'd left it so long—too long—that only the most intense therapy would stand a chance of effecting change. Even then, there was no guarantee of a full recovery.

With that situation unresolved, she turned her thoughts to something she could influence, which was care of the horses. 'I have no idea how the ponies will react until we're in the air,' she admitted honestly. 'I'll feel more confident when we land, especially if your facilities are as good as I hear they are—'

'They are,' Dante assured her.

'Then I don't foresee any problems.'

'And I'm happy to welcome you on board.'

He was proud of his jet. He owned a couple of smaller aircraft as well as several helicopters, one of which was kept on his yacht, but this huge aircraft with its custom fittings and long-range capabilities was his particular pride and joy. It enabled him to be anywhere in the world on a whim—with or without his horses. There were stalls rivalling any in the world on the lower level, and a fully staffed veterinary surgery in case of emergency. The upper level was more like a super-luxe apartment than anything resembling a plane. One of the foremost interior designers had kitted it out to Dante's specific instructions to include bedrooms, a galley manned by a Michelin starred chef, as well as a couple of luxurious bathrooms. In addition to this, he had a full working office and a spacious lounge where he could relax.

'Wow,' Jess gasped when they had boarded and she could look around. 'This isn't so much an aircraft as a flying palace. And you need all this...why?'

'Because I'm a very busy man.'

'I can see that,' she agreed, viewing the tech in his office as he took her on the tour.

'Would you have my horses walk home?'

'Of course not, but it does seem...how can I put this?... very big for one man.'

'How kind of you to highlight my regrettable bachelor status,' he mocked lightly.

'Don't mention it,' Jess returned, matching his tone and adding a grin.

At least she was relaxed. 'Make yourself at home,' he invited. Cabin attendants were standing by with trays of the finest Cristal champagne, as well as delicious canapés designed to tempt a flagging appetite.

'I'd rather see the horses settled, if you don't mind,' Jess told him matter-of-factly, managing a warm smile for the attendants at the same time. 'Could you show me the way, please?' she added.

'Of course.' There were many things he'd like to show Jess, and not with stabling as his first stop. He wanted to introduce her to his world, to show her that it was as purposeful as hers, and that it just had more trimmings. No woman had ever made him feel the need to justify his wealth. Because they took it for granted, he concluded as he led the way to the lower deck. Jess took nothing for granted.

'This is incredible,' she breathed as she stared with interest at his state-of-the-art equine facility. 'I'm even more impressed than I was on the upper deck. 'You've thought of absolutely everything.'

'Horses are my life,' he confessed, dragging deep on the familiar and much-loved scent of warm horse and clean leather.

'Do you mind if I stay down here while we take off? I'm concerned that the noise might spook Moon.'

'The pilot won't allow you to wander around at will. You'll have to be strapped in for take-off. The grooms have their own drop-down seats, much like the cabin attendants on a regular flight.'

'So long as Moon knows I'm here,' she agreed. 'Why don't you go back upstairs and relax? There's no reason for both of us to be here. I'm sure the grooms and I can handle everything. Why don't you take the chance to rest that leg?'

'I'm not an invalid,' he retorted sharply.

'No. You're anything you choose to be,' Jess agreed with a pointed look at his cane.

'I hope you're not suggesting that it's my choice to use this?'

'You don't have much alternative at the moment,' she pointed out. 'Nor will you until you accept treatment.'

'I'll be staying down here too,' he gritted out, keen to change the subject. 'These ponies represent a huge financial outlay—'

'Don't give me that,' she flashed back. 'You love them as much as I do.'

'I care for all my animals,' he conceded, 'and I've noticed, as you must have done, that Moon is particularly edgy, so I'll be staying with her when we take off.'

'One rule for you and another for me?' Jess challenged. 'Don't *you* have to be strapped in?'

'It's my jet and I do what the hell I like.'

'Regardless of safety?'

'Don't make me send you upstairs.'

'Why don't we both stay with Moon to reassure her?' she suggested mildly, refusing to rise to his threat.

'Because spending time with a woman who appears to take pleasure in sticking sharp words into my leg and shattering glances at my cane holds zero appeal.'

'Oh, I think you can take it,' she said. 'As you must shortly take some painful treatment.'

'You know a lot about me. Or think you do.'

Jess ignored this too and as she slipped into Moon's stall he followed her.

Moon became agitated when the jet engines screamed, eyes rolling back in her head.

They stood either side of the anxious mare to soothe

her. Perhaps the combination of two people who cared got through to the spooked animal. Moon settled and allowed him to scratch a favoured spot beneath her chin. By the time the jet had levelled out everything was calm again. Which was why Jess's tense expression surprised him.

'You okay?' he asked.

'Of course.'

He was going home, but Jess was taking a step into the unknown, he reasoned as she worried her bottom lip.

'You've been standing long enough,' she said, switching the spotlight to him.

Who was in charge here? His concern for Jess evaporated. 'You don't give orders on my flight.'

'Agreed,' she said without objection.

'But?'

She braced herself as if preparing to drop a bombshell.

'Spit it out,' he advised.

'You're in my care.'

'I'm sorry?' he queried, frowning.

'This is as good a time as any to explain that your siblings hired me to treat your leg. Which means obeying my instructions,' she went on before he could answer. 'The alternative is to throw their care and love for you back in their faces.'

'How long have you known this?' he asked in an ominously measured tone.

'I swear I haven't had chance to tell you before now. Yesterday flew by—'

'And you could not have made time?' he queried, controlling everything in his manner and voice to avoid upsetting the skittish mare.

'I didn't want anything to worry my father.'

'And how would this news have done that? Surely he'd be glad you've got another high-profile client?'

'All right,' she admitted. 'I anticipated your reaction,

and I'm worried about you. You need this treatment badly, so please don't be angry. I'm very good at what I do. Your brothers and sister wouldn't have hired me otherwise.'

He shook his head. 'You should have told me at the first opportunity.'

'And I have.' She held his stare without blinking. 'You can always refuse treatment, but for your sake I hope you don't.'

Truth might be blazing from Jess's eyes, but that wasn't enough to stop him feeling deceived and wrong-footed. 'We'll pick this up another time.'

'This is surely not a complete shock. You knew you would be undergoing treatment.'

'Not with you. I was expecting a physiotherapist, yes.'

'And you've got one,' Jess pointed out. 'One with three years' experience at a prestigious London teaching hospital before I went into private practice to allow for more flexibility.'

So she could take care of her father, he presumed Jess meant by that. He couldn't knock her for something he would have done. Family meant everything to both of them.

'I'm known for my good results if people listen to me,' she went on. 'That's why your family contacted me. Word of mouth is the most effective marketing tool.'

He didn't trust himself to discuss this yet, and Moon, sensing discord between them, was fast becoming restless.

'You're unsettling her,' Jess murmured as if he needed this pointing out.

'Is that why you chose to tell me here? Because I couldn't make a fuss.'

'I think you'd better leave,' Jess told him in the same calm tone.

'No one tells me to leave.'

'It's best for the horse.'

'And you,' he pointed out with a sceptical huff. 'You go.

I'll take care of Moon. She should know me. You can't cling to her for ever. It isn't fair to the horse. Go,' he instructed Jess as the pony grew increasingly agitated. 'If you love her, you'll entrust her to me.'

Jess's eyes were wide, and threatened tears. 'You'll take good care of her, won't you?'

'The well-being of my animals is paramount.'

'Just one more thing,' she said, and Dante paused for a moment. 'What would you have said if I had introduced myself as your therapist in the first place?'

Based on ten-year-old memories? He would have laughed her out of the room.

'Don't be angry with your family for caring about you,' she said as if reading his mind. 'I'm the best chance of recovery you've got.'

'We'll see, won't we?'

Swinging around, he turned his attention to the horse. The mare was soon quiet again. Moon trusted him instinctively. What she didn't like was friction between him and Jess. 'We'll have to do something about that, won't we?' he murmured in one silken ear.

Moon rewarded him immediately by calmly resting her head on his shoulder and whickering softly, as if to say yes.

CHAPTER FIVE

PERCHED TENSELY ON the edge of a deeply upholstered seat in the lounge area of Dante's super-jet, Jess brooded on whether she should have blurted out sooner, *I'm your therapist. I've been booked by your brothers and sister. Suck it up.* Well, maybe not that last—

'Are you sure you won't have another sparkling water, *señorita*?'

'No, thank you.' Suddenly aware of the empty glass she was nursing, Jess handed it over with a smile. The cabin attendants couldn't have been more helpful. Her surroundings were beyond impressive, from the plush leather and polished wood to the space. There was just so much space. She definitely wasn't used to that in the cheap seats. The interior of Dante's jet was more impressive than a mansion in a magazine. All light and bright and pristine, everything was of the highest quality.

Dante's expression could be described as anything but light and bright when she'd left him on the lower deck; trust was crucial between a therapist and their patient. Had she sacrificed that? Heaving a sigh, she wondered when she could have told him. Things had moved so fast, because that was what her father wanted.

She could have made time.

Maybe, but that might have spoiled yesterday for her

father. And, selfishly, she had wanted time to get to know Dante, and hadn't wanted to put a spike in that either.

And now? What did she want now?

To get through this, and for Dante to accept treatment.

He was perfectly entitled to send her home.

What would be the point in that? Why delay his recovery when he had a therapist on hand? She would be on the *estancia* to see the horses settled, so he might as well accept treatment. Even Dante Acosta wasn't superhuman.

He just looked that way...smelled that way...acted that way—

'Excuse me, *señorita*...?'

It was the cabin attendant again. Jess looked up and smiled. 'Yes?'

'Señor Acosta is waiting in the dining room.'

'I'll be right there.'

Jess's mouth dried. Did Dante's summons herald a reprieve, or was she about to receive her marching orders? Pausing only to smooth her hair and firm her jaw, she set off to confront the wolf in his lair.

Dante had seated himself at the head of a full-sized dining table, where he was ravenously devouring a baguette and cheese. When Jess walked in he looked up briefly. Indicating 'Sit' with a jerk of his chin, he swiped a linen napkin across his mouth. 'Are you hungry?'

'A little,' she admitted.

The look Jess was giving him suggested she couldn't deal with so much charm. Tough. He wasn't about to sugarcoat his manner for someone who had kept vital information from him.

'Eat,' he rapped, 'and then we'll talk.'

'That sounds ominous.'

Ignoring her comment, he finished his food and swilled it down with a large glass of water.

Jess made no attempt to take anything from the laden platters in front of her. 'Do you want something else?' he probed, frowning. 'If you do, ask.'

She looked uncomfortable. 'I don't want to put anyone to any trouble.'

'Really?' he said, sitting back. Keeping his stare fixed on Jess, he waved the attendants away and reached for some fruit.

'I'm not here to eat,' she insisted. 'You wanted to talk to me.'

He shrugged.

'You think I've taken advantage,' she stated tensely.

'That's exactly what I think,' he agreed.

'I'm sorry you feel that way.'

He held up a hand. 'Don't be. We're not so different, you and I. Why shouldn't you seize an opportunity? I would have done exactly the same thing.'

Her frown deepened. 'So…?'

'So we're complicated.' Easing his shoulders, he stared at her. 'Do I have to put something on a plate and feed you myself?'

Her eyes darkened. 'No, I'm—'

'Fine?' he suggested.

'Yes.'

'Relax, Jess. I have the greatest admiration for the caring profession. You should have told me from the start, but it's done. You're here. Now you have to put your manner of telling me behind you, as I do.'

'I didn't mean to deceive you. I just want to help.'

'My leg's aching,' he admitted. 'Why shouldn't you help? Grapes and cheese?'

She looked bemused for a moment, but then she relaxed. 'Thank you. I am hungry, and that would be good. I know I haven't made the best of starts, but I will make up for it.'

She certainly would, he thought.

* * *

The cheese was delicious and Dante was too. He was such a distraction she had trouble remembering important things, like why she was here and what she had come to do. He'd showered and his hair was still damp. It curled in thick black whorls that caught on his stubble. His earring glinted in the overhead lights, while the scent of lemons and something woody surrounded him. On home territory Dante was relaxed, wearing just a loosely belted robe after his shower. When he moved she caught glimpses of his tattoos…an edge of the snarling wolf across his heart and, when he turned to pour another glass of water, a glimpse of the skull and cross mallets tattooed across the back of his neck. How was she supposed to make easy conversation with all that going on?

'Eat up—take more,' he insisted. 'From what you've told me, I'll be working you hard.'

Jess's throat tightened. Shouldn't it be the other way around?

'If my treatment can't wait, I'm sure you're eager to begin,' he suggested dryly, with a long amused yet challenging look.

'Yes, of course,' she agreed in a voice turned dry.

'You have access to my medical history?'

'Scans, X-rays and a full set of notes,' she confirmed.

'Then there's no reason why you can't start right away. We're not going anywhere until this aircraft lands, so you might as well make a start. As you can see,' he added lazily, playing her like a minnow on the end of his rod, 'I dressed with that in mind.'

The thought of laying hands on Dante's body sent Jess's heart into a spin. Would she ever be ready to do that? She was a professional, with a job to do. Of course she could do it.

'I'm happy to start your treatment right now,' she said evenly.

It wasn't just Dante's sporting future she was holding in the palm of her hand, Jess realised. She wasn't so naïve that she didn't understand the boost her CV would receive if Dante's treatment resulted in him returning to world class polo.

'Second thoughts?' he suggested.

'None.'

'Then…' Dante was viewing her with amused eyes, as if he knew every thought in her head. 'You'll need a firm surface to work on, I presume?'

'Correct,' she confirmed.

'I'll make sure you have one. We will begin in half an hour.'

'That's good timing,' she agreed. 'You should digest your food first.'

'It will also give you chance to examine all the reasons you chose to come to Spain.'

'I have a contract,' she countered swiftly. 'And the lower deck of your aircraft is full of ponies that mean the world to me and my father.'

One of Dante's sweeping ebony brows lifted. 'You have an answer for everything, *señorita*. We will soon see if you have a solution for my damaged leg.'

Get over yourself, Dante mused as the minutes ticked slowly away. He shouldn't have allowed the situation to reach a point where his brothers and sister had been forced to intervene. But that was how the Acostas were. If one needed help and refused it, the others stepped in. Jess was stuck in the middle of a forceful, powerful family. He shouldn't be taking out his frustration on her. He'd been difficult since the polo accident. Hell, he'd always been difficult. He'd been the wayward son before his parents' death. It was only after the tragedy that he realised how much grief he'd given them. Now that grief was his. Verbal jousting with Jess had lifted him. He liked a challenge, and Jess was full of it. Without polo there was no conflict in his life. Jess gave him all he needed. Feeling her hands on his body was something he anticipated with interest.

'My bedroom?' he stated when she appeared at the appointed time.

'Perfect,' she agreed without batting an eyelid. 'We'll have privacy there.'

'So no one will hear me scream?' he suggested dryly.

'The treatment will be painful,' she admitted evenly, 'but I don't imagine you show your feelings as easily as that.'

They stared at each other for a moment. *Pot, kettle, black*, he thought, but at least Jess didn't shy away from her obligations. 'Lead the way,' she said pleasantly instead.

'I'm going to put a towel over you to preserve your modesty,' she told Dante in the reassuring tone she used with all her patients.

'What modesty?' he growled.

She blinked as she turned back to her patient and was confronted by an iron butt. Her heart thundered like crazy at the sight of something that would normally pass her by. A butt was a butt. They came in all shapes and sizes, and she had never judged anyone yet. Before now. In her defence, Dante had an exceptional butt. And the sooner she covered it with a towel the better.

His body was all over magnificent. Dante Acosta was as close to male perfection as it got.

'I'm ready,' he announced.

Are you? she felt like saying, but at least he'd bounced her out of the self-indulgent stare. Members of his crew had arranged a board on top of the bed and she'd added a cover on top so it was comfortable.

'Well?' he prompted. 'What are you waiting for?'

She would have to be made of stone not to appreciate the sight in front of her. 'I'll be starting on your calf and working up.'

'Great.'

'Don't get too excited. According to your notes, there's nothing wrong with your groin.'

'Very witty. I rather thought I would be staying here on my front anyway.'

'You will; don't worry,' she replied as she hauled his legs into a position to suit the upcoming therapy. 'Now lie still and don't move again. And please don't talk. We have less than an hour for this treatment, if you want to take a shower when I've finished.'

'What are you using?' Dante asked suspiciously as she slicked her hands with oil.

'Horse liniment. My bag's in the hold—'

'You're doing *what*?' he roared.

'Joke?' she said mildly, chalking one up for the therapist. 'This is straight out of your bathroom.'

'No more jokes,' Dante growled, which was her signal to dig deep into the muscles on his injured calf.

Applying her skill, she soon discovered the seat of the problem. Starting gently, she built up the pressure until Dante let rip with a violent curse.

'You're supposed to be curing me, not torturing me!'

'If you'd started treatment sooner your muscles wouldn't be in such a knot.'

'Then make allowances for that knot.'

'Stop deafening me. Stay still. Keep quiet,' she instructed. 'This will hurt if you don't submit—'

'*Submit?*' he roared, almost exploding off the bed.

She pressed her weight against his back...his warm, tanned, hard-muscled back. 'Lie back down,' she insisted.

'I could shake you off in an instant,' he warned.

'You could,' she agreed. 'But what good would that do? Meanwhile, I'm hearing your treatment time ticking away.'

'You're cool; I'll give you that,' he conceded.

Thank goodness that was how she appeared. It wasn't how she felt.

'Continue,' Dante instructed as he rested back on the bed. 'Though I imagine you're going to make me pay.'

An unseen smile hovered on her lips. 'Whatever makes you think that?'

'My infamous intuition,' Dante informed her.

He bit back a curse as Jess—or Skylar, as he preferred to think of her in this merciless mood—dug her fingers deep into a nerve.

'This is the price you pay for neglecting follow-up treatment,' she informed him when he snarled a complaint.

He didn't care for the tone of her voice.

'What do you think you're doing?' Jess demanded when he rolled off the bed.

'Getting a few things straight.'

'Like what?' she demanded, lifting her chin to confront him. But her glance dipped to his lips before it returned to his eyes.

They continued to stare at each other until her eyes sparkled and she couldn't hold back a laugh. He laughed too because this was real, this was Jess. She wouldn't have known how to flatter him if she'd tried.

'Down,' she instructed, pointing to the bed. 'I haven't finished with you yet. Take your treatment like a man.'

'With pleasure,' he agreed, smiling.

'There won't be too much of that,' she assured him.

'Pleasure?'

That one word was all he could get out before the torture began, but he had to confess that she was good by the end of the session. 'My leg feels a little easier,' he remarked with surprise.

'You'll pay for it tomorrow,' she predicted. 'One session isn't a cure. It's only the first step in a very long treatment.'

'Excellent.'

'Excellent? I can't promise to be gentle with you.'

'Please,' he said, staring into her eyes, 'don't hold back.' Jess was blushing deeply as he added, 'At least my siblings haven't wasted their money.'

'Wait—I want to check something before you go,' she said as he straightened up. With that, she knelt at his feet.

'You don't have to bow to me— *Mujer!*' he exclaimed as she dug her fingers into an area he had so far treated with the care he might show an eggshell.

'There you go,' she announced with satisfaction. 'It is that muscle at the root of your problem.'

He had more muscles with more problems than she knew.

'And you had to prove it,' he observed as Jess stood up.

'Yes, of course I did. I know what I'm doing, you know.'

There was no doubt in his mind of that.

Something incredible had happened while all this was going on. The anger that had dogged him since the accident—an accident caused by his recklessness, as well as that of his opponent—evaporated and was replaced by good humour. Jess had released something in him. It was the same knack she'd had ten years ago when he was an overconfident youth of twenty-two. She could burst a bubble of entitlement with a flash of her emerald eyes. Maybe she had been in awe of the Acosta brothers when they strode into her father's stable, but she'd hidden it beneath a mix of teenage attitude—and one surprisingly bold action. She hadn't even been fazed by the little fluff-ball disgracing itself all over her clothes, or if she had, she hadn't shown it.

'Don't you see the funny side of this?' he enquired with

interest. 'Teenage Jess turned regimental sergeant major where my treatment's concerned?'

'No, I don't,' she said flatly. 'Treating patients is a serious occupation for me. I don't find any of this amusing.'

'Liar,' he reprimanded her softly. 'You must be gloating deep down.'

Jess's expression remained unchanged.

Now the session had ended they went their separate ways, Jess to check on the horses, while he went to take a shower and get changed. Had he met his match? The thought that he might have done pleased him as he stared into the glass above the basin. Would she get the better of him? No. That would never happen and it was something Jess still had to learn.

But… As he eased his leg, and for the first time in a long time felt no pain, he thought his accusation of Jess gloating over her control of him had gone too far. Yes, she was in charge of his treatment; that was what she'd been hired to do. Early signs pointed to her therapy being effective. Instead of trying to wind her up, he should be thanking her. Jess was alone on new territory, where he controlled everything outside Jess's treatment plan. A little humility on his part wouldn't go amiss.

CHAPTER SIX

'THANK YOU,' Jess whispered as she stroked Moon's ears. She loved the contrast between sharp-edged cartilage and sleek, velvety hair and, even more than that, she loved the communion between them. The healing power of animals could never be overestimated in Jess's opinion. She only had to be in the stall with Moon to know that this closeness between them was a gift, a space, a special place to be— it was a place where she could always see things clearly. Except for Dante.

All those years she'd dreamed about him, without making allowances for the man he would become. In her mind, Dante had remained the dangerously attractive youth who hovered unseen, and yet so forcibly present, over every relationship she'd ever had. How was she supposed to have a successful love life with Dante Acosta as her template?

That kiss hadn't stopped him when it came to relationships.

No. Far from it. Following Dante's career meant following a great many stories of his private life, which ran alongside his success, both in polo and the tech world. While she applauded his many triumphs, she was forced to see him dating, and that cut deep.

It still did.

It hadn't damaged the connection between them. That was real and strong, at least on Jess's part, but did Dante feel it too? He was impossible to read. Even blazingly alive in front of her rather than haunting her mind, Dante was as intangible as he had ever been.

Could there ever be anything between them?

'Look at the state of me,' she murmured as Moon nuzzled her neck. 'Does that seem likely when women across the world are hammering on Dante's door? Why waste my life on pointless dreaming?'

'So here you are—'

She jumped at the sound of Dante's voice.

'I knew I'd find you with the ponies.'

Her swift intake of breath must have betrayed the fact she'd been thinking about him. If that wasn't enough, her cheeks were blazing and her lips felt swollen, while her breasts were aching for his touch.

Dante appeared totally unaffected. Ditching his cane to come into the stall, he lounged back against the wall to inform her, 'Look, no stick. I'm cured. You can go home now.'

'By parachute?' she suggested.

He laughed, a flash of strong white teeth against his dark, swarthy face, which was the cue for heat to rush through her. If there was one thing more dangerous than a grim-faced Dante Acosta, it was this version. She couldn't resist this one at all.

She must, Jess reminded herself. Professionalism was paramount. 'It's too soon to discard your stick,' she observed. 'I've already warned you that you'll suffer tomorrow if you put too much stress on that leg. You could pay the price with a setback.'

Dante's answer was an easy shrug. 'Relax. I left my cane outside to avoid spooking Moon.'

'And you delight in teasing me. Don't forget that.'

Dante almost turned serious. 'I delight in the improvement I can feel in my leg. You can claim a miracle if you like.'

'I prefer to work steadily until I'm sure that any improvement is lasting. I don't throw up my hands and cheer at the first sign of change.'

'Tell me, how do you remain so controlled?'

'It counters your teasing,' she said honestly. 'As for miracles? All I see in your future is more therapy, hard work and pain.'

'Sounds irresistible.'

'I thought you'd prefer to hear the truth.'

'Did you?'

The look he gave her now made Jess's cheeks flare bright red, while her body responded with far too much enthusiasm. 'I take it you're here to see Moon?' she said in an attempt to distract both of them from the mounting tension.

'I'm here to see you also.'

'Oh?'

'There's something I forgot to say to you.'

'You're fired?' she suggested dryly.

'Now, why would I do that when I think we're making progress?' Dante viewed her steadily. 'Small steps,' he explained.

Was he still referring to his leg? 'Small steps,' she agreed. 'Truce?'

She tensed as he pulled away from the wall. As he came closer and his heat wrapped around her, Dante's energy pervaded the atmosphere.

'I just want to say thank you,' he soothed.

He dipped forward to brush a kiss against her cheek, but she turned her head at entirely the wrong moment and their lips met. It seemed like for ever, though it could have been no more than a heartbeat, that she didn't move, breathe or register anything apart from the fact that Dante was kissing her and seemed in no hurry to move away.

'You okay?' he prompted, pulling back.

The penny dropped. No wonder he was frowning. In

Dante's sophisticated world kisses were exchanged as easily as handshakes. 'Of course I'm okay.' She shrugged as if men like Dante Acosta kissed her every day of the week, when what she really wanted was for him to kiss her as if he really, *really* meant it. 'There's no need to thank me. It's my job.'

'You're very good at your job,' he observed in a tone that bore out every thought she had about the meaning of that kiss. There was no meaning beyond *Thank you*.

'And now it's time to strap in for landing,' he added briskly.

You can say that again, Jess thought, curbing misplaced amusement as Dante's dark stare lingered on her face.

'Now?' he prompted. 'We'll be touching down in a few minutes.'

His wake-up call was badly needed. She wasn't his type. If his perfunctory kiss hadn't proved it, any magazine in the world would show that Dante went for glamorous women, more at home on the front row of a high fashion show than the back row of the stalls.

Heading off to find a seat to strap into, she was surprised when Dante did the same. She'd already decided to stay on the deck with the horses so she was ready to help the grooms as soon as the plane landed. 'Why don't you strap in upstairs?' she suggested to Dante. 'We can manage here, and if you don't rest after treatment you'll never get better.'

'If you don't learn that I don't accept orders you and I are in for a bumpy ride,' he shot back.

Pressing her lips together so she didn't say something she might regret, Jess reflected tensely, *You don't frighten me, Dante Acosta, and, whether you like it or not, for the duration of your treatment I'm in charge.*

With the horses safely arrived in Spain and loaded into transporters waiting on the tarmac, it was Jess's turn to climb into Dante's flatbed alongside.

Flinging his cane into the back, Dante hauled himself into the driving seat beside her. 'You'll be in pain for some time yet,' she explained when he grimaced and paused to knead a cramped muscle. 'I dare say I've woken up nerve endings you'd forgotten about.'

'No chance of that now,' he agreed grimly. 'How long must I suffer cramp?'

'Until you're cured.'

'Then you'd better get on with it.'

'I intend to.'

As Dante shook his head with exasperation, Jess knew she was dealing with a warrior, a man who had thought himself invincible until the accident.

'You'd better make sure I'm ready for the new polo season,' he threatened, grimacing.

'I'd be lying if I said I could guarantee that. It's largely up to you, and how seriously you take my treatment plan.'

'Do you have to be so honest?'

'Always.'

'I can hire a therapist any day of the week.'

'Then go ahead and do so, though I can't imagine you'll have many takers if that expression settles on your face.'

'*Ha!* And what about the ponies? Or have you forgotten about them?'

'I've forgotten nothing,' she fired back. 'I'll stay on your *estancia* until they're settled, but that doesn't mean you have to keep me on as your therapist. Go ahead and hire someone else.' *At least I wouldn't have to tolerate you as a patient*, she thought, though deep down she knew it was the frustration of Dante's injury driving him to lash out at her. Better he did that than he took it out on someone who didn't understand him. 'I'm here to help and until you fire me that's what I'm going to do.'

'So you can put Acosta on your CV?' he suggested with an ugly snarl.

'So you can walk without a cane, and ride again, and maybe even play polo at international level again,' she argued calmly.

'Only maybe?' he said with a narrow-eyed look.

'There are no guarantees where the body is concerned,' she said honestly, 'but I've never shirked in my attempt to heal a patient yet, and I don't intend to start with you. I'm not a quitter, Dante.'

'Just my bad luck,' Dante murmured beneath his breath. Releasing the handbrake, he gunned the engine and they were off to a future even Skylar would find hard to predict.

While they were driving, Jess called her father to reassure him they'd landed safely and the horses had been loaded successfully without drama and were now on their way to Dante's ranch in Spain. It would have been a lie to add that things were going well, she reflected, and so she confined herself in a very British way to talking about the weather. 'It's warmer here in winter than Yorkshire in summer,' she told her father with a laugh.

'You enjoy yourself,' he said before cutting the line. 'All work and no play et cetera.'

'Thanks, Dad, I'll remember that.'

Dante glanced at her as they ended the conversation and she huffed a rueful laugh. 'Everything okay?' he asked.

'My father seems fine—on top of the world, in fact. I've never heard him sounding quite so optimistic.'

'Good. That's good.'

They both fell silent and she tried to relax, but it wasn't easy when she was trapped in the confines of a cab with so much man. Dante's lean tanned hands effortlessly tickling the wheel while his biceps bulged and his iron-hard thighs rested a hair's breadth away from hers would have tested the endurance of a saint. His machismo was like a living thing that sucked the air from her lungs, leaving her nothing to breathe but pure sex.

'I'm fast but safe,' he stated.

She laughed inside, wondering if she should feel quite so disappointed about the fast reference in that statement.

'You drive very well,' she said in an attempt to blank images of her life becoming fast and extremely unsafe. Her body wanted one thing, while common sense dictated caution. Twenty-seven years old and she couldn't boast a single successful sexual relationship, and that was all down to one man setting the bar at an unattainable height. Dante hadn't made things better with his most recent kiss. Even if it was just a token to say thank you, she was still buzzing with awareness and kept touching her lips with the tip of her tongue, as if to recreate the moment.

Okay, so she had been one hundred per cent guilty of sabotaging any potential love affair in the past by picking unworthy men. She didn't have time for love, she'd tell herself as she concentrated on her studies. Though she did have time to dream about Dante Acosta. And the failed love affairs? Were down to not wanting to tarnish that first romantic image of a memorable kiss in a stable. And who could blame her, when even a routine 'thank you' kiss from Dante Acosta set her heart pounding? He knocked the competition out of the park.

But there was no point in falling for a lost cause. She had to find a way to get him out of her system, or she'd never move forward and have the chance to love.

Not that she was in danger of falling in love with Dante Acosta. No way! Jess assured herself in the most forceful manner possible. Sucking in a deep breath, she made herself relax.

They'd been driving for around an hour when Dante announced, 'We're here.'

Anything Jess had imagined was obliterated by what

she saw in front of her. Having left the bustling coast behind, the peace of this much lusher, greener interior held
immediate appeal for Jess. 'How lucky you are,' she murmured as high gates swung back to reveal a crown of snow-
capped mountains circling Dante's land. Neatly fenced
paddocks full of ponies stretched away as far as the eye
could see.

'I can ski in the morning and swim in the sea in the afternoon,' he said as they passed through the gates and drove
on down an immaculately maintained road.

Lush green was fed by a glittering river, while clusters
of trees provided shelter for the ponies. Jess was rendered
speechless, and wondered how Dante could ever bring himself to leave.

'I spoke with my brother while you were busy with
Moon. He says they booked you for a month.'

'I can't predict how long your treatment will take, but I
would expect a substantial improvement by then.'

Dante hummed, leaving Jess to wonder if, for him, a
month was too long or not long enough. Either way, she
must separate her personal feelings from what she'd been
tasked to do.

Each bend in the road revealed a new vista of contented
animals and tidily maintained land. 'I've never seen so
many ponies in one place before,' Jess admitted on an incredulous laugh, 'but what about security?'

'High-tech.'

Like everything else in Dante's life, she imagined.
'You've got a lot of plates to keep spinning, and once you
return to full fitness I suspect you'll want to spin even more.
Do you ever take a break?'

'Do you?' he countered with a swift sideways glance.

They fell silent after that, which allowed Jess to appreciate how big his ranch was. It was like a small country within a country, and when she contrasted that with

the small hill farm where she'd grown up she got an even greater sense of the yawning gulf between them.

'Do you like what you see?' Dante enquired.

'The more I see, the more I understand why you chose to come here to lick your wounds.'

'It's my home,' he said, as if this were obvious.

But it was more than that, Jess suspected. This was Dante's retreat from the world, where he could live free from comment or the cruel gossip that suggested he might never play again. That gossip made her doubly determined to heal him.

Though there might be more to heal than Dante's leg, she accepted. He was a complex man who had famously run wild in his youth, only to be drawn to a shuddering halt by the death of his parents. Since then, it was well documented that Dante had done everything he could to help his oldest brother take care of the family. That took its toll as well, she reflected, thinking of her father's distressing retreat from the world when he'd lost his wife. Nothing hurt more than seeing someone she loved suffering as much as her father had, and Dante had gone through that same torment with his brothers and sister, which made her wonder how much time he'd taken to grieve.

'Another couple of miles and you'll be able to see all the facilities, as well as the ranch house and the stables.'

Meanwhile, she would feast her eyes on Dante's hands, lightly controlling the wheel, and his powerful forearms, shaded with just the right amount of dark hair.

Another couple of miles?

Could she control her breathing for that long?

She must, and she would. It wasn't a gulf between them; it was an ocean. She had entered a kingdom for one, which would be forced in the short term to play host to an invader with a medical bag.

And a will every bit as strong as Dante Acosta's.

CHAPTER SEVEN

'MY FATHER TAUGHT me that the handing over process is as important as the sale, so I'll see the ponies settled in before I go to my accommodation, if that's okay with you?' Jess said as Dante drew into a courtyard the size of a couple of football pitches.

'Don't worry. Your father's ponies have come to the best home in Spain.'

'I can imagine,' she agreed, 'but I promised that I would see them settled, and then ring to reassure him. After that, I'll concentrate on you.'

'That sounds ominous,' Dante said as he rested his hands on the wheel.

'You're my patient, and that makes you my primary concern.'

'I'm very glad to hear it.'

The way he spoke, the way he looked at her, was going to make it hard to remain immune to the infamous Acosta charm.

Make that impossible, Jess thought as Dante climbed down from the driver's side and came around the vehicle to help her out.

'I can manage, thank you.'

Ignoring her comment, he lifted her down, leaving her with the overwhelming and inconvenient urge to be naked with him, skin to heated skin.

'When you've reassured yourself regarding the ponies, my housekeeper will show you around the ranch house. Or you can sit on the fence and watch as I allow the ponies to stretch their legs. They've been cooped up and will appreciate some carefully controlled freedom.'

'Sit on the fence?' she queried wryly. 'Does that sound like me?'

'No,' Dante admitted, 'but the sooner the ponies get used to new handlers, the happier they will be.'

For a moment Jess felt excluded, and had to remind herself that interaction with her father's ponies was to reassure him and that her main job was to treat Dante.

But she couldn't help herself, and when she noticed Moon playing up she walked over to the wrangler. 'Let me do this,' she insisted as the tricky mare reared. 'I know Moon. I understand her.'

'*Está bien*, Manuel. Back off,' Dante instructed as Jess took charge.

The ease with which she was able to calm Moon was almost embarrassing. Everyone stopped to watch as she brought the pony down the yard but, not wanting to start off on the wrong foot, she explained to the assembled wranglers, while Dante translated her words from English to Spanish, that the mare trusted her because she'd known Jess since the day she was born.

'They appreciated that,' Dante remarked as he led the way into the quarantine area where Moon would be allowed to roam.

'No problem. I know the ponies, and soon they will too. 'Treatment after supper,' she reminded him as they removed Moon's halter and set her free.

'I'm braced and ready,' Dante assured her dryly, 'but I'm handing you over to my housekeeper, Maria, while I catch up with what's been happening on the ranch.'

Maria gave Jess the warmest of welcomes, but even the

most informative tour of the spacious and luxuriously appointed ranch house, with its burnished wood and richly
coloured furnishings, failed to distract Jess from thoughts
of Dante. She had to find a way to put him out of her mind.
At least until his next treatment when, for a short time only,
he would be the focus of her mind and not her heart, she
determined.

'I see you've made yourself at home,' Dante commented
later at supper. He had lined up in the cookhouse with everyone else, while Jess was behind the counter, serving
with Maria and Manuel, the wrangler she'd met earlier.

'And what a home,' Jess commented, smiling as she
handed over Dante's loaded plate. 'Maria invited me to
throw myself in at the deep end, which was exactly what I
wanted to do. So here I am.'

Dante glanced around. 'You approve?'

'Who wouldn't?' she enthused. Dante's ranch had an
air of purpose and everything was of the highest quality,
including the delicious food.

'You don't have to do this,' he said bluntly.

'But I want to. I'm not used to idling my time away.'

His eyes took on a darkly amused glint. 'I'm not enough
for you?'

'Even with two therapy sessions a day, that's only a few
hours of my time.'

With a shrug, he moved on and she attended to the line
behind him.

When it came to Jess's turn to eat, there was one space
left and Dante was sitting at the same table. It was a table
for two, and their knees brushed when she sat down. An attempt to tuck her legs away failed. There just wasn't enough
room. 'Sorry,' she said wryly.

'Too close to the fire?' Dante suggested.

'I can handle it,' she assured him.

'I'm sure you can,' he agreed.

Brooding and aloof was easier to deal with than a decidedly relaxed man, Jess reflected as she got stuck in to the spicy paella.

'One last check on the ponies and then I'll be ready for my treatment,' he said, pushing his plate away and standing up.

'I'll come with you.'

'As you wish.'

Dante stabbed his cane impatiently against the cobbles as they crossed the yard. She guessed his leg was giving him hell, as she had predicted. Her treatment on the plane had been deep and thorough. The memory of her hands on Dante's body made a frisson of anticipation rip down her spine at the thought of doing it again. Could she resist him for an entire month? Would Jess, the coolly professional therapist, do her work and go home, or would all that longing locked inside her break free at some point?

She could do this, she told herself as she followed Dante into the isolation block where her ponies would be kept until they had been checked over and passed fit by his veterinarians. The past had formed her and made her strong. The present brought new challenges, but so far she'd seen them through. There was no reason to suppose she'd falter now.

The facility resembled a top-class equine hotel. She turned full circle to take it in. 'This is wonderful.' Spotless surroundings, spacious stalls and animals contentedly resting was Jess's idea of heaven. She told him so.

'You can move in,' he offered, lips tugging in the hint of a smile.

'If I liked hay for a bed and oats for supper, I might just do that.' But she was laughing and relaxed; they both were.

His libido shot through the roof at the sound of Jess laughing, but his leg let him down by yowling on cue. He couldn't wait long for that treatment.

They checked each pony in turn. When Jess ran capable hands over them, murmuring soft words of encouragement, he craved the same attention. When they walked out of the stable block even the resident cats in the yard came to wind themselves around her legs. 'Next time I'll come prepared with treats,' Jess promised her feline admirers, kneeling down to give them a fuss.

'You have quite a menagerie,' she commented, smiling in welcome as one of his older dogs heaved itself up from its vantage point in front of the kitchen door. Animals were the best judge of character, he knew, and from then on Bouncer stuck close to her side as they completed the tour.

Several members of staff greeted Jess as if she'd lived on the *estancia* all her life. Light spilled onto her auburn hair in the veterinary hospital, setting it on fire as she chatted easily with his veterinarians in the sick bay. When they left the facility she reminded him he was due a treatment. 'Another session tonight, and then I'll leave you alone until tomorrow morning,' she promised.

Drawing her into the safety of the shadows as a truck loaded with sacks of feed trundled past, it was Jess who broke free first. 'Sorry,' she said as if she'd done something wrong.

He gave a relaxed shrug. 'Don't apologise.' He could get used to the feel of Jess beneath his hands. 'See you in half an hour for my treatment? Ask Maria to show you the way to the sports complex. There are treatment rooms there we can use.'

'Fine,' Jess confirmed. 'I'll do that.' But her emerald eyes were as dark as night and her tone was breathy.

Had that just happened? Almost happened. She was still tingling with awareness where Dante had held her out of the way of the truck. She had wanted to stay in his arms but couldn't do that and remain professional. This was only the start of her contract and she was already in danger of melting.

Entering the empty kitchen, she leaned back against the door and closed her eyes briefly. These might be fabulous surroundings and Dante was definitely the most attractive man she'd ever come across, but that was no excuse for her to lose her grip on reality. She couldn't afford to do that, even for a moment. She was here to treat a patient, and though the urge to continue what they'd started ten years ago—what *she* had started ten years ago—was overwhelming, it must remain locked in her mind. Maybe she would have to remain unsatisfied for the rest of her life, but better that than throw away everything she'd worked for on a dream that could never come true.

'Can I get you something, Señorita Slatehome?'

She jumped guiltily as Maria entered the kitchen. 'Jess. Please call me Jess.'

Quickly reorganising her features into those of a woman who hadn't been thinking heated thoughts, she smiled at Maria. 'I'm sorry to invade your beautiful kitchen, but Señor Acosta said you would be able to tell me where to find the sports complex.'

'He didn't have the patience to tell you himself?'

Maria's raisin-black eyes twinkled with laughter, as if this was the Señor Acosta she knew. 'You are a very welcome invasion, Señorita Jess, and I'm happy to direct you.'

But it was a struggle to concentrate when Maria began to explain. Jess felt as if her life had taken on a new and rapid speed and she had no way of slowing it down.

'If I can do anything else for you…' she realised Maria was saying.

'No, no, that's fine—to the side of the stable block, behind the yard—'

Maria laughed and corrected her indulgently. 'Señor

Acosta is enough to make a saint lose concentration,' she reassured her.

'I'm hardly that,' Jess admitted.

'But you are a great improvement on previous visitors,' Maria told her with a significant look.

'Thank goodness for that.'

As they smiled at each other, Jess felt as if the bond that had formed the moment they met had tightened.

'Señorita Jess,' Maria added, catching hold of her before she left the kitchen, 'I would appreciate it if you could let me know if there's anything else you might need over the weekend, as I'm taking the day off on Saturday to start the preparations for my wedding.'

'Oh, how exciting!' And how good to have something to think about, apart from Dante. And a wedding was the best of all distractions.

'You're invited, of course,' Maria told her.

'Me?' Jess's hands flew to her chest.

'Of course you,' Maria confirmed. 'Everyone on the *estancia* is invited.'

Even Dante?

Jess's smile lost some of its sparkle. The less she saw of him in social situations, the better. Seeing him in the stable with horses was safe. Safe-ish, she amended. But weddings were emotionally charged affairs, infused with romantic overtones.

'Please say you'll accept,' Maria pressed. 'I think you'll enjoy it. I'm planning a traditional *gitanos* wedding with a Christmas theme. It will be held before Christmas in the marquee Señor Acosta has arranged here. He's so kind… so generous—'

So The Wolf had a heart after all, Jess reflected wryly as Maria continued to enthuse about Dante's many virtues. 'I'd be honoured to celebrate the day with you, Maria.' Whatever she thought of Dante, Jess wouldn't dream of offending her new friend, and the prospect of attending an authentic *gitanos* wedding was a bonus she had never expected. 'I'm really excited for you,' she admitted as she and Maria shared a hug. 'It's a privilege to be included in something so personal and romantic when I'm a newcomer to the ranch. Please let me know if I can do anything for you.'

'Just be happy here,' Maria implored her with a long thoughtful look as they released each other and stood back.

'Being welcomed like this, how could I not be happy?'

Dante. Wanting more than he could ever give her.

So, Jess reflected as she made her way to the sports building, twice daily physio sessions with Dante, and now a wedding. Was it even ethical to continue treating him, when all she could think about were the possibilities ahead?

These were early days, Jess reassured herself as the sports complex loomed in front of her. All stark steel and glass, it appeared more than fit for a billionaire's purpose. Which was more than could be said for her, Jess concluded with amusement when she caught sight of her reflection in a sheet of glass. She doubted many of Dante's companions went to meet him dressed in scrubs and clogs, carrying a medical bag—unless he had kinks she didn't know about. This thought made her smile, made her determined to get used to seeing him, touching him. She would rein in her feelings. She had to.

But could she?

CHAPTER EIGHT

DANTE PICKED UP some calls while he waited for Jess in the sports block. Each supplied another small piece of the jigsaw that was Jess. He already knew she was a complicated woman, driven, successful and determined. She was also beautiful and he wanted her, but these shreds of information supplied by his team fleshed out the back-story of who she was.

He should have known the bold teenager would rise above the tragedy of losing her mother and develop into someone whose only thought was helping others. Competent and organised, Jess's reputation in her profession was second to none. But did he want to get close to her? Did he want to get close to anyone? The loss of his parents had been unbearable. Grief had frozen his heart.

With nothing but his racing thoughts for company, he soon became impatient. Before the accident he'd had many outlets for his energy: riding horses, women, working out in the gym. That appetite was only slumbering. Flexing his muscles, he turned on his stomach to rest his face on folded arms. Closing his eyes, he breathed steadily and deeply in an attempt to block Jess out, and then flinched, feeling her cool hands on his skin.

'Apologies,' she said in her best no-nonsense voice. 'Are my hands too cold for you?'

'You'll soon warm up,' he predicted.

Telling his body to behave was unnecessary when she began work on his muscles. '*Infierno sangriento!* Hold off!' he warned as she delved into the site of his injury with all the finesse of a commando in the gym.

'I know what I'm doing.'

And with that she put the flat of her hands between his shoulder blades and shoved him down again. 'Don't worry,' she soothed. 'This will soon be over.'

More accustomed to caresses and hungry, urging grips, he growled a soft warning as she kneaded and probed his tender damaged leg.

'Try to relax,' she insisted.

'Are you enjoying this?'

'It's my job.'

'Then improve your bedside manner,' he rapped, 'and while you're at it refine your touch.'

'It's my intention to heal, not pleasure.'

He huffed a cynical believing laugh.

'Settle down,' she instructed.

'Don't tell me what to do.'

'Are you going to take over the session?' She stood back.

'Get on with it,' he growled ungraciously.

'No more talking. Or laughing,' she added as he shook his head and huffed with incredulity that he was still here, still tolerating her torture.

'You've got enough to think about,' Jess assured him. 'As I do, if these leg muscles are ever going to heal.' To prove her point, she applied even greater force to her pummelling and kneading.

'I'm not a lump of dough.'

'No. You're a lot noisier,' she observed. 'And far less pliable. So be quiet.'

'I could fire you.'

'Really?'

She sounded far too enthusiastic about that idea, so reluctantly he submitted, but not before he had acknowledged how quickly charming Jess could revert to Jess the therapist. That impressed him. In the ability to disconnect, she was very like him.

'If you don't obey my instructions,' she murmured as she worked, 'these sessions will be endless.'

'Really?'

'Stop that,' she warned in response to his amusement. 'Any slight improvement you've noticed after our session on the plane only signals the fact that certain muscles and nerve endings are being called into use again. That's a good sign, but it doesn't mean you're cured.'

He gritted his teeth as she gave him a good workout.

'Turn over. I need to work on the front of your leg,' she explained.

He couldn't turn over until his body took the hint. 'Give me a minute,' he ground out, before silently reciting the alphabet backwards.

'Maybe I can help you,' she suggested with concern.

She certainly could.

'Do you have cramp?'

He had something. The mother of all hard-ons meant taking longer than he'd thought. 'Don't touch me,' he warned when Jess attempted to turn him over. 'You might strain your back, and then what happens to my treatment?'

'I'm overwhelmed by your concern,' she murmured with a smile in her voice. 'But if you co-operate I won't need to strain my back.'

'Wait,' he insisted.

'As you please.'

She wouldn't sound so prim if she knew the extent of his problem. She was killing him in more ways than one.

At last he could turn over. 'Carry on.'

* * *

Dante had the most beautiful body she'd ever seen. How could she ignore that—ignore him? Patients were at their most vulnerable on the couch beneath her hands, and Dante was no exception. She wanted to heal him and she knew what to do. She also wanted to touch and pleasure him, but that was off the menu. Thankfully, he behaved himself for the rest of the session, which allowed her to concentrate on her work.

Most of the time.

'I'm done for today,' she announced as she satisfied herself that progress had been made.

'Exhausted?' Dante suggested, turning his head to look at her.

'It would take more than a single session with you to do that.'

'You sound very sure.'

His expression made her blush, made her smile…made her smile broaden. It was impossible not to find some humour in this situation, and it seemed the harder she tried to remain aloof from Dante, the harder fate worked to screw up her plan.

Trapped in the beam of very dangerous eyes, she said firmly, 'I'm done for today.'

'*Muchas gracias, señorita*,' Dante murmured as he rolled off the couch.

'Don't mention it,' Jess said politely as he straightened up and towered over her. 'It's what I do. First thing tomorrow morning, back here, around eight?'

'I'll be in town tomorrow,' Dante said flatly as he snatched up a robe.

'What about your treatment?'

'It will have to wait.'

'But I need to establish a routine.'

Dante grunted. Was this his way of dismissing her? Was

she going to be ditched like the doctors in the hospital? Was he really going to risk his future mobility?

'You can't afford to miss a treatment.'

'You decide this?' he asked with a narrowing of his night-black eyes.

'Yes,' Jess said bluntly. 'I decide your treatment programme. You're not cured yet. If you have to go into town, I can start earlier. Name your time.'

'Six o'clock.'

He made it sound like a challenge. 'Earlier, if you like,' she suggested mildly.

'The time suits me.'

'Then it suits me too,' she said pleasantly, as she seriously considered stamping on Dante's one good foot.

Rewarded by a grunt of assent, Jess had to admit the banter and contest of wills between them was arousing. Dante was a patient like no other. And there was no law against dreaming. No code of ethics could find fault with that.

'Excellent,' she confirmed, turning to go. 'I look forward to seeing you in the morning.'

Delay was the servant of pleasure, Dante reminded himself grimly as he took note of the resolve in Jess's expression. Next stop the pool. He glared at the loathed cane, hating that he needed it to balance as he thrust his feet into sliders.

'You won't need that soon,' Jess called across on her way out.

He hated that she witnessed his plight. But Jess of all people was bound to, he accepted reluctantly. That was why she was here. His siblings would hear more of this. Why had they chosen this disturbingly beautiful woman on a mission, when a troll would have suited him better? Were Jess's soft hands even capable of delivering pleasure? He was beginning to doubt he would ever find out. And that was a first for Dante Acosta.

So. That went well, Jess reflected grimly.

Instead of blanking Dante's brazen sexual appeal, she had thought of little else throughout that entire session. And now it was a struggle not to stare at him through the floor-to-ceiling windows as he sliced through the pool like the hottest thing in black swimming shorts. Even with one leg below par, Dante's body housed an immensely powerful engine. Massive shoulders, rippling muscles and those steel girder arms required supercharged apparatus to drive them on.

'Don't overdo it!' she yelled out as he performed a neat turn at speed. Maybe he heard, probably not, but she doubted he was in the mood to heed advice. There was only so much instruction Dante could take before needing to paddle his own canoe.

A wave of unaccustomed uncertainty washed over her. The prospect of curing him seemed more elusive than ever.

'On your head be it,' she muttered as she walked on. If this was the first day, it would be a long month.

A long month of reliving what had happened between them all those years ago, and wondering if it would ever happen again. She had never forgotten the feeling of his lips on hers at the farm and that brush of his mouth on the plane had only served to intensify her longing.

Get a hold of yourself, Jess; it's never going to happen. And you shouldn't want it to. The man is a nightmare. It would never work.

Look on the bright side, Jess decided as she headed to the kitchen for a snack. In just a few weeks' time there'd be a wedding and lots of new people to meet. She didn't have to spend time with Dante. She could skirt around him between treatments; she'd do it. There was no excuse not to work hard and enjoy herself while she was here.

He felt peckish after his swim. Having checked the new ponies for the last time that day, he headed back to the house to find Maria baking in the kitchen, with Jess clearing up. Jess tensed when he walked in.

Helping himself to a handful of Maria's delicious *churros,* he watched the two women, marvelling at the speed with which they'd formed an easy friendship. He took years to get the measure of a man, and had no reason to get to know women in any depth. Since being misled about his parents' condition at the hospital, he'd found it hard to trust anyone outside his immediate family and staff. Jess was in the group marked pending.

He still remembered the vultures swooping at his parents' funeral, and how he and his siblings had quite literally stood back to back to defend from their greedy demands. The general thought had been that young headstrong youths couldn't hope to take care of themselves, let alone handle a family fortune and land. The scavengers soon learned that the Acostas might have been headstrong at one time, but duty had changed them for good. Some, like Maria, said the change was for the better. Others said not. One thing was sure. No one crossed them.

'I'll miss this woman when she leaves,' Maria told him in Spanish, distracting him as she fondly squeezed Jess's arm.

He grunted a response. His leg twinged. He flexed it.

Jess noticed.

'Better or worse?' she enquired, brushing a loose strand of hair back from her face.

'I haven't decided yet.' If anyone could look sexier with flour on their nose he had yet to meet them.

'I think you're feeling an improvement.'

'Oh, do you?' he said, indicating her nose.

She swiped at it. 'Better?'

'I think I liked it better before.'

His reward was her paint-stripping look.

'Didn't I give you exercises to do?' she prompted. 'Why are you here?'

'I choose to be.'

Their eyes met in a combative glance, accompanied by a now familiar tug in his groin. Jess's eyes had darkened. She could act professional all she liked, but Jess was a woman too.

'If you will excuse me?' he said politely as he made for the door. There was no rush. She was here for a month, and it was no longer a question of *if* Jess would yield to the hunger inside her, but how long it would take.

Stabbing his cane into the long-suffering yard, he conceded that even after one day of treatment his leg was beginning to show faint signs of improvement. He'd probably be stiff tomorrow, as Jess had predicted, but as she was around to sort it he wasn't too concerned. Anticipating more banter between them, he smiled. There was only one problem. Celibacy didn't suit him.

He took out his frustration in the gym. Boxing shorts, boots, strapped wrists, bandaged knuckles and a bandana to keep the sweat out of his eyes. He gave the bag hell. Jess had stressed no violent exercise, but Jess wasn't here. to hell with the programme. She should have taken his frustration into account.

And now he was aroused. He stopped, swore and resumed his vicious pounding until the heavy bag almost swung off the hook. Pausing to stare in the mirror, a monster stared back: Dante Acosta in his most primal form. He checked his leg with a scowl. It was still attached to his body. That was good enough for him.

Muscles pumped, his body covered in ink, signalling his

allegiance to team Lobos; there was nothing genteel about men who played polo at his level. Or the level at which he'd played before the accident, he grimly amended with an explosive curse. Retrieving the hated cane, he swung around to find Jess watching him. 'Yes?'

'I thought I told you not to exercise, apart from the regime I gave you. Did you forget, or do you still imagine you can go your own way?'

'As I did when I left hospital?' he suggested, easing his neck.

'Look where that got you,' Jess countered, hands on hips. 'You shouldn't be standing without a cane so soon, and you certainly shouldn't be putting so much pressure on your leg.'

'You put unnecessary pressure on my patience,' he snarled.

'So, get out? Leave me alone?' she suggested with a lift of her brow.

'You put the words into my mouth.'

He glared down. Jess lifted her chin. Daggers drawn, they stared at each other until he murmured, 'Well? Are you going to punish me?'

She shrugged. 'If I must, I will.' Her words were casual, but the sexual tension between them had soared. This wasn't Jess the therapist but Jess the sexually aware woman. Smiling faintly, he raised a brow and waited. Her blush deepened, as he knew it would, but that didn't stop her mouthing off. 'So the great Dante Acosta knows better than a trained professional?'

'I stand by all my decisions.'

'Stubbornness doesn't seem to have worked for you,' she observed coolly with a pointed look at his leg. Then her gaze tracked up to his half-naked torso. She studied the snarling wolf tattooed in all its dramatic splendour across his heart. 'If you care about your team at all, you should listen.'

'And obey?' he suggested with a tug of his mouth.

'If you don't co-operate you won't progress and I can't extend my contract.'

'Did I ask you to?'

'No,' she admitted. 'But you should know I'm very busy.'

'And likely to be more so,' he observed shrewdly, 'if you succeed in curing me.'

'True,' she admitted. 'But I do have other successes.'

'Or you wouldn't be here,' he pointed out.

'Don't mess up, Dante,' she warned. 'I really think we're getting somewhere with your leg.'

It was good to see her tiger claws. To walk again without a limp, and play world class polo, was all he wanted, and Jess's expression was absolutely firm.

'What do you want from me, Jess?' he asked as he swung a towel around his neck. 'What do you really want? You could have refused to treat me—recommended someone else. I'm not easy, and that's putting it mildly. You must have known you were taking a chance on complications after our encounter all those years ago.'

'If by complications you mean that foolhardy kiss…'

He hadn't expected her to be so blunt.

'I've come a long way since then. I'm a lot older, and successful in my own right. I viewed the chance to work on your leg as an interesting and challenging opportunity. Curing you remains my aim. It's not such a coincidence that your family hired me, or that you saved my family farm by buying up the best of the breeding stock. The Acostas and Jim Slatehome have a history of trust that extends back a number of years. I'm part of that.'

'So your agreeing to treat me had nothing to do with money, publicity, sex or bragging rights?'

'Correct,' she said with a huff of disbelief. 'Wow,' she

added. 'You really do have a high opinion of yourself. You're not my only celebrity client. And if I wanted sex it wouldn't be here, and it wouldn't be with you.'

'You sure about that?'

'Let's get one thing straight. My focus remains returning you to full fitness. I don't accept *if*, only when you are cured. You may not like my regime. You may not like me, but that's irrelevant because if you do as I suggest you will be cured, if a cure is at all possible.'

Jess was all heat and anger as she stared into his eyes, but then, as if she'd been clinging to the edge of a cliff with her fingertips, she exhaled and closed her eyes. The result should be inevitable. It might have been, had he been a different man.

CHAPTER NINE

HAD SHE REALLY been that close to falling under the notorious Acosta spell? Her body confirmed the lapse by softening and yearning.

Dante made it easy to snap out of the slip when he murmured, 'You think I want to kiss you now?'

'I'm just hoping and praying that you see sense.' They had to work together, and it was crucial for Dante's injury that there were no more interruptions in his treatment.

His harsh laugh suggested there was no warmth inside him, but they had both suffered loss and unimaginable grief, and that could so often lead to closing down feelings. She wasn't exactly a dab hand at showing emotion herself. Since her mother's death it had been a relief to lose herself in work, where caring for the individual was paramount, and personal feelings had no place. Dante was challenging her isolation, making Jess want things she had never believed possible, like learning to love and daring to show it, and having the courage to lay her heart on the line.

Maybe they could help each other.

In another universe, she concluded. One where she wasn't a medical professional treating a patient, and Dante actually wanted to lower the barricade he'd built around his heart.

She jerked to attention when he spoke. 'Tired?' she queried. 'I guess I'm running on fumes too. Could I join you in town tomorrow, though, after our morning session?'

'So you do need something from me,' he remarked dryly.

'Yes, I could do with some advice on what to buy Maria for her wedding. She's invited me. I don't have anything to wear, or a gift to give the bride.'

'You don't have to give her anything. You weren't to know about this. You've just arrived from England. I'm sure Maria doesn't expect a gift.'

'That's not the point. I wouldn't dream of turning up without something nice after all her kindness to me. And I can't go dressed like this...' Jess ran a hand down her scrubs. 'This is all I've got with me, apart from spare uniforms and gear for riding.'

Dante dismissed her concerns with a shrug. 'Order what you like and I'll pay for it. The gift too.'

'That's not how it works,' she informed him bluntly. 'I set my own budget. The gift for Maria must come from my pocket, not yours.'

Dante's impatience showed itself again. 'You wouldn't be borrowing anything from me. Just think of it as a bonus on your charges.'

'Your brothers and sister have already paid me.' *But not danger money*, Jess thought as Dante speared her with an impatient stare. He was wealth-blind, and didn't have a clue how patronising he sounded sometimes. 'If it's not convenient to take me into town, just say so. Maybe I can borrow a car or a bike?'

'A bike?' he queried. 'Why not take a horse? You could tether it to the nearest lamppost while you shop.'

'Is there a bus?'

'No,' he said flatly. 'We're deep in the countryside and the nearest town is around twenty miles away. Why the rush? Must you go tomorrow?'

'It seems like a good opportunity. I'd like to start looking for a gift sooner rather than later, so if I don't find anything tomorrow I can always try again.'

'Nothing daunts you, does it?' he remarked.

'You'd better hope not,' she countered.

'I'll take you into town. Get some sleep. We leave first thing.'

'After your treatment,' she reminded him.

'At seven we leave.'

'Deal,' she said happily. It would be tight, but she'd make it work.

The next morning's physio went without a hitch—when you were on the clock there was no time for banter. There would be chance for plenty of that on their journey into town, Jess anticipated as they set off, but she would confine herself to bland remarks and try not to look too hard at Dante.

The sparring didn't take long to start.

'You shop, and then I'll take you to lunch,' he stated.

'There's no need. I imagined you'd drop me—'

'Over a cliff?' he suggested.

'In town, close to the shops,' she said evenly, refusing to rise to the bait. 'And don't worry. I'll make my own way back. A taxi or something.'

'Am I driving too fast? Are you frightened?'

Not of his driving, though Dante's skilful handling of the low-slung muscle car as it blazed a trail down the tarmac was surely at the limit of what was possible. 'I'm not frightened of anything.'

'Except yourself,' Dante suggested as she remembered to release her fingers from the edge of the seat. 'Don't worry. I won't hold you to my schedule.'

'I'm not worried, but you really don't have to buy lunch. I'm not dressed for somewhere fancy.'

'Am I?'

She had vowed not to look at him, study him, drink him

in, but Dante had just made that pledge impossible. Even in jeans and a form-fitting top, he could go anywhere and be treated royally. With a body made for sin and a face to launch a thousand fantasies, Dante's piratical good looks would open any door.

'Can I trust you not to get lost?' he said when they arrived in town. 'Or had I better show you around first?'

'I'm sure I can manage,' she said, holding up her phone. It was time to escape from temptation.

Unfolding his formidable frame with annoying ease from the confines of the vehicle, Dante swore, retrieved his cane and swore again. Then, with a jerk of his chin, he led the way. She maintained space between them, but the streets were crowded. There seemed to be some sort of festival going on.

'It's market day,' Dante explained. 'Anything goes. Any excuse for a party.'

Jess glanced down at herself self-consciously. She certainly wasn't dressed for a *fiesta*. She'd had a quick shower and changed her clothes after Dante's treatment session, but her hair remained tied back and she was still make-up-free. She yelped as he held her back as a motorbike with a youth on board roared past within inches of her toes. Dante's touch was like an incendiary device to her senses.

'Careful,' he advised. 'You must remember what it was like to be a teenager—wild, reckless, risk-taking?' Her cheeks burned up as he added, 'There'll be a lot of them around today.'

'They grow up,' she said tensely.

'Some of them very well,' he agreed with a long, steady look. 'What made you decide to be a physiotherapist?'

It was a relief to have a question to answer. 'I promised my mother I'd finish my studies, whatever happened. I always had an interest in sports-related injuries, and equine sports in particular. When she died it made sense to have regular money coming in. My father went to pieces. I could help him.'

'So you tore yourself in two, working in London and spending your spare time on the farm.'

'I was lucky to land such a prestigious job,' she argued. 'I didn't want to leave my father, but my friends in the village promised to keep an eye on him. We needed the money, and I'd promised my mother. We all do what we must.'

'Your father's very lucky.'

'And so am I,' Jess insisted. 'My father was the first to encourage me to take the post. He reminded me of my mother's wishes, saying they were as one in that, and he'd never forgive himself if I stayed in the village because of him.'

'He struggled that much alone that you would have needed to?'

Jess hesitated, but then drew herself up tall. She was so lovely, Dante reflected, and so very proud. 'He loved my mother very much. It was…hard. I guessed he was lonely, so I returned home permanently. If it hadn't been for the help of the local village, I don't know what we'd have done. While I was freelancing, one of our neighbours would make sure to keep him company, and somehow we made it work.'

'Did London fulfil your expectations? Do you want to go back?'

'To living in one room in someone else's house?' She laughed. 'Don't get me wrong—the job was brilliant. I learned so much and had the most wonderful colleagues. I made lots of friends…'

'I'm sure you did.' There was an edge to Dante's voice. What did he imagine she meant?

'The type of friends you share a pizza with, maybe pick up some restricted-view seats in the West End to see a show.'

'Sounds…'

'Interesting?' she suggested with a grin. 'You've got no idea. It was fun and it was formative. You don't need money to enjoy life. And I appreciate the quiet of Yorkshire and the peace of your *estancia* so much more now. The calm certainty and trust in the eyes of the animals we both love is enough for me. And yes, London's hectic and crowded, but it's fabulous too. There's so much to see, and not all of it has to be paid for. I always think that people like me with hardly any money can have the very best of London at their fingertips.'

Dante frowned. 'How's that?'

'There are so many opportunities available if you search them out. Loads of places are free to visit. There are beautiful parks and glorious buildings, and the river—' Was she boring him with her ultimate guide to the simple life? Dante's life was so very far removed from Jess's experience, it was hard to tell.

But his life on the ranch was low-key.

True, she conceded.

'Anyway, enough about me. Why don't we turn the spotlight on you?'

'I'd have to want you to do that,' Dante pointed out, 'and I don't.'

Undaunted, Jess pressed on. 'I don't imagine you have to hunt for parking spaces, catch a bus or miss the last Tube home.'

'I do have a house in London,' he revealed, 'but that doesn't mean I wouldn't like to see your side of London one day.'

'I'd be a flat-out liar if I didn't admit I'd like to see yours,' Jess admitted on a laugh.

'Are we talking compromise?' Dante enquired with a frown.

His expression was more amused than disapproving. 'We're talking,' she conceded with a smile.

Dante's sideways look made heat rush through her. 'It must have been hard for you.'

'No harder than it is for other people. What's hard about working alongside people I really liked and admired or being taught the skills that allow me to help people like you? I count that as a real privilege.'

'A vocation?'

'If you like.'

'You must miss your colleagues now you're self-employed.'

'We keep in touch, and I meet new people all the time. My life is rich and varied, so please don't feel sorry for me.' *It's one heck of a sight better than your life in your grass-fed ivory tower*, Jess concluded. Dante's inactivity was obviously eating away at him. She didn't need to be a medical professional to see that.

'So why physiotherapy?'

'Why specialise? It seemed an obvious choice. I grew up in the horse world where, like any extreme sport, there's always a need for medical professionals on standby. My skills allow me to work close to the animals I love, with the people surrounding them.'

'An introduction from me into the world of top-class polo wouldn't hurt your career,' Dante stated bluntly.

'No, it wouldn't,' she agreed, 'but that's a very cynical view. This isn't about me; it's about you, and returning you to fitness. I don't know who's used you in the past, but please don't tar me with the same brush. What you see is what you get with me. Take it or leave it.'

'But there's another side to your character.'

'Skylar?' she queried, cocking her head to one side to smile up. 'That's just a childhood nickname.'

'That suits you,' he said.

'Sometimes,' she agreed, 'but a name doesn't change me.'

'Just how you act,' he suggested.

'In a fortune-telling tent, maybe,' Jess conceded, 'but doesn't everyone have two sides to their character—private and public?'

He stared at her long and hard.

'There are a lot of genuine people out there,' she insisted, feeling she was being judged. 'You don't have to look any further than your ranch.'

'I hand-pick my staff.'

'While I was foisted on you?' Jess suggested lightly, but Dante didn't answer.

They had reached the main square. Guessing he must be desperate to break free, she suggested a plan. 'Leave me here. I'll take a cab back to the ranch.'

'I have something to drop off at my lawyer's office. You can shop while I do that, then we'll eat and I'll drive you back.'

A restaurant was a public place. There was no harm in eating with a patient and if he caught up with her shopping, Dante could advise on what Maria might like.

'Okay. I'll see you around here,' she agreed. 'But please, no swanky eateries. I'm not dressed for it; I'd feel uncomfortable.'

'I've got a restaurant in mind,' he informed her. 'Don't worry; it's casual. I think you'll like it.'

Nothing like her local greasy spoon, she guessed, but anything was fine by her.

She stood to watch as Dante made his way across the square. Taller than most, he was a standout figure. It was impossible for him to pass unnoticed. Plenty of people recognised him, and some asked for a photograph with the famous polo star. Not once did he swerve their attention or pretend not to see his fans. Dante behaved at all times with unfailing courtesy, as if he had all the time in the world to stand and chat. What she'd seen of him so far suggested Dante could be brooding and difficult, but who could blame him when he was reliant on a cane? This was the true side of him, she suspected, and it was a side she longed to see more of.

Caught out, she gasped when he swung around and pointed to her. The man he was talking to joined his hands together and shook them in the air, as if to praise and congratulate Jess. *We're not there yet*, she wanted to say. *We're a long way off.* But Dante telling people she was helping him gave her a thrill of pleasure that had nothing to do with boosting her CV.

Dante was back from his appointment before she knew it. She'd been so busy scouring the market stalls for likely gifts and trinkets she'd lost track of time. 'You haven't been away long.'

'Long enough to do what I needed to. That guy in the square,' he added, neatly side-stepping any potential questions, 'used to work for me before he retired. He asked how I was getting on, so I told him you'd get me back in the game.'

'That is my aim.'

'If I do as you say?' Dante suggested, dipping his head to direct a stare into her eyes.

'That will be the day,' she observed good-humouredly. 'But you will improve immeasurably. I'll make sure of it.'

'For some reason,' Dante confessed, 'I believe you.'

Having steered her towards a cobbled passageway leading off the square, Dante ushered her through a stone archway leading into a modest courtyard. Decorated with simple clay pots overflowing with flowers, the quaint wrought iron tables and chairs made eating outside a real treat for Jess at this time of year. But, to her disappointment, the restaurant was full. 'We can go somewhere else,' she suggested with a rueful shrug.

Dante's answer was to put his hand in the small of her

back and usher her forward to where a small, capable-look-ing woman, wearing a mob-cap-style chef's hat and a crisp white apron, was cooking up a storm on an outside grill.

Catching sight of them, she passed her dishes over to an assistant and bustled forward to greet them. 'Dante, *mi amor! Cómo estás?*'

Jess knew enough Spanish to understand that the chef was asking how Dante was getting on. Concern showed clearly in the woman's eyes. When she turned to shake hands with Jess, she clasped both of Jess's hands in hers when Dante explained that it was Jess who was treating his leg. 'Your poor leg,' she exclaimed in English for Jess's benefit. 'Still no improvement?'

'Some,' he said, 'according to Skylar here.'

'Skylar?' she queried, studying Jess. 'What an inter-esting name.'

'Chef Ana,' Dante explained, introducing them.

'It's more of a childhood nickname,' Jess explained to the cheery-faced older woman, 'but Señor Acosta likes to use it.'

'Does he now?' Chef Ana murmured. Her smile broad-ened as she glanced between them.

'We're hungry,' Dante stated, as if eager to break the spell.

'When are you not hungry?' Chef Ana commented with a shrug. 'It will take all your skills to heal him,' she added in a stage whisper to Jess, before adding in a far more dis-creet tone when Dante had turned away to greet the wait-ers he knew, 'Dante has wounds you cannot see.'

'I know,' Jess whispered back.

The two women exchanged a lingering glance as a table and chairs were hastily set up for Dante and Jess, and then, with a squeeze of Jess's shoulder, Chef Ana gave Jess one last smile and left them to it.

Chef Ana's food was absolutely delicious. Platters of

finger-food to share lightened the mood and made banter between Dante and Jess inevitable as they jousted for the last morsel of deliciousness. By the time the platters were empty all Jess's sensible resolutions had floated away. Was it even possible to sit across from Dante and not want their legs to touch or their fingers to brush, or their glances to meet and hold? With his hunger satisfied, Dante was a different man. Easy and charming, he made Jess relax to the point where she really believed they were beginning to know each other. She couldn't find much that was sensible in that, but if she were sensible what was she doing here?

Leaning back in his seat, Dante stared as he stretched out his legs. Part of her could have stayed like this all day, but her sensible head won through. 'What time does the market pack up?'

'Is that a hint?' he enquired.

'Yes,' Jess admitted, digging in her bag for some high value notes. It might be a small, modest-looking restaurant, but the food was top-class and the prices reflected this.

'Put your money away,' Dante insisted, but on this occasion she was too fast for him.

'I prefer to be independent,' she reminded him as she handed her money over to a waiter. 'You gave me a lift into town, so I pay for lunch. It's only fair.'

He seemed to find this amusing and exclaimed, '*Dios me salve de una mujer independiente!* God save me from an independent woman,' he translated when she gave him a look.

'You prefer a woman to be dependent?' It was a loaded question.

'Tell that to my sister and I'm a dead man,' he said. And Dante was smiling…laughing. 'I invited you to lunch, so I should pay.'

'Sounds to me as if you need more independent women in your life.'

'*Dios!* I have enough of them,' Dante exclaimed. Standing, he snatched up his cane. 'Okay, this is the deal. You pay for the meal, I pay for your dress.'

'Okay. But nothing fancy,' she insisted. 'And I buy Maria's wedding present with my own money. That's not up for discussion,' she added, 'though I would appreciate your advice as to what she might like.'

'We have a deal,' Dante confirmed.

This time Jess was sensible enough to nod rather than shake his hand and risk the consequences of touching him. 'I believe we do,' she agreed.

CHAPTER TEN

THE TOWN WAS more packed than ever by the time they left the restaurant. There were so many stalls she hadn't visited, Jess wasn't sure where to head first.

'Here,' Dante prompted, drawing her attention to a group of women on a stall full of beautifully crafted items.

She had set out to buy Maria's gift from what many would call a 'proper shop', but it soon became apparent that the items on the stall were unique. A tablecloth with drawn thread work was absolutely exquisite, but Jess doubted she could afford it. The cloth was so intricately worked the price would surely reflect the hours of dedication involved.

'Why don't we give it as a joint gift?' Dante suggested, seeing Jess's disappointment when she read the price tag.

'I couldn't do that,' she protested. Her mind raced as she considered how that might look.

'Why not?' he asked with a shrug.

She could give him a dozen good reasons. 'Don't worry; I'll find something else.'

'Here's another suggestion. Why don't I buy the cloth and you buy the napkins? You'd be helping me out,' Dante added. 'I don't have a clue what Maria might like, but I do know she loves to entertain, so this seems right to me.'

'And to me,' Jess agreed.

She loved the way Dante's mouth tugged up when he got his own way, but this suited her too, Jess reminded herself as they completed the transaction. She truly hoped Maria would love the tablecloth as much as Jess did.

More people recognised Dante as they left the stall. He stopped to chat, which gave Jess the chance to pick up some more things from neighbouring stalls.

'Have you found a dress?' he asked when the pack around him moved on.

'Not yet.'

'Follow me.'

How many times had he done this? she wondered before scolding herself for being so obviously jealous. Was it likely the type of glamorous women Dante was renowned for dating would pick out their clothes from a market stall?

He took her to what turned out to be the most popular outlet on the market. 'My sister loves this stall,' he explained, which put Jess firmly back in her box.

'Your sister has excellent taste.'

'Yes, she does. And I'm sure Skylar would approve.'

The clothes were certainly more colourful than Jess would usually choose, but no less attractive for that. There was no harm in combining Skylar and Jess for a harmless day out shopping, Jess decided. Her father sometimes accused her of not having a life outside work, and this was her chance to prove him wrong. She longed to try on something different, and Dante had predicted Skylar's taste to a tee. Her gaze did linger on a sensible mid-length tea dress, but that was definitely out of the running, she realised as Dante shook his head.

'You don't seriously expect me to wear one of these?' she protested when he handed over his selection. They were flirty and flimsy and quite definitely eye-catching, when Jess's preferred choice would suit a mouse.

His mother used to say he was an old soul, Dante remembered. He called it intuition. With no idea how he knew things in advance of them happening, he just accepted that he did. His gift was invaluable today when it came to choosing an outfit for Jess. 'We'll take the red dress,' he stated before Jess had chance to argue. That was the one she wanted. She could stare all she liked at the dull, sensible dress, but he wasn't buying it. As if to confirm his decision, her gaze strayed again to the racy red.

'Seriously?' she exclaimed. 'But that's the most expensive dress on the stall.'

'You want it, don't you?'

'What about this one?' she suggested, pointing to the dowdy offering she thought she should have.

'I'm not buying a dress for my grandmother.' And his decision was final.

The bright red dress with its spaghetti straps and a length barely south of decent was perfect for Jess, in his opinion. Handing over the cash, he ignored Jess's complaint that the dress was too short, too revealing, and that she'd probably catch a chill. 'This is the south of Spain, not the wild moors of Yorkshire,' he said as he pressed the package into her hands. 'And you want this one,' he pointed out with a shrug. 'Why pretend otherwise? We'll take the shawl too,' he told the stallholder, indicating an exquisitely worked length of smoke-grey lace. 'For decency's sake at the ceremony,' he explained to Jess. 'And for when it grows cool in the evening.'

'But the shawl's even more expensive than the dress,' she protested. 'I can't possibly accept these gifts when you've picked out the two priciest items on the stall.'

'You don't want them?' His expression remained deadpan.

'I can't accept them,' Jess insisted, tightening her lips.

'Hard luck. They're paid for. They're yours.'

'Ask for your money back,' she pleaded as he walked

away. 'Please, Dante,' she begged, chasing after him. 'Don't embarrass me like this.'

'The stallholder's packing up.'

'Then catch her before she leaves!'

'So she loses the last sale of the day? Is that what you want?'

Jess deflated in front of his eyes. She was far too considerate to allow that to happen. 'Well, you shouldn't have done this,' she said with a shake of her head.

'I can. I did. And I should,' he argued. 'After all, you have to put up with me.'

'There is that,' she murmured dryly, 'though I'm determined to pay you back.'

As they passed the impromptu dance floor in the middle of the square, one of the local bands struck up. 'If you insist on paying me back, do so with a dance. It would be a great boost to my self-esteem.'

Like that needed a boost, he reflected with irony. 'It would prove your therapy's working.' True. It would also ease the ache in his groin. He had to put his hands on her soon, or he'd go mad. Delay might be the servant of pleasure, but it was also an aching test of his endurance.

'I can't dance,' Jess protested. 'I've got two left feet.'

'What about my self-esteem?' He delivered the words deadpan, with just the right edge of vulnerability in his tone to appeal to Jess's generous nature.

Her cheeks flushed pink. 'Put like that...'

'You can't refuse,' he confirmed.

'But just one dance,' Jess insisted with a concerned look in her eyes. 'You've been on your feet a lot today.'

He'd settle for that. 'I'll put your parcels behind the bar, and then we'll dance. If I feel the strain, I'll lean on you.'

He'd gone too far and she laughed. 'That'll be the day!' she exploded. 'But I do owe you for steering me towards such beautiful gifts.'

'That's right,' he confirmed, 'you do.' *Now, let's get on with it*, he silently urged. But his attitude towards Jess soon mellowed when he reviewed the sincerity in her eyes when she thanked him. Was he the first man to treat Jess as a woman should be treated? She should be spoiled. Jess had been working her ass off for years. What was wrong with cutting loose now and then?

'The dress wasn't a gift; it was a necessity,' he insisted. 'I brought you here—I landed you in this—'

'Fabulous and unexpected wedding invitation with a lovely new friend,' Jess interjected.

'Agreed. But you have to wear something at the wedding, apart from jodhpurs or scrubs.'

'True,' she conceded, smiling. 'And I'm thrilled to have such a pretty dress to wear at Maria's wedding, and I'm very grateful—'

'You don't have to be grateful. You've earned it. If there's a shortfall...' he pretended to ponder this '... I'll make sure you earn it. Does that salve your delicate conscience, and soothe your touchy pride?'

She shrugged ruefully. 'Whether I'll have the courage on the day to wear that particular dress remains to be seen,' she admitted with a grin. 'And I can't see it coming in handy at the farm.'

'Skylar would wear it,' he remarked.

'Yes, but she's a shameless hussy whose only skill is telling fortunes,' she dismissed.

'Can she dance?'

Jess's kissable lips pressed down as she considered this. 'Skylar can dance,' she confirmed.

'Just to be clear, when we hit the dance floor, am I dancing with Skylar or Jess?'

'Which would you prefer?'

'A freestyle combination of the two.'

'I'll have to see what we can do,' Jess offered with a grin.

'Knock yourself out.'

'I'll try to make things interesting,' she promised.

His lips curved. 'That's what I expect.'

But the best laid plans, et cetera, et cetera...

They'd barely reached the dance floor when his leg cramped. Seeing his grimace, Jess quickly reverted to professional in a trice and found him a seat. Kneeling on the cobbles in front of him, completely unconcerned by the people who had gathered to watch, she worked on the spasm, oblivious to everything but easing his pain.

Hell. This was not how he'd planned the evening to end.

'Better?' she asked, gazing up at him with concern.

'Much better,' he admitted in an ungracious low growl.

'No dancing for you,' she told him. 'It's time to go. That cramp was a warning. I'll get the rest of our things—' She handed him the cane.

He had never hated it more. 'I can manage without your assistance.'

Jess opened her mouth to reply, then thought better of it and stood back while he levered himself up.

They didn't speak a word for the first part of the journey home. He was in a foul mood, thanks to the cramp in his leg, and Jess had more sense than to attempt conversation. At least she showed more sense to begin with...

'You have to accept that your leg will take time to heal,' she ventured after they'd covered a few tense blocks. 'There will be setbacks, sometimes when you least expect them.'

'Thanks for the advice. Can we leave it now?' To emphasise the point he played some music. Jess talked over it.

'You're not invincible, Dante. You're a man, you're injured and you hurt. That isn't something to be embarrassed about.'

'Embarrassed?' he spat out with affront.

'If you tell me as soon as you get these cramps, maybe I can help.'

'Like you have done so far?' he derided.

'You're in pain now,' she intuited, 'so, rather than take it out on me, stop the car and let me drive.'

A short incredulous laugh shot out of him 'Are you serious?'

'Never more so,' she stated bluntly. 'It isn't a weakness to admit you need help. Open up. Trust someone—'

'Trust you?'

She blushed, but that didn't stop her asking, 'Why not? You have to start somewhere.'

'That's rich, coming from you, Jess. And no, you can't change places with me, either to drive this vehicle or to see things the way I do. So let's just agree to disagree and restrict our comments in future to subjects connected to my treatment.'

'Fine by me,' she bit out.

'Good.'

'Good,' she echoed before sinking back in her seat.

His mood didn't improve. If anything, it grew worse. If it hadn't been for the setback with his leg, he would be planning to mark the successful business deal he'd signed off at his lawyers round about now.

With Jess?

The connection between them was undeniable, but they were worlds apart. She deserved more than he could give—more than he wanted to give. Casual relationships suited him. His siblings were the one constant in his life. He doubted he'd ever be tempted to extend his family. After the tragedy of his parents' death, he chose to fiercely protect what he had.

He glanced across at Jess. They couldn't avoid each other. He needed more treatment, and they'd meet socially at Maria's wedding, where he'd be polite, nothing more. His world was constructed around practicality with no space for pointless emotion. A good night's sleep should sort him out, he reasoned as they hit the highway and headed out of town. He'd attend Jess's therapy sessions religiously, and he'd be civil when they met away from the treatment couch, so when Jess's contract ended he'd say goodbye without regret.

Jess felt the need to beat herself up. How could a day that had started so well end so badly? She and Dante were further apart than they had ever been, which made it hard, if not impossible, to work with him. If she didn't have Dante's trust she had nothing, and right now the gulf between them felt wider than ever.

What more did she want?

To put it another way: what more could she expect? Try nothing and she'd be close. Dante had spelled out exactly what he wanted and expected of her, which was for Jess to heal him in the shortest time possible.

Frustrated by Dante's impatience, for which she had no answer, and by the black cloud surrounding them, Jess realised that she was gripping the packages they'd bought on the market as if they were comfort blankets. She desperately wanted Dante to be free from the shackles of his past. The loss of his parents was a scar he'd wear for ever, but would his parents have wanted him to pay a penance for their death every day of his life? She refused to believe it, but how could she help when Dante had shut her out? Perhaps he was right to do so and being professional from now on *was* the only way forward.

When Dante was under her hands on the treatment couch later that evening she marvelled at the miracle of healing. It had nothing to do with rich or poor, privileged or not, and had everything to do with training. Staring down at one of the most brutally physical men on the planet, currently resting on his stomach buck naked with the small exception of the towel she'd placed across his buttocks, she realised it was possible to separate her two selves and concentrate solely on healing. Manipulating his muscles until she felt the knots release was all the satisfaction she would ever need.

Was it? her cynical inner voice demanded.

It had to be.

'Well done,' she said, standing back when the session was over. 'That can't have been much fun.'

'Fun?' Turning over, he grimaced. 'If torture is fun, that was hilarious. You're a lot stronger than you look.'

Wasn't that the truth? Helping her father out of his financial difficulties was only half the story. When her mother died he took to drink, thinking this might numb the pain. But it was still there in the morning, only now he had a hangover to cope with, while Jess changed his sheets, washed his clothes and begged him to please take a shower. She suspected that these were secrets many other families were forced to keep.

As much as it had hurt like hell, the whole sorry experience had made her strong: physically strong as well as mentally robust. The first time she'd picked him up off the stairs, she'd strained her back. A refresher class in recovering unconscious patients from the floor had reminded her of techniques she should use to avoid injury. One step at a time, she'd told herself as she came to grips with caring for the broken man her father had become. 'One step at a time,' she'd whispered when he sobbed in her arms.

Now, thanks to the sale of the ponies, those dark nights were behind him and her father was back on top. He'd stopped drinking and took a shower every day. The washing machine went back to its regular cycle. Jess rejoiced to see him recover, but if she was totally honest she could see that being strong for her father had left her with no time to grieve. Just as well, she determined, firming her jaw. She had responsibilities, and a job to do, which she was good at.

What had caused the shadows in Jess's eyes? Dante reflected. Had someone hurt her?

Dante didn't invite questions into his life, and if Jess wanted to tell him she would. He wasn't used to dealing with women who had so many onion skins to peel away before their true self was revealed, or maybe he'd never had the time or the inclination to do so before. Compared to Jess, those other women seemed like mannequins to him now. Jess was real—so real he missed the rapport they'd shared before their spat in the car. Their banter enlivened him, lifted him, and the pointless argument had been largely down to him and his frustration at not snapping back to full fitness immediately. That wasn't Jess's fault. She was doing her best to help.

'Don't rush off,' he said as she packed up her kit. Swinging off the couch, he tested his leg…not too bad. 'A lot of water has passed beneath the bridge since that kitten peed down your front, and you've shared so little with me.'

'While you've been incredibly forthcoming,' Jess observed dryly.

'Touché,' he conceded with a shrug and a smile. Then, after another few moments, he added, 'I apologise.'

That stopped her dead in her tracks. 'I'm sorry?'

'I was unreasonable in the car.'

'You were in pain.'

He didn't want understanding; he wanted a return to the up and down relationship they'd shared before. That was never boring. Professional civility was borderline. 'We can continue to snipe at each other or—'

'I must have stank in that stable,' she said, softening into the woman he wanted to know better. 'Belated apologies,' she added.

'For caring for a kitten?' He grinned. 'Apology unnecessary.'

'They were cute, weren't they…?'

She looked wistful as she thought back, no doubt remembering her mother alongside her in the barn, introducing her to the miracle of birth and teaching her how to care for kittens. How lovely she was.

'I have to go,' she said, breaking the spell. 'Apologies again, but I can't stay to chat. I promised Maria I'd call by to see if there's anything I can do to help with the wedding.'

'That's very kind of you.'

'I am kind.'

Yes, she was, and he'd almost lost her. Even now it was as if the connection between them had been reduced to the slimmest of threads. He wanted to kiss her, reassure her, and banish that sad look in her eyes, but not yet. This was not the time.

'Dante?' she queried. 'What are you thinking? You look so far away, yet so intense.'

He snapped to immediately. 'Just thinking about your charity event.'

'It was a good day, wasn't it?'

'A very good day. Successful, I hope?'

'Massively,' she admitted. 'Mostly thanks to you.'

He shrugged this off. 'It was your day. You organised it.' Jess was always thinking up ways to help others. Why hadn't someone helped Jess?

'The main thing to me is that it lifted my father.'

He nodded in agreement. Everyone in the horse world knew the saga of Jim Slatehome, and how the great man had been devastated by the death of his childhood sweetheart. When his wife had died Jim had gone to ground and hadn't been seen for several seasons. Surely someone must have noticed that Jess was reeling too? He guessed she'd put on a brave face because that was who she was.

Her father had relied on her completely, and anything Jess had achieved personally, or for him, was a result of sheer willpower and grit. She didn't deserve to be abandoned now with no one to confide in.

'Three sessions tomorrow,' she reminded him brightly before she turned to go.

'Am I supposed to cheer?' he asked dryly.

'You're supposed to get up bright and early and set your mind to accepting three sessions a day from now on. If you attend each one and follow my exercise regime, I predict that in around a month you'll be back on your feet without that cane.'

His stare followed Jess as she walked away. There was such an air of purpose in her stride. He couldn't go right ahead and seduce her because Jess was special, unique, precious and oh, so tender beneath her onion skins of professionalism and grit. There weren't many he held in high regard outside his immediate family, but Jess Slatehome was right up there.

CHAPTER ELEVEN

A LOT COULD happen in a month. The run-up to Maria's wedding seemed to fly by. Jess had grown to feel at home on the ranch. In her free time she helped out wherever she could.

Dante had been as good as his word, attending each treatment session promptly, before fulfilling his quota of exercises as diligently as Jess could have wished for a patient.

She did a lot of wishing that month—that their banter could progress beyond amusing and superficial to something deeper, and that the man beneath her hands might somehow wake up one day to find her totally irresistible. This led to a lot of sleepless nights, but if she hoped for Dante to act on the ever-strengthening bond of friendship between them she was to be disappointed.

They learned more about each other for sure, but the facts remained these: Dante worked on his leg. She worked on him.

He rode more and more, which was amazing to see, while she made notes on his progress, revelled in his surprisingly wide-ranging library, walked the ranch, rode out on her own, which was what she was used to in Yorkshire, and spent time with Maria, who was the closest thing to a sister Jess had ever had.

And today was the morning of the wedding.

Jess stood, hand clasped to her mouth in shock, in the

middle of Maria's cosy sitting room. 'Me? Be your brides-maid? Are you serious?'

Jess was overwhelmed, while Maria was clearly em-barrassed at having to ask Jess at the last moment to stand in for her one and only bridesmaid, who had gone down with a bad cold. 'It's such an honour! I can't believe it. Of course I'll hold your flowers at the crucial moment. I'll do anything I can. Are you sure? Isn't there anyone else you'd like to ask?'

Maria bit down on her lip. 'Can I be completely honest?'

'Of course,' Jess said warmly.

Pulling a face, Maria laughed and blushed. 'You're the only one who'll fit into the dress.'

Jess's peal of laughter set Maria off. 'I can't think of a better reason,' Jess admitted as the two women hugged.

'But the best reason of all,' Maria said in all serious-ness when they parted, 'is that I like you and trust you to do this for me.'

'Then I'm honoured and thrilled to accept,' Jess con-firmed. 'Do you think I should try on the dress, just to be sure it fits?'

'Of course...'

Crossing the room, Maria returned with a dream of a gown.

'This is so beautiful,' Jess breathed in awe. The deli-cate confection comprised of lace and tulle and was lovely enough for any bride to wear on her wedding day.

'I hope you like it?' Maria asked with concern.

'I love it.' Jess sighed as she stroked the peach lace and chiffon. 'I've never had the chance to wear anything like this.'

'Wait until you see my wedding dress,' Maria exclaimed happily. 'Señor Acosta insisted that the gowns came from Paris, so he flew me and my mother there, saying she must have a special outfit too.'

'He's very generous,' Jess murmured thoughtfully.

'Oh, yes, he is,' Maria enthused. 'Everything was hand-made in the atelier of a very famous designer.'

'If only he weren't so obstinate and remote. If he just let people in and…' Her voice tailed away. Maria was looking at her as if she sympathised and yet wanted Jess to come to some conclusion by herself.

'I'm sorry,' Jess said gently. 'He's always been kind to both of us. I didn't mean to criticise him—especially not to you, and not on the morning of your wedding. How selfish you must think me.'

'Not at all.' Maria took Jess's hands in hers and held them tightly. 'Like you, he's hurt and scarred by loss and, like you, he says nothing. Both of you lose yourselves in work, and it's only this accident that forced Dante to pause and take a proper look around at things that matter. Like you—'

'Me?' Jess exclaimed incredulously.

'Can't you see it? Can't you see how much he needs you—how much you need him? You complete each other. You're the missing parts to each other's heart. Perhaps I can see it clearly because I have The Sight, but you do too, don't you… Skylar?'

Jess smiled crookedly as she stared into the eyes of a woman she trusted like no other. 'Who told you my mother's name for me?'

'Dante. He doesn't open up very often, but when he does and I see the man behind the scars I love him like a brother. Neither of you is looking for pity, Jess, I know that, but what you should be looking for is love to fill the hollow in your heart.'

They hugged and then Maria whispered, 'Okay now?'

'Okay,' Jess confirmed, burying her face in Maria's shoulder. 'And so honoured that you've asked me to be part of your special day. Are you sure you trust me to wear this?'

she asked as they broke apart and Maria took the beautiful gown she wanted Jess to wear off its hanger.

Jess viewed the intricately worked creation with awe. The beading was so delicate, and the cut of the gown so flattering it belonged in a costume museum rather than on the sturdy body of a hill farmer's daughter.

'Of course I'm sure,' Maria stated firmly. 'You'll look beautiful. Pale peach is the perfect foil for your fiery auburn hair.'

'I'll take good care of it,' Jess promised, vowing silently not to step on the hem and rip it, or snag the beading with her ragged nails.

As if reading her concerns, Maria added, 'Señor Acosta has arranged a beautician and a hairdresser to attend me, and I hope you'll join in the fun. I'm guessing you're not used to that sort of thing any more than I am. It would give me confidence,' she insisted. 'Señor Acosta has made the premier guest suite on his *estancia* available for our use.'

'I… Oh…'

What was wrong with getting changed into a bridal outfit in Dante's house, apart from the fact that it was a reminder that Jess had no happy occasion on the horizon, or anywhere close, for that matter?

'It would really help me,' Maria said, having no doubt interpreted Jess's expression as stage fright. 'Neither of us is used to dressing up in such finery, but I'd feel so much better if you'd share this experience with me. I'd really value your honest opinion.'

'You can be sure of it,' Jess promised warmly. This was Maria's day and she'd give her all to it.

Dante had offered to act as father of the bride and give Maria away, but Maria had refused, saying she would walk herself down the aisle. Maria's attitude reminded him why he had hired her. No-nonsense and capable in so many ways, Maria, in turn, reminded him of Jess, a woman he confidently expected to appear at any moment, dressed in a provocative slip of a bright red dress. It was too late to wonder why he hadn't agreed to purchase Jess's staid choice, which would at least have given him chance to relax.

As if by some silent signal the excited chatter surrounding him died down. There was a rustle of best clothes as everyone stood up. A few more tense seconds passed and then a guitar began to strum, announcing the arrival of the bride. A collective sigh went up, but Dante was facing forward. He was no romantic and was more concerned about Jess's absence. The seat he had saved for her was still empty. Was something wrong?

He focused his attention of Manuel, Maria's soon-to-be husband. The man appeared to be overwhelmed with emotion. He'd never seen Manuel cry. He might well cry with a lifetime of hen-pecking ahead of him, Dante reflected.

A waft of unbelievably agreeable perfume accompanied by the rustle of delicate fabric finally forced him to turn around. To say he was stunned by Maria's arrival would be seriously understating the case. But he was looking past Maria to her one and only bridesmaid, Señorita Jessica Slatehome.

This was Jess as he'd never seen her before. Dressed in a gown so ethereal and lovely it belonged in a painting rather than on a living, breathing woman—or it would have done, had that woman not been Jess. He was also struck by the fact that Jess had made no attempt to overshadow the bride. He'd seen that before, but Jess had chosen to wear very little make-up, and must have directed the hairdresser to draw her hair back demurely at the nape of her neck, rather than allow it to cascade down her back in all its fiery rippling glory. She wore no jewellery to catch the eye, though it occurred to him she might have none to wear...

Sensing his interest, she turned her head to look at him.

Her face was perfectly composed, though her emerald eyes held enough of Skylar to make him anticipate the rest of the day even more than he had expected.

And then she was gone.

Moving on down the aisle until she came to a halt behind the bride and groom, Jess shattered his honourable resolutions and left Dante counting the seconds until he could be with her again.

Jess hadn't been to many weddings, and though she had a few ideas about the high-octane atmosphere on such occasions she could never have anticipated the level of testosterone at this one. Dante's wranglers were young, tough and high-spirited, while Maria's relatives were *gitanos*, experts in the art of flamenco with their own customs and language.

Maria's people had enriched Spanish culture for centuries with their valuable contribution of music and dance and finely crafted wares, and many of the young women who had travelled down from their mountain villages were extremely beautiful. Safe to say, Dante's ranch hands were on full alert.

Dante had instructed his people to erect the marquee on the paddock closest to his ranch house. The path leading up to it was lined with candles and flowers while the inside of the tent was a riot of music, excited guests, colourful clothes and flashing jewellery. Blooms so perfect they hardly looked real filled the air with exotic scent, but what touched Jess the most was the sight of the toughest men with their recently smoothed-down hair and newly shaven faces. All except for Dante, who had gone for his customary rugged look, and who, apart from his dark, custommade suit, managed to look as swarthy and as dangerous as he ever had.

Concentrating fiercely on Maria so as not to be distracted by him, Jess found tears pricking the back of her eyes. Maria had never looked more beautiful in a wedding gown that gave more than a passing nod to the flamenco tradition of her kin. It would be no exaggeration to say that Maria had been transformed from diligent housekeeper to fairy tale bride.

Who didn't love a wedding? She couldn't help but glance at Dante, and there was her answer. Maria had already told her he'd refused a seat of honour at the front, as Dante believed that was where Maria's relatives should be seated. In a position halfway down the aisle, he was already restless. Dragging her attention away, she was just in time to take Maria's bridal bouquet as the ceremony began.

Incense swirled while soft words of praise were spoken, though through it all an underlying tension and discreet glances suggested the congregation's thoughts were already turning to more earthly pleasures.

When the ceremony ended Maria called out excitedly, 'I'm married! I'm married!'

To which her new husband replied in a rather different tone, '*Terminado! Ya he terminado!* I'm done for! I'm done for!' which set the entire place rolling with laughter.

'You may kiss the bride...'

The poor priest battled in vain to restore order to a congregation that was more interested in partying. Everyone was on their feet, cheering and applauding, while Maria, being tiny, disappeared completely behind a wall of guests. The first intimation Jess received that the bride was safe was when the bridal bouquet came sailing over the human barricade to land squarely in the centre of her chest. Cradling it close to keep it from being trampled, she backed straight into a roadblock that turned out to be Dante Acosta.

'I'm getting you out of here before you're squashed to a pulp,' he informed her.

'You're not using your stick.'

'Thanks for reminding me,' Dante growled as he forged a passage for them through the crowd. The throng parted like the Red Sea to allow him through, and it was only when he had her safe on the fringes that Dante relaxed and turned to face her. 'You sure you're okay?'

'Thanks to you, even Maria's bouquet made it through.'

'You know what this means, don't you?' Dante prompted as he stared at the lush arrangement Jess was holding close to her heart.

'Maria can dry the flowers and keep them?' Jess suggested, tongue in cheek.

Dante huffed at this. 'Trust you to strip the romance out of it.'

'Me?' Jess queried. 'Like you're so romantic?'

'I do have my moments, given half a chance.'

Excitement and jealousy roiled inside her. It was a flippant remark. Dante made it while they were eyeballing each other, but it was enough to rouse Jess. Neither emotion was appropriate, so she quickly moved on to professional concerns. 'Where's your cane?'

'Thanks to you, I don't need it so much.'

'You'll need it tonight. You'll be on your feet a lot.'

Dante speared her with a look. 'Okay, *señorita*, so I left it by the table. Is that good enough for you?'

'You're learning,' she approved, holding his fierce look steadily.

'I've got the best of teachers,' Dante conceded with a look that sizzled its way through her veins, leaving her breathless.

Approachable Dante was far more dangerous than grim Dante, Jess concluded. His smile and the way he dipped his head to whisper in her ear made all her good intentions turn bad.

'Aren't the decorations lovely?' she blurted in a lame attempt to distract them both from the sexual tension between them. The boisterous congregation had spilled out of the seating area in front of the altar, which meant the quiet place Dante had found for them would soon be swamped.

'These pine cones remind me of home at Christmas,' she admitted wistfully as they moved on to the shade of an awning decorated with swags and bows.

'Maria's people brought them from the mountains where they live. It was Maria's dream to have everything reflect her heritage today.'

'Which you've helped her achieve, and beautifully.'

'She's worth it. I'd trust Maria with my life.'

'What will you do for Christmas?' Maria had explained she was taking time off for a honeymoon, so there would be no one else living in the house, as far as she knew. 'Will you join family?'

'Why are you so interested?'

Jess shrugged. 'I'm not. I just don't like to think of people being alone at such a special time of year. I'd never leave my father at Christmas, but don't worry, your treatment can safely be handed over by then,' she hurried to reassure Dante. 'And if you stick to your regime you could be back on the polo field by New Year.'

Breath shot from her lungs as Dante lifted her up in his arms. Until she realised he was moving her out of the way of the wait staff.

'Don't squash the flowers!' she exclaimed to cover her breathless shock and excitement.

'I'll have them delivered to Maria,' Dante offered. 'Or do you want to hang on to them for some reason?'

'What reason?' Jess demanded. 'Do you think I'm going to take a turn around the marquee to try and drum up some interest?'

'Now I'm offended,' Dante protested, hand on heart.

She thought of the snarling wolf beneath. 'You?' she queried. 'The only certainty about you is that you enjoy teasing me. Would you care to accompany me so you can make a list of my potential suitors?'

He stared at her darkly for a moment, then laughed. They both laughed, and both relaxed. 'I think the bride's calling you,' Dante prompted. 'You'd better go and attend to your duties. How lucky am I,' he added as Jess turned to leave, 'to be spared the ordeal of trying to find you a mate?'

'A mate?' Jess queried, stopping to throw him a paint-stripping look. 'You should be so lucky.'

Dante's lips pressed down but his eyes were firing with laughter. 'When I lifted you, that was what your body told me you needed.'

'You and my body don't speak the same language,' she assured him in a flash. 'And now, if you'll excuse me—'

'And if I don't?'

She stared at Dante's hand on her arm.

'It would be my pleasure to escort you to Maria's table,' he murmured.

'There's no need. I can find my way.'

'As I'm sitting next to you and it's my table too, it would seem sensible for us to walk there together.'

There was nothing sensible about this, Jess reasoned as she paused. 'It seems I have no option,' she said at last.

'None at all,' Dante agreed.

Conversation between them and the other guests was lively at the top table, but on one of their many tours around the marquee to make sure everyone had everything they needed it was inevitable that Jess encountered Dante. What she hadn't expected was that he would catch her around the waist and whirl her on to the dance floor. 'You can enjoy yourself too,' he insisted when Jess protested that she had her duties to attend to.

'Your duty is to check on me and make sure I don't overdo it,' he informed her.

'And how am I supposed to do that when you never listen to a word I say?'

'My recovery would argue otherwise. You can gauge the extent of my recovery as we dance.'

And a number of other things, she thought hotly as Dante drew her close. 'I'm not sure it's appropriate.'

'Uncertainty doesn't become you, Señorita Slatehome. Should I doubt your prowess now?'

'Not where my therapy's concerned.'

'What else should I doubt?'

Jess's cheeks burned.

'If you don't want to dance with me, that's another matter,' Dante told her with a relaxed shrug of his powerful shoulders, 'but this is our promised dance—to celebrate my recovery,' he reminded her.

'I don't remember promising that.'

'Amnesia can be a terrible thing.'

'Don't make jokes. I know you're teasing me again.'

'Am I?'

Dante's voice was so warm and coaxing, and his body so hot and strong, that just for a moment she allowed herself to relax.

Of course she should have known better.

'I won't allow you to play the professional card at a wedding,' Dante warned, 'or assume the role of Cinderella. You can't run out on me at midnight.'

'So you're Prince Charming now?'

'I have a white horse.'

'And an answer for everything.'

'I do my best,' Dante agreed.

'If I agree to dance, it's only on the condition that you sit down and rest afterwards.'

'Rest?' Dante's lips tugged up at one corner in a smile. 'Not a chance,' he murmured dangerously close to her ear.

'A resting wolf is still a dangerous animal. Your treatment worked, and now you must take the consequences.'

Why did she choose that moment to stare up into Dante's laughing eyes?

'That's better,' he whispered, drawing her attention to his mouth. 'Relax. You have permission to enjoy yourself without feeling guilty.'

She drew in a shaking breath while Dante continued in the same soothing tone, 'You look beautiful tonight and, as Maria is happily entwined around her new husband, you're free of your duties, and free to dance with me.'

Oh, but this was dangerous. And irresistible. Wearing such a fabulous gown made Jess feel different, as if anything might be possible for the woman who wore the gown. When morning came she'd be a farmer's daughter again and see things differently, but for now...

Something fundamental had changed between them, Dante reflected as Jess quite clearly debated whether or not to move into his arms. She knew what that entailed as much as he did. It was line crossed that could never be redrawn. The tension between them was too much for that to happen. They knew each other better, and yet in some ways not at all. There were still too many pieces of the jigsaw missing. He had pledged to keep everything professional, and so had Jess. He wasn't satisfied with that. Was she?

What did she think about while he lay on the treatment couch beneath her hands? He had to try very hard not to think. Thinking was dangerous because the sight of her was enough to arouse him. Even the pain he suffered beneath her probing fingers aroused him. Everything about Jess was arousing, but the stakes were high because slaking his lust would never be enough where Jess was concerned. She was a special woman who demanded more of him emotionally than he had ever been prepared to give.

* * *

Banked-up feelings exploded inside her as Dante drew her into his arms. There was something so compelling and right about it, and that in itself made her wary. This wasn't just a dance; it was a barrier crashing down. It was permission to feel, to respond, to hope for something more. She'd been so careful around him up to now, not just because of professionalism. Natural caution played its part. Dante was a player in every sense of the word. His relationships were famously many and short-lived, though at the moment he was making her feel as if she was the only woman capable of reaching him. How many others had he made feel that way?

He knew how to tease. Dante's grip was frustratingly light and stirred a primal need inside her. *Leave it at dancing or regret it in the morning*, were inner words of caution she ignored. Dancing like this was a prelude to sex. Every inch of her body was moulded to his. Dante was exerting no pressure, but Jess's body had its own ideas. His thigh was threaded through hers, bringing them into the closest contact possible outside of sex. But how—*how*—was she supposed to resist him? And did she want to?

'You seem distracted,' Dante commented when the first dance ended.

'Nothing could be further from the truth,' she assured him. 'I'm wide awake.'

'And firing on all cylinders,' he observed, bringing her with him as the band started playing again.

She should have stopped at that point, excused herself politely and left the floor. Instead, she warned, 'Behave yourself or I'll make you sit down to rest that leg.'

'I love that you're so masterful,' Dante mocked in a husky whisper, bringing his mouth very close to hers.

'And I love that you accept my authority,' Jess countered with a half teasing smile. She couldn't be serious all the time. 'At one point I thought I'd have trouble with you.'

'You will,' Dante promised, drawing her closer still.

Dancing with Jess was like seizing hold of a red-hot brand and asking to be consumed by it. Any lingering thought he might have had that they could rewind to achieve their previously careful and polite relationship was now implausible, impossible; it just couldn't happen. It only took millimetres of subtle shift in their bodies to tell him Jess felt the same. There was no need for grandiose gestures or unnecessary words between them. Coming together like this was enough. No woman had ever felt so right in his arms or been so receptive. There were a lot of beautiful women at the wedding but there was only one Jess. Who made him laugh as she did? Who had the wit to exchange banter that could be funny but was never cruel?

'This is better than I thought,' she whispered, surprising him with her boldness, and yet not really surprising him at all.

'Better still,' she murmured when he drew her close.

Jess's duties as bridesmaid were the only obstacles he faced. She had a keen eye for detail and noticed everything, which meant leaving his side on a number of occasions to help the wait staff or to answer a guest's query. Nothing was too much trouble for Jess. Apart from dancing with him, apparently. By now they should be somewhere else, but he hadn't bargained on dancing with a Girl Scout.

God bless the Scouts, he reflected, shaking his head with amusement as Jess embarked on yet another mission. He might as well go rest his leg.

The party went on late into the night. When Maria teased Jess into joining her in dancing on the table, Jess laughed. 'I hope you know I've got two left feet.'

'Too late now,' Maria told her as the bridegroom, Manuel, lifted Jess and deposited her next to his bride. Guests had gathered to watch the spectacle, which meant Jess couldn't let her new friend down.

'Lift your gown like this,' Maria instructed as she picked up the hem of her wedding dress to strut a few dramatic flamenco steps. 'Arch your back and stamp your feet in time to the music. Clap your hands like this.'

Having been forced to borrow shoes that were becoming increasingly uncomfortable, Jess confined herself to a series of poses and enthusiastic shouts of *'Olé!'* Carried away by the excellence of Maria's dancing, she acted on a wave of enthusiasm, so when the music ended and Maria jumped into her bridegroom's arms, Jess jumped too—straight into the arms of Dante Acosta, who'd been standing watching with a look she found impossible to interpret. Catching her with no effort at all, he carried her away through the crowd.

So much for her resolve to keep Dante at arm's length, Jess mused, excitement mounting. This was a night to remember, and whatever came next she was more than ready for it.

CHAPTER TWELVE

THE HUNGER TO be alone with Jess had been burning a hole through his head throughout the entire wedding. He could think of nothing else but being alone with her, but once they were inside the ranch house he reined in the wolf. Lowering Jess to her feet, he stood in the shadows staring down. 'Another drink?'

'I haven't had a drink yet. Bridesmaid duties,' she reminded him. 'Clear head and all that?'

'Keeping a clear head is always wise.'

'With you around,' she agreed cheekily.

Angling her chin to stare up at him with that same playful, challenging look in her eyes, she plumbed some deep, untapped well inside him. This couldn't end here. It wouldn't end here. They continued to stare at each other until the tension snapped, he seized her hand and they headed for the stairs—ran, rushed, with no sign of his injury now. Jess was the woman who'd broken through his reserve, and they were both laughing. It felt good after so long of having nothing to laugh about. Humour was a healing balm, and it was a glorious irony to want Jess so badly and yet be laughing so much that they couldn't get there fast enough. Tears of laughter were streaming down Jess's face as she finally dropped down on the stairs. He joined her and when eventually she fell silent that silence was charged with sexual energy. Who needed a bed?

'May I?' she asked, her voice hoarse with laughter.

'Do I have a choice, *señorita*?' he asked as she reached for his belt.

'None at all.'

Those were the last few moments of calm. The next saw them tearing at each other's clothes. Several of the tiny buttons down the back of the bridesmaid's dress bounced down the stairs and skittered across the floor in the hall-way.

To hell with this! He had no intention of making love to Jess on a staircase.

'Dante! Give your leg a break,' she protested as he swung her into his arms.

'Why? If I injure it again, you'll have to stay on.'

'Dante, I can't do that. You know I can't—'

That was the last sensible conversation they had. It was as if an atomic force had consumed them both. Crashing into his room, he rocked back against the door, slamming it behind them. Lowering Jess to her feet, he wrenched off his jacket and tossed it on a chair as Jess slipped off her dress with catlike grace. Tugging his shirt free, Jess started work on his zip. At the same time they were kissing wildly, lips, teeth clashing in a dance as old as time. Animal sounds of need escaped their throats until finally he cupped Jess's face in his hands and silenced her with kisses that were deep and long.

'You're overdressed,' she complained when they came up for air.

'So are you,' he growled as he viewed her flimsy thong.

Cocking her head to one side, Jess smiled a witchy smile. 'Do you like it?'

His groin tightened to the point of pain. 'Depends on how easily it rips.'

'Why don't you try it and see?' she suggested.

It ripped.

* * *

When Dante touched her she was his—right away, no hesitation. Fears and consequences were instantly banished to a place so deep in her mind she doubted they'd ever break free. This was right. This was how it should be. Falling back on the bed, she pulled him down on top of her. Guiding his hand, she directed him shamelessly. Not that Dante needed much direction. Moving her hand away, he continued to pleasure her in more ways than she knew existed.

'Don't,' she begged when he pulled away. She needed this—needed Dante. The world she had previously inhabited made no sense now. Without emotion, sensation or risk, it was empty, as everything else was without Dante.

'There are rules,' he informed her in a husky whisper.

'What? Like you make me wait? You leave me frustrated?'

'I make you show me what you want,' he added to her list.

'I can't do that.'

'Why not?' Dante enquired with his mouth very close to hers.

Jess's heart thumped wildly. Surely Dante couldn't mean she should touch herself in front of him?

'You're not shy,' he observed in a clinical tone, 'and we both know how hungry you are.'

'Just as I know you're teasing me.'

'Am I?'

Emotion churned wildly inside her. All her adult life she'd had disappointing sexual encounters, and these had left Jess with the firm belief that the pleasure everyone talked about must be overrated. So what did she want Dante to do about it? Prove her wrong? Prove her so wrong she'd be in a worse state than before—wanting him with no possibility of ever having him? She'd end up as chaste as a nun.

'I feel as if I've lost you,' he remarked, staring down. 'If you've changed your mind—'

'I haven't changed my mind.' This was what she wanted. At least she'd have something to think back on.

She shivered with pleasure as Dante ran one slightly roughened palm down the length of her back. 'You're beautiful. Why make such a deal out of denying yourself pleasure?'

She was wedded to her career? That was a flimsy excuse. She wouldn't be the first professional to cross the line, nor would she be the last.

Dante had spoiled her for all other men when she was just seventeen. Being older made the risk greater. Making love with Dante would reopen that wound and leave her worse off than before. So she was a coward, Jess concluded, destined to live out her life without knowing if sexual pleasure was even possible.

'I get that you need time,' Dante murmured, but that didn't stop him continuing to waken her body until she doubted it would ever sleep again.

'Not too much time,' she admitted dryly.

'What are you doing?' he asked as she moved down the bed.

Putting off the moment? Pleasing Dante? Both of those things.

What she discovered slowed her right down.

Were all men this…built exactly to scale?

'You'd better stop,' he advised.

'I've no intention of stopping.' Brave words, but was this even possible when it took both her hands to encompass him?

Jess won and for the first time ever he was glad to be on the losing side. Tangling his fingers in Jess's hair, he urged her on. Beyond intuitive, she knew everything about pleasure.

Exploring with her lips, her hands and dangerously thrilling passes of her tongue, she cupped him with exquisite sensitivity, and then she teased him with the lightest flicks of her tongue. The instant she took him firmly in both hands, moving them steadily up and down the length of his shaft, she brought him to the edge in seconds.

Sucking the tip brought his hips off the bed. The master of control was finding it hard to hold on. Pleasure built until it refused to be contained and with a roar of relief he claimed his release. What he hadn't expected was that Jess would scramble off the bed.

'I shouldn't be here,' she blurted out.

'Why not?' Catching her close, he searched her eyes. 'Jess, what's wrong?'

'You know this is wrong. I know it's wrong—'

'I know nothing of the sort,' he assured her. But the mood had changed and couldn't be recovered.

Swinging off the bed, he crossed the room naked. Jess was right to call a halt. What could he offer her? Very soon he'd be back on top, with a fast-paced life that demanded selfish focus. Polo took him around the world, as did his business. Jess deserved a man who'd be there for her, someone kind and steady who would treasure her as she deserved. He was not that man, though the thought of some unknown goon pawing her made him sick. That didn't change the facts. He had no right to hold her back from the happiness she deserved.

Bringing a robe from the adjoining bathroom, he wrapped it around her shoulders. He couldn't bear seeing her looking so vulnerable. He'd secured a towel around his waist, for her sake rather than his.

'I'm sorry if I led you on,' she blurted as she moved about the room, gathering up her belongings.

'What are you talking about?'

'You must know,' she insisted, halting with clothes bundled in her arms to turn and stare at him.

'I'm afraid I don't. You didn't lead me anywhere I didn't want to go. I thought that applied to both of us.'

'I should go,' she declared, scouring the room to make sure she hadn't left anything behind.

'Go,' he invited, spreading his arms wide.

He frowned as he watched her leave. Jess was a sensualist, and beautiful, and he had thought her eager to be with him. What on earth was going on in her head? Yes, she was a professional woman with a successful career, but why was she denying herself a life?

Why couldn't she accept pleasure for pleasure's sake? Jess reasoned as she rushed to her room in the guest wing of the *estancia*. Wasn't that what other people did? Where was it written that every relationship must be everlasting? Why couldn't she accept a night of passion with Dante and leave it at that? Was she really bound by duty, or by fear that her teenage dreams could be dust by the morning? Would any man succeed in challenging her belief that she was better on her own, to sort out her life, care for her father, progress her career—

And still be lonely?

Well done, Jess. Everything and nothing has changed.

After a sleepless night she went to the stables to check on the horses. It was early and the yard was mostly silent. The *estancia* had that morning-after feeling that so often hung over a venue after a big event like a soothing web of remembered music and laughter. The door to the facility slid open on well-oiled hinges, and it didn't take long for Jess to satisfy herself that her father's ponies were still happy and contented. Dragging deep on the familiar scent of warm horse and clean hay, she went to take up her usual perch on a hay bale. Tucked away in the shadows of a stable had always been Jess's safe place of choice. It gave her chance to think, to plan, to reflect, and thankfully not regret too much this morning. Life could continue as it always had, a Dante-free zone with no more wild thoughts at a wedding or anywhere else.

With a sigh, she rested back. Going without sleep had left her exhausted. The sound was a cue for Dante's big old dog Bouncer to come and nuzzle her leg. As if he understood the turmoil inside her and was determined to soothe her troubled mind, he settled himself down beside her. Resting his head on her lap, Bouncer exhaled heavily, which made tears sting Jess's eyes at the thought of leaving the *estancia*, and all the many things she would miss. When she should be thrilled that Dante was cured…

'Stealing my dog now?'

Breath shot out of her lungs, with surprise at seeing him and the horrified response to the film reel playing behind her eyes of their aborted love scene last night. 'Dante? What are you doing here?'

'Checking on the animals, like you. I didn't expect to find you here. But then again…'

'What?'

'This is exactly where I should expect to find you.'

'You know me so well,' she teased, trying to keep things light.

'Hardly at all,' he argued. Staring down with concern, he added, 'Are you okay?'

'Of course,' she blustered, stroking Bouncer's ears furiously.

'Hey, leave some of that for me,' Dante insisted as he hunkered down beside her. 'You're spoiling him.'

'And so are you,' she remarked with a smile as Dante fed his old dog some treats. How did anyone manage to look so laid-back and gorgeous so early in the morning—after everything that had happened last night? She felt like a failure, like a ragbag in banged-up jeans and a faded top. It didn't help that Dante was wearing exactly the same sort of clothes, because they only made him seem more tantalisingly attractive and out of reach than ever.

'I'm glad I caught you,' he said in the most relaxed tone ever. 'I have to cancel my eight o'clock therapy session because of some pressing business.'

Her face was burning red with thoughts of last night, and it was a relief to have this shift of focus forced on her. 'No problem,' she blurted on a tight throat. 'We can change the time.' Gently moving Bouncer's head from her knee, she stood up. Dante stood too. 'Any time to suit you,' she offered.

'Hey, you've fulfilled your contract, remember?'

Dante was smiling down as warmly as ever, so why was ice flooding her veins?

'Have this one on me?' she offered awkwardly.

'I would never take advantage of you.'

'Even if I want you to?' So now she sounded desperate. The humiliation of last night put another thought in her mind: Dante was done with amateur hour.

'I've arranged your flight home,' he said as if confirming this.

Yes, she'd half expected it, but still she was stunned into silence. It was as if the floor was dropping away beneath her feet, and she was dropping away with it.

'Thank you. That's very kind of you. I appreciate it' She spoke all the expected words on autopilot. Her lips felt numb, and she had to remind herself that she had always intended to be home in time for Christmas. 'Time flies,' she murmured distractedly.

'When you're enjoying yourself?' Dante suggested wryly.

'I enjoy seeing you without a cane,' she said honestly.

'My PA will be able to tell you all the details. You'll be escorted every step of the way—taxi home, et cetera.'

'Thank you,' she said again as Dante pulled away from the wall. He was clearly in a hurry to leave. 'Don't let me keep you.'

Instead of leaving, he took hold of her hands. 'Jess, this isn't over. I really do have business to attend to.'

'You don't have to explain to me.'

'I think I do. I'm not punishing you or sending you away. Last night was a learning experience for both of us.'

When he learned how unsophisticated she truly was and she learned that Dante was way out of her league.

'It's time for you to get on with your life,' he continued gently. 'You can't be on call here for ever. I don't want to restrict you, but I don't want to lose what we've got either.'

What had they got? What had she allowed them to have? She'd gone into something without thinking it through. Dante wasn't a half-measures man and she had tried to short-change him. And now she could do no more than stand rigidly to attention, not trusting herself to say anything more than, 'Thank you again. It's very kind of you to see to the arrangements.'

'It's not kind,' Dante argued. 'It's in your contract. You'll leave tomorrow morning. The car will collect you prompt at six. That should still give you time to pack your things and say your goodbyes today.'

How could she have forgotten that this was Dante Acosta, a member of the famous Acosta family, tech billionaire and world class polo player? Having recovered full use of his leg, Dante was no longer dependent on anyone, and he was obviously keen to move on—especially from an ingénue who knew next to nothing about sex.

'I thought you'd want the first available flight back, so you can prepare for Christmas at home with your father.'

'That's right. That's so thoughtful of you.'

'Will you need an extra suitcase?'

For two outfits and some knick-knacks she'd bought on the market? 'That won't be necessary, but thank you again.'

'Flight time okay for you?' Dante prompted.

Jess could only hope she didn't look the mess she felt inside. 'Perfect,' she lied. 'The flight's perfect.' Even Bouncer was looking at her with concern. Trust a dog to sense trouble. You couldn't fool an animal. 'I'll be ready to leave at six.'

'Good. Please don't worry about my ongoing treatment. I've already hired someone else to carry on where you left off.'

'Good idea,' she confirmed mechanically. Dante hadn't wasted any time, but when did he ever?

'I won't be slacking,' he promised with a smile.

'I would never think that of you.' To her horror a tear stole down her cheek.

'It's a big, burly man, in case you were wondering,' Dante informed her with a grin.

Try as she might, she couldn't feel light-hearted. She had to get away before a complete meltdown happened and she betrayed her true feelings with huge racking sobs. 'Physios come in all shapes and sizes,' she agreed with a tight smile. 'And I'm sure that whoever you've chosen will be very good.'

'He'd better be,' Dante agreed with a crooked smile. 'You set the bar pretty high.'

But her contract had ended. *Deal with it.* 'I'll leave my notes, though doubtless your new therapist will have his own ideas.'

'Jess—'

'That's okay. I always intended to be back home for Christmas.'

Extricating herself gently from Bouncer, who had wound

himself around her like a comfort blanket, she dipped down to give the big yellow dog one last hug.

Dante blocked her way as she stood up to go. 'Your father will be pleased to see you.'

'I'll be pleased to see him,' she said on a throat turned to ash.

'I'd fly you back myself,' Dante explained as he held the door for her when they left the stables, 'but I have this business deal, and then my first team practice the day after tomorrow and I want to get some training in before then.'

'That's wonderful news,' she said truthfully.

'I know what you're going to say—don't overdo it,' Dante supplied. 'I promise I won't. I owe my recovery to you, and I'll never underestimate what you've done for me.'

And you for me, Jess thought as the curve of Dante's lips twisted her heart until she wanted to cry out in pain. *You've taught me never to be naïve again*, she concluded with her usual sensible self back in charge.

'It's my job,' she said, pinning a smile to dry lips as she shrugged.

How much more of this could she take? She was breaking up inside and desperate to put space between them. The last thing she wanted was to break down in front of Dante. What good would it do, other than make her look even more pathetic than she felt?

She was halfway across the yard when Dante caught hold of her arm. 'Was this just another job for you, Jess?'

There was no chance to hide the tears in her eyes, nor did she even try. 'I'll miss you,' she blurted. To hell with pride! What did pride count for in the end? What did she stand to lose when there was nothing left to lose?

'I'll miss you too,' Dante admitted.

'Just take care of those ponies—and yourself,' she insisted. 'Take care of Moon for me in particular. She needs a lot of attention.' Unlike her human counterpart, thank-fully, Jess thought as she firmed her jaw.

'How can you doubt it?' Dante queried.

'I don't,' she said honestly. When it came to his animals, Dante's love and desire to care for them was as acutely honed as her own. It was just human beings outside his family and staff he had a problem with.

'We won't forget you on the *estancia*, Skylar,' he said dryly, standing back.

An ugly swearword came to mind when Dante men-tioned Skylar. Sadly, her mother had been wrong. There was no magic in the name. There was just Jess. Hurting like hell.

CHAPTER THIRTEEN

SHE WOULDN'T CRY, Jess determined as she stood at the kitchen sink on Christmas Eve in Yorkshire. This wasn't about her, or missing Dante so much it made her heart drum a lament in her chest. This was about the village where she lived, and about her father and the wonderful pals who had kept him afloat while she was working. This year, thanks to the sale of the ponies, they could afford a real Yorkshire Christmas, which meant she could thank everyone by holding open house as her mother used to do.

The scene beyond the steamed-up window would be perfect for a Christmas card. The snow fairies had arrived early this year, frosting the paddocks with pristine white, capping the fences with sparkling meringue peaks of snow. Her father had been out most of the day with the other local farmers, scouring the moors for stranded animals. They deserved a good feed when they got back.

No longer a lonely widower crushed by grief, Jim Slatehome was part of the village again, and part of the horse world too, just as her mother would have wanted. Of course he felt sad and still missed his wife, but now, thanks to all his friends and the medical help he had finally agreed to accept, he had strategies to deal with black moments, which was the most anyone could hope for.

Everything was right with the world, Jess told herself firmly as she put the finishing touches to the feast she'd prepared. Everything apart from one notable thing, she accepted with a pang. Where was Dante? What was he doing this Christmas? It made her unhappy to think of him alone. Surely he'd be with his family? It was such a big family.

Dante playing gooseberry? Did that seem likely?

If only he lived closer, she would have swallowed her pride and invited him over. *If only.* What an overworked phrase. It was no use to anyone, because it spoke of regret and things left undone.

So where was he?

According to her most reliable informant, the *Polo Times*, Dante Acosta had already whupped three types of hell out of his arch rival, Nero Caracas.

He'd better not have damaged that leg.

She'd researched the man who had taken over Dante's treatment and, to be fair, his reputation was impeccable. Trust Dante to choose the best.

It was the most frustrating thing on earth to care as deeply as she cared for Dante, Jess reflected as she pulled away from the sink, and yet be prevented from caring *for* him. He'd never played so well, according to *Polo Times*. And in a direct quote from Dante, that was all thanks to his physiotherapist, Jess Slatehome, who, together with her close associate Skylar Slates, had raised him up when he'd been down.

Dante had more than kept his promise to let the polo world know that Jess was good at her job. The phone had been ringing off the hook since the article was printed. Admittedly, most of the calls had been from reporters wanting to know what the 'real' Dante Acosta was like.

'He's such a loner and an enigma,' they'd prompted, 'while you were a young woman on her own.'

'I'm a medical professional with a job to do,' she had reminded them, remembering to add, 'Happy Christmas,' genuinely and warmly—because, like her, they were only doing their job.

Happy Christmas.

Jess's mouth twisted with the pain. She missed Dante so much the words meant nothing. Swiping tears away, she cleaned down the kitchen until it gleamed like never before. Checking the fire, she hung up her apron. With a shake of her head, as if that might knock some sense into it, she thought through the rest of the day. The food was ready. There was nothing more to do, and she longed to get outside. There could be more sheep to find.

He could go anywhere for Christmas. Invitations were stacked up in a pile on his desk at the *estancia*. Those from his family had received polite refusals. Those who craved Acosta glitter to brag about went in the bin.

He checked again. Nothing from Jess.

Why should there be?

Shifting position impatiently, he picked up a call from his sister, Sofia. 'Yes?'

'Compliments of the season to you too,' she said dryly. 'I gather you're in a good mood.'

'What do you want?'

Accustomed to his stormy moods since the injury, Sofia gave his bad manners a bye. 'I'm ringing to tell you not to buy so many presents. A truckload arrived today, when all we want is you.'

'Another year, perhaps,' he promised gruffly.

The Acostas always gathered at Christmas to remember their parents, though all five of them under one roof for any length of time could be a recipe for disaster. To put it mildly, they could be fiery. Dante's eldest brother always referred them to the Argentinian branch of the family which, he insisted, was far better balanced since all the brothers had married. He tried this same lecture each year but, as he remained unattached, it lacked bite.

The problem, Dante reflected, was that none of them was prepared to risk their heart after the crushing grief of losing their parents.

Even him?

Why couldn't he date Jess in a way she'd find acceptable? What was stopping him giving her the future she deserved?

Only his stubbornness. And possibly Jess's too.

Glancing at the phone, he felt a stab of regret. He loved his sister, and would miss catching up with Sofia and his brothers at the annual get-together, but this year there was only one place to be.

Why the change of heart?

Try living anything approaching a normal life with one exceptional woman, with whom he had unfinished business, permanently lodged in his mind.

Everything was ready for whoever dropped by, Jess reassured herself as she left the farm. Gifts for her father were wrapped and ready, together with the 'little somethings', as her mother used to call them, for his pals, and for any surprise visitors. She'd brought in extra folding chairs from the barn, so all that remained was to tempt her father back to the house with the promise of a delicious feast.

Financially, the year had ended on a high, mainly thanks to Dante's purchase of their ponies. It was a real treat to have enough money to buy her father things he'd denied himself for far too long. There would be a satisfyingly large heap of gifts beneath a tree laden with baubles that carried memories. Everything was warm and welcoming, just as her mother would have wanted it to be. The tradition of open house at Bell Farm would continue.

She paused at the top of a rise to stare out over the winter wonderland with its coating of snow and inevitably her thoughts turned to Dante.

Where was he? Who was he with? What was he doing? Would he be lonely? Was his leg still okay?

'Stop it,' she said out loud. This was going to be a wonderful Christmas, to which her broken heart was most definitely not invited.

Dante's flight through thunderclouds on his way from Spain to England was, to put it mildly, interesting, even in the luxurious surroundings of his private jet. The drive to the farm was even more so. No one was prepared to release a helicopter in such uncertain weather, so he hired a big workhorse-style SUV, but even that was brought to a sliding halt by snowdrifts on the exposed Yorkshire moors.

Grinding his jaw, he grabbed some belongings and set off to walk to the farm. According to the satnav on his phone, he was close to his destination. This wasn't the way he'd planned to arrive, but Jess wouldn't care less if he arrived in a helicopter or on foot. Unimpressed by shows of wealth, she was the most down-to-earth woman he'd ever met. She demanded an entirely new rulebook. He was still finessing the detail as he ploughed on through the snow.

He thought about Jess with each step, and what he owed her for restoring the strength in his leg. Most of all he thought about holding her. Maybe that was a stretch. There were no guarantees where Jess was concerned. She'd pick her own route through life.

Pausing to look around and get his bearings, he was grateful for the map on his phone. There were no recognisable landmarks. Everything was covered in a blanket of snow. Even the road had become one with the field. Jess's home turf seemed determined to show him an increasingly hostile face. If Jess did the same, he was wasting his time.

Pulling up his jacket collar, he pushed on. There was an

occasional flicker of light and a glimpse of colour down the hill, where a cluster of homesteads sat squat in the snow. He exhaled on a cloud of humourless laughter. Why was he surprised that a woman from such a bleak and forbidding landscape would be anything but strong and self-determining?

It had occurred to him that Jess might refuse to see him. Who rocked up unannounced on Christmas Eve? It couldn't be helped. He wasn't going anywhere until they met up face to face. Jess had rocked his world on its axis and there was no way he'd let this go. If he reached the village—*when* he reached the village, Dante amended—he'd surely find lodgings for the night. The roads were impassable, so he was stuck here whether Jess agreed to see him or not.

After another half a mile or so, he stopped to blink and rub snow from his eyes, seeing shadows moving in the distance. As he drew closer, he realised the shadows were men working in the field. Driven almost sideways by gusting wind, they were attempting to heave sheep out of a ditch. Several more animals were stranded, and he didn't hesitate before pitching in.

Fate had dealt him a kindness, Dante concluded as he worked with the other men. Rescuing the terrified animals built an instant camaraderie that allowed him to ask the way, enquire about lodgings and even learn something about Jess.

The moors had a peculiar stillness that only descended after a recent fall of snow. It was like being alone on the planet, without even birdsong to keep her company, Jess mused as she trudged on. She was keeping a lookout for her father and for his friends, as well as any stranded animals she might find along the way. She'd come prepared, with a snow shovel strung across her shoulder on a strap.

She paused for a moment when she got to the brow of

the hill. The view was immense. Now the snow flurries had died down she could see right across the moors to Derbyshire. But it was only a temporary respite because snow had started falling again.

Bringing her muffler over her mouth, she prepared to slither down what was now a treacherous slope. Halfway down, she dug in her heels and skidded to a halt. An SUV was stuck in a snowdrift and tilted on its side. Thoughts flashed through her head. Uppermost was saving whoever was in the vehicle before they froze to death. Hurtling down the bank regardless of safety, she sucked in great lungsful of air. She had to conquer that panic. She'd be no use to anyone like this.

Once she'd gathered herself, another question occurred: who drove a flashy SUV in the village?

Could it be Dante?

Don't be ridiculous, she railed at her inner voice. Why would Dante come here on Christmas Eve? There were no ponies to buy. He'd bought them all. And would a billionaire's Christmas include the simple pleasures of a small isolated village on top of the Yorkshire moors? He had absolutely no reason to come here.

That didn't stop her wading through the sometimes thigh-high snow. She had to reach the SUV. Not only would the driver and any passengers be in danger of freezing inside the vehicle; if they left it they could quickly become disorientated, and the result would be the same. Wind chill was deadly, and it was vital they reached safety and warmth soon.

Fast progress was impossible, which gave Jess's thoughts the chance to run free. Maybe Dante had somehow heard that Bell Farm was throwing its doors open to all-comers at Christmas. It wasn't beyond the bounds of reason that he'd spoken to her dad but, whoever was in that vehicle, or maybe wandering around lost on the moors, she had to do her best to find them.

There were times when Jess thought her feet would freeze into icicles and break off. This wasn't helped by the local brook being covered by a thin layer of ice beneath a concealing carpet of snow. She yelped as her feet sank beneath the surface yet again, but now she was within touching distance of the vehicle and she pressed on.

Swinging the snow shovel off her shoulder, she braced herself for whatever, or whoever, she might find inside. Was she too late? What if Dante had driven up to the moors? Why hadn't she had the courage to tell him how she felt before now? It wasn't as if she was shy or retiring. Tears froze on her face as she frantically dug out the snow. Why had she never told him she loved him? Why had she held back?

Why had they both held back?

It wasn't as if Dante had plied her with words of love and reassurance, any more than Jess had unleashed her true feelings for him.

Straightening up, she eased her aching back. It wasn't as if they hadn't talked, but neither of them was comfortable talking about feelings. They'd both built grief-driven barricades. Was that what those they'd lost would want for them?

Please, please, please! Don't let it end like this, she begged the fates and anyone else who was listening. *Please let me have one last chance to tell Dante how I feel. I promise I won't shy away from it.*

There was no way of predicting, of course, how Dante might respond to that, but as he was hardly likely to be the driver of the vehicle that hardly mattered.

But there was no one in the SUV, and fresh snow had covered any footprints around it. Planting her shovel, Jess flopped down in the snow. Exhausted and dispirited she might be, but she couldn't spare the time to catch her breath. Getting up again, she resolved to solve the mystery of the abandoned SUV because whoever had been driving was still in danger.

She'd search the whole damn moor if she had to, Jess determined as she stumbled on. Thank goodness she knew the terrain.

CHAPTER FOURTEEN

'JESS?'

'Dante!'

Out of the blizzard came a shape: a man—the only man—a powerful, healthy, vigorous life force in a world grown so bleak and frightening even Jess had begun to doubt that it would ever be summer again.

She went rigid at first and then started laughing and crying at the same time, before launching herself at Dante. 'I can't believe you're here! I'm so glad you're safe!' Pulling back, she searched his eyes with relief.

'Believe,' he said dryly, gently disentangling himself.

'Were you in the SUV?' she demanded, swinging around to look over her shoulder.

'I had that pleasure.'

'Of landing in a ditch?' she suggested, laughing with happiness now.

'That was somewhat unexpected,' he conceded.

'So why are you here?' She was breathless with excitement.

'I keep asking myself that same question.'

Her eyes narrowed with suspicion. 'No one arrives on top of the Yorkshire moors in a blizzard without a very good reason. And it's Christmas Eve,' she pointed out, 'so it must have been something big to bring you here.'

Something small, he thought, measuring her fragility

against the frozen landscape, but if you added spirit into the mix Jess was a match for any and all conditions.

'Are you saying I've got no excuse to be here?'

'Not unless you're hiding the reindeer.'

His lips tugged with the urge to laugh. Suddenly the trip was more than worthwhile. But there was something he had to know. 'Good surprise, or bad?'

'Lucky for you that you're in time to eat with us,' Jess exclaimed happily without attempting to answer his question.

'I wouldn't dream of putting you to that trouble.'

'No trouble,' she said, cocking her head to one side to bait him with a grin. 'We've got enough food for an army, so I could do with another mouth.'

'*Dios*, no!' he murmured dryly. 'I can't imagine you with another mouth. One is enough to contend with.'

She smiled and relaxed at this. 'But you will come and join us?' she pressed.

'I'd be delighted to join you. Solely in the interest of helping you out on the food front, of course.'

'Of course,' she teased back. 'Great!' Biting down on her bottom lip, Jess shook her head as she smiled up at him, as if she couldn't believe the evidence of her own eyes.

The force of Dante's personality alone was like a blaze of fire in a frozen monochrome landscape. Jess's feelings were in danger of overflowing. It was as if her world had exploded into a blizzard of happiness. Beyond relieved to have solved the mystery of the missing driver in the stranded SUV, she knew now that nothing could be better than discovering the driver was Dante.

'You're safe,' she marvelled as they walked along.

'That I am,' Dante confirmed while she imprinted every rugged detail of his face on her mind.

Of course he was safe. Dante Acosta would never set out on a mission without proper planning first. Hence the backpack and the storm-proof clothing and the tough work-manlike boots. The question was: what was his mission this time? Jess wondered.

Meeting up with her father and his friends a little way closer to the farm was such a happy reunion. 'So you found her!' Jess's father enthused, slapping Dante on the back as if he'd known him all his life.

'Have you two met already today?' Jess asked, cocking her head to one side to study both men.

'We met in the field where your father was rescuing sheep,' Dante revealed.

'And you joined in,' Jess guessed. Her father confirmed this with his customary grunt that reminded her so much of Dante.

Dipping his head, Dante whispered in her ear, 'We have to stop meeting like this.'

You have to stop sending shivers spinning down my spine when my father is watching, Jess thought. 'Suits me,' she said coolly.

Meaningful glances exchanged between Dante and her father made Jess instantly suspicious. 'What's going on?' she prompted. 'What aren't you telling me?'

'This is no place to linger for a chat,' her father scolded gruffly.

There was nothing underhand about Jess's father. If he knew something he spat it out. This behaviour wasn't like him. She frowned. Her father wasn't frowning. A smile had spread across his face as he walked along with Dante. It was almost as if he had expected their visitor—if not today, then at some point soon. What weren't they sharing? Why had Dante come to Yorkshire?

'We'll take these sheep back to the barn,' her father was telling Dante. 'And then I hope you'll join us for our first Christmas feast.'

'I'd love to,' Dante confirmed.

'Excellent,' her father exclaimed, slapping his hands together to keep them warm. 'With Jess's cooking I can confidently guarantee you a very happy Christmas!'

'Happy Christmas to you too,' Dante echoed with an unreadable glance at Jess. 'And the best of everything in the New Year.'

'The New Year's going to be so much better for us,' her father enthused. 'You made sure of it,' he told Dante.

How had Dante made sure of it? The sale of the ponies would only take them so far. Jess didn't have chance to think it over as the group of men with her father chorused in a shout, 'Happy Christmas!'

Having seen the sheep safely gathered in, they ended up at the packed pub where, as Jess might have expected, her father invited everyone back to the farm. Steam rose from their clothes as the roaring log fire did its work. While the general air of celebration and good-humoured complaints about the weather rang out around her, Jess's focus was all on Dante. He bought a round of drinks for everyone and was soon swapping stories with the best. Not once did he let on that his life was extraordinary, and though the locals might have known he was a polo-playing billionaire, as far as they were concerned he'd helped them save the sheep, and that made him one of them.

It was wonderful to have Dante here in the place she loved best. And at Christmas, Jess's favourite time of year. Most important of all, he was safe. Why he'd come to the village didn't matter. All she cared about was that they were together. Dante was the best Christmas gift of all.

The farmhouse kitchen was almost as crowded as the pub and definitely as noisy, and in all the right ways. He was instantly struck by the warm and homely atmosphere Jess had created. She was special. This was special. With enough delicious food to feed an army and an assortment of chairs and stools gathered from who knew where, she soon had her visitors munching happily.

'I'm sorry,' she said as she squeezed past with yet another oven dish brimming with crunchy golden roast potatoes. 'This can't be what you're used to.'

She was gone before he had chance to tell her that this was so much better than anything he had, and that he envied everything about it. No Michelin starred restaurant could better the happy family atmosphere Jess had created here.

He'd never eaten food like it, and he prided himself on his chefs. If the way to a man's heart was through his stomach Jess had the route map down. They didn't have chance to speak as Jess was so busy, but he pounced on the cue when a rather attractive widow from a neighbouring farm invited her father over. 'I've got a room at the pub,' he told Jess, 'if you'd care to join me for a nightcap?'

'Why, Señor Acosta,' Jess challenged with a smile, turning her bright eyes up to his, 'are you propositioning me?'

'I'm offering to buy you a drink to thank you for the meal. Then I'll walk you home.'

And I'm supposed to believe it's as simple as that, her narrowed eyes clearly told him. Who could blame her when testosterone was firing off him in spears of hot light?

'Do you have people to look after the animals?' he asked.

'We drafted in some extra help over Christmas. They'll take it in turns to keep a watch through the night.'

'Then you have no excuse.' His lips pressed down as he shrugged.

'Apart from natural caution, do you mean?'

'What would Skylar say?' he challenged.

She laughed. 'I'm not sure I want to know.'

'You need a break so you can enjoy Christmas too,' he pointed out.

'You think?' Jess laughed as she wiped a forearm across her glowing face.

'I know it,' he stated firmly.

Her cheeks pinked up even more but she was in no hurry to give him her answer. *Brava*, Jess. This woman was exactly the challenge he wanted.

Should she go with Dante? Life was complicated, and he had made it even more so because she wanted to go with him, more than she'd ever wanted anything before.

There were so many reasons not to go. The kitchen was a mess—inevitable after a successful party—and she would have liked to stay and clear up.

'You go,' her father's friend Ella told her, having intuited Jess's dilemma. 'I'll handle this first thing tomorrow morning—and I'll handle your dad too.'

Jess could believe it as she exchanged a smile with the older woman. Ella coped with a farm on her own so there was no reason why she couldn't take on Jess's dad. 'If you're sure?'

'I'm positive. You've more than put the effort in to making today a great success, and if you can't go and have a quiet drink down the local pub I don't know what's wrong with the world.'

But would it be a quiet drink down the local pub? 'Thank you. You're very kind—'

Before Jess had chance to continue, her father interrupted with the surprising news that she shouldn't wait up for him.

'I don't know what time I'll be back,' he explained.

'Oh.' Jess's jaw must have dropped. She quickly pinned on a smile. Yes, she was surprised. Things seemed to be moving quickly between her father and Ella, though she'd been away in Spain and, with work and the animals, maybe it was Jess who was guilty for being out of the loop. She had never asked the relevant questions. Her father had been lost and lonely without her mother; why shouldn't he be happy now?

'See you, Dad,' she called out as he left with Ella. With all her heart, she wished them well, and her father a much better future.

They'd all come a long way, Jess reflected as the rest of their guests left for home. Dante was waiting by the door with her coat. So what was she going to do? Turn him down? She could stay here and nothing would change. He'd probably be gone by the morning. And what would she have missed?

That remained to be seen, she concluded, firming her jaw.

Glancing around the familiar kitchen, she couldn't help feeling that, whatever happened next, her life would never be the same again.

When he planned something, he planned down to the last detail. He'd taken the top floor of the pub in advance and had Christmas gifts for Jess and her father in his emergency backpack. He would arrange the recovery of the SUV as and when; meanwhile, champagne was on ice and, as he'd also requested, tasty snacks were in the icebox he'd had installed in one of the rooms. This wouldn't be his only visit to the village, so home comforts were essential. As for him and Jess? It was crucial they had a chance to talk in private.

Inviting her into the cosy sitting room, where the landlord had the good sense to light the log fire, he took her coat and then they stared at each other in silence.

Jess made the first move. Moving closer, she stood on tiptoe to brush her lips against his. 'That wasn't a mistake,' she informed him. With a shrug she added, 'Maybe it was as reckless as when I was seventeen, but I think I'm old enough to handle the consequences now.'

'You expect consequences?' He smiled and shook his head.

'You'd better not disappoint,' she warned cheekily.

'What's been holding you back?'

Jess's mouth twisted as she turned serious to think about this. 'Duty—like you? Career—like you?'

'Disappointments in the past?'

'If you think you can do better...'

She was only half joking, he suspected. 'Try me and find out.'

'I intend to.'

'Do you think you should take your boots off first?'

'My boots?' she echoed with surprise, glancing down.

'Your feet must be frozen.'

She stared at him and laughed. They both laughed, and were still laughing when he brought Jess into his arms to kiss her—gently at first, and then as if he would never let her go. Whatever doubts had been in Jess's mind, it soon became clear she'd given them the night off. Having left her boots by the door, she informed him, 'My heart is set on undressing you.'

He held his arms out. 'Be my guest.'

She did this slowly and deliberately, as if every button took her closer to a personal goal that had less to do with sex and more to do with establishing trust between them. His urges were far less worthy. He wanted to strip her naked, throw her on the bed and make love to Jess until she was too tired to move, but this was such a pivotal moment for both of them he decided to run with Jess's approach. Until she sank to her knees in front of him.

'Did I do something wrong?' she asked, wounded eyes fixed on his as he brought her to her feet.

'You've done nothing wrong,' he said gently. Now he understood why Jess's sex life had been so disappointing. If she'd had to do all the work, what pleasure was there in that for Jess? Sex should be a shared experience with mutual pleasure.

Swinging her into his arms, he carried her into the bedroom. 'Now it's my turn,' he warned as he peeled off the heavy socks she was wearing beneath her boots. 'These are disgusting.' He tossed them aside as she laughed, and then she took turns smiling and groaning with pleasure as he warmed her feet in his hands.

'You know all the best routes to a girl's heart.'

'Dealing with frozen feet is my speciality,' he conceded as he bathed her tiny feet in kisses and hot breath.

'How many hearts have you broken with that technique?'

'I've never been much interested in finding my way to anyone's heart,' he admitted.

She seemed surprised so he asked, 'Why do you find that so hard to believe?'

'Your reputation precedes you?' she suggested.

'Do you believe everything you read?' When she shrugged, he explained, 'I love my brothers and my sister, Sofia. And, before you ask—no, I have never put their feet near my mouth.'

Everything changed in that moment. Jess's smile broadened until it lit up her face, and he knew that the biggest hurdle had been crossed. Before sex came trust, and he had won Jess's trust.

CHAPTER FIFTEEN

DANTE UNDRESSED HER with as much care as he might have shown a skittish pony—if that pony had been wearing ten layers of Arctic gear. And with each item of clothing he removed, he kissed her. When she was naked the room seemed to grow very still. The only sound was their breathing—Dante's steady and Jess's interrupted by short gasps of pleasure when Dante found some new place to kiss.

It was possible to soothe and arouse at the same time, she was fast discovering, and Dante was a master of the art. Long, soothing strokes down her back quietened her, but made her want so much more. He gave her chance to feel her body waking to his touch, but his restraint was a torment. The urge to take the lead began to overwhelm her, but each time she tried to make a move Dante dissuaded her with kisses, telling her to concentrate on sensation and nothing else.

She hadn't just stepped over that line; she'd leapt over it, Jess concluded as a soft moan of pleasure escaped her throat. They could never be close enough and when Dante's hand found her she cried out loud with excitement. He'd made her wait so long she was right on the edge. 'Please don't stop,' she begged when he moved his hand. His answer was to kiss her neck, her lips, her cheeks and her eyes, while she trembled with anticipation beneath him like a greyhound in the traps. Then he turned her and, holding her hands in one giant fist above her head, he made control impossible. As she bucked uncontrollably beneath him Dante released her pinned hands and captured her thrusting buttocks in one hand while he helped her to extract every last pulse of pleasure with his other hand. Having found her slick warmth, he made her take the short journey again, until she found herself right on the edge.

'Again?' he suggested in a low growl.

She had no chance to do anything but cry out, 'Yes!' Dante's fingers were magic and he knew just what to do. Grinding her body frantically against the heel of his hand, she claimed her second powerful release. He silenced her panting and groaning with a kiss that was as deep as it was tender.

She loved the way he held her buttocks firmly in place with one hand as he pleasured her with the other. 'Are you going to be as greedy as this all night?' he teased in a deep, husky tone as he loomed over her, swarthy and dangerous, and so impossibly sexy.

'You made me insatiable,' she said, marvelling at how gentle he could be, how persuasive. She was half his size and Dante treated her as if she were made of rice paper, which was frustrating but also reassuring.

'I want to taste you,' he growled, moving down the bed.

She laughed softly. 'Do I have a say in this?'

'No.' Lifting her legs onto his shoulders, Dante dipped his head.

She thought she knew pleasure? She was wrong. *This* was pleasure. This was something beyond anything else.

'I can't,' she protested, speaking her thoughts out loud. 'Not again.'

'Is that a fact?' Dante queried with a wicked look, pausing.

His tongue, his mouth and fingers continued to work their magic. This time the pleasure waves were so strong she was tossed about on a wild tide of sensation that stole away every thought except one: could she remain suspended in Dante's erotic net for ever?

Jess...

Holding himself back was the biggest test he'd ever faced. Jess took even longer to recover and when she did her eyes were heavy. She wasn't just tired; she was exhausted. It had been a long day, with the shock of seeing him and the rescue of the sheep. Then she'd gone on to cater a meal for who knew how many before allowing herself downtime. Who wouldn't be exhausted? Taking her now would be taking advantage. She was sleepily sexy but her conscious mind was taking a well-earned breath. He'd waited a long time to make love to Jess and when it happened he aimed for special, not something to tag to a long, draining day.

'You're smiling,' she commented drowsily.

Because he wasn't used to waiting, but Jess was different.

'Well?' she prompted softly, reaching out. 'Are you going to explain?'

Turning off the light, he drew her into his arms.

'Are you asleep?' she asked when some quiet time had passed. 'Do you regret this?'

'No.'

'Then...?'

'You're tired,' he murmured.

'I'm not,' Jess protested.

'Exhausted, then.'

'I do need a hug,' she admitted.

To reassure her, he tightened his grip.

'I don't want you to think I'm having second thoughts,' she whispered.

It was obvious she wanted to talk. Releasing her, he sat up beside her. 'Talk to me,' he encouraged her gently.

'About loss and grief and duty, and how there's never enough time to mull over those things?'

'There hasn't been a right time for either of us, I'm guessing,' he admitted, raking his hair.

'Stop distracting me,' she scolded, smiling, 'or we're wasting another chance to talk it out.'

'I'm not even sure we should be talking about it now, when you so clearly need to sleep.'

Searching his eyes, she explained, 'I need to talk first and then sleep.'

'Go ahead,' he said softly, waiting.

'I didn't cry when my mother died,' Jess eventually revealed in a small voice, as if she still felt guilty about it. But then, remembering his loss, she reverted to her customary warm, concerned self. 'I don't expect you showed any emotion either when you lost your parents.'

'Oh, I was angry,' he confessed, thinking back. 'When I arrived at the hospital one of the doctors told me, "Where there's life there's hope."'

'And of course you desperately hoped he was right and believed him.' Her eyes were in that moment as she stared into his.

'There was no hope,' he confirmed flatly. 'My parents were already dead, as I discovered when I barged into the room where they had been treated.'

'You were how old?'

'Old enough to know better—seventeen or eighteen. I've found it hard to trust anyone outside my inner circle since that day.'

'And who could blame you?'

'Not you, apparently,' he remarked as he stared into Jess's eyes. 'So, what's your excuse for being so bottled-up?'

'Events,' she said succinctly in the way people did when there was a world of trouble hidden behind a single word.

'Tell me about those events,' he said gently. 'The grief you hid I know about, so I'm guessing we're talking about your father.'

She was silent for a while and then confessed, 'He was such a proud man...'

'Was?' he prompted.

'You must remember...' Her eyes were big and wounded.

'I do. Everyone's brought low by grief, so I'm guessing your father took some time to pull through.'

'It wasn't easy for him.'

'Or for you,' he observed quietly.

'Don't they say love makes anything possible?'

She looked so sad as she asked the question. His imagination could fill in the blanks for now. Jess wasn't ready to tell him the detail. Maybe she never would be. She was right about her father being a proud man, and Jess was as protective of family as he was. It was up to her to decide if and when and how much she told him.

'I trust you,' she admitted before falling into a thoughtful silence. 'I know you won't say anything to harm my father's reputation,' she added at last, staring into his eyes, unblinking.

'Never,' he pledged.

He let the silence hang until Jess was ready to continue. 'I built my adult life on the promises I made to my mother, which were to continue my education and to qualify so I could earn a living and look after my father and the farm. That didn't leave much time to mourn my mother's loss, but it was a relief to be busy because the alternative was to sink into grief and achieve nothing, which would have betrayed her trust.'

'We all need time to mourn.'

'Says you,' she rebuked him with a sad smile.

'Let's build on the past and remember those we loved

happily, positively, knowing that's what they'd want us to do.'

'You always find a way to make me smile,' she observed thoughtfully.

'Do you want to punish me for that?'

'Do you want to be punished?'

His smile darkened. 'Not for that.'

Her gaze flew to the rumpled bed. 'You spoiled me for other men ten years ago.'

'That kiss in your father's stable?'

'That was just the start,' she admitted. 'And now you've spoiled me all over again.'

'Don't expect me to apologise.'

When he fell silent she asked, 'Dante, is something wrong?'

This was not the right time to explain what was happening with the farm. 'No. There's nothing wrong. We'll talk again in the morning.'

'Promise?' she asked softly.

'I promise.' Drawing Jess into his arms, he settled down on the bed. Feeling her tears wet his chest, he turned to look at her. 'Why are you crying?'

'I'm happy,' she confessed.

Cradling her in his arms, he kissed the top of her head. 'Sleep now. I'm not going anywhere.' She was possibly already asleep, he thought as Jess's breathing steadied, and he was surprised by the deep sense of satisfaction that stole over him at the thought that she could relax in his arms.

Was this love?

Deep trust was love. Unpacking memories that had wounded them both and entrusting them to each other was closer to love than anything else he could think of. The warm contentment inside him felt like love. How else could he be lying here, wanting this woman as he did, without the slightest intention of disturbing her?

* * *

Had there ever been a better way to start Christmas Day than this? Jess woke slowly to find she was naked in bed with Dante in the dark quiet hours of early morning. Naked and contented, she amended, though not for long. It was a small step from lazy contentment to making her wishes clear, and Dante was as eager as she was. With a soft growl of cooperation, he shifted position to make things easier for her.

Guiding him, she used Dante's body to rouse a place that could never get enough of him, and now badly needed more.

'Hey,' Dante whispered, 'take it easy.' Moving over her, he whispered, 'There's no hurry.'

She was way past listening to advice, but when he allowed her the smooth tip of his erection she was more than ready to bow to his greater knowledge, especially as he had moved her hands by this time and taken over.

'When I say and not before,' he instructed.

How could she answer when all her concentration was focused on getting him to probe a little deeper? Dante's jaw was set, she noticed, glancing up. He was suffering too. So much restraint had to be torture for him. Damping down the urge to thrust forward and bring their torture to an end, she settled for doing as he suggested, which was to let everything go and allow Dante to set the pace.

'That's right… Relax,' he encouraged. 'Sensation will be so much greater if you allow me to pleasure you, while you do absolutely nothing.'

Heaving a shaking sigh, she knew at once he was right. Each touch was amplified by her stillness. She could concentrate on every feeling as Dante pleasured her at his own pace. She tensed momentarily as he sank a little deeper, stretching her beyond belief. They weren't even past the smooth, domed head of his erection yet but, feeling her concern, he stopped to allow her to become used to the new sensation. When she was ready to move on, he cupped her buttocks and took her a little deeper still. There was no pain. He'd prepared her too well. There was only pleasure—wave after wave of incredible pleasure, fired by the overwhelming need to be one with him.

Sinking deeper still, he took her to the hilt in one slow, firm thrust. She couldn't help but gasp, but Dante had an answer for the shock of his invasion. Massaging her with rotating movements of his hips, he brought her swiftly to the point of no return and then he commanded in a low voice, 'Now.'

She didn't need any encouragement and plunged into pleasure with repeated cries of relief. Even when the waves crashing down on her eased off, Dante was still moving. He took her steadily and gently until her hunger built again, when she grasped his buttocks to work him faster and harder, and he pounded into her as if they would never ever stop.

Now the dam had burst their lovemaking was fierce. They enjoyed each other in as many ways as they could, gorging on pleasure, sometimes on the bed and sometimes not. A shared shower to cool down after more heated activity proved another excuse for lovemaking, only this time she scrambled up him and Dante slammed her against the wall to take her deep. Towelling dry was another opportunity to test the resilience of the black marble countertop, and when they returned to bed they didn't quite make it.

'Not so fast,' he said, dragging her close. Bending her over where she was standing at the side of the bed, he encouraged her to brace her hands against the mattress so he could take her from behind, while using his hand to encourage somewhere that needed no encouragement. He allowed her cries of release to subside before turning her so she was sitting on the edge of the bed, facing him. Moving between her legs, he pressed her back. Grabbing a pillow, he placed it beneath her buttocks.

There was no end to pleasure with your soulmate, Jess reflected some considerable time later when she sank back, gasping, on the bed.

What else could she call Dante? Could fate be so cruel that it had thrown them together again for no reason? The gulf between them remained wide in terms of financial success and lifestyle, but were these the most important measures? Wasn't the way they played off each other, and improved each other, far more important than that? Would this feeling of euphoria last? she wondered as she stared at Dante. Why not, she reasoned, when his care of her, and his sheer damn sexy self, was so different to the grim face he showed the world? Was that a coincidence too? Couples could destroy each other, while others were improved in every way just by being together. She wanted to believe that she and Dante were builders not destroyers, and that they would be stronger together than they were apart.

'It's your turn now?' she teased as Dante joined her on the bed.

She reached for him. They reached for each other. Dante took them both to the edge, and over it.

They slept for what must have been hours. When she woke the light was filtering through the curtains. Could it really be Christmas morning? Tiptoeing across the room, she tweaked back the edge of the curtain.

'Hey,' Dante complained huskily as light poured into the room. 'Don't you ever need to rest?'

Bouncing back on to the bed, she threw her head back with sheer happiness. 'Says the man who keeps more plates spinning than anyone I know?

'Happy Christmas! The best Christmas ever!' Tossing her hair back, she laughed with sheer happiness at the dawning of this special new day.

'Ah,' Dante said, sitting up. 'Thanks for reminding me—'

'You needed reminding? You are a lost cause.'

'Not quite,' he assured her. 'Let me grab a robe.'

'Wow. This sounds serious,' she said as Dante rolled out of bed. Her spirits took a dive when he didn't answer. 'While you do that, I'm going to take a quick shower.'

Freshen up, think, organise her brain cells. Last night had been spectacular, but now it was another day. And she was determined to remain optimistic.

One of the advantages of Dante taking the entire top floor of the pub was that they didn't have to share a bathroom, so she luxuriated for quite a while before dressing and returning to the bedroom to find Dante seated at the desk. He'd showered too, and was dressed in jeans and a form-fitting top—a pairing that pointed up his spectacular physique. She didn't have long to dwell on that. There were some documents on the desk that somehow made her nerves twang. And Dante was looking serious. This wasn't good.

'Why are you frowning?' he asked.

'Am I?'

He gave her one of his amused, forbearing looks. 'I'm not allowed to give you a Christmas present?' he queried.

'Depends what it is. And I feel terrible,' she added.

'Oh?'

'I don't have anything for you,' she explained.

'But I'm not expecting anything,' Dante told her with a shrug. 'You didn't know I was coming.'

'I could have sent a card.'

'Write one now,' he suggested with a casual jerk of his chin in the direction of the pub's info pack, which would almost certainly contain some of the striking postcards they sold at the bar.

'I wouldn't know what to say,' she admitted honestly.

'Really?' Dante barked a short laugh. 'You being short of words must be a first.'

She hummed while her heart raced. What was Dante hiding in that case?

'Well?' he prompted as she hovered by the door. 'Are you coming in properly, or are you going out again?'

She shut the door, but stayed where she was.

'Don't you want to know what your gift is?' he coaxed.

'A halter and a bag of pony nuts?' she ventured, unable to rip her gaze from the official-looking papers.

Dante pulled a mock-disappointed look. 'Is that your best guess?'

'It's my only guess.'

'How would you feel if I said that this document is my way of gifting you the farm?'

As Dante held out an official-looking envelope time stood still. Jess didn't speak or move a muscle, and was completely incapable of rational thought.

'Well?' he prompted.

She attempted to moisten her lips so she could reply, but her mouth had turned as dry as dust. 'I'd say you were teasing me,' she said at last. 'But it isn't a very funny joke.'

'I'm not joking, Jess,' Dante assured her with a long steady look. 'That's why I've come here. Well, partly, anyway. I guess I could have sent the contract, but I wanted to hand it to you in person.'

'Why?' she demanded faintly. 'Why have you done this?'

'Your father needed help. He asked me for help.'

She was confused. 'You mean more help after the sale of the ponies?'

'You must have known that buying his stock would only temporarily bail him out of trouble. He needed more. The bank needed more.'

'So what are you saying?' She shook her head as if none of this made sense.

'I'm saying I bought the farm, paid off your father's debts and cleared his overdraft at the bank. He's a wealthy man now, so he can breed and train ponies to his heart's content. That's what he's good at, Jess. It's what he should be allowed to do. Business isn't his thing. And you need a life too.'

She frowned. 'And you decided this?'

'It was the best way to help your father and help you too.'

'Help yourself, don't you mean?' she flared. 'My father owns the best pasture in Yorkshire, the best gallops, the best ponies—or he will once the new foals are born and brought on. Anyone would want to buy Bell Farm.'

'Then why haven't they?' Dante asked bluntly. Jess blanched as he went on, 'According to your father, there hasn't been a single offer. He explained that not everyone has the appetite to live up here and cope with the climate and unrelenting work involved.'

'So what will be his position?' she demanded. 'Lackey to you?'

'He will do the job that suits him best, leaving my professional team to handle the business side of things. It's time to face facts. Your father needs more help than you can give him. You can't go on like this, working on the farm, caring for your father, maintaining a practice—you're running yourself ragged. And you would still have the bank hounding you.'

'It's not up to you to decide how I handle this, or what I need,' she gritted out, filled with fury that any and all decisions had been made, irrespective of her opinion.

'So you don't want this?' Dante held out the document.

She waited for the red mist to clear before trusting herself to speak. What he said made a certain amount of sense. It was the way Dante was looking at her now that chilled her. So many people must have seen that same stare—in Dante's office, his boardroom or in his lawyer's office. It was a cool and decisive look that contained no emotion. Dante had struck a deal and that was that. Even half an hour ago she would have said it was impossible for him to treat her like this.

'It's a done deal,' he said as if to confirm her thoughts. 'It's what your father wanted, so there's no going back. You might as well accept—'

'I don't have to accept anything,' she interrupted. 'And I'm not prepared to say anything more to you until I've spoken to my father.'

'Be my guest,' Dante invited, glancing at the phone. 'I'll leave you to it,' he added, standing up. 'But I can assure you that your father is extremely happy with our deal. He sees it as a great way forward—for both of you.'

'So the two of you have decided my future without discussing it with me?'

'Your father didn't want to give you anything more to worry about. He wanted to present it to you as a *fait accompli*. It's his farm to sell, Jess. He thought you'd be pleased. His knowledge and experience is invaluable to me, and now he'll have a wider role as advisor to all my equine facilities.'

'I can't deal with this right now.' She held up her hands, palms flat. 'I can't believe you've done this. I trusted you.'

'I'm not the enemy here, Jess.'

How could she deny her father what would be the most wonderful opportunity? She couldn't. She loved him too much. Protecting him was her mother's last wish, and this was a chance beyond their wildest dreams. But there was one thing she could refuse. 'You can take that contract with you. I don't want the farm. I haven't earned it.'

'You don't want your family farm, free from debt and with money in the bank?' Dante asked, frowning.

'If you're such a philanthropist, why didn't you give the farm to my father?'

'Because this was what he wanted, what he asked for. And this is what I want to do for you.'

'Seriously?' Jess shook her head. 'How do you think that makes me feel? Will you call by each time you're in Yorkshire to accept payment in kind?'

'*Dios*, Jess! Is that how little you think of me?'

'I don't know what to think,' she admitted, grabbing her coat. 'I'll speak to my father face to face, and then I'll decide what to do.'

CHAPTER SIXTEEN

IT TOOK JESS a while to catch her breath as she rushed down the lane leading home. Dante's offer was too much to take in. *He* was too much. She should have known better than to give way to feelings that had been ten long years in the making. Dante wanted more than she could give.

Huge sums of money passed through his hands on a regular basis, but his offer of the farm was incredible to Jess. It didn't seem right. She had to hear directly from her father that it was his wish too. Maybe he'd been blinded by the fact that Dante's offer put him back on top and hadn't thought things through.

She would do anything not to spoil his chances, but pride alone would stop her accepting Dante's gift. In monetary terms, she accepted that it was probably equal to Jess shaking out a few coins from her piggy bank, but that didn't make it right.

What made Dante's offer sting the most was that all she wanted was him, but Dante hadn't put that on the table. That wasn't part of his deal.

Jess marched towards the farmhouse entrance before suddenly hesitating. It was Christmas morning. Was she really going to ruin it with a blazing row with her father? Was that really what she wanted after all they'd been through? Changing course, she headed for the stables, made for it like a homing pigeon flying back to its roost. She had some serious thinking to do.

Diplomacy had never been his strong point, but he would not allow things between him and Jess to end like this. Tugging on his jacket, he headed out. It was a straight road to the farm and the directions were imprinted on his memory. He guessed he'd find Jess in the stable with the animals, where their company would warm her better than any brazier.

As he had expected, he found her hunched up in the bleak grey light on a hay bale. 'Hey…'

'Dante!' Jess didn't appear to breathe, and then noisily dragged in a huge gulp of air. 'I told you I needed time to think. Don't do this. You stunned me. I need space.'

'I'm here to make sure you got home safely.'

'I do know the way.'

'It can still be dangerous in this weather.'

'You're concerned about me now?' she challenged with a sceptical sideways look.

'Always.'

'Then why drop the bombshell about the farm as you did? Why cut me out of the discussions in the first place?'

'I could have led up to telling you with more grace,' he conceded, 'but I was impatient for you to know. As for cutting you out? I did what your father asked, but keeping you in the dark didn't sit well with me—hence my impatience to make things right.'

'It's all a mix-up,' she flared with a shake of her head. 'The only thing not in doubt is that you're an impatient man. Leaving hospital too soon. Riding before you could walk.'

He conceded all these comments with a shrug—all except one. 'I'm not always impatient. Not when it comes to you.'

She blushed at the reminder.

'You must see me as overbearing,' he confirmed with a shrug.

'You think?' she fired back.

'This was something I had to do for you, Jess.'

'I haven't had chance to speak to my father yet,' she admitted in an attempt to close the conversation down.

'What are you waiting for?' he challenged.

'You are overbearing, and you should have run this past me,' she stated hotly, 'but I won't disturb my father when he might have a second shot at happiness.'

'He's not here?'

'He's with Ella.'

He let that hang for a while and then remarked, 'It's good he's finally got his life back.'

'Meaning I haven't?' Jess suggested with an accusing look.

'You can do anything you choose to,' he said evenly. 'In the words of the cliché, the world is your oyster.'

'You mean, if I sell the farm back to you?'

'That's a novel idea.'

'I'm full of them.'

'I'd prefer you to keep the farm as your security going forward,' he said honestly. 'You don't have to live here. You can live anywhere you like.'

'Your people will move in to help out,' she intuited.

'If you want them to—they're waiting for your instructions.'

'You've thought of everything, haven't you, Dante?'

He remained silent.

Averting her face, Jess chewed her thumb before turning back to face him. 'This is all about trust,' she said.

'Without it we're going nowhere,' he agreed.

'*We?*' she queried.

There was a long silence, and then she said, 'Isn't time supposed to heal all wounds?'

'Some cut deeper than others and leave scars we have to deal with, but they do get better over time.'

She looked at him as if she wanted to believe him. 'I didn't mean to make this about me. I just wish I had my mother to confide in sometimes.'

'I understand that. It's as if we've both been set adrift. I was without an anchor for years until I got my head together and knew we must pull together as a family. You've changed and grown too,' he reminded Jess. 'You completed your training, as you promised your mother you would, and now you're an excellent physiotherapist. Here's the living proof,' he added with a flourish as he spread his hands wide.

'No cane,' Jess agreed with the glimmer of a smile. 'Your return to polo's been well documented, though playing like the devil on horseback so soon after your recovery is asking for trouble.'

He seized on her cue. 'That's why I need you. See what happens when you leave me to my own devices?'

'As I remember it, my contract ended and you appointed someone else in my place.'

'To take over your good work,' he pointed out.

'Yet now you risk that good work by launching yourself like an avenging angel on Nero Caracas and his team.'

'The important thing is, my team won.'

'Of course it did,' Jess agreed with the lift of a brow. 'And by some miracle you survived.'

'No miracle,' he argued. 'My recovery is thanks to extremely effective therapy from a certain Señorita Slatehome.' He didn't want to talk about that. He wanted to talk about Jess. She was all that mattered. He wanted her to trust him and relax in his company. He'd handled things badly when he told her about the farm, but his remorse was genuine and he wanted her to have security in the future, whatever choice she made next.

'Just don't take too many chances in the future,' she warned.

He shrugged. 'See what happens when you cut me loose? There's only one way to sort this. The next time I play polo you'd better be there.'

'What are you saying, Dante?'

'I'm admitting I need you,' he confessed.

'As a therapist?'

'What do you think?'

'I think it makes sense from that point of view to keep me on speed dial.'

'Speed dial?' His lips pressed down as he considered this for all of a split second. 'I'm not sure that would suit either of us.'

Even in the dim light he saw her blush at this reminder of their inexhaustible appetite for each other.

'Will you be heading home now?' she asked on the way to recovering her composure.

'Not until I know you've spoken to your father, and I feel confident you're reassured about what's happening with the farm.'

Then he would leave, with or without Jess. If he'd been in doubt about the nature of love, he understood now that it sometimes involved sacrifice, and if staying here was what Jess wanted he had no option but to let her go. He had been overbearing with his purchase of her family's farm and in trying to help her father he'd only succeeded in railroading Jess. She couldn't fight him. The sale was a done deal, and she wouldn't do anything to upset her father's future.

'Dante—'

'Yes?' He hardly knew what to expect. Jess's face was tight with tension.

'I can't let you go without telling you I love you.'

Her eyes snapped shut after this statement. She didn't move. She didn't breathe and then, with a ragged exhalation of air, she opened her eyes and zoned in on his. 'I love you,' she repeated with fiery emphasis.

His entire body thrilled. Jess's words were a statement, a challenge, a baring of her soul that rang in his head like a carillon of happy Christmas bells.

'I'm not going anywhere.' Closing the distance between them in a couple of strides, he lifted Jess into his arms. Sacrifice was one thing, but he was the kind of man who always had to fight tooth and nail for what he believed in. He should have known that all along.

Urgency consumed them both. Jess met him with matching fire. She was already reaching for him. They didn't trouble to undress completely. Just enough to fall back on the hay and mate like wild animals. It was a wordless, mindless coupling that said everything about how far they'd come, and how deep was their trust.

'It feels as if we've come full circle,' Jess murmured as they put their clothes back in order.

'This is where we first met,' he agreed with a grin. 'And things get more interesting each time.'

'There's a new litter of kittens,' she warned, 'so watch out.'

She smiled. So did he, and as they stared into each other's eyes he knew the situation could be rescued, but lovemaking wasn't enough. He had to prove to Jess that when it came to business he might be brusque, brisk and to the point, but he hadn't meant to hurt her over the farm, as he so obviously had.

Stable cats and dogs stood by, ready to assist him. Jess's motley assortment of strays and beloved pets had sensed they were needed and had gathered around them to provide a welcome distraction. Neither Jess nor he could remain immune to them for long, or remain tense, not with animals around.

When she'd fed them some treats Jess held up her grimy

fingernails and grimaced. 'I'll never make it in your world. I'm just too down-homey and—'

'Chilled out?' he suggested. 'Don't you think that's what I need?'

'Just as well,' she commented, grimacing as she took in the damage to her sweater from a new naughty kitten.

'I still love you,' he said as she pulled a face.

Her gaze flashed up to his. 'Please don't say that unless you mean it.'

'I love you,' he said again, his eye-line steady on Jess's.

'Don't make this any harder than it has to be,' she said firmly. 'especially when I know you're about to leave.'

He shrugged. 'What's so hard about leaving with me? Or are you more concerned about dealing with the damage from a leaking kitten?'

'Don't make a joke of this,' she said softly.

'Because…?'

'Because I love you too much for that.'

'Then be with me always.'

'Always? As in for ever?' she exclaimed, incredulous. 'As your therapist?'

'As my wife. I can't think of anyone else who'd have you,' he teased with a pointed look at the stain on Jess's sweater. 'Let me love you as you deserve. Let me spoil you. Let me lavish things on you.'

'You should know by now that's not me. I don't need any of those things.'

'But you'll grow to love being spoiled, I promise,' he insisted.

'I love *you*,' she stated firmly, 'not what you can give me.'

'As I love you,' he said, 'but you must allow me to have the pleasure of giving you things. Love, and gifts like the farm are not mutually exclusive, so get used to it because there's a lot more coming your way. The farm is just the beginning.'

'But I haven't given you my answer yet,' she pointed out.

'I'm not a patient man,' he warned.

'So I shouldn't push you too hard?' she suggested.

'Unless it's in bed.'

'Do you take anything seriously?' she scolded.

'I'm extremely serious when I take you.' And when she shook her head, he added, 'I love you for everything you are, and everything you will be in the future. So what's your answer?'

Jess gasped as he dragged her close. 'My answer's yes. I'll come with you wherever you go.'

'You can depend on it,' he promised.

A few potent seconds ticked by while they laughed and took in the trust that was the bedrock of their decision to be together for ever, but then, as might have been expected, their control snapped at exactly the same moment and as Jess reached for him he drove his mouth down on hers.

It was a long time later when Jess fell back, exhausted. They could never get enough of each other and had made love fiercely, tenderly and, last of all, and most affecting of all, they had made love slowly and deliberately, with love and trust in their eyes, while Dante told Jess she was the only woman he could ever love and that he would be proud to have her at his side for the rest of his life.

'There's so much we don't know about each other,' she whispered, frowning as she turned languidly in his arms.

'Great,' Dante approved. 'So much to learn about each other. New surprises each day.'

She had to be certain. 'Are you sure I'm enough for you? I'm not fancy. I live a plain life in plain clothes, surrounded by plain-speaking people.'

'Enough for me?' he exclaimed softly. 'You're perfect for me. And to prove I'm serious I've got something for you.'

'Nothing expensive, I hope?' Laughter pealed out of her as Dante produced a wisp of hay.

'Jessica Slatehome, sometimes known as Skylar… I'm prepared to be adaptable when it comes to you, so I'm asking again, formally this time, will you marry me?'

'You know my answer, but I'll happily give it again *formally*,' she teased, knowing her face must betray her feelings. 'My answer's yes.'

'Now, I've just got to get this to stay on,' Dante said, frowning as he secured the hay ring around her marriage finger with a few well-judged twists.

Jess stared at her hay ring. She loved it as much as any diamond a fashionable jeweller.

'This is just a start,' Dante insisted, 'We can't change who we are, and it would be wrong to try and change each other.'

'But how will I fit in to your glamorous life?'

'You'll fit in perfectly. We fit together perfectly,' he added, though as he'd moved over her to prove his point, Jess kept her opinion to herself. Providing therapy for injured athletes was her life's work. Riding the horses she loved was her passion. That was the world where she belonged.

Was it? Was it really?

How could she live without Dante? How would she feel if she saw him with other women, knowing she hadn't even put up a fight for the best thing in her life? Were her dreams dust? Was it even possible to hold on to her familiar world while sharing his? 'You're at the top of your field in the tech world, and on the polo circuit,' she mused when they were quiet again. 'And although I could happily fit into your equine world, I belong backstage, not out front with the beautiful people.'

'Is that a fact?' Dante queried with a long sideways look as he set about repeating what he did so very well.

'In my opinion,' he added much much later, 'you out-shine anyone I've ever met. When men on the polo circuit are as dazzled by your beauty as I am I'll have to flatten them. Is that good enough for you? There's no question of you being backstage. You'll be at my side and for ever, I hope.'

'Dante—'

'What?'

She gave a long sigh of pleasure.

'I hear you,' he reassured as he brushed her mouth with lingering kisses. 'You don't want to talk now. You want this, you need this, so please don't ever stop?'

'For ever is a long time,' she reminded him in between hectic gasps of breath.

Dante shrugged as he moved firmly towards the inevi-table conclusion. 'That's one thing over which we'll have to agree to disagree. For ever with you can never be long enough for me. Merry Christmas, Jess.'

CHAPTER SEVENTEEN

MORE THAN A week later, when Jess had spent quality time with her father and Dante had spent earthy, intimate, getting to know her every which-way time with Jess, they boarded his private jet to return to Spain. He was happy to think Jess was doubly reassured—not just by the news that the arrangement for the farm suited her father, but by something even better than that.

'It's never too late to fall in love,' Jim Slatehome had explained to both of them, saying he'd been struck by lightning when he had the opportunity to get to know his neighbour Ella again.

Confident that her father was not only financially secure but was happy and well looked after, Jess was ready to embark on her new life. Everyone, including the animals, was on tenterhooks at the thought of her return to what Maria described as Jess's home.

Dante owned numerous properties across the world. Jess could take her pick. He imagined she might choose his simple shack on a Pacific island, judging by the way she'd held on to the wisp of hay he'd tied around her wedding finger.

That was Jess. That was the Jess he loved. The woman who had insisted she needed no other ring. He'd taken her at her word. For now.

It had taken him a short time or a little over ten years, depending on how he looked at it, to win Jess's trust and now she could have whatever she wanted. Nothing could corrupt her moral compass and, with their lives ahead of them, she'd have plenty of opportunity to counter his riches with hay bales and sound common sense. They were like two pieces of a jigsaw that fitted together perfectly and he could never repay her for what she'd given him.

They'd slept at the pub each night after Christmas, and each night before she slept he told Jess how much he loved her, and how much he owed her, not just for healing him but for teaching him how to trust, and to give his heart deeply and completely. Those quiet times alone had allowed him to reassure her that she would never have to give up her career. His proposal was that Jess headed up a travelling clinic, so they could be together wherever he played polo. She had instantly approved the idea and was excited to make a start. He was confident she'd soon build up a regular practice, especially with him around as visible proof of Jess's excellence as a therapist.

She was playing with the hay wisp, he noticed, turning it round and round her finger. 'I can't believe you managed to hold on to that,' he admitted. 'You can have a ring of your choice as soon as we land in Spain. You can design your own, if you like.'

She gave him a teasing smile. 'It would have to look exactly like this one.'

'I'm sure that can be arranged.'

She remained silent for a while and then she said, 'Could we have a Christmas wedding?'

'You can have a wedding whenever and wherever you like. We don't have to get married at all.'

'Is that your get-out?' she half scolded, half teased him. 'Are you tired of me already?'

'I will never tire of you.' His heart had found its home and wanted no other.

'Then next Christmas it is,' she declared happily, clearly

brim-full of excitement. 'There's something special about the holiday season, don't you think?'

'It won't be snowing in Spain,' he cautioned.

'Not where you live,' she agreed.

He thought of his ski chalet, high in the Sierra Nevada, and conceded, 'Snow can be arranged.'

Jess laughed. 'Is there anything you can't do?'

He huffed a sigh as he thought about this for the time it took to kiss her neck and then her lips. 'Resist you?' he suggested. 'But remember, if you're set on this idea of a Christmas wedding, there's almost a year to wait.'

'For the veil and the dress,' she pointed out.

He laughed as he got the picture. 'You are a shameless hussy.'

'You made me so.'

'I plead innocent,' he fired back with amusement. 'It must have been Skylar who led me astray.'

'Can she do so again?' Jess suggested as the aircraft levelled off.

'There are several bedrooms in the back—take your pick.'

'Lead the way,' she whispered.

A little less than one year later

Christmas Day was approaching fast. Since moving to Spain to live on Dante's *estancia*, Jess had travelled the world. Watching Dante play polo and dispensing necessary therapy, both to his polo-playing associates and to Dante under rather more intimate circumstances, had given her a new insight into the lives of the super-rich.

They had the same worries and the same ailments as everyone else, but some were so remote and removed from the realities of everyday life she felt sorry for them. Rather than envy their so-called gilded existence, she thought of them, locked in their ivory towers with their sights set on some far-off horizon, missing the little things down on the ground that, in Jess's opinion, made life worth living.

Dante's sister Sofia was a glaring exception. They thought alike, and Sofia had become Jess closest friend. Sofia had persuaded Jess that she could navigate the role of star player's wife, and billionaire's soulmate, with the same grace with which Jess handled her job at the mobile clinic. 'You love him. That's all that matters,' Sofia had pointed out. 'And my brother adores you. I love you because you brought him back to us. I've never seen Dante like this before. He wants to be with his family. He wants to share us with you. You've healed him in more ways than one.'

Both Jess and Sofia were excited that Maria and her relatives had agreed to play a major role in Jess's wedding ceremony, providing music and dance. Jess wanted a real party and for everyone to join in. As Dante had promised, their marriage would be celebrated high on the Sierra Nevada mountain range, where snow and fiery passion went hand in hand.

Sofia's wedding gift for Jess couldn't have pleased her more. It was a new horse blanket for Moon. The mare had fretted for Jess, Dante had explained, and so the pony she'd loved since the day Moon was born was his wedding gift to Jess.

Sofia had insisted on giving Jess a few more small presents—or 'thingamajigs' as Sofia liked to call them.

'I want to spoil you with bits of nonsense,' she'd said.

'Not nonsense,' Jess had protested as she opened the boxes of accessories—hairbands, bracelets that jingled and Spanish mantilla combs with filmy, lacy veils. 'These are lovely, thoughtful gifts.'

She only wished Sofia could find the same happiness she had.

'Here comes the groom. He's going to be late,' Sofia announced tensely.

Looking out of the window, Jess saw Dante and his brothers skiing up to the door of his magnificent chalet. Her heart sang at the sight of Dante, as skilful on snow as he was on Zeus, his mighty black stallion. He had to do something first thing in the morning, Dante had told her last night, or he wouldn't be capable of staying away from his bride before their wedding.

The year leading up to this moment had been packed full of polo and patients and horses and Dante, which was pretty much everything Jess could ask of life. Dante hadn't forced the issue when he asked her to marry him and, predictably, that had made her want him all the more. The ring she would wear when they were married remained the only bone of contention between them.

'A plain gold band will do me,' she'd insisted, while Dante had countered by assuring her that the first time they made love as man and wife Jess would be wearing nothing but diamonds.

'The first time?' Jess had queried with amusement.

'The first time as husband and wife,' Dante had countered before taking her in the most delicious way.

Would she ever get enough of him? Not a chance, Jess concluded as she watched him shoulder his skis. There was a sense of purpose and a particular speed to his actions she recognised. Dante wouldn't be late for his wedding, because he was already thinking about taking her to bed.

'Jess? Your gown,' Sofia prompted.

Jess turned to see the sparkling lace and chiffon dream of a dress Dante had insisted must come from Paris. It was a restrained and beautiful creation, a fairy tale dress, as Sofia described it, and one that made dreams come true.

Arranging the gown reverently on the bed, Sofia stood

back. 'I can't wait to have you as a sister,' she admitted, glowing with pent-up excitement.

'I'm already your sister,' Jess insisted as they exchanged the warmest of hugs. 'Skylar too?' Sofia teased as they broke apart.

'Of course. We can't leave her out, can we?'

'And now this dream of a dress,' Sofia said as she lifted it carefully from the bed.

Jess had dreamed of this moment since that first encounter with Dante in her father's stable ten years ago and now, quite incredibly, those dreams were about to come true.

'Not incredible,' Sofia argued when Jess voiced these thoughts. 'My brother is lucky to have found you. A woman less likely to be cast about by the winds of fate, I have yet to meet. You are a strong, determined woman who will bloom wherever you're planted, and I'm proud to be your friend.'

Jess was so popular on the *estancia* everyone had made a special effort to travel to the mountains to attend her wedding ceremony, which was as relaxed and authentic as Jess had always dreamed it would be. to make things easier for their guests, Dante had laid on two of his aircraft to bring them in from far and wide. Sofia had dipped into her billions too, to ensure the most magical scene.

A huge pavilion had been erected in the deep snow in the garden of Dante's chalet overlooking the dramatic mountain range. Fairy lights were strung lavishly around, while a pathway of pink rose petals, edged by sweet-smelling country flowers flown in from Yorkshire, filled the air with delicate scent. The ambient temperature inside the pavilion was cosy, thanks to heaters hidden in the roof, and the guests agreed they had never been more comfortable at a wedding than they were on the deeply upholstered white seats. Haunting music from a single acoustic guitar set the romantic mood, while candles glowed on the altar and jewel-coloured lanterns cast a magical glow across the excited congregation.

Peeping through the entrance, Jess saw her father seated with Ella on the front row. They looked so happy together and, never one to miss a business trick, her father had flown in from England on one of Dante's specially adapted jets accompanied by not just his lively and down-to-earth partner but by several promising ponies as well.

There was a Christmas tree in the entrance covered with small gifts for their guests. Dante had told Jess that her gift was the small brown paper-covered box at the top of the tree and that she must claim it and open it before she came down the aisle.

One of the taller attendants got it down for her, and when she opened it she gasped. It was a perfect replica of Jess's hay twist ring, but crafted in pure rose gold.

Her wedding ring was perfect and so was the groom, Jess thought when Dante turned at the moment she appeared and their eyes met.

Every seat was taken by Dante's family and staff, and by a select number of guests. Maria had settled into the chalet weeks ago to prepare food and the mix of delicious cooking smells had stayed with him, making him hungry, and hungry for Jess. *Dios*, where was she? When could they get away from here?

At last!

His heart filled with love as he caught sight of his bride, who looked beyond ravishingly beautiful as she walked up the petal-strewn aisle.

'Thank you for my ring,' Jess whispered when she reached his side. 'It's absolutely perfect. I have something for you...'

'What?' he demanded as Jess turned to hand over her bouquet to Sofia, thinking of all the small, thoughtful gifts

Jess had bought him in the lead up to the wedding. Her answer was to take hold of his hand and rest it gently against her stomach. A lightning bolt of excitement struck him as Jess stared up with eyes full of trust.

'You…?' He was stunned into silence, and not just because the celebrant had indicated that the ceremony was about to begin.

'Yes,' Jess confirmed. 'We're having a baby. We're going to be adding to the Acosta clan soon.'

'Oh, *Dios*!' he exclaimed on a hectic rush of breath. 'Thank you! Thank you!'

'You may *not* yet kiss your bride,' the priest scolded them with a twinkle in his eyes.

But Dante Acosta had always broken the rules, as had Skylar, so they kissed passionately and everyone applauded until at last, with love surrounding them on every side, Jess and Dante were married.

* * * * *

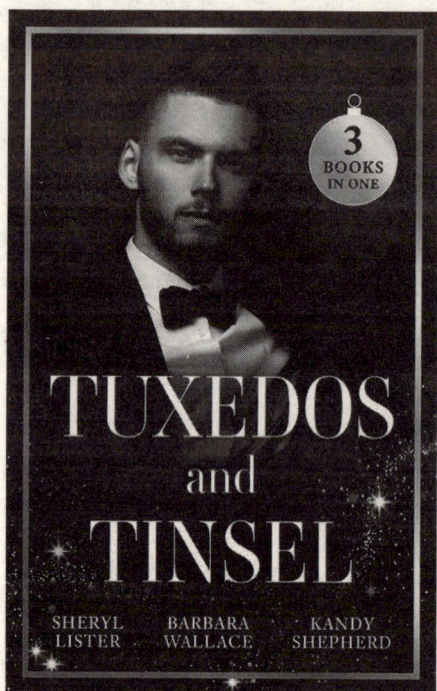

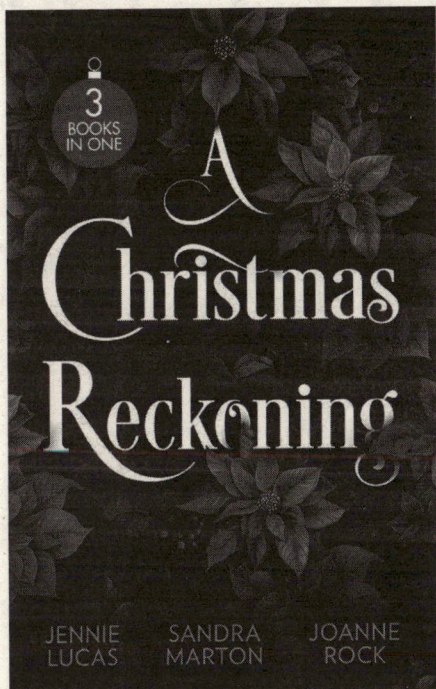

LET'S TALK

Romance

For exclusive extracts, competitions and special offers, find us online:

- **f** MillsandBoon
- **X** @MillsandBoon
- **O** @MillsandBoonUK
- **♪** @MillsandBoonUK

Get in touch on 01413 063 232

For all the latest titles coming soon, visit
millsandboon.co.uk/nextmonth